Mr. Frosty Pants

(Mr. Christmas #1)

BY LETA BLAKE

An Original Publication from Leta Blake Books

Mr. Frosty Pants
Written and published by Leta Blake
Cover by Dar Albert
Formatted by BB eBooks

First Print Edition, 2018
ISBN: 978-1-626226-5-24

Other Books by Leta Blake

Any Given Lifetime
The River Leith
Smoky Mountain Dreams
Angel Undone
The Difference Between
Omega Mine: Search for a Soulmate
Raise Up Heart
Heat for Sale
Bring on Forever

The Mr. Christmas Series
Mr. Frosty Pants
Mr. Naughty List
Mr. Jingle Bells

The Training Season Series
Training Season
Training Complex

Heat of Love Series
Slow Heat
Alpha Heat
Slow Birth
Bitter Heat

Stay Lucky Series
Stay Lucky
Stay Sexy

'90s Coming of Age Series
Pictures of You
You Are Not Me

Co-Authored with Indra Vaughn

Vespertine

Cowboy Seeks Husband

Co-Authored with Alice Griffiths

The Wake Up Married serial

Will & Patrick's Endless Honeymoon

Gay Fairy Tales

Co-Authored with Keira Andrews

Flight

Levity

Rise

Audiobooks

Leta Blake at Audible

Free Read

Stalking Dreams

Discover more about the author online

Leta Blake

letablake.com

Gay Romance Newsletter

Leta's newsletter will keep you up to date on her latest releases and news from the world of M/M romance. Join the mailing list today.

Leta Blake on Patreon

Become part of Leta Blake's Patreon community in order to access exclusive content, deleted scenes, extras, bonus stories, rewards, prizes, interviews, and more.
www.patreon.com/letablake

Acknowledgements

Thank you to the following:

Mom and Dad, without whom I couldn't be following this dream of being a writer. Brian and Cecily, my lights to travel home to. All the wonderful members of my Patreon who inspire, support, and advise me, especially Sadie Sheffield. Keira Andrews for the editing work. DJ Jamison for proofing. Stacey McDonald for another set of proofing eyes. Neta and Einat for the early beta reading work. Robert Winters for early reading and advice. Emmy the Great and Tim Wheeler for the song that inspired the book, and Knoxville, TN for the setting inspiration.

Most of all, thank you to my readers for making all the blood, sweat, and tears worthwhile.

For Emmy and Tim

This Christmas, can true love warm his frozen heart?

When Casey Stevens went away to college four years ago, he ghosted on his straight best friend, Joel Vreeland. He hoped time and distance would lessen the unrequited affection he felt, but all it did was make him miss Joel more.

Home for the holidays, Casey hopes they might find a way to be friends again. But Joel's frosty reception reminds Casey of just how hard he had to fight to be Joel's friend in the first place. It's going to take a Christmas miracle to get past that cool façade again.

Joel isn't as straight as Casey believes, and his years of pining for Casey have left him hurting and alone, caring for his abusive father and struggling to get by. Unable to trust anyone except his rescue dog—and with no reason to believe Casey is interested in him for more than a holiday fling—Joel's icy heart might shatter before it can thaw.

Can Casey and Joel's love overcome mistrust, parental rejection, class differences, and four long years apart? *Mr. Frosty Pants* is a Christmas gay romance by Leta Blake featuring a virgin hero, childhood friends-to-lovers, second chances, and romantically steamy scenes.

Chapter One

I F CASEY STEVENS ignored the gaudy multicolored Christmas lights strewn through the bushes and trees—and the massive air-blown, glowing Santa popping in and out of a big, green box in the front yard—his old house looked the same as it had before they moved out. Although his dad would suck his teeth in disapproval if he saw how the new owners had decorated for the holidays.

All Casey's life, Jonathan Stevens had insisted on keeping Christmas "classy": single, white electric candles in each window, expensive greenery on the window sills, and a big wreath on the front door. To Casey's dad, strings of lights all over the house were the epitome of tackiness, and colored ones? Well, they were downright trashy.

Casey slowed his Lexus RX—last year's Christmas present from his parents—as he passed his old home. Nostalgia dug its nails into him with a bittersweet grip. His folks had moved out of the upwardly mobile Manor Crest neighborhood and into the uber-uppercrust Pearlwood community the autumn after he'd left for NYU. This was his first visit to Knoxville in almost four years, and his folks' new neighborhood seemed nice enough, full of shimmering near-palaces, but it didn't satisfy him or feel like home. Not the way the old Manor Crest house did.

In the new house, Casey didn't have his own bedroom anymore. Instead, he had a generic, perfectly appointed guest room to crash in, complete with cream walls, cream bedspread, and cream carpet. Impersonal and threatening in its purity, it was nothing at all like the messy room in the Manor Crest house where he'd kicked back to watch

YouTube videos of cats climbing into boxes and squirrels raiding bird feeders. The place where he'd first jerked off, fretted about the fact that it'd been to thoughts of Joel, and coped with the angst of falling in love for the first (and only) time.

Leaving his former house behind, Casey drove over the next hill, his eyes gobbling up the old, familiar sights. These were the streets he'd biked on as a kid, the houses he'd passed every day on the way to the bus stop, and the neighbors he'd ultimately lost track of.

He noticed Mrs. Weinstein had put her menorah in the window like she did every year. And Mr. Maples had put out his giant, glowing Nativity scene again. The same one Casey and Joel had stolen the baby Jesus from during their senior year. They'd hidden it in Joel's garage for a night or two and then brought it back to Mr. Maples's yard on Christmas Eve wrapped in a big, red bow.

Casey's stomach fluttered remembering the way Joel had laughed as they'd run off into the cover of night, leaving the glowing baby Jesus behind where he belonged. Joel's slanted smile had glinted like a knife in the darkness.

Joel.

Casey stopped the car and gazed longer at Mr. Maples's nearly life-size Nativity scene. The shining Mary was pretty with her long, brown, painted-on hair and blue painted-on dress. Her rosy, holy lips were open in astonished joy as she gazed down at the child in the manger.

Casey's cheeks heated. Those were the lips he'd stupidly kissed "for practice" on Joel's dare the night they'd stolen the Christ child. Joel had knelt solemnly by the manger, his pale skin glowing and dark hair messy, clutching the baby Jesus in his arms as he'd watched Casey's clumsy attempt with hot eyes. Casey would never forget how his adorably asymmetrical face had lost all its usual crabby irritation.

A shiver shot up Casey's spine like it always did whenever he thought of that night: the clarity of feeling in Joel's shining gaze. He'd looked holy too—holier than Mary even—lit from below by the glowing, empty manger.

In that moment, Casey had almost let himself think…

Yes, for a second he'd really *believed* it was possible that his own tender feelings were returned. There'd been something so undeniable in Joel's eyes, something he'd never seen there before and never let himself look for again.

God, *Joel's eyes.*

During an elective poetry class at NYU, he'd tried to describe them once. The best he'd come up with was a sad metaphor describing Joel's eyes as akin to muddy water—dark, reflective but clear.

Obviously that poem never saw the light of day. He was better at ad copy than whimsical explorations of feelings and fanciful descriptions of nature. Poetry class had turned out like life in general for Casey: an exercise in pretending to show everything while actually showing as little as possible.

Which was why he was getting a degree in marketing. He could shine up shit like no one else. Maybe it was because when it came to ad copy, design, and branding assignments, he actually *wanted* to draw people in. In day-to-day life, he'd learned long ago that to "keep up appearances," he had to hold people at arm's length.

Ann, his therapist in New York, said he was a master at presenting a smooth, likable façade instead of showing his raw humanity. And he agreed. There was a reason for that, after all. He'd been brought up in a household that prioritized image over reality, and it wasn't like anyone was clamoring to know his personal shit anyway—not his parents, not his acquaintances at NYU, and hardly any of the guys he'd dated.

Even coming out hadn't changed how alone he felt. There was something holding him back, keeping him from connecting. Something he was bound and determined to change because that was another issue he was working on with Ann: Coming to terms with the fact that at twenty-two, he no longer had anyone to blame but himself for his disconnected loneliness.

The fact was, there'd only ever been one person he'd ever been tempted to be entirely authentic with, even if he died from the humiliation of it. But he'd chickened out and pushed Joel away with both hands.

Putting the car back in gear, he eased past Mr. Maples's Nativity scene and then past Mrs. Westfield's gold-bow-and-holly-encrusted house—keeping it classy too, he guessed. Snowflakes drifted in hazy circles, flecking his windshield. Not enough to turn on his wipers and definitely not enough to stick.

Just the usual Tennessee tease.

He winced, thinking of his ex-boyfriend Theo packing up the small box of things he'd kept at Casey's apartment. "*Being with you is just a tease of the real thing, babe. You don't love me. You act like you do, but you don't.*" Theo had run his hand through the fuzzy black curls on top of his head, sighing in frustration. "*To be fair, I don't love you either. We both deserve someone who wants more than 'this doesn't suck.*" He'd smiled sympathetically, his white teeth shining starkly against his dark complexion. "*We deserve someone we're crazy about.*"

He'd had a point. Casey hadn't even cried when Theo left for good, and he supposed that said something.

No, it said everything.

It'd been six months since Theo put a definitive end to their yearlong, off-and-on relationship. Casey didn't really miss *him* so much as he missed knowing there was someone he could rely on to hang out with every weekend. Someone that meant Friday and Saturday nights were handled. Someone he enjoyed sexually and liked as a person, even if he wasn't in love. In a city as big and bustling as New York, the appearance of intimacy was *something*. It beat being alone.

At this point in his senior year, he was ready to agree with Ann that his parents had done him a disservice in getting him an apartment instead of letting him live in the dorms. He'd at least have gotten to know more people in a communal situation. Probably. But Jonathan

Stevens wouldn't have it. Not when he could afford "better." Not for his son.

But now, months after his and Theo's breakup, Casey's ridiculously expensive one-bedroom apartment, just a few blocks from busy Washington Square, felt so lonely that, despite Ann's warnings that he might regret it, he'd been eager to accept his mom and dad's invitation to come home for Christmas break. Spending time with his family, putting up the tree, catching up with old acquaintances, and being back home in Knoxville again? It seemed like it would be a great change from the isolation of his life at college.

Until yesterday when he'd actually arrived after a tedious, twelve-hour car ride—something he'd rebelliously insisted on rather than accept his father's offer to foot a ridiculously expensive, last-minute plane ticket—and discovered his parents' new house wasn't *home* at all.

God, he knew he shouldn't complain. So many people struggled and did without, and he was lucky as hell his parents had money. It was his own fault he was lonely. Maybe he was just broken inside. Maybe he was just *wrong*, and all the therapy in the world wouldn't fix him.

Maybe Joel was far better off without him.

Breathing against the ache in his chest, Casey braked by the stop sign where he'd shivered on cold mornings waiting for the school bus. He'd waited there with Joel, of course.

He sighed and pressed the heels of his hands to his eyes. He was set to graduate from NYU in May. It'd been almost four years since he'd said goodbye to Joel. And yet he still couldn't move on with his life. They'd never even been together! Joel had dated girls for fuck's sake. Whatever Casey felt, it was his own burden to bear, and it was ludicrous.

Ann said he needed to either let the past go or confront it head on. When he'd told her he was taking up his parents on their invite, she'd replied, "*If you insist on returning to the scene of the crime, now's as good a time as any to be more transparent with the people in your life, Casey. Consider it.*" He'd known she was talking about his folks, but when he considered being transparent with anyone, the only person he could think about was Joel.

He rounded the corner and entered Belmont Hills, the neighborhood behind Manor Crest, built twenty years before it. The houses there were smaller and more rundown, and the neighborhood amenities existed in a state of disrepair. The playground and tennis courts were overrun with weeds and punctuated with litter. The swing set had no swings to speak of, and the pool was roped off with yellow caution tape. Not much different than when Casey had last driven through four years ago.

He took a deep breath as he turned onto Elder Lane and passed a multicolored blizzard of over-the-top Christmas joy hosted by the house on the corner. He was almost there. Icicle lights dripped from the rooflines of the ranch style home next to Joel's dad's place.

One more driveway to go...

Casey pulled in front of the split-level house in need of a paint job. He gripped the wheel and swallowed hard, biting down on the inside of his cheek.

The garage door was open, exposing the place where Casey used to sit on the cold, hard concrete floor to watch Joel practice his bass guitar. But now the interior was packed with children's toys: tricycles, bikes, balls, and scooters galore, as well as a big, pink toy kitchenette and a chalkboard. Holy shit, did Joel have *kids*? His heart clenched hard.

But then two lanky teenagers, a blond girl and boy, came bursting through the front door with unopened boxes of Christmas lights tucked under their arms and pouty expressions on their faces. A flustered woman followed with a stepladder, pointing at the porch roof and directing them with swooping motions of her arms.

After a few moments, she turned to stare curiously at Casey's car lingering by the curb. When a man came out to join them, he kissed the woman, and she motioned at Casey. His heart lurched, and he swallowed against the lump in his throat, easing his foot off the brake.

It was clear. Joel didn't live here anymore.

It'd been foolish to think he would still be in his father's old house. Why would he be? It'd been nearly four years, and he was a grown man now. He'd probably gotten married or at least moved into a place of his own. But deep down, Casey had always assumed Charlie Vreeland, Joel's dad, would still live in the house, that he'd be there forever as a tether to the days when Joel and Casey had hopped the fence between their backyards, violating their fathers' common belief that Manor Crest boys and Belmont Hills boys shouldn't play together.

Wiping at his face, annoyed by the sting of unwanted, stupid tears, Casey headed toward the corner of Belview Drive. There was just one more thing he wanted to see before he drove back to his parents' house. He hoped it was still there. It had to be. It was the one thing in the world that had been theirs alone.

The bench.

But as he approached what used to be the empty lot he and Joel had claimed, his stomach dropped. Someone had cleared the trees to make way for a new house going up. And, from what he could see, the wood-and-iron bench—*their* bench—on the formerly wooded lot was gone. His breath caught. The bench where they'd hung out to smoke Joel's stolen cigarettes. The bench Joel had only ever shared with him. Their secret. Gone.

He'd never again sit on the garage floor and watch Joel play bass.

He'd never again sit beside him on their bench, as they smoked cigarettes and eyed each other.

He'd never again crawl through Joel's window after his dad had gone to sleep and huddle with him in his twin-size bed listening to a Gaslight Anthem album and aching all over with unexpressed feelings.

Never ever. It was done. Over.

Gone.

Minutes passed. He straightened up and wiped again at his traitorous eyes. The snow came down harder, threatening to stick. He flipped on the radio, his chest tight and throat aching.

If he could change the past, he would. He'd do everything different-ly. Maybe Joel wouldn't have ever cared for him *that way*, but Casey could at least have had Joel in his life as a friend. And that would have been something, wouldn't it? Better than the big, fat nothing he had now.

Leaving Belmont Hills and heading back toward his folks' new place, he turned up the radio. A barrage of Christmas songs washed over him—bells and harps, familiar choruses and verses—but none of them touched him. He carefully stuffed his memories of Joel back into the box he'd built for them in his heart. But they didn't seem to fit inside anymore. They poked out with sharp, rough edges.

As Casey crested the hill leading to his parents' new house, he gazed at the hazy Smoky Mountains in the distance. He was "home" for the holidays. But he hadn't been prepared for how much it hurt.

Chapter Two

"**D**ID YOU KNOW the Vreelands moved?"

Casey sat across from his mother on a stool at the wide, polished granite kitchen counter.

"Hmm?" She evaded his question by focusing on the pile of recipe cards she was sorting so that Heather, her new housekeeper, could come later that night to prepare the following week's dinners in advance.

As Casey waited for her to choose between a lamb and beef soup, he studied her closely for the first time since he'd arrived home. His mother's hair was freshly cut in a bleached-blond pixie style. It stood out against her trim black sweater, and the contrast brought out a cunning spark in her blue eyes. Her red, corduroy skirt hugged her yoga-sculpted hips, and black tights rounded out her casual look. She looked good, but then she always did.

Casey's own red sweater felt too warm and his jeans too tight. He shifted awkwardly in his seat, tapping his fingers on the counter restlessly. He'd kept his tone carefully neutral when asking about Joel, shoving down the insistent *feelings* that had risen when he drove by the Vreelands' old place. But now, overstuffed with them, he felt like he might burst open and spill everything out all over the counter anyway.

"Mom?" he asked again, several long seconds later. "Did you hear my question?"

"Sorry, honey. What did you ask?" She flipped between a pumpkin pie recipe in Grandmother Johnson's handwriting and one in Grandmother Stevens'. "I wish Heather would hurry and finish the recipe spreadsheet I asked her to make. It'll be so much easier when she has every dish all sorted by season."

His mom had told him during a phone call several weeks before that she'd begun designing her menus around seasonally themed dishes because she'd read it was the newest meal trend amongst the wealthiest families in Atlanta and Dallas. And Deanna Stevens wanted little more than to be both wealthy and on trend.

Casey took a deep breath and steadied himself. "The Vreelands moved." Stating it as a fact hurt enough that he turned his face away, pretending to look out the wide windows to the gray lake rippling by the edge of his parents' new property. "Did you know?"

"Oh? Well, yes. I suppose I did," she said. Casey turned in time to see her dark blue eyes soften as she glanced up from the recipe cards. She sent him a sympathetic smile. "Did you visit the old neighborhood today, honey?"

There was no reason to deny it. Still, he felt horribly exposed as he nodded. He remembered the shining armor displays at the Met in Manhattan and wished for a suit of it to cover his soft places, protection from his mother's often unwittingly hurtful words.

"I see. Visiting old haunts." She smiled sweetly at him again. "I used to do the same thing when I first moved to Knoxville. I'd go back home to Friendsville to visit." Her eyes went distant. "It truly doesn't seem that long ago. I can't believe it's been fifteen years since I last saw the old family home. Now *that* was a true loss when we had to sell Papaw's land. Not like when we left Manor Crest at all."

Casey cleared his throat, determined not to be led off course. "After I drove by our Manor Crest place, I swung by Joel's old house." He fought the tremor in his voice. "They don't live there anymore."

"Well, of course not," his mother said, blinking at him slowly, as though he were stupid. "Joel had to sell the house when his father went into the nursing home." She pursed her lips. "Something about qualifying for Medicaid, maybe? I can't recall."

Casey furrowed his brow. He hadn't known Joel's father was in a nursing home now. Why hadn't anyone told him? Sure, Charlie Vreeland had always been a jerk to him, and to Joel for that matter, but he'd been Joel's dad. "When did that happen?"

"A year ago? Maybe two? I'm not sure, honey." She shrugged. "I overheard something about it a while back when I was at my stylist." She patted her hair, making sure the pixie was still perfectly mussed. "I made a mental note to tell you at the time, but I suppose I forgot."

"What else have you heard about them?" Casey knew his voice was pitched too high—that it gave away all kinds of things he normally tried to hide. But even as he tried to temper it, Ann's voice rushed in, reassuring him that he was a grown man now, and it was safe to be himself, along with other therapist bullshit like "breathe" and "be yourself."

"Mmm. Let me think." His mother narrowed her eyes, casting back. "There was some speculation that Vreeland's Home and Garden was going to close down too. The new nail artist at my salon—Melissa, I think her name is? Anyway, she swears upside-down and backwards that Vreeland's carries the best summer annuals selection and that if the store went under Knoxville would suffer a terrible loss." His mother rolled her eyes, finally chose Grandmother Stevens' recipe, and tossed Grandmother Johnson's aside, turning her attention to seasonal sides next. "And maybe it would be. How would I know?" She shrugged. "I get everything through the landscapers now, and I think they buy from Lowe's."

Casey schooled his face. Even though he'd asked, he hadn't really expected his mother to be so in the know about the Vreelands. Joel and his father weren't society people and thus not on her usual radar. Besides, she'd always called Joel "that boy" and radiated icy displeasure whenever Casey told her he was jumping the fence to go hang out. Or, worse, whenever he invited Joel to come over to their place.

"Your aunt Courtney can't make it until Christmas Eve. Did I tell you?" his mother said, flipping over a card for a seven-layer salad in her youngest sister's handwriting. "But at least she'll be here for the party."

"You said."

They studied the recipe cards together as a Christmas carol playlist he'd helped her create on Spotify drifted through a black, cylindrical Bluetooth speaker placed in the middle of the counter. All the mentions of snow in the lyrics made Casey almost miss Christmas in New York. For the last three years, his parents had flown up to spend Christmas Eve and Christmas Day with him in the city. They'd all enjoyed the limited time together.

But this year Casey's father had been promoted to executive VP, and one of his new positional duties was to throw a massive Christmas Eve party for his underlings, nevermind that most of them would probably rather be at home alone or with family on the night before Christmas. It was a company tradition. Casey's parents had invited friends and family to the event as well, and, if his mother's planning was any indication, it would be a great night. But two weeks in Knoxville without Joel, enduring the sticks and mud of a Tennessee winter, lacked the magic of the colorful bustle of New York and the potential for a white Christmas. *Why did I think this was a good idea?*

"I can't believe Courtney's the only one of my siblings living close enough to travel to Knoxville now. Remember the old days when the whole family used to get together for the holidays?" his mother asked wistfully, her eyes going soft again with memories. "I miss that."

"It's a shame the holiday rituals all fell apart after Grandma Johnson died." And it really was. His mother's side of the family was warm and loving, full of big voices and giant hugs.

It was his dad's side he'd never enjoyed spending time with. Mainly because their hillbilly, Appalachian ways left his class-obsessed father wallowing in a paroxysm of shame. Unfortunately, on the ride home from those visits, his irritation usually got taken out on Casey in volleys of criticism and complaints.

His mother's smile tightened, a grief spasm Casey recognized from the year following Grandma Johnson's death. "At least Courtney's coming," she said again. "I've missed her since she moved to Atlanta."

Casey let that sentiment rest on the counter between them long enough to gather a bit of dust before he came back to what he really wanted to know. "So, what happened to Joel? After his dad went into the nursing home, I mean? Did he go to college? Is he still around town? Does he run Vreeland's?"

His palms began to sweat in the small silence that followed his questions while his mother chose between an acorn squash casserole dish and a nutty chicken stew recipe. "Yes, I think he runs the store or at least owns it. I'm not sure how much time he spends there, though. He definitely didn't go to college." She tsked quietly and rolled her eyes. "He never had much ambition."

Casey bit back a retort.

Joel always had plenty of ambition, just in ways parents never understood. He remembered how Joel had loved to write gory short stories and had once shared with Casey a great idea for a terrifying horror book. He'd wanted to get into writing screenplays too. Joel had been committed to his little high school garage band for as long as it had lasted, and he'd have been willing to see it through if he'd ever gotten a record contract. Most of all, Joel had wanted to travel the world. But that obviously hadn't happened for him.

Casey wondered what kind of life he *had* made. "Did he get married? Have kids?"

"I'm not positive, but I think he's still single. Why?"

"Just curious. Hope he's happy. That's all."

She put down her recipe cards and gazed at him warily. "I admit I was surprised when you didn't keep in touch with him. Though, in retrospect, I suppose your father was always right. It's one thing to play together when you're young, or to hang out when you're teenagers. That's a matter of proximity." Her light eyebrows rose pointedly. "But it was only natural to discover as adults that you have absolutely nothing in common."

Ah, there was the sharp pain of a word arrow well-landed. Casey rubbed his chest, an ache over his heart, and said nothing in reply.

After a long silence, he picked up the recipe card for his favorite autumnal dish: sweet potato casserole. Studying it carefully, like he was putting it to memory, he recalled the time he took a scoop of it over to the Vreelands' house. Joel had warmed it up in his dad's messy, food-encrusted microwave before eating the casserole like it was ice cream, moaning with each bite.

"*You don't know how good you have it, man,*" he'd said enviously as he'd polished off the bowl. "*Having a mom who makes something like this?*"

Casey had wanted to share every good thing in his life with him after that. For almost a year, every time Casey jerked off, he'd thought about the noises Joel had made eating that casserole. They'd been sexier than any sound he'd ever heard—sexier even than the moans men made together in the gay porn he'd dared to watch in the dead of night on his phone.

But *everything* about Joel had been sexy back then. Like the way Joel's lips curled up in a snarl when he played bass, or how his eyes softened whenever he really looked at Casey—instead of looking at everything *but* him. Or how his face brightened with excitement when he told Casey the storyline to one of his dark, morbid stories. Or the way he said Casey's name all gruff, while they sat side by side on the bench and shared their forbidden cigarettes.

Hell, Casey'd been half-hard nearly constantly around Joel back then.

"I always knew it was a puppy crush," his mother said, eyeing him. "Your father, of course, was terrified your obsession with Joel meant you were gay."

"I *am* gay."

She laughed. "I know, dear. And now that you're out and your father's come to terms with it, his terror has subsided. It was just such an uncertain time for him, you understand."

"It was an uncertain time for me too."

"I'm sure it was." She cocked her head, trying to peer into Casey. He tightened his walls, battened the hatches, and endeavored to make himself unreadable. Screw Ann. What did she know about the relative safety of his parents' home? Nothing.

His mother asked, "So you *did* have a crush on him then?"

Crush? Hardly. He'd been madly in love with Joel and still was if the barely restrained pain in his heart was anything to go by. Casey wasn't going to give her that much, though. She hadn't earned it with her behavior so far today. So he only met her gaze and held it silently. Even that said more than he really wanted her to know.

"Never say I don't understand my son." She patted his hand. "But it's good he's in the past now. You deserve so much better than someone like him. Speaking of… Have you heard from Theo? He's such a delightful young man. And your father likes him so much."

Casey almost laughed. Theo was the only reason his father had "come around" about him being gay. Even the "black thing," as Theo had called it, hadn't been an issue in the end. As the son of a famous black NBA player and a wealthy New York City heiress, Theo had brought a certain caché that the crushes of Casey's past, especially Joel, lacked. Casey's dad had enjoyed flaunting Casey's glamorous connection amongst his pals, especially when that connection led to some pretty amazing courtside tickets.

"Mom, I know you both liked him, but he's not coming back."

"We liked him, yes, but what about *you*? I'm sure it's been hard for you since he left. You were quite serious about him, after all. You were living together."

"We weren't, actually."

"He was there all the time!"

"Just on the weekends." Casey frowned. "And now we're not seeing each other at all. There's a reason for that." He picked up another card. Chess pie—Theo's favorite. He rolled his eyes. Wasn't the universe just full of jokes today? "We weren't a good fit. It's better this way."

"Is it, though? You always sound so lonely when I call."

Did he? He hadn't realized he was letting it show. Maybe he'd lost his touch at keeping his emotions tucked away. Maybe living alone had made him soft. Ann would be proud. "I'm fine. You don't need to worry about me."

"I can't help it. You're my baby."

Casey raised a brow. "I know, I know. Let's not go there, okay?"

"Oh, men. Always so afraid of their feelings." She sighed and returned to her dinner planning.

Casey couldn't argue with that. He'd been terrified of his feelings since he was eight and…

Nope. Not going there. He ruthlessly shoved away those useless thoughts and moved over to the window by the kitchen table. The view of the lake was undoubtedly better in summer when everything was lush and green, and the blue sky was reflected in the water. But it wasn't bad in winter either, with the fuzzy gray of the leafless trees gentling the edges of the water and softening the winter ashen sky.

God, he hated how quiet he had to be here. At least in New York, he was so alone these days he could speak freely. No one gave a shit what he said or did. Ann called it the liberation of anonymity. Seriously, why had he thought it was a good idea to come back to Knoxville?

His heart beat faster, and he shoved his hands into his pockets. A strange urge crept up his spine, not unlike the one he sometimes got on swarming subway platforms or in the middle of crowded New York streets. What would happen if he started screaming? What would happen if he made a huge, loud, painful scene? What would his mother do? What would she *say*? What would happen if he stopped being Casey Stevens and started being *free*?

"Speaking of home-and-garden stores," his mother said, interrupting his shadowy turn of thought with a smile, "will you do me a favor today? Can you run by Costco and pick up a Christmas tree? I haven't had time, and your dad wants a real one this year." She waved her hand dismissively. "Something about it just not feeling like Christmas without the real-tree smell."

Casey smirked. "He didn't say it was classier to have a real tree?"

His mother shot him a sharp glance to see if he was being a jerk. He softened his smirk into a genuine-looking smile. She laughed warmly. "You joke, but, well, there's a reason it's funny."

"I'll pick one up, sure."

"Costco makes it easy. Just swing by there. I want it to be at least eight feet tall, if possible. Oh, and grab a few wreaths. Two medium-sized and one large. But nothing gaudy. Make sure it's something that will look nice on the front door." She winked and chuckled. "Keep it classy."

Twenty minutes later, Casey passed Costco without even slowing down. Enough with feeling sorry for himself. It was time to act. He held the steering wheel tightly, and his gut churned. He had another destination in mind—a place he should have gone as soon as he crossed the Knoxville city line. Where, if he were lucky, he'd get a glimpse of the brown eyes he couldn't forget.

And sure, he'd get his parents a tree and some wreaths while he was at it. Classy ones.

Chapter Three

JOEL HAULED THE five-foot Fraser fir from the half-full tree lot and out to the blue 1982 Volvo waiting in front of his store. The temperature dropped fast as the sun skimmed the horizon, and he wished he had gloves on his numb fingers while he tied the tree to the rack on top. The late afternoon light, orange and bright, glared into his eyes as he worked the final knots.

"That'll hold 'er." He turned to his former neighbor, the sweet and old-for-as-long-as-he-could-remember Mrs. Hendrix. "You sure you don't need me to follow you home to get her down and into the house?" He brushed the pine needles from his fleece-lined jean jacket before sticking his hands into the pockets of dirty blue jeans, smiling at her. "I'm happy to do it."

"You're a good boy, Joel." She patted his arm with her arthritis-gnarled fingers. "But my grandson Troy—you remember him?"

Joel raised a brow. Remember Troy? How could he forget? Troy Hendrix had been bucktoothed, acne-pocked, and a nicotine fiend. He'd given Joel his first smoke during one of his summerlong visits to his grandma's back when Troy was nineteen and Joel sixteen. Joel could never forget heaving and gagging after he'd smoked that cigarette or how he'd thrown up afterward, dizzy and overcome. For some reason, he'd taken the whole pack Troy had offered him even after that. "How could I forget Troy?"

"He's going to meet me at the house to help me get it inside and decorate it."

Joel shrugged. The Troy he'd known wasn't always reliable, but maybe he'd changed. They were both grown men now. Supposedly. "If you're sure?"

"Absolutely." Her crinkled rose-petal cheeks glowed in the chilling air, and she winked at him. "You close up shop here and get on home now. Surely you have a young lady waiting with a good dinner for you?"

"Ladies and me? We don't seem to hit it off, Mrs. H," Joel said, grinning slyly. "I'm too much of a player, I guess."

She pshawed and slapped his arm. "Silly boy!"

"Actually, I've got a crockpot, and it's been simmering some nice bison chili since early this morning. From what I hear, that's almost as good as having a wife. Maybe better."

"Oh, law, Joel! You make me laugh, honey." She rubbed his arm affectionately. "Too bad about the ladies. Though, I'm sure you'll find the right one someday. I'm glad to hear you can fend for yourself in the meantime." Her eyes crinkled with her smile. "I bet you'll enjoy that chili."

"I hope so. I sank my grocery money for the week into it."

Mrs. Hendrix laughed like he was joking, and he let her think he was. She didn't need to know how tight things were for him now that Pop was in the nursing home. A crockpot meal to get through the week was hardly the worst of it.

Between the weekly expenses associated with his father's care and the way the big companies like Lowe's and Costco had cut into Vreeland's Home and Garden's bottom line, Joel was just barely keeping the place alive. He'd reduced staffing down to just him, his assistant manager Brandon, and three employees. He'd even cut back on his smoking habit. He allowed himself a mere half-pack a week and limited himself to a six-pack of beer a month.

"If you need any more string lights for your bushes out front, I'm running a sale on the white ones. Half off."

"Oh, white Christmas lights!" Mrs. Hendrix snorted, waving the idea away. "Who wants those? So boring! Put a sale on the colored ones and you've got a deal."

He chuckled as she walked around to the driver's side of her car and climbed in. He rubbed his hands against the cold wind and watched her pull onto Kingston Pike with the Christmas tree he'd just sold her shivering and shedding on top.

Turning back toward the brightly lit store, he whistled low under his breath. A shiny, white Lexus SUV pulled into the parking lot with the wide, telltale swing of an entitled S.O.B. with money to burn. It was late and he was hungry, but he couldn't close up quite yet, no matter what Mrs. H seemed to think. Not when there might be customers to sell trees to, like this rich asshole. Hopefully, he'd buy more than a tree and make staying open worth Joel's while.

Joel plastered on a "welcome to Vreeland's" smile that didn't quite reach his eyes as he rearranged a table of poinsettias positioned near the Christmas tree lot. He glanced at what he had in stock and made a mental note to get Angel—his annoying, goth-brat employee from hell—to contact the nursery for another dozen fresh trees tomorrow.

The SUV door slammed shut, and Joel's back stiffened. Pivoting to greet the new customer, his breath caught in his throat and his heart skipped a beat. The young man standing in front of him was about six feet tall, slim, and as all-American as they came, with light-brown hair that was almost blond, a straight nose, creamy skin, and a pouty-looking mouth that Joel had always wanted to—

Oh, crap.

Casey Stevens.

Just standing there smiling at him like he'd never gone away, wearing clothes that could probably fund Joel's father's stay in the nursing home for a month or more, and glowing like he'd been spit-shined and polished. Brighter than a shiny nickel. Brighter than the plastic glowing Virgin Mary statue Casey had kissed that night so long ago in Mr. Maples's yard.

Dammit. Why now?

Joel didn't have time for the pain twisting through him like a snake curling up tight in his chest, hissing and protective. Promising him that, *yes*, he still had the same unmanageable feelings, and *yes*, he still had a heart that could break. Alas, he hadn't managed to kill off that weak part of himself quite yet. Not for lack of trying.

"Hey," Casey said, smiling and sticking out his fist like a grenade, the start of an old handshake they'd made up the summer they were fourteen. The same summer Casey got braces, and Joel had agonized over his own crooked—*still crooked*—teeth. And the same summer he'd fallen in love with the boy from the "right side of the tracks," and his father had punched him in the mouth for being a moon-eyed sissy about it.

Joel tossed his chin up, withholding his hand. "S'up. Long time, no see."

Casey left his fist out long enough for it to become awkward, but Joel only raised an eyebrow and didn't put him out of his misery. Finally, Casey let his arm fall. His brows dropped, and the corners of his pillow lips drew down. Joel's brain itched with irritation that some part of him wanted to smooth Casey's brow and shush his discomfort away.

Instead, he put out his hand and Casey took it. After shaking like Casey was any old customer, Joel sighed. He'd always given Casey too much leeway. "How's the big city?"

"New York is, uh… It's fine."

"Good. Glad to hear it." Joel pursed his lips and flicked a strand of his dark hair out of his eyes. He put on a smile, but it felt tight and wrong on his face. His heartbeats were all wonky, and the air seemed to whir in his ears, making his own breathing sound strange.

He cleared his throat, trying to get a handle on what to do and where to look. Not at Casey's face—anywhere but in his amber brown eyes. *Get it together. Treat him like he's just another customer.* "Can I help you find something? We have a lot of Christmas items discounted in the back of the store."

He's driving a Lexus, dumbass. Like he needs your stupid discounts! Joel wiped a hand over his upper lip. What the fuck was Casey doing here anyway? Why wasn't he in New York City where he fucking belonged?

Casey frowned, and Joel knew he was probably coming across like a total dick. He shook with the effort to keep himself together. Tight voice, tight chest, barely holding back the betrayal and hurt he'd felt when Casey had up and left him behind. Never even looked back. Like Joel had been nothing and no one at all. Joel chewed the inside of his lip, adrenaline rushing cold in his veins.

It's not like he was your boyfriend. Get a grip, dipshit.

"My mom sent me for a tree."

The uncertainty in Casey's voice and the wavering hurt in his eyes awoke Joel's stinging sense of self-righteous anger. Who was Casey to act hurt? He was the one who'd left, who'd never replied to Joel's last text, who'd cut him off like deadweight.

Joel jerked his chin toward the organized rows of Fraser and Douglas firs and fresh Scotch pines. "Have at it."

He turned back to the poinsettia display, shifting a few pots around. His gut tangled and his chest ached. His sweaty palms nearly lost grip on one of the pots as he moved it slightly left. Wiping his hands against his jeans, he ignored Casey, who stood rooted in the spot, Christmas lights reflecting in his golden-brown hair, apparently struck dumb by Joel's rudeness.

"Oh. Well, right. I guess you're busy." Casey flicked a pointed glance around at the nearly empty parking lot. "With all these customers…"

Since when did earnest little Casey Stevens grow a snarky tongue? Joel almost admired it, except that it meant Casey was still standing there reminding him of feelings he never wanted to have again. It hurt too much when people just up and left. Like his mom had when she died. Like Casey had when he graduated.

If Joel had learned it once, he'd learned it over and over again: everyone left eventually.

"The work's never done when you're the boss," Joel bit out, but his voice shook. "So, like I said, please, have at it. When you've picked out a tree, we'll be happy to help you load it." He gestured at the tree lot again before turning on his heel and stalking into the red brick block of Vreeland's Home and Garden without looking over his shoulder.

"Fuck," he whispered as the door swung closed behind him. His knees shook, and his stomach twisted up hard. He swiped a hand over his face, fingers raking over his scratchy whiskers, and squeezed his eyes shut. "Fucking fuck *fuck.*"

Joel's mind raced. How was it that all the feelings he thought he'd stomped to death and buried deep beside painful memories of his mom came roaring back at just the sight of this grown-up Casey?

It was like a hand had popped out of the grave he'd marked "Love for Casey Stevens," and in an instant the head and shoulders had emerged too, surprisingly intact and handsome. The creature's face was smudged with a bit of dirt, but no sign of decay was in evidence as the rest of the zombie body emerged. Love for Casey Stevens approached, hands outstretched toward him, offering a friendly smile drawn out over straight, white teeth. Joel shuddered. He could feel fingers around his throat, choking him.

The plot for a new book dropped into his head. He'd call it *Merry Christmas From Your Undead Lover,* because why not? When his first (and of course unrequited) love rose from the dead during the holiday season, he was obligated to work it into a novel, wasn't he? It was either that or burn the world down around him. One or the other. No in between.

His employee Angel stood next to the life-size Blow Mold Nativity scene he'd set up near the register. He'd chosen it for their inventory because it was reminiscent of the one in Mr. Maples's front yard. Now, with Casey fucking Stevens wandering the length of his Christmas tree rows, it made his heart wring again.

Oblivious, Angel held a Sharpie in her fingers, a pensive expression on her face. A silver ring glinted in her thick, dark brow, and her blue eyes shimmered with mischievous anticipation. That expression faltered as she caught sight of him. "What's wrong?" she asked.

"Nothing."

She tilted her head, obviously not believing him, but then she shrugged. Her black sweater dotted with white skulls stretched tightly over her ample bosom and wide shoulders. "Then I'll carry on." She leaned forward, shoved her chin-length, dyed black hair behind her ears, and stuck out her tongue in concentration. The Sharpie descended toward Mary's face.

Joel pointed at her. "I swear to God, if you draw a mustache on Mary or put 666 on the Baby Jesus's forehead, I will fire you so fast you won't know what hit you."

Angel sighed and capped the Sharpie. She blinked curiously at him. "You're grouchy tonight. Why?"

"This is a job, not a game," Joel barked, pointing between her and the Blow Mold set. "That's merchandise, not a toy for your amusement. Stop trying to turn my store into your goth performance art piece." He pulled his still-trembling hands through his hair in frustration. "Just sell things to people, Angel. That's what you're here to do."

"But I'm bored," she said, as if that was a reasonable statement to make to an employer. "And this isn't merchandise to sell. It's our display model, and you said I could give it to my mom after the season was over."

Joel grimaced. "I said you could *buy* it from me for sixty percent off, not just take it. And does your mom want her gift vandalized?"

"Maybe. She thinks I'd make a good tattoo artist one day."

"You can draw on it when it's in your mom's yard, then." He took a deep breath, trying to hold it together. Sometimes he thought Angel acted more like a fifteen-year-old than the nineteen her paperwork proclaimed her to be. He was only twenty-two after all, but he felt a dozen years older than her most days. "It's almost closing time. You can get through a few more minutes without vandalizing anything."

"Can I please put 666 on the baby's head? Just long enough to take a selfie with it?" She blinked at him with wide blue eyes popping brightly between the dark black eyeliner on her lids. "I'll use some hair spray to clean it off before I leave."

"No. For one thing, that's blasphemous or something." He wanted to escape into the backroom and get his crap together before he had to go back out there and help Casey load a tree into his SUV. Assuming Casey even wanted to buy a tree from a rude asshole like him. He struggled to come up with another reason. "For another, just no. Absolutely not."

She rolled her eyes and wrote 666 on her left hand instead, and then returned to stand behind the register, smiling to herself as she began to draw what appeared to be a bat on her forearm.

Joel took a slow breath, walked over to the register, and grabbed a red Sharpie from the tin can of pens. He handed it to her and said with a gentler tone, "It's Christmastime. If you're going to draw a bat on your arm, at least put a Santa hat on it."

She rolled her eyes again, this time with a heavy sigh for embellishment, but she uncapped the red pen and complied. Done with his ridiculous employee, Joel stomped off into the backroom and plopped down at his small desk crammed with paperwork and an out-of-date computer. He tugged his hands through his hair before burying his face in his arms. His blood zipped through his body like it was being chased.

Casey Stevens. In town. At his store.

He swallowed hard. Fuck, maybe Casey would just leave without buying anything. Leave and not come back the way he had when he left for NYU three and a half years ago. Why had he come here anyway? To rub it in? To make sure Joel was living the loser life he'd always been destined for despite his stupid adolescent dreams of getting out?

Humiliation rode him hard. Joel's throat tightened. He wished Casey had never come around. But showing up uninvited had always been a habit of Casey Stevens's.

"Can I watch you play?"

Joel looked up from where he was noodling on the new-to-him pawnshop guitar he'd bought with his own money from working in his dad's store. The garage door was open, and the cool winter air mixed with the stale smell of old cigarettes and the relentless scent of diesel oil.

Casey stood there, flushed and handsome, holding a banged-up sketchbook with the winter sun backlighting him like an angel. Joel hated that he thought things like that about Casey. As if he were some kind of queer.

But he was a queer, actually.

If he were being honest.

Because there were plenty of other thoughts he cherished about Casey, too. Uncomfortable, sinful, and exciting thoughts. Thoughts that apparently showed on his face sometimes; thoughts which his dad couldn't resist trying to beat out of him.

"I won't distract you," Casey promised, shoving one hand into the pocket of his khakis and lifting up the sketchbook with the other. "I'll just draw a little."

"The rest of the band will be here soon," Joel warned him. "That'll be your cue to scram."

"I know." Casey's expression went thoughtful as he gazed at the drum kit, amps, and guitars taking up nearly the entire garage. Joel's father might have thought the band was a waste of time, but there were several good reasons he was generous with the use of the garage space. Reasons Joel preferred not to think about—like one massive black eye that had required a cover story for a few weeks—but they were reasons all the same.

Casey scratched at his pink-tipped ear and hesitantly met Joel's eyes. "Or I could stay? I like to listen to the band. Sometimes I don't go home, you know. I hang out around the corner where your friends can't see me, and I listen."

"Stalker."

"Y'all are good."

"Don't go talking like a hick. That'd be low class." Joel teased Casey with the words he'd heard Mr. Stevens use a lot over the years of being Casey's only neighborhood friend, but his heart swelled at the idea that sometimes Casey stayed behind to secretly listen to the band play.

"I'm not a stalker. I just want to hang out with you. Why is that a problem?"

It was a problem because if Joel didn't ditch Casey as soon as they got off the bus at school, if Joel's band pals acknowledged him with even a head nod in passing in the hallways, Casey Stevens might go from having the reputation of an anxious-but-cute nerd boy to…what? The pet geek of the angry, bitter, and going-nowhere-fast crowd?

It wasn't like Joel had any illusions about who he was and what his future held, even if he liked to talk big about his dream career as a writer. But it didn't have to be that way for Casey. He'd go to some fancy college, find a career, make a million dollars before he was twenty-five, and wonder why he'd ever looked at Joel with the hero-worshipful eyes he was flashing now.

And that was the way it should be. The way Joel wanted it to be. He cared too much about Casey to drag him down in the gutter with him. RJ and Becca were already gutter kids. They didn't have anything to lose by being friends with Joel. But Casey sure did.

Besides, maybe he didn't want to share Casey. Not even with his bandmates. But he couldn't admit that to anyone and barely even to himself.

Joel sighed. "If listening around the corner is what you normally do, why not just keep doing it?"

Casey deflated a little and tweaked the collar of his white, long-sleeve polo shirt worn beneath his navy-blue Timberland coat. His clothes were so bland, so personality-free, that sometimes Joel wondered if Casey was actually trying to make himself invisible by wearing them. He figured Casey would have some geek pals by now if he ever wore some T-shirts with science jokes on them. Though Casey was more of an art guy. So T-shirts with art jokes, whatever.

Joel huffed. He knew Casey would be better off if he had other friends, and, frankly, so would Joel. He'd have fewer black eyes and bruises, that was for sure. But Joel couldn't shove Casey away either. Because he was dying to know what Casey Stevens looked like naked, what his mouth tasted like, and what noises he made when he came. Hell, he'd have done anything to just hold Casey in his arms and smell his hair, touch his skin, and get to love him. But wanting those things was a lot like breathing underwater. It was going to get him killed. And also like breathing underwater, in the end, it was inevitable. A person could only hold their breath for so long.

If he were smart, he'd beat the shit out of Casey and kill this thing between them once and for all, instead of letting him stay. But that was another thing he'd never do, just like he'd never kiss Casey or let him glimpse how he really felt.

Because a queer wasn't something he could ever be. Even if Casey let him. Even if the world allowed it. His dad had made it more than clear with his fists that Joel couldn't ever be a queer and live. Not ever.

"I want to stay here to listen when the band comes," Casey said, his amber eyes flashing and his jaw setting stubbornly. Joel knew that look. It meant Casey Stevens was about to get what he wanted, and Joel Vreeland wasn't going to stop him. "And I don't care if you're an asshole about it."

Joel's lips twitched as Casey sank down to the cold concrete floor of the garage to sit with his legs crossed. His tight jaw dared Joel to do something. Defiantly, Casey opened up his sketchbook, revealing the doodles and small, fake ads that he made up for fun. His talent wasn't huge with a pen, but Joel had seen what Casey could do with the digital art apps on his iPad, and it was good stuff. He caught Casey's eye and raised a brow.

"Not leaving," Casey said again, his pouty mouth thinning.

Joel shrugged, elated and scared at the same time. "Fine. Be stubborn." His heart beat faster, and his palms started to sweat.

Casey broke into a smile, and damn if that didn't make Joel's stomach churn with strange, messy excitement. He might puke if Casey didn't stop looking kissably obstinate like that. Joel concentrated on strumming the chords of the band's new song "King's Pride," and Casey sang along quietly. Casey's tenor was sweet like honey, and Joel held himself back from putting the guitar aside, sliding down to his knees, and grabbing hold of Casey's cheeks to kiss him.

He cleared his throat and schooled his mind again. Kissing Casey was a super queer thing to want to do. Really damn queer. Why couldn't he just stop imagining it and wishing Casey wanted it too?

Then the dark thoughts descended. The ones he tried to ignore almost as much as he tried to ignore the kissing thoughts. What if someone else saw Casey's special beauty one day? What if that someone was a girl? How would he ever survive if Casey fell in love with someone? Held hands with her in front of him? Kissed her?

He'd curl up and die, that's what, if he were being honest.

Sitting up and rubbing his face, Joel groaned. Honest about his feelings for Casey Stevens was something he'd never planned to be, and with Casey suddenly returned, he sure as hell wasn't about to start now.

Chapter Four

CASEY COULDN'T BELIEVE what a dickwad Joel had turned into. Yeah, he'd always been cranky like his old man, and he'd been a jerk sometimes, but that was when they were kids. They were adults now. Grown men. And Casey hadn't expected Joel to treat him like a stranger. Not that he'd thought Joel would give him a giant bear hug, pat him on the back, and welcome him home either. But a few minutes of his time? The chance to make amends and reconnect? He'd thought he'd at least get that.

Should have known better. Casey berated himself for hoping and tried to banish the knot of pain that tightened in his gut.

But, if he was honest with himself—something Ann was teaching him how to be—maybe he deserved the reception he'd received. Friends grew apart, true enough, but most did it naturally. He couldn't claim that the end of his friendship with Joel had been natural at all. No, Casey had turned his back on Knoxville and everyone in it after he came out as gay to his parents and headed off to NYU still shaking with the fright.

Frankly, he'd been too scared to look back. He'd always thought if Joel really knew how he felt and the things he wanted to do with him, he'd be disgusted. Joel was straight after all, and most straight guys in Knoxville didn't have a very open mind about gay sex.

So maybe that was it. Joel *was* disgusted. Joel had probably heard through the grapevine about Casey being a big ol' queer who enjoyed sticking his dick up tight, sweet man-butt. Maybe that idea grossed Joel out so much he couldn't even be polite to Casey. Maybe he hated him now. That was probably what this cold shoulder was all about. Casey's heart ached.

Casey couldn't be too surprised. Homophobia was a real thing, after all, and he'd experienced it before. Though he hadn't expected it of Joel, who'd always been cool with both RJ and Becca being gay. What could have changed? Had he found religion? Been saved? Gone conservative?

Casey's chest went tight the way it always did when shame clawed into him. He closed his eyes and breathed through it, trying to listen to his inner Ann-voice. What would she say about Joel? She'd probably suggest that Casey not jump to conclusions, and then she'd ask if this kind of cold, distant behavior was normal for Joel.

And, yeah, Casey would have to say that it absolutely was. Even if he didn't want it to be. There hadn't been a single time Casey could think of when he hadn't been initially rebuffed by Joel when they were kids. But if he persisted, Joel always came around.

Maybe instead of Joel turning into a giant homophobe, he was doing what he always did: playing the straight-guy friendship version of hard-to-get. Like back in the day when Joel used to tell Casey he should leave the garage before Becca and RJ showed up for band practice, but then was secretly happy when Casey stubbornly stayed anyway. Casey hadn't missed those subtle smiles or the flash of amused satisfaction in Joel's eyes when Casey had just *stayed* and been his friend, no matter how Joel grumbled about it.

Casey stalked up and down the rows of Christmas trees. At the end of one identical line, he glanced back toward the store. Joel had initially disappeared somewhere deeper inside, but he was visible now through the well-lit windows, instructing a teenage girl wearing a black sweater with white skulls, helping her arrange some fir and holly wreaths. The girl frowned and sucked on her finger like the holly had pricked her.

Joel motioned with his hands. He no longer wore the thick fleece-lined jean jacket he'd had on when Casey pulled up. He'd taken it off, revealing a white short-sleeve shirt and jeans that clung to his ass. His arms bore tattoos that hadn't been there the last time Casey had seen them bare.

Casey couldn't make out the details of the tats, but they were all black and most were in script, clearly words of some sort, except for one on his right forearm that was bright red. An upside-down heart—depending on which direction a person looked at it. It would be right-side up to Joel and upside-down to others.

Swallowing hard, Casey shook his head and turned back to the rows of Christmas trees. Dejection seeped into him from the cold soles of his tennis shoes up to the top of his head. He walked more slowly back down the next row. He looked more carefully at the trees this time.

They were all of good stock. Many tall enough to choose for home. He could stuff one in the back of the SUV, leave some cash half-tucked beneath a poinsettia pot, and get going. It might be better to cut his losses and forestall further humiliation. Or, hell, he could always go to Costco like his mom had asked. The employees there might not give him a big ol' hug either, but they wouldn't make him feel like a total piece of shit by just walking away like he wasn't worth their time.

Instead, Casey sat on a wrought-iron garden bench decked out with glowing, colored twinkle lights, and counted his breaths. Each exhale was released in giant, white puffs. It was a trick Ann had taught him during his first winter in the city: he could endure any amount of loneliness or pain for five good puffs of frigid air. And then he could do it again.

"Still here?" Joel asked, voice terse, shattering Casey's concentration. His eyes were hot, though, as he stood at the other end of the row of trees, hands stuffed into his re-donned jean jacket's pockets and one dark, thick brow arched questioningly.

"So many to choose from." Casey stood and dusted off his ass. His cashmere trench coat didn't provide the same warmth that Joel's denim and fleece probably did, but he shoved his hands into his pockets all the same, mirroring Joel's stance. "I gave up. Maybe you could help me out? You know, with your tree expertise?"

Joel stared at him.

He should just take the hint and leave. What compelled him to stay here and stare down Joel's dark glare when he obviously wasn't wanted? But he was still Casey Stevens, still that boy in Joel's garage at heart. And he wasn't going to leave until he got what he wanted. Not unless Joel actually outright told him to go. "Mom said it was up to me to choose. But, I mean, what's the difference between Scotch Pine and Douglas Fir anyway?"

Joel shifted to his other foot and shrugged. "It's just a matter of what kind of needle you prefer. The longer Scotch Pine or the shorter Douglas Fir."

"Why would someone prefer one over another?"

"Some people think the Scotch Pine is prettier and has a nicer color, but the ornaments slip off the long needles. Others say the Douglas Fir has a stronger pine scent, though it isn't as attractive. But the short needles hold the ornaments better. It's all a matter of what you want."

Casey smiled. A matter of what he wanted? He wanted Joel to talk more. He wanted to break through to him and be friends again. The length of needles was as good a place as any to start. "What do you like?"

Joel stared at him, his pale cheeks flushing before he broke eye contact. "It doesn't matter what I like. You should ask your mom what she wants." He started to turn away.

"Hey!" The word burst out of him before Casey could stop it.

Joel turned back, brows lifted in surprise.

"Want to hang out while I'm in town?"

Joel cocked his head. "Excuse me?"

"You heard me."

Joel's expression fluttered through a dozen different shades of irritable shock and flabbergasted surprise. None of which matched Casey's own disbelief that he was actually standing here talking to Joel again, asking him out—in a way—and he wasn't going to let him get free without answering.

Casey strode closer until they stood face-to-face, surprised to find that Joel was a few inches shorter than him now.

Joel's chin lifted, eyes intense as he held Casey's gaze. "Why?"

Casey decided not to mention Joel's muscles or tattoos. And he definitely was not going to mention how tough (and hot) Joel looked these days with his unshaven five-o'clock shadow and his callused hands. All he could spit out around the tightness in his chest and the dizzy rush in his veins was, "I've missed you, man."

Joel tossed his hands up incredulously. "Are you serious?"

Casey swallowed hard, trying to get a grip. "Why wouldn't I be?" He crossed his arms over his chest.

Joel scoffed. It sounded nothing like the rough giggle that used to send shivers up Casey's spine. "Are you kidding me right now? You haven't contacted me in almost four years." He pierced Casey with a glare. "Now you want to 'hang out'?" He snorted. "I repeat, why?"

"Because we were friends…" Casey trailed off. What had he been hoping for? A Christmas miracle where Joel was gay too and had been pining for him as well? He was insane.

"Ha! Before you left, I sure as hell thought we were friends. But after? Not so much," Joel snapped. "Do you need me to remind you why? Or do you think you can remember on your own?"

Casey's head spun. He'd never been unkind to Joel. He'd only ever wanted Joel to like him. He'd only ever *wanted* Joel. He'd left Knoxville and turned his back on their friendship so Joel would never know how much. *So why are you here now, idiot?*

"Forget it." Joel shook his head.

"No." Casey stepped even closer. The scent of pine and fir filled his nose, and he wanted to drag Joel close and hold him against his body. He wanted to find out what he smelled like now, what he tasted like.

Joel frowned and shrugged. "No what?"

"No, I mean… I remember how I left and… Joel, what I did, ghosting like that? It's not how friends should treat each other."

"Glad we sorted that out." Joel said, shoving his hands into his jean jacket pockets and shrugging. "Now grab your tree and get out of here, man."

Casey could practically feel the heat coming off Joel's body. "You're treating me like a stranger or, worse, like someone you hate." Casey tried to calm his voice. He sounded shrill even to himself. "I know I didn't keep in touch these last few years, not like I should have, but is this really how you want it to be?"

Joel blew a hank of dark hair off his cheekbone and swallowed audibly. He darted a glance back toward the store's big, bright windows and eyed the goth girl he'd been counseling on the wreaths earlier. She appeared to be drawing a tattoo with a black Sharpie on one of the shepherds' arms in the Blow Mold Nativity scene. Joel shook his head and sighed. "For fuck's sake."

"Well?" Casey pressed. In addition to the inches he'd grown in the last few years in New York, he'd also grown an even stronger spine. He couldn't have survived the city if he hadn't. And Ann had helped with that, too.

"No, this isn't how I want it to be," Joel admitted. His voice was drained of rage for the moment. "But I don't know why you came here."

"Why *wouldn't* I come here?" Casey gestured around at the trees and the store. "My mom asked me to get a tree and some wreaths. I always came here before."

Joel's eyes hardened again. "I mean, yeah, sure. Come on over to Vreeland's if you want a tree, or a Christmas cactus, or some icicle lights for the outside of your folks' big, honking, new house, but otherwise…?" He licked his lips and sputtered, gesturing with his hands like Casey was a nuisance. "We were friends a long time ago. Now, I got nothing for you, man."

Casey reached out, his fingers so close to touching Joel's jacket, but he fell short. "Look, my mom said to go to Costco, but I came here instead."

"And?"

"Can't you see what I'm getting at?"

Joel shook his head. "No. I can't."

"I'm not here for a tree, Joel." Casey shoved his hands through his hair; frustration and another stunted emotion stuck like shrapnel in his chest. "I mean, yeah, I need a tree. For my mom. But I came here to see you. I thought we..." He swallowed, his heart squeezing. He felt light-headed. "I hoped maybe..."

"Yeah?" Joel's eyebrow went up again, and this time there was a glimmer of something less angry in his eyes. "You hoped what?"

"That we could hang, I guess. Like I said."

"Hang. You *guess*." Joel shook his head and crossed his arms over his chest. "Wow. What are we? Fifteen? Or are you slumming it?"

"Slumming it?"

Everything was pear-shaped. Casey had walked into some upside-down world where it was an insult to want to rekindle an old friendship. Where was the exit and how did he get out?

"Sure. Slumming it. You know, piss Daddy Stevens off by rubbing elbows with a proletariat like me. Isn't that what you used to get off on?"

"I don't understand." Casey scrubbed a hand over his mouth. "You actually think... I mean, are you really angry that I've missed you? That I wanted to hang out with you while I'm in town for Christmas? That's crazy!" Casey threw his arms wide. "What's your problem, dude? Yeah, I should have stayed in touch, but this shit happens when people go to college." He knew that wasn't necessarily true—that he'd cut Joel out of his life to protect himself from heartbreak—but he couldn't exactly admit that to Joel now if he wanted to revive their friendship. "What do you want from me?"

"Nothing." Joel's dark eyes didn't look at all like mud anymore. They were cold and hard as stone. "I don't want anything from you."

He stepped close enough to stab his finger against Casey's chest. "Go to Costco and buy your mom a tree. Take it back to your fancy, giant house. Decorate it in gold-dipped fucking glass balls for all I care. Go back to New York. Become a hotshot lawyer, or whatever you're going to be, and get on with your life. Me? I don't fit in with you, Casey. I never have, and I never will."

He brushed past, stormed toward the parking lot, and climbed into a beaten down old, gray Chevy. The goth girl from inside came running out after him, shouting for him to wait as he started the truck and drove away, but it was too late. She and Casey stared after Joel until his taillights disappeared around the bend.

"Well, crap. I guess I have to close up then," she said, shoulders slumping. "I hate when he does that."

"Sorry."

"Why?" she asked, snapping her gum and shoving her black hair behind her ear. "Is it your fault he left?"

"I think so. Yeah."

Her blue eyes sharpened, and she smiled with a gleam of interest. "Really? What did you say to him?"

"Nothing much. I asked if he wanted to hang out. We used to be friends, but…apparently we aren't anymore."

She laughed. "Don't sweat it, dude. Mr. Frosty Pants doesn't like anyone, really. Or at least he likes to pretend he doesn't." She shoved up the sleeves of her sweater, revealing what appeared to be a drawing or a tat of a bat wearing a Santa hat on her left forearm. For her sake, Casey hoped it was just a drawing. "I'm sorry if he was rude to you. Normally he's pretty great with customers. He saves his assholery for his employees and friends."

"Maybe I rank as a friend after all."

"Maybe." She eyed him speculatively. "Does he have a good reason to be mad at you?"

"I left for three and a half years and never got in touch."

"Huh. Never pegged him for being sensitive about niceties and shit like that, but, then again, I don't actually know him that well." She lifted her chin higher and nodded once, a smirk twisting her lips. "That's it. I'm putting 666 on the baby Jesus's forehead, and I'm gonna get that selfie. He owes me for making me close without him." Without another word, she stomped back into Vreeland's, leaving Casey alone amongst the Christmas trees.

He consulted his inner Ann and got nothing.

After breathing in and out twenty times, he grabbed the nearest eight-foot tall tree, dragged it toward his SUV, and shoved it in the back, heedless of broken limbs or damage. Then he headed in to pay the goth girl. Inside, he grabbed some decent-sized wreaths—one with a giant red bow.

Then he climbed back into his SUV, ready to return to his parents' house with all his hard-won greenery. As he pulled out of the parking lot, he resolved to write the whole incident off as a mistake. Take it as a lesson. This time, he'd be done with Joel for real, and he wouldn't ever look back.

"You utter asshole," he muttered, as snow again flirted with his windshield.

He wasn't sure if he was talking about Joel or himself.

Chapter Five

THE PRIOR WEEK, Joel had decked out his trailer for the holidays. He'd draped solar-powered colored lights along the gutters and added a wreath with a hanger on the front door. But nothing really took away from the fact that it just didn't feel like home.

No place had in a long time now.

The house in Belmont Hills hadn't felt like home once Casey left for college. Then it'd been ripped away from him entirely after Pop's stroke when he'd been forced to sell it to help fund his stay in the nursing home.

Joel climbed out of his faithful gray Chevy Silverado and took a good hard look at the trailer on the two-acre lot where he lived now, trying to see it through Casey's eyes. It was a decent piece of land he'd inherited directly from his granny on his mother's side when she passed away. In the gloom of night, illuminated only by the motion-sensor lights he'd put along the edge of his property, he noted the line where the lingering grass turned muddy down by the lake. The water shimmered in the moonlight, dancing in the light breeze. The fishing was good there in the summer, and he often caught his own dinner, which went toward cutting down the grocery bill.

Over to the right, near a thicket of overgrown bushes and shade trees, tumbled-down walls indicated the spot where Granny's old cabin had once stood. To the left was a flat area that led to the ridge of train tracks running along the eastern side of his property.

A layman unfamiliar with the ins and outs of Knoxville real estate might have thought Joel could solve his money troubles by selling these two acres of lake property to a developer. But the close presence of the train tracks and the fact that the property was on the "wrong side" of the lake made it worth very little. Joel was proud of the land, though. It was his, and no one could take it away from him.

Admittedly, the trailer wasn't his dream home. Once his financial tides had finally turned, he planned to build a log cabin to his own specifications—a home that would do his grandmother's gift justice and make a nice place for him to retire into old age. He'd write his books by the window, looking out on the lake, surrounded by peace and quiet.

Maybe he'd never move out of Knoxville like he'd dreamed when he was a teenager just a few short, hard years ago, but he could make something good out of what he had here. He looked around and saw possibilities. It was one of the only areas of his life where he felt optimistic.

But if Casey saw the place as it was now, he wouldn't see Joel's dreams. All he'd see was Joel's current poverty, and he'd pity him. Or, worse, he'd loathe him. Casey's face would take on that sour look rich people always wore when confronted with the unwashed masses. That haughty sneer. Joel never wanted to see Casey's all-American, gorgeous face twisted up like that.

And damn, if it wasn't somehow worse that Casey'd grown up so handsome and tall. He'd lost all his old nerdy scrawniness. The boy Joel had found confusingly attractive had become the kind of man who could make Joel's head spin. Because, yeah, Joel was gay as hell. It'd taken him a long time to fully admit it to himself, but it was the truth. And one day he was going to have to do something about it.

But not with Casey Stevens. *Never* with Casey Stevens.

He stalked up the stairs to the trailer and jerked open the door. The welcoming scent of spicy chili greeted him. Saliva flooded his mouth, and he groaned hungrily. He'd forgotten to eat most of the day—not that he had a lot in the tiny fridge at the store anyway.

His dog Bruno flung himself at Joel desperately. His golden, sleek, muscled body wriggled like mad and his whip-long tail whapped from side to side, catching a stack of bills on the entryway table and knocking them to the floor.

"Well, hello to you too," Joel said with a laugh, rubbing Bruno's silky ears and gazing into his wide-set golden eyes. He'd taken Bruno in when he found him wandering the edge of his property, skinny and starving, with twine knotted around his neck. It'd never crossed his mind to send him to an animal shelter.

He knew a pit bull mix would face a death sentence at most shelters or, worse, be "adopted" out to dog fighters. Besides, he'd been lonely, and taking in a dog seemed a far better choice than actually doing something scary like downloading one of those gay dating apps.

So, a dog it was. Unlike with some meaningless hookup, Joel had no regrets. Bruno was a great pet. He waited patiently all day for Joel to come home, never running off too far, and always using the dog door Joel had installed to do his business. Plus he greeted Joel just like this. Every day. No matter what.

To Bruno, Joel mattered—*more* than mattered.

Bruno didn't care if Joel had been away for sixteen hours at Vreeland's doing his work. He didn't care if Joel was hungry, tired, and not sure where the next paycheck was coming from. Bruno was just happy as hell every time Joel came back, period. He didn't know they lived on the "wrong" side of the lake in a trailer with not enough food. He just loved bounding in the woods after squirrels and splashing in the water. His nonjudgmental love, incredibly low expectations, and unconditional trust had saved Joel's life too, if he were honest.

Which, as Joel was all too aware, he didn't tend to be.

Not about the scary things. And not about important ones. Like how he'd *really* felt when he saw Casey Stevens get out of his stunning white, brand-new SUV that evening. It'd been a kick to the gut, and then to the nads, and then to the gut again. Fuck. He was still winded from it.

When Bruno calmed down from his greeting, Joel said, "Let's get some dinner, yeah?"

Bruno agreed, enthusiastically bounding around in a circle, knocking more mail onto the floor before hurtling into the kitchen. Joel followed, cleaning up the mess Bruno left in his wake and laughing as Bruno shook himself and whined eagerly. A cloud of hair rose and fell around him, joining the clumps of dog hair already breeding big, fat dog-bunnies in the corners.

"I should vacuum later," he said to Bruno, who stood at his feet grinning up at him with his tongue lolling out. "But, man, Bruno. I'm tired. Sixteen hours a day for three weeks straight will do that to a guy."

Luckily, his assistant manager, Brandon, would be returning from his poorly timed vacation the next day. Then Joel could finally get a break from the endless work. Not that customers were a bad problem to have. He'd rather the store be busy and the money be coming in than to have plenty of leisure time and no way to pay his bills. Even though he loved writing, his books never sold more than a handful of copies each.

Soon enough he'd take a whole day off and leave the store in the hands of Angel and Brandon and his other three employees, and he'd spend it writing. If only he could hire a couple more part-time employees like his dad had back in the old days, then he'd be set. He might even finish more than one novella a year.

Unfortunately, once Christmas was over, he knew they'd hit a few lean months again before the spring planting rush started. Maybe by summer he'd be eating more than a crockpot of chili for a week. Maybe he'd even be able to afford to see a movie in the theater and reactivate his streaming services.

So many pipe dreams.

Maybe one of them could come true.

After filling Bruno's dog dish, Joel prepared his bowl of chili, sprinkling the top with the corn chips and grated cheese he'd splurged on. Slumped on the sofa, he aimed the remote control at the TV, but navigating the paltry, free offerings of his HDTV antenna was uninspiring. Sighing, he turned it off.

As he reached for his laptop and powered it on, he knew he should open his latest manuscript and start adding more words to where he left off. But he also knew he wasn't going to do that. He had another plan for his evening, and he almost hated himself for it. Chili spread over his tongue in spicy bursts of flavor as he logged into Facebook and typed a name into the search bar.

He allowed himself to do this every six months or so. A few times he'd even let his mouse linger over the Facebook messenger icon before he hastily closed down the screen and shoved his computer away. This time, he wasn't even tempted by that button. No, tonight he planned to torture himself with Casey's photos again.

There.

Casey and a tall, good-looking black guy who was obviously his boyfriend. They both wore tuxedoes and had their arms around each other. Big grins spread across their stupidly handsome faces, glittering like the New York skyline behind them.

Was it taken on top of the Empire State Building or someplace else? Joel didn't know. He'd never gone anywhere but Sunset Beach, North Carolina, once with his mom before she'd died. He'd just been a little kid. He still remembered the feeling of the waves crashing over his toes and the sucking sand beneath his feet. Eventually, he'd stood in one spot long enough that the waves had left him in a hole, mired deep enough that his mom, laughing, had to come tug him out.

Joel clicked to the next picture. He'd seen it before, but he wanted to see it again.

It was Casey and the same guy—tagged as Theo Frasier—dancing at someone's wedding. He didn't think it was theirs. Surely Becca would have told him if Casey had gotten married. Because while Becca didn't keep up with Casey per se, she did keep up with RJ, and RJ was in several pictures on Facebook with Casey, so obviously they were still in touch.

And how had that happened, anyway? How had *his* group—his band—fallen apart like that? And why had everyone but him seemed to go on to do just fine? Even Becca, now his closest friend, had her life together a thousand times over compared to him. Not that Casey had been part of the band, really. But he might as well have been. He was always there, every practice, staring up at them, his head moving to the beat and his eyes gleaming with fannish adoration.

God, Joel missed that. Even if he'd never deserved it, he'd *lived* for that look in Casey's eyes. A huff from his feet reminded him that Bruno gazed at him adoringly now, but he was just a dog. He'd gaze at anyone who fed him with the same devotion. Casey had been…Casey. And Joel had flown high as a kite on his gaze, even if he'd always been too afraid to admit what that meant.

Speaking of what it meant…

Why hadn't he taken the risk four years ago and kissed Casey that last night they spent together on their bench before Casey left for NYU? If nothing else, he'd have felt those lush lips pressed against his own before the punch came. And what if there hadn't been a punch at all? What if Casey had kissed him back? After all, he looked so fucking comfortable kissing this Theo Frasier.

Joel clicked to that picture next.

In it, Casey and Theo kissed playfully in front of a small Christmas tree. Half of Casey's mother's body was visible at the edge of the shot, and Casey's tiny aunt, Courtney, stood on a chair behind them giving bunny ears and grinning widely.

The picture was clearly taken in New York City in a fancy hotel room and not Casey's parents' new house—the gleaming, shining, ridiculously big place Joel had driven by out of curiosity at least a half dozen times. The house that was actually right across the lake from his own property. He could see their bright, back windows glowing in the darkness right now if he went to his bedroom and looked out.

Joel stared at the picture and shook his head, beating himself up for wanting so much that he couldn't have.

Casey kissed this man—this obviously wealthy, well-connected man—in front of his parents in their super upper-class hotel room, decorated expensively for the holidays, while his accepting aunt stood behind them—literally. *That* was Casey's life now. That was the kind of man Casey got to be.

And all the while, back home in Knoxville, across the wrong side of the lake, Joel was alone. He'd dealt with his father's stroke alone. Ran Vreeland's Home and Garden alone. And admitted his gayness alone. He'd done it all—faced his fears, dealt with his anger, and endured the endlessly looping sense of betrayal—alone.

Bruno jumped up on the sofa beside him and snuffled at Joel's almost empty bowl of chili. Joel must have been hungrier than he realized if he'd eaten that much without noticing and despite his heartsick jealousy. Bruno's jowls dripped with slobber.

"I know. I'm a sad sack," Joel muttered as he let Bruno lick up the last of the chili. "Wah, wah, wah. I tell you what, Bruno. It's better to be alone than…"

He had no idea.

Snapping the laptop shut, he closed his eyes. The truth was he didn't want to be alone and never had, but he knew he didn't get to be friends with Casey Stevens either. That wasn't how the world worked.

Not today anyway.

Chapter Six

"CASEY, MY MAN, to what do I owe this honor?" RJ was clearly a touch high; his voice through the phone sounded a little spacy. Casey wasn't sure how he felt about that, but he supposed it was part of the rock 'n' roll lifestyle.

"Yeah, it's been a while. Sorry about that."

"S'okay. How's your boyfriend? What's his name, Tad?"

"Theo. We broke up."

"Because he was uptight and weird?"

"No," Casey said, laughing and rubbing at his face. He'd parked in his parents' driveway with the tree and wreaths he'd purchased from Joel's store filling the SUV with needles and pine scent. The new neighbors' houses were dressed up for the holidays—very tastefully, of course. He watched the moon reflecting on the lake beyond the house. "We ended things because we weren't in love. We both thought we deserved more."

"He got tired of you phoning it in?"

"I did more than phone it in!" Casey protested. He'd tried to be a good boyfriend to Theo, but love wasn't something you could force.

"Fair enough. But I guess he's a little right about you not opening up. Take me, for example. I knew you all through high school while you worshipped at Joel's feet, but even then I couldn't say for sure you were gay. Not until you showed up at Knitting Factory that night when I was playing in New York."

"Well, I wasn't out in high school."

"Obviously. And maybe I just wasn't looking closely enough. Sorry about Theo, though."

"Thanks. It didn't hurt as much as it should have. Which probably says it all."

"Yeah."

The neighbors on the right turned on their Christmas tree lights, visible through the big picture window facing Casey's folks' house. "Um, so I have a question."

"Hit me."

Casey tried to sound casual. "You keep up with Joel at all?"

"Oh, Joel. Your one true love," RJ teased.

"I should never have told you about that." He'd confessed it that night after the show at Knitting Factory back in RJ's hotel room while Theo was in the bathroom.

RJ took a long sucking inhale on something. Probably a joint, since RJ had never smoked a cigarette in his life as far as Casey knew. "But you did."

"Mistakes were made."

"Maybe. But, no, man, I haven't talked to him in a few years. Becca keeps up with him, though."

"Ah." Casey swallowed hard. "Did you tell Becca what I told you?"

"Tell 'er what?"

"About my crush on Joel?" Becca followed him on Facebook, so she knew that he was gay.

RJ chuckled deeply. "Nah. I kind of forgot about it until just now, to be honest. I was pretty drunk that night."

"True."

"But, I admit, I'm surprised Joel never came out."

"Came out?"

"Yeah. I'd always hoped he would, you know?" He sounded sad and fond all at once. "From what little I know, though, he's as closeted as ever."

Casey frowned. "Joel's straight."

"Uh no. The way he used to look at you? Are you kidding me?" RJ laughed again. "I mean, I didn't know if *you* were gay, but Joel? C'mon." He clucked his tongue.

Casey swallowed hard, hope hurting as much as hopelessness ever had. "Spell it out for me, RJ. Pretend I'm dumb." Casey rubbed his fingers over his eyebrows, straining for patience. His breath came tight and fast.

Why was it that the acute heart-pangs he'd tried to run away from years ago started up again with every mention of Joel's name? It'd been almost four years, for God's sake, and Joel had basically just told him to kiss off. How could he be so pathetically in love still? It made no sense.

"Ah, I don't know, bro. I'm high. Probably saying things I shouldn't." RJ sighed heavily. "But Becca and I always thought Joel's claims about hooking up with girls in high school were all bullshit. Especially since he never got a second date with any of them. And *especially* since I never had any reason to believe he really had a first date in the first fucking place."

"What are you talking about? Girls loved him," Casey muttered, rubbing at his eyes. His mind whirred. "They were always coming onto him at school. Flirting. Following him around." It used to drive him nuts, waiting for the day Joel did choose one of them to date for real and not just screw like he claimed.

"Yeah. True. They did chase him, you're right." RJ took another puff of whatever he was smoking. "What do I know? I just always thought we'd have heard *something* from one of those girls if he'd actually taken them out. Like, you know, drama because he used them and walked away. That sort of thing." RJ coughed. "Becca always said it was all bullshit. Just Joel fronting. You know how he was—all bark about everything. Never any real bite."

Casey sat quietly trying to absorb RJ's words. It wasn't possible. Was it? "So you think he's gay?"

"Maybe. Could be bi. He sure had some kind of thing for you back then. Becca and I used to talk about it all the time. Though we haven't discussed it in years. She's too busy telling me the gruesome details about her latest lady hookups to gossip about Joel, or you for that matter."

"Why wouldn't Joel have told you he was gay? You and Becca were out already."

"Like you told us?"

Casey groaned. It was a fair point, but he didn't want to admit it.

"Scared probably. Joel's dad had some pretty big hang-ups about queers. Joel always told me and Becca to never mention it around him or we'd never be allowed back again. Hell, Becca used to pretend to be Joel's girlfriend in front of his dad. And he punched Joel sometimes, you know?"

"Wait, what?" Casey tasted bile. "He did?"

"Yeah."

Casey's head spun. How had he not known any of this? Not about Becca pretending to be Joel's girlfriend, and definitely not about Joel's father being abusive. He'd been Joel's best friend. They'd hopped the fence for each other. They'd watched YouTube videos in each other's bedrooms. They'd listened to Gaslight Anthem albums and talked about horror movies.

Why the hell did RJ know something so important and he didn't?

RJ went on, "His dad didn't hit him enough for anyone to call Child Protection or whatever, but... Well, I don't know." RJ scoffed, annoyance slipping over the line. "It seemed like enough to me. I wanted to call, but it wasn't my business. Or that's what my mom said when I told her about that black eye he had that time—remember? You even asked him about it."

The glaring purple bruise had forced Joel's eye shut and lasted over a week. Casey's chest tightened. "He said he fell cleaning out the gutters."

RJ spoke softly, like he didn't want to spook Casey. "Joel lies. That's what I'm telling you. He lies for good reasons, I guess. Well, good reasons *to him*. But they're lies all the same."

"Lies," Casey echoed, feeling pieces of their past clicking into new and strange positions, making a fresh puzzle, a different map.

"Yeah, tons of lies. Everything from acting like he didn't want us around to dating girls to where those bruises came from." RJ sounded desperately sad, and the echo of it filled Casey up. "As for him being queer like us? Well, what other straight boy was hanging out with me and Becca? Not you. Am I right?"

"Not me," Casey conceded. "But it's not impossible. It's not like every friend I've ever had in the world is gay."

"True. Some of the guys in the bands I've toured with have been mostly or even all straight. I prefer it that way, actually. It means more hot ass for me."

"Ha!"

"Opening for The Cure was my best gig ever. I got so much tail. All those old farts went to bed so early, and the band I was playing for at the time was totally straight. I was taking men home in handfuls. It was amazing."

"You're a slut." Casey laughed.

"And proud of it." RJ laughed with him before he spoke again, a tender sympathy in his tone. "So, you're really still carrying a torch after all this time?"

Casey's throat tightened. His instinct was to deny it and make up an excuse to get off the phone, push RJ away along with everyone else. But he had to face it. "Yeah. But I think he hates me."

"Why the hell would he hate you?"

Casey leaned back against the headrest and studied the pristine ceiling of the car's interior. The pine scent from the tree sticking out the back enveloped him. "Pretty sure it's because I didn't contact him for almost four years after I went to college."

"Huh. Might not be the coolest thing you've ever done, but given your big old unrequited love, I understand why you did it."

"Yeah. I stopped by Vreeland's tonight to pick up a Christmas tree for my folks. He wasn't happy to see me."

RJ laughed. "Pissy little shit, ain't he?"

Casey huffed and rolled his eyes. "You know what? He really is."

"Yep," RJ agreed and then hummed with a sweet gravelly purr that soothed Casey's hurt.

Perking up, Casey asked, "Hey, where are you right now? Are you home for Christmas? Maybe we could get together. Hang out. Talk." He and RJ hadn't spent a ton of time together over the years, but Casey felt closer to him than anyone he'd met in New York. Which was really pathetic when he thought about it.

"Unfortunately I'm in Boston tonight. Then I'm spending Christmas in Cinci, gigging for a friend's local band, and after that I'm heading out to London. Going on tour with Pearl Necklace."

"Never heard of them." That wasn't a shock. RJ played guitar for almost any band that would take him on. He'd seen the world that way, though sometimes Casey wondered if he missed making his own music.

"Queer grunge-rock. Doesn't pay as well as my last gig, but it's a passion project for me." RJ laughed with rough joy. It made Casey smile, despite his spinning head. "The lead singer's my new boyfriend."

"Oh? Awesome. Well, congratulations. What's his name?"

"Pan Soldier."

"No, it's not."

RJ cracked up. "No. It's not. But that's what he goes by onstage and that's what he makes me call him in bed. 'Yeah, Pan! Take it like the soldier you are!'"

Casey snorted. "You sure know how to pick 'em."

"Don't I, though?"

Settling into the driver's seat again, Casey watched as a string of colored lights blinked to life on a trailer across the lake. "Remember back in high school when you lusted after our English Composition teacher? Twitchy Mr. Danvers?"

"Oh, man. Don't even bring him up," RJ groaned. "I still get hard when I think about his hot little ass in those tailored tweed pants. Christ."

"You loved his bow ties."

"His bow ties gave me life. It's true. Shit." RJ moaned again. "Why'd you bring him up, dude? Now you've got *me* riding the old crushes train again." He sighed wistfully. "I won't get any sleep tonight for stalking his Facebook and Instagram. He has both, by the way. And he's as adorable now as he was back then." RJ chuckled. "I've been on this particular ride before."

Casey laughed. "Does he have a Twitter?"

"Guess I'll have to find out."

The front door to Casey's parents' house opened, and the golden foyer lamps illuminated his mother's form. Her white-blond hair shone, and at some point she'd changed into red-and-green silk pajamas. She waved at him from the doorway, and he rolled down the window to shoot her a reassuring thumbs-up and to let her see he was on the phone. "Hey, I should go."

"You sure? You know I'm here for your Joel-related heartache, buddy."

"Thanks. I appreciate it. But I just got back to my folks' place and my mom's eager for me to bring the tree in."

"Text anytime. FaceTime, whatever. Whenever. I'll always be ready to spill tea about our love lives."

"Why would we want to do that?"

RJ gave a long-suffering sigh. "Show some pride, Casey. Own up to being a human being. Admit you're sick with the love disease. Accept that Joel is your weak spot."

"I don't even know him now." Casey's mother gave up and went back inside. He really should go join her, but he wanted to hear RJ deny Casey's words first.

"He's Joel. Of course you know him. Now go decorate the tree with your mommy like a good little boy."

"Safe travels. And hey—thanks. I... You're a good friend. It's nice to catch up."

"Anytime, man. Don't be a stranger like usual, okay?"

"I won't." This time, Casey meant it. Ann would be proud.

Before Casey climbed out of the car, he opened up the Facebook app on his phone and typed in Joel's name. It brought up the profile Casey had set up four years prior. There he found the same profile shot he'd originally uploaded. A picture of The Millennial Yodels—Joel, RJ, and Becca's old band—stretched across the top of the page, and the single, solitary post was the one Casey had typed up on Joel's behalf years ago.

But there was one new picture now. Something Becca had tagged both Casey and Joel in ages ago: an old shot of the band practicing in Joel's garage, with Casey sitting on the concrete floor staring up at Joel with stars in his eyes.

But Joel himself had posted nothing on his Facebook page at all. Typical. He'd always been a closed book. And now Casey had taken a page from that book and closed himself off too. And he was sick and tired of it. Sick and tired of feeling alone and disconnected.

The idea that Joel might be gay or bi and that he'd actually crushed on Casey in high school? Casey couldn't process it. How the hell had Joel kept that all locked away?

Probably the same way you did.

Maybe RJ was wrong. Casey closed his eyes, telling himself not to get excited or hopeful. Not even a little. Even if somehow Casey's greatest wish had come true and Joel liked guys, he'd made his opinion of Casey crystal clear. Whatever he may or may not have felt back then, he clearly didn't feel it now. No point in wishing for anything where Joel was concerned.

But what if...

Tamping down the flare of hope, Casey put his phone away and stopped torturing himself. Freeing the Christmas tree from his SUV was easy enough. It was maneuvering it into the house that was hard. The short Douglas Fir pine needles tugged and clawed at him, and when he went back out to grab the wreaths, the holly stuck him good. A bright bead of blood welled to the surface of his thumb when he dropped them on the front porch.

Staring at it, Casey thought of Joel's pinched face glaring at him from down the row of Christmas trees. He stuck the wound into his mouth and sucked the blood away. It wasn't a big deal. Just a small stab from the holly.

But damn if that little prick didn't hurt like hell.

Best thing to do was stay the hell away from Joel. Don't think about him—and the incredible possibility that he could be gay too. RJ had to be wrong. No, Casey definitely wouldn't try to see him again. *Definitely* wouldn't look up his current address.

With the metallic tang of blood on his tongue, Casey pulled out his phone.

Chapter Seven

J OEL COULDN'T SAY he was surprised so much as annoyed when he stepped out of his trailer the next morning to find a gleaming white SUV parked in the yard next to his own gray Chevy. As for Casey, well, he looked ridiculously gorgeous leaning back against his Lexus, his arms crossed over his broad chest. The sleeves of his pale-yellow button-up shirt were folded to expose his strong forearms, and his long legs were crossed casually at the ankles.

Bruno, traitor that he was, dashed past Joel, bounding excitedly at the prospect of a new friend. Where were his pit bull roots now? Where was the big booming bark that would scare Casey into his car and away from here?

"Sic, Bruno!" Joel called out. "Attack!"

Bruno didn't know those commands. He was a giant teddy bear. And despite Joel's best effort to sound like Bruno might be an actual killer, Casey wasn't perturbed at all. In fact, he squatted down to pet and rub Bruno's ears while the turncoat dog pranced and slobbered all over Casey's nicely pressed khaki pants. At least he'd sullied him a little. If only Bruno would jump up and put his muddy paws on Casey's pristine shirt, then they'd be getting somewhere.

Speaking of Casey's shirt, it was clear the guy still had no fashion sense. What sane person their age—Casey was almost twenty-two now—dressed like that? He looked like he took fashion advice from his grandpa. And yet he was still so fucking handsome.

Ducking back into the trailer, Joel left Casey to deal with Bruno. He tugged his fleece-lined jean jacket on over his black short-sleeve T-shirt and checked that his wallet was still in the back pocket of his jeans. Then he glanced at himself in the mirror, relieved by what he saw. His dark hair was on point, his skin remarkably clear given his crap diet, and he looked mussed enough that he could easily pretend he didn't care what Casey thought of his appearance at all.

"His name's Bruno?" Casey asked with a friendly smile when Joel came back out.

"No, it's Murder. Which is what he's going to do to you in a few seconds. Once he stops slobbering all over you."

"Right." Casey smiled as he rubbed Bruno's head and talked to him in that high-pitched voice that everyone used with dogs and babies, except for Joel. Well, he *did* use it with Bruno when they were *alone*. But never where other people might hear him. How humiliating for Casey that he didn't know how ridiculous he sounded. How humiliating for Bruno to have to hear it. And how damn annoying that it was all kind of cute.

He took in the whole of Casey again. The morning sun loved Casey. It reflected the gold flecks in his light brown hair and, damn, all along his exposed forearms. It wasn't fair how beautiful he was. It wasn't *fair* that Casey's rich boyfriend got to enjoy all that shiny glow and probably took it for granted. Joel's gut did flip-flops, but he fought against it and made certain his sour expression held.

"So, are you stalking me now?" Joel asked, stomping across his yard and glancing at his cell phone to check the time. He didn't want to be late. Angel was opening Vreeland's this morning, which was nice of her given the fact that he'd left her to close on her own the night before. The shit show of texts she'd sent, including the picture of the Blow Mold baby Jesus with Satan's numbers Sharpie'd on his forehead, had made her irritation beyond clear.

So he didn't have to rush in to work, but he did need to go by the nursing home to bring his father breakfast first. He stuffed his cell back into his pocket and took a deep breath, preparing for emotional battle before meeting Casey's eyes. "Well, stalker?"

"No, I'm not. Well, maybe." Casey grinned sheepishly.

"Maybe? I'd say definitely. How'd you find me?" Not many people knew where he'd moved after selling the house. "Was it Becca?"

"Google."

"Oh. Right." Joel rolled his eyes. "I forget my privacy is nil since Congress overturned all those crucial Internet privacy regulations just so they could line some big companies' pockets. Thanks, 'Merica."

Casey said nothing, continuing to pet Bruno, who stared up with all the adoration Joel had once felt for Casey. He couldn't even blame the dog for being smitten. He still was, despite his better judgment.

"Well?" Joel asked again. "Why are you even here?"

Casey rose, muddy paw prints on his pant legs and his formerly pristine shirt wrinkled and covered with dog fluff. Joel wanted to feel some sort of satisfaction in that—he *should* have felt it—but instead he had to hold back from scolding Bruno for doing what dogs do. Casey bit his lower lip, a gesture that shot into Joel like an arrow straight to his heart, and when he gazed up at Joel from beneath golden lashes, another arrow went straight to his dick. *Fuck.*

"I wanted to apologize for last night," Casey said. "I shouldn't have surprised you that way."

Joel barked a laugh and gestured at the SUV and Casey standing there beside it. "So, this is better?"

Casey winced. "Right. No. Probably not."

"Christ." Joel turned his gaze from Casey's plump lips and earnest eyes. He shifted to look out at the lake instead, the dark water reflecting the winter-gray sky. "You were always like this. You'd just *come over.* Like you were allowed. And then you'd just *stay.*" And he'd liked that about Casey. Always had, and, fuck his own stupid heart, always would. He even liked it *now*, for fuck's sake.

"I wanted a chance to talk to you. Face-to-face. Something better, more honest, than last night."

"You couldn't have used the phone?"

Casey ignored that. "I barely slept. My mind kept turning over everything you'd said to me. I hated that you… That I made you feel that way, Joel. By ghosting on you, I mean. And I guess I thought face-to-face would be more productive. I thought you'd be less likely to ignore me." He grinned, and the light caught his eyes. "Plus, I don't exactly have your number. The Internet didn't cough that up."

Joel rubbed a hand over his upper lip. His stomach flipped over. Why was it so damn hard for him to say no to Casey, much less stay mad at him? He really wanted to be mad. But…

Bruno took off across the yard, barking hard at the wild turkey he'd spotted in the woods. Joel let him go without whistling him back. Bruno was a terrible hunter, but at least he'd get some exercise trying to catch the bird before Joel shut him back up in the trailer for the day. He had his dog door for necessities, but typically he was a lazy lump and mainly slept.

"So what do you say? Can we talk?" Casey asked when Bruno's barks had faded and his clumsy rustling in the woods calmed down.

Joel tilted his head back, studying the steel-colored clouds, and finally shrugged. "C'mon." He gestured with his head for Casey to follow him. "We can sit at least."

Casey's sharp intake of breath as they came around the corner of the trailer and into the shade of a massive oak tree by the lake brought a grim smile to Joel's face. At least Casey recognized it. That was something.

"Is that…?"

"Yeah. I took it before the construction crew could demolish the entire lot for that new house they're building."

"Isn't that stealing?"

"I figured it belonged to me more than to anyone else. Don't you agree?" Joel sat and gestured for Casey to join him. "Like the good old days." The sarcasm wasn't intentional, and he felt a little guilty when Casey's smile faded again before he folded his now ridiculously long limbs to sit on the wood-and-iron bench—*their* bench.

"Huh. Looks like you've outgrown it," Joel said. "Like a lot of things."

"I can still fit." Casey leaned forward, resting his elbows on his knees, then looked out over the lake. "This was your grandmother's land, right? I remember when she left it to you."

"Yep."

"It's a great view. Really good property here."

"Eh. Not as prestigious as the other side, of course. It's got a decent view but nothing like the one your folks have of the mountains to the east and lake to the west." He nodded at Casey's parents' place across the way.

Casey gasped. "Wait, what?"

Across the narrow neck of the lake, the Stevens' windows reflected the pale gray sky, but in the daylight Joel could clearly make out the big wreaths hung on the porch and patio doors. Both looked to be Vreeland holly-and-fir wreathes, if he wasn't mistaken. Vicious stickers protruded from some of those. He was always warning Angel and his customers about them. A bitter, hateful part of him hoped Casey's folks had gotten poked while hanging them up, but the angel on his shoulder hoped they hadn't.

"I didn't realize you could see my parents' house from here." Casey narrowed his eyes against the gray glare as he peered toward the fancy neighborhood on the opposite side of the water. "That's bananas."

"Yeah, bananas." Joel snorted.

Casey's eye roll was fairly satisfying, so Joel let it drop. They stared at the water together, and when the silence grew uncomfortable, Joel patted his jacket pockets and pulled out a mostly empty pack of cigarettes. He'd planned to quit this year, but most days seemed to bring a new reason to grant himself the gift of one more cigarette. He shook one free and then, glancing up at Casey, he shook out another.

He doubted Casey had any idea what a gift he was giving him in one of his preciously parsed out smokes. But never let it be said that Joel was a scrooge with what he had. He might be curmudgeonly, but he was generous.

Lighting both cigarettes in his own mouth, enjoying the hot smoke as it swirled into his throat and lungs, he closed his eyes. When the nicotine hit his veins, he felt steadier. Opening his eyes, he handed the second smoke over to Casey, who took it as gingerly and inexpertly as he ever had. Joel tried to hold back a laugh as he watched Casey's plump lips wrap around the end and take a small draw.

The reaction wasn't as intense as it had been the first time Joel had convinced Casey to share a smoke with him, though. Coughing until tears came to his eyes, Casey covered his mouth and shook his head hard. "Wow. It's been a long time," he croaked. Then he took another drag and coughed less, exhaling in a jerky stream. "Oh, yeah," he moaned gently. "There's the rush I remember."

"Good?"

Casey shrugged and considered the cigarette before taking another puff. "Kind of like an Oreo: not good at all, but at the same time, fantastic."

"I hear you."

They smoked their cigarettes in silence. Joel was on the verge of making a smartass comment about how Casey could go by the gas station and buy his own pack the next time he needed a smoke, instead of dropping in where he was unwanted. But it wasn't true that he was unwanted, and while Joel had no problem being a liar, he didn't want to turn into a hateful man like his dad. So, he kept that unkind comment to himself, which was better than he'd managed last night.

A sad shame filled him as he remembered the things he'd said. So what if he'd been hurt by Casey ghosting him after high school? He didn't have to be an asshole. He wanted to be better than that.

Eventually, Casey turned to him, all amber-eyed seriousness, and announced without preamble, "I'm gay."

Joel glanced his way. "I know."

"You do?" Casey swallowed, his Adam's apple bobbing.

"Yeah."

"How?" Did he sound scared or was that just Joel's imagination?

"Google," Joel fibbed.

Close enough. He wasn't going to admit to Facebook-stalking Casey like a lovesick psycho. And he'd never own up to the fact that he'd even downloaded the Instagram app once just to see if Casey had an account. (He didn't. Or at least, he hadn't at the time.)

Casey's eyes brightened. "You looked me up online?"

"Curiosity. Killed the cat." He flicked the ash from the end of his cigarette. "You know how it is."

"Oh, yeah, man. I know how it is." Casey nodded meaningfully, his eyes bright and yet somehow shy. "I've tried to look you up, but there's nothing. Just stuff about Vreeland's and that old Facebook account I made for you."

"Just the way I like it." Joel smiled tightly. He wasn't a big fan of the Internet. At least not for anything other than streaming TV shows and watching porn. Why did people want to share their every waking moment with the world? Privacy was a thing he cherished. So was his dignity.

"So you know?" Casey took another drag on his cigarette and released it slowly. "About me?"

Joel nodded and let smoke stream from his nostrils.

Casey ashed his cigarette, opened and closed his mouth a few times, and then asked, his voice shaking vulnerably, "Is that what your attitude yesterday was all about? Do you have a problem with me being gay?"

"Why the fuck would I have a problem with it?" Joel glared at Casey, flicking ash on the ground between his feet.

"I don't know. You were friends with RJ and Becca, so it's not like you're a bigot. Or you weren't."

"Still not."

"Okay. Good. But I thought maybe you couldn't handle it if it was, you know, me, who was gay." Casey licked his lips, his shoulders drawing up higher. He managed to curl his limbs tighter on the bench, like he was bracing himself against something.

"You? What's so special about you?" *Oh God, everything.* Joel internally rolled his eyes at himself.

"Nothing. But did you…maybe you…" Casey groaned, thrust the cigarette back in his mouth, and raked his hands through his hair before dropping them to hang between his knees. After a few puffs, he pulled the cigarette free. "This is stupid. It shouldn't be so hard."

Joel studied Casey carefully—the tension in his eyes and back, the pleading need for acceptance in his eyes—and he didn't want to have this conversation anymore. It was too much like the last time they sat on this bench, so close to confessions that would have come too late to make a difference anyway.

Joel took a steadying drag from his cigarette before exhaling hard. "Go back to your boyfriend, Casey. Leave me the hell alone, okay?"

Casey tilted his head, brows knitting together. "I don't have a boyfriend."

Joel narrowed his eyes. "You don't?"

"What made you think I did?" Casey's smile broke open knowingly, and he chuckled. Worse, he *winked*. "Oh. Right. Google."

Joel shrugged, tamping back the horrible, electric satisfaction currently flash-bombing his soul at the words "I don't have a boyfriend." He concentrated on keeping his fingers from shaking when he sucked on his cigarette again.

Casey stubbed his cigarette out and tucked the butt into the pocket of his pants. "His name was Theo, and we've been over for a long time."

"Whatever. Like I care." Joel sighed and shifted uncomfortably on the bench. The wooden slats dug into his ass. The combination of hope and satisfaction faded quickly. Nothing worked out for him. It never had, and it never would. This conversation was pointless. He stubbed out his cigarette and flicked the butt into the grass. Irritably, he spit out, "Why aren't you leaving yet?"

"Because I want to stay."

Joel sighed glumly and gazed out at the narrow lake again. Bruno came trotting along the water's edge with a doggy smile on his face and his tail wagging happily. Joel watched him and pondered. His heart tripped over itself, and he licked his lips nervously. "Well, since you're not going anywhere, let me ask you something."

"All right?"

He didn't take his eyes away from Bruno's progress toward them. "Why'd you leave me behind like I was trash? Like you didn't have use for me anymore?"

Casey's breath caught. "How could you think that?"

"Who wouldn't?" The only way he could say the words was to fully focus on the lake. The small ripples in the water as the wind blew across the top. The sparkle as the clouds broke and the sun peeped out. "One minute we're friends. Best friends, even. Or that's what you said. The next minute you're gone. Then your folks moved. You didn't text. You didn't call."

"You didn't either."

"I did. Once."

"No, you…" Casey trailed off, recollection flitting through his eyes. "You're right. You did. Just once."

"You didn't text back." God, how pathetic did he sound? How *gay*? He could imagine his father's sneering taunts. Joel popped up the collar of his jacket and ducked into it like he could hide.

"No. I didn't. Do you know why?" Casey's mouth twisted bitterly. "It was my first week at NYU, and I was scared shitless. I knew no one. The city was overwhelming. I'd come out to my parents before I left, and my dad didn't take it well."

Joel swallowed hard, the click audible between them. Mr. Stevens could be scary. Not like his own dad, not violent, but demanding all the same. Intense. If he hadn't taken Casey coming out well...

"Yeah," Casey said, nodding. "You have no idea how much that last night before I caught the plane to New York sucked. And in the midst of dealing with all *that*, what did I get from you? My best friend, the boy I... The person I was dying to hear from? I got an asshole text saying, 'So, you some frat boy's bottom bitch yet?'"

"Oh." Joel's stomach dropped. He'd somehow forgotten that little detail in his butt-hurt understanding of what had happened. Or maybe he'd blocked it out. It hadn't been his finest moment, that text. He'd been scared too. Ashamed.

"Yeah. *Oh*." Casey raised a brow. "It proved my biggest fear back then: that you'd hate me if you knew the truth."

Joel cringed. He opened his mouth to apologize, and instead what came out was, "What was I supposed to say? 'I miss you already.' How gay would that have been?"

Casey's eyes flared brightly, a hint of rare anger. "Can you not use that word that way? You're talking to a *gay guy*."

"Funny. So are you."

Casey coughed, choking on his own spit apparently, and didn't stop until Joel pounded on his back. "Really?" Casey gasped, eyes watering.

"Yeah, I'm a fag," Joel snapped, but it didn't hold much fire. "Sue me."

"Wait, wait. Slow down. Just..." Casey turned to Joel and reached out tentatively. For a frozen moment they only stared at each other. Then Casey inhaled and took one of Joel's hands in both of his.

A shiver rocked Joel. Casey's fingers were soft and smooth, the hands of a student, and a wealthy one at that. He clenched his own callused hand tight around them, hard, hurtful—*hoping* it hurt—but desperate not to let go.

Casey returned the grip. "You're gay."

Joel's head swam. How to answer that? Hadn't he already said, for fuck's sake? "It's untested, but...yeah."

"Untested?" Casey's brows lowered as he cocked his head. "What's that mean?"

Joel's mouth went dry, and he darted his eyes away from Casey's, heat rising up his neck. He could stand up now. Go to work. Forget all about this conversation and Casey fucking Stevens. He didn't have to tell him anything. He owed him nothing. Not a single damn raw truth.

His voice was ragged as he replied, "Never met a guinea pig I thought was worth the effort of fucking, I guess."

"You've never...with a guy." Casey didn't phrase it like a question, but his voice was so gentle that Joel's heart ached.

"With anyone." Jesus, why was he saying all this? Why did Casey make him so weak?

Casey's head dropped back, and he stared up into the branches of the oak above them. "RJ was right," he whispered. "Wow."

"About?"

"About everything." Casey lowered his chin to gaze at Joel again. "I think. Maybe not *everything*."

Joel shrugged, his fingers aching, and he pulled his hand away from Casey. He crossed his arms and tucked his fingers beneath his armpits to try to wipe away the sensation of Casey's touch. He was weak to want it. Stupid to think he could ever have it. So what if they were both gay? Casey was rich and living in New York, and Joel was...Joel.

"So those girls you talked about going out with?"

Joel scoffed. "Covering for my super-duper queerness, dude. It's pretty obvious."

Casey laughed quietly, shaking his head, his eyes wide in amazement. It tore Joel's gut up. He wanted to touch that lightness. "Apparently obvious to everyone who isn't me."

"Everyone? Who else knows my private business? Besides RJ." Joel studied Casey's face. "I think I've managed to keep it off Google."

"Just RJ and maybe Becca."

"Oh, Becca." He shrugged, a small smile tugging involuntarily at his mouth. "Yeah. She knows. We're close. I came out to her first. And, until now, only." He forced his lips wider, but the fake smile felt weird on his face. "Hope you're happy. You're the second person I've told."

Casey leaned in closer and whispered, "Does it feel good to say it?"

Joel couldn't handle the open curiosity on Casey's face. He turned his attention back to Bruno, who'd just finished digging a hole by the water. He studied his emotions. "No. It feels shitty. Like it always has."

"Why?"

Joel breathed slowly, wishing he dared dip back into his cigarettes for another smoke. He didn't look Casey's way, shrugging again. "I don't know."

"It doesn't have to feel shitty. It can feel…good."

"I guess you'd know."

"Meaning?"

"You've had sex with guys, right? Probably with more than one?" Joel shoved down a surge of jealousy that anyone had touched Casey—felt his soft skin, heard his cries of ecstasy. It should have been him. It could *never* be him. "Innocent, nerdy Casey Stevens getting more ass than me. Who'd have ever seen that coming?"

"Do you even *want* to get ass?" Casey asked, sliding his fingers over Joel's hand again, trying to take hold and sending sparks spiraling up his arm. "I mean, you could. You're hot enough, and there are apps for that." A frown crinkled Casey's forehead.

"Call me old-fashioned, but I don't want do that stuff with just anyone." Joel pulled his hand away from Casey's tantalizing touch and crossed his arms over his chest again, not sure when he'd uncrossed them anyway. He frowned at Bruno's happy dogface as he dug a second hole nearer the tree line. He'd need to fill those in later. There was always something more that he needed to do, another hurdle in his way, another hole to fall into.

"But it doesn't have to be like that. You can take it slow. I've found all kinds of guys on those apps. Some guys just want hand jobs. Or blow jobs. You don't have to jump in with both feet right away."

"Apps for blow jobs." Joel shook his head. "What has this shitty world come to?"

Casey whispered, "And some guys are really into kissing. They're happy to do that and nothing else."

Joel stiffened.

"What? Kissing?" Casey asked. His voice grew even gentler. He leaned in, and Joel felt his breath brush against his ear as he whispered, "Has anyone ever kissed you, Joel?"

Joel's pulse beat insanely in his temples and behind his eyes. Dizziness swept over him as Casey touched his cheek.

"What are you doing?" Joel choked out.

Casey slid his fingers down to take hold of Joel's chin. He stared into Joel's eyes, giving him time to see the kiss coming, to avoid it if he really wanted. Joel gasped. It was slow motion, like molasses. It felt like he was dying as he waited for Casey's mouth to dip and press, damp and soft, against his own.

Joel shuddered as Casey's mouth touched his. The sweet kiss lingered. Then Joel moaned when Casey's lips parted and the kiss grew wet. He didn't know what to do, how to respond, and so he let it happen. He let Casey kiss him again and again. Softly, gently, carefully, and with soul-destroying tenderness. Joel shook, and his dick grew hard, pressing against his jeans.

"Wow," Casey breathed against his mouth, and then he kissed Joel again.

Joel's hands trembled as he raised them to Casey's shoulders and finally kissed him back. His pulse thrummed wildly, and his cock ached. Time stretched out. Casey's taste and the tingling sensation of his breath, his lips, and his gentle fingers broke Joel open until he was panting and shaking with need.

"Now you can't say you've never been kissed," Casey murmured as he pulled away. His eyes were blown wide, and they were glossy with emotions Joel didn't feel confident enough to name.

The cool morning air tingled against his now-wet lips, and the only thing Joel could think to do was pull out another precious cigarette and light it. "I'm running low," he whispered in explanation of not offering Casey a second smoke too. His hands shook as he took a draw. "Sorry."

Casey watched him carefully, and Joel looked anywhere but at those questing eyes. What the hell had that been about? What was he supposed to say? Or do?

"We can share," Casey said, plucking the cigarette from between Joel's fingers and breathing in a puff. Joel's stomach somersaulted seeing Casey's plump, kiss-reddened lips wrapped around his cigarette. He wanted to kiss him again.

And that was no good at all. That was terrible, in fact.

Casey handed the cigarette back. "I shouldn't smoke more. I might puke." He smiled softly. "I don't do it much now."

"You never did it much back then either." Joel let the cigarette dangle between his index and middle finger. His mind raced as he asked unsteadily, "So, what? Do you expect me to thank you for that?"

Casey laughed softly. "I should thank *you*, actually. I've wanted to kiss you forever." He slipped gentle fingers through the hair at Joel's temple, pushing it back, and gazed at him with so much feeling in his eyes that it made Joel dizzy. And maybe a little sick like he'd been the one to smoke too many cigarettes after years of abstinence. It was scary as shit.

Joel stood and threw the barely smoked cigarette into the lake. He didn't usually litter, and he didn't usually fail to finish his death sticks, but he didn't know what to do with all his jail-broken feelings now that Casey was here acting all…

He shuddered. Now that Casey had kissed him. Now that Joel was facing the wretched specter of some kind of fucked-up hope. The thing he'd never let himself indulge in when it came to Casey Stevens, and the thing he'd mostly banished from the rest of his life too.

Casey didn't rise. He stayed put, studying Joel carefully. "What are you thinking?" Concern thickened his voice.

Joel sounded rough, like he'd smoked a whole pack, when he ground out, "I have to get to the nursing home."

"My mom told me about your dad yesterday. I didn't know."

"Yeah. Well. Life happened. Whether you were here for it or not. It happened."

Casey's brow furrowed. "I'm sorry."

"Don't say that. It makes it weird." He'd never liked it when people told him they were sorry about his mother's death, and he didn't like hearing that they were sorry about Pop now. It just made things awkward.

"Right. I remember. Sorry."

Joel shifted to relieve the pressure in his pants where his cock still hoped that the kiss meant more than it did. "Yeah, well, Dad expects me to bring him breakfast by nine, so..." He pulled his phone out of his pocket to check the time and waggled it at Casey. "I have to go."

He didn't wait for Casey to join him as he walked away. Bruno raced to his side, panting, with muddy front paws.

"Just to be clear, I left you behind *because* I wanted to kiss you," Casey called from his seat on the bench.

"And I let you go because I *wanted* you to kiss me," Joel called back. He turned around slowly to meet Casey's eyes for the next bit. "And I wanted a hell of a lot more than that back then."

Casey bit his lower lip. It made Joel's balls tighten again. "And now?"

"And now it's been almost four years and, fuck, Casey. I don't know. I need to go."

Casey rose and trotted after him, breathless. "I'm in town until the new year. Can I see you again?"

Joel's heart leapt eagerly, but he clenched his fists. Hope was pointless. This thrill of joy screaming through his body was stupid. It could never go anywhere good. They could never *happen*, not really. Casey was, just as Joel had claimed last night, slumming it during his winter break. He was horny and lonely and bored. That's all it was. All it could ever be.

But Casey didn't let up. "For lunch? For dinner? For anything?"

"What? You got my first kiss, Casey. You want to be my first everything now?" Joel rounded on him, hands shoved deep in his pockets so he didn't grab Casey's broad shoulders and kiss him again. His heart skipped wildly.

"Would that be so bad?" Casey gazed at him with a heat that made Joel's dick swell and his heart twist up hard.

Joel tried to glare. He was pretty sure he failed. "I don't need a pity fuck."

"You think that's what I feel for you? Believe me, it's not pity, it's lo—"

"Don't say it." Joel held out his hands, stopping the word halfway out of Casey's mouth. "Don't leave for nearly four years, come back here like you're something special, and think you have any right to say that word to me." Especially when Casey didn't mean it. Couldn't mean it. Not the way Joel wanted him to anyway.

Joel let out a slow breath and called to Bruno, "C'mon, boy. Back inside."

Casey lingered silently as Joel used a dirty towel he kept by the trailer door to wipe off Bruno's feet, opened the door, and let Bruno in. Of course Casey followed at Joel's heels again once he started toward his truck.

"What time do you eat lunch?" Casey asked when they reached their vehicles at nearly the same time.

"Same time as most folks, I guess."

"I'll see you then. And I'll bring you something good." He pointed at Joel with a commanding finger, forestalling his protest. "I'll be there." Then he climbed into his SUV and buckled up.

Refusing to look at Casey, Joel tried to steady his frantic mind by taking his time checking the ties holding a wheelbarrow he'd borrowed from Vreeland's in the back of his truck.

After Casey drove off, Joel sat in the driver's seat of his Chevy and stared at the Christmas wreath on his door and the colored lights around the gutters. His lips tingled, and his chest burned with a screaming sensation. Fear and excitement combined.

Casey Stevens had left town because he'd wanted to kiss him.

And today Casey *had* kissed him. With his beautiful mouth that Joel had admired since they were just kids playing in their backyards.

"Merry fucking Christmas to me," he whispered, touching his lips. He could still feel the sting of Casey's prickly stubble against his chin. In a daze, he backed out of his lot and started on the road toward the nursing home. His head was a spinning, cascading, maddening mess of amazement.

CASEY'S PALMS SWEATED on the steering wheel as he drove aimlessly away from Joel's plot of lakeside property. He turned on a country road and kept going, taking the winding curves, his heart racing and his breath coming in sharp gasps.

When he was a good five minutes into his stunned retreat, he rolled down his window, stuck his head out into the crisp winter air, and yelled as loudly as he could out across the rolling fields.

His engine and the wind rushing down from the Tennessee hills swallowed the sound, but his throat relished the strain. Giddy and wild, he yelled and yelled until his own laughter cut him off.

He'd done it.

He'd kissed *Joel Vreeland!* With his mouth!

On Joel's mouth!

Multiple times!

Maybe he should have slipped him more tongue, unbuttoned Joel's jeans, and taken the kiss to a more passionate place. But that hadn't seemed right. It'd been a pure moment, vulnerable and sweet. Joel had seemed almost childlike in his acceptance of it.

Eventually he'd kissed Casey back, but barely. Just teased his tongue into Casey's mouth and then back out again, like a scared thing. The memory of it made Casey's heart pound. Casey had taken the risk and gone for it. Had opened himself up to possible rejection despite his fear. Goddamn, he was proud of himself. Proud of Joel too.

He laughed, shaking his head. What a fucked-up pair they were, but they'd actually *kissed*! He stuck his head out the window again and howled with delight.

When he was relatively calm again, Casey drummed his hands on the steering wheel. He had to figure things out. He needed to excavate the truth between them. He wanted to crack Joel open. He wanted to see all of that beautiful, scared vulnerability again and again. He wanted to explore him slowly, breaking down his fears and resistance, until he was soft and sweet under Casey's hands. That would be amazing. Beautiful. It was all he'd ever wanted.

Casey groaned. His cock grew hard, and he yelled out the window again.

What if this was exactly right? The two of them together. A couple. It could be a *thing*. They could happen. His entire future opened up in front of him with a brightness he hadn't imagined possible. His heart flew, his blood rushed, and he pushed the gas pedal down harder.

Ann would say not to get his hopes up. Joel was skittish on a good day, and with his boundaries being tested, he was sure to push back against this amazing, perfect, gorgeous thing that could happen between them. It was his nature.

And yet Casey couldn't remember the last time he'd been this excited. About anything. Kissing Joel had supplanted every moment he'd previously deemed "best" in his life.

He screamed out his window again. He shouldn't get ahead of himself. But it was too late. He wanted Joel. And Joel wanted him in return. And it was Christmastime.

They both deserved a miracle.

Chapter Eight

"CASEY STEVENS KISSED me."

The nine-story tower of the nursing home loomed over where Joel had parked the truck in the gloom of a tall beech tree still clutching some frail, bleached-brown leaves. He adjusted the heating vent and waited for Becca's reaction to this improbable news.

"Wait, *what?*" Becca spoke loudly into the phone. In the background, Joel heard women's voices, hairdryers, running water, and a door chime. "Hold on. I need to go somewhere quiet. I don't think I heard you correctly."

Joel pictured Becca strolling past her fellow stylists' flying scissors as they sculpted beauty out of birds' nests. He knew she'd be reeking, as always these days, of some new line of expensive hair products and made up in lip and eye colors like a fever-dream. He loved that about her. Becca was beautiful and wild at heart. Something he envied more and more every year.

He wondered if she was also wearing one of her trademark dresses with the sweetheart neckline that revealed the giant Korean magpie tattoo on her chest, a nod to her biological family's roots. He rubbed his arm where his upside-down heart was inked, remembering how they'd gripped each other's hands from adjacent tattoo chairs, enduring the pain.

"Heading outside for my break," she said to someone in the store, and then there was the door chime again, followed by a cessation of salon noise and a burst of traffic sounds. "Okay, I can talk." She sounded breathless. "What did you say when I picked up? I think I hallucinated or something."

Joel let out a shaky laugh. Half the reason he'd called her was to prove to himself he hadn't hallucinated the kiss either. Because if he told another person, it had to be real. "Casey Stevens kissed me."

"What?" she gasped. "I don't understand. *Our* Casey Stevens?"

"I don't recall us owning him, but yeah."

"I thought he was—wait, you said—okay, hold up. He's supposed to be in New York."

"Home for the holidays." A leaf flittered down from the beech tree and landed in the parking lot.

"Wow. Holy shit. Tell me the whole story. Beginning to end. And start now because I only have a fifteen-minute break, and I don't have time to pull the truth out of your snarling face."

Still shaking with disbelief, Joel told Becca about Casey's visit to Vreeland's the night before and how he'd showed up at the trailer that morning. And then he told her about the kiss, glossing over most of the conversation that led up to it.

She whistled. "Well, hot damn, our Casey is all grown up."

"He's twenty-two. The same as you and me."

"With smooth moves. And soft lips. *And* you said he put his fingers on your chin to hold you steady. Swoon!" A car honked in the background on her end.

Joel chuckled. She was right. His trembling knees and racing heart told the whole swoony story.

"Do you have to work today?" she asked. "I've got a light load this morning. Want to come over and tell me more in person? Strategize about how you're going to get into his pants?"

Joel left aside the question of whether he even wanted in Casey's pants and glanced at the clock on his car dash. His dad's Egg McMuffin cooled in the bag next to him in the passenger seat. "Sorry. Wish I could, but I've gotta go into the store, make up to Angel for last night, and get everything set up for Brandon's return. And right now…" He glanced at the clock in his car dash. The sweet giddiness in his gut soured. "I have to go in and see Pop."

"Ah. Right. McMuffin time." She clucked her tongue to chide him. "You're gonna be late. It's past nine. Better hustle."

Joel didn't say goodbye, though. "He's bringing lunch to me today at Vreeland's."

"Your pop?"

"No. Casey, duh."

"Oh my gosh. He's courting!" She laughed, and he could just imagine her leaning against the painted concrete blocks at the back of Salon Bohème, her eyes crinkling up with her smile. "Sounds like we don't need to strategize at all. He's got his aim set on your cute bubble butt. *Someone* won't be a virgin for long!"

"Screw you."

She crowed, laughing even harder.

Joel waited patiently in silence, trying to figure out if she was right. Did he have a chance of getting laid? With Casey Stevens of all people? Maybe this *was* a dream after all and he'd wake up any minute now.

After Becca stopped laughing, she asked, more seriously, "Honestly, though, didn't he turn out handsome?"

"God, yes." He knew she kept up with Casey on social media. She must have seen all the pictures with Theo and knew exactly how gorgeous Casey was. She just wanted to hear him say it.

"Is he still into art?"

"He's still…" He couldn't find the words.

"Oooh, he's still your shiny, isn't he?"

Joel grunted. "Whatever that means."

Becca teased, "One day you'll be a grown-up boy and learn to express your emotions without insults or deflection."

"And on that day, we'll also achieve world peace."

She laughed again. "Can't wait. Hey, as much as I'd like to continue talking with you, the clock is ticking. I have to get back to work and, well, Daddy Asshole awaits."

Joel glanced toward the miserable-looking building ahead of him and sighed. "You're a bitch. But I love you."

"Love you too, Joely." She disconnected her end of the line.

Joel smiled at the little nickname she'd blessed him with. She'd started calling him that after she'd returned home from Nashville once the dream of a record deal fell through. She was a fantastic drummer, and RJ was a great guitarist, but their songs together had only been so-so.

RJ had chosen to stay behind and start up a career as a touring and studio guitarist, but Becca had had enough of people trying to change her for the sake of a brand. She'd hightailed it home to start cosmetology school. Though she still drummed with some local groups for fun and extra cash, she'd otherwise let music fall by the wayside.

Joel was grateful to have her in his life. She made everything brighter just by being herself.

The nursing home smelled like horror, cleanser, and a spritz of death. It always gave him the creepy-crawlies whenever he came to visit. Merry Hills Towers wasn't the best nursing home in town, not even close. Joel wished he could afford better for his father, but at this point, his father was a Medicaid patient.

They'd had to sell off everything, and Joel had been forced to buy Vreeland's with his savings to get his pop's net worth down low enough to finally get the government support they needed. Hell, even bringing him an Egg McMuffin every day was potentially suspect to auditors, but the nurses turned a blind eye to small violations like that.

"You're late," Katie, his pop's morning nurse, whispered. Her brunette hair was pinned up tight, and her bright-red, Taylor Swift-esque lipstick shone like a beacon under the fluorescent lights. "He's pissed."

"I figured." Joel rolled his eyes as rushed past with the cold breakfast.

She winked at him and smiled encouragingly. He smiled back. The nurses always treated him with extreme sympathy, not because his father was on the verge of death like so many in this place, but because, Joel assumed, they felt bad for him growing up with such an asshole as his only parent.

In that way, the stroke had been a relief. For the first time ever, everyone finally saw the real Charlie Vreeland. The one Joel had grown up with. The one who raged. The one who punched him hard enough to see stars when, at twelve, he'd said something about Casey being a cute kid.

Before the stroke, everyone knew Charlie as the sweet old man who ran Vreeland's Home and Garden. Funny, charming to the old ladies, and good with children too. The stroke had robbed Joel's pop of the ability to put on that show. For that, and that alone, Joel was grateful to the stroke. Relieved. Validated. Because, yeah, Charlie Vreeland was an asshole.

Joel was very late, and Pop's room was empty. That meant they'd already taken him down for his physical therapy and he wouldn't be back up for—Joel looked at the clock—twenty minutes.

Pop's room on the fifth floor had a view of cars zooming past on Papermill Drive. The tan walls were sparsely decorated with photos Joel had torn from an old album and hung around the room with putty stuck to the back.

There were pictures from his pop's time in 'Nam and a wedding photo of both of his parents. His mom, Jennifer, looked so young and happy. Her curly black hair had been tamed to straightness for the day, and her dark-brown eyes glinted with joy. She wore a strapless white gown with beading down the front and a veil that made her look like a princess. Joel wished he remembered more about her. He only had a few precious memories, and sometimes he worried he'd made those up.

And his father? Well, he looked like an old man marrying his daughter. Fifty-eight to his mother's twenty-six, he was already balding, but he had a handsome grin and a possessive arm around Jennifer's shoulders. His knuckles were white with the force of his grip, and Joel sometimes wondered if he'd ever hit her too.

He hoped the violence was just for him. Somehow it made Joel feel better to think his mother never knew how mean Pop could be.

In the end, he supposed it didn't matter. His mom was long dead, and soon enough his pop would be as well. Inexplicably, given how much of an asshole Charlie was, Joel still kind of hoped Jennifer would be waiting for him on the other side. Becca had asked him not long ago if he even loved his pop, and Joel guessed *that* was love, holding that hope for him. It was the only kind of love Joel gave the man who raised him. Unless you counted the Egg McMuffin. And he did.

After a few more minutes, Joel chose not to wait. He was going to get reamed out anyway. It might as well be tomorrow.

Placing the McDonald's bag on his father's pillow, golden arches up, he beat a retreat to his truck and drove to the store, memories bubbling up like old poison.

"Most rich assholes are queers," Pop snarled. "Cowardly queers who hid behind books instead of fighting in the war."

He was deep in a bottle of Christmas rum, so Joel knew better than to contradict him, but he was itching to anyway. He was no fan of Casey's stuck-up dad, but the man wasn't cowardly and he wasn't a queer. He was just born twenty-five years too late to go to Vietnam, for God's sake.

"You keep hanging out with that sissy boy, and you'll be licking his balls and begging like a bitch before you know it."

Joel blinked at his pop, taking in the way his muscles bulged even as he reclined in his La-Z-Boy. Joel bit down on his cheek hard. He wasn't going to say anything. Nothing at all. He wouldn't give anything away.

"You think I don't know? You think I don't have eyes that see?"

"What do you see, Pop?"

Joel wanted to knock himself unconscious for being stupid enough to ask a question. If he'd been smart, he'd have gone to his room long before now, before his father's attention even fell on him.

"I've seen all kinds of things. Like you and that boy wrestling in the backyard back when you were kids. And I see you now." He waved his glass

Joel's way. "I see you looking at him all moony-eyed. You a fuckin' queer? You better tell me so I know what to do with you."

Joel never wanted to know what that meant. "I'm not a fucking queer, Pop." He was a queer but not a fucking one. He was a virgin all the way. So it wasn't even a lie.

"That's what they all say," Pop slurred.

In all likelihood, his pop wouldn't remember any of this in the morning. But Joel hoped like hell he did. Whenever Charlie drank enough to get his asshole out and show it around, he felt guilty as sin the next day.

That's how Joel had convinced Charlie to agree to let the band practice in the garage, and that's how he wrangled his first bass guitar and amp too. He'd been hoping to pick up a tube preamp so they could make better-sounding demos to put up on YouTube. If his pop remembered these accusations tomorrow, he might be able to buy it.

"Your mom's brother was a fuckin' queer," he whispered, taking a sip of his drink and eyeing Joel angrily. "Died like the rest of 'em in the eighties. Should've known better than to knock Jenny up. Should've never given in and let her have you. Maybe she'd still be with me."

Joel didn't know what the hell that meant since her death had literally nothing to do with him. How was it his fault that his mom died in a freak electrical accident while visiting a friend? He hadn't even been with her. He'd been at home with a babysitter.

"Go to your room. Come out when you're not a damn faggot."

Joel did as he was told, though when his alarm went off the next morning, he ignored the last part of his father's injunction. He grabbed his iPhone, backpack, and the freshly pinched pack of cigarettes before heading out the door to wait at the bus stop with Casey. Queer as ever.

Gripping the steering wheel, Joel choked down the mix of shame and anger and resentment. He thought of kissing Casey and managed to smile, even if it was more of a smirk. He was still a damn faggot, and Pop could go to hell.

Chapter Nine

"*GLORIA IN EXCELSIS Deo!*"

Casey's mother had a light voice that bounced around the living room as she unboxed all the ornaments for the tree. The Bluetooth speaker sat in the middle of the giant glass coffee table and spewed Christmas carols all around. They'd strung the tree with lights the night before, but everyone had been too worn out—and Casey too distracted—to hang the ornaments.

The tree was the one thing about Christmas that didn't have to follow his father's rules. That was because his mother had developed a story about the decorations, one that his father bought into. She told anyone who commented on the wild mish-mash of ornaments and colors that it was tradition in their home to have a tree that reflected the life and love a family shared, *not* to reflect the décor of the house. So, their tree had ornaments from their travels and his childhood, his grandmother's old tree, and his mother's time in college. Handmade items that barely stood the test of time now.

"Hey, Hank. Glad I caught you. I'm thinking of upsizing our boat next summer. If I did, would you want to buy the old one?" His father paced like a tiger by the windows that overlooked the lake. He looked older than the last time Casey had seen him, when he'd popped up to New York for a business meeting over the summer, but no less powerful. Still an inch taller than Casey's six feet, his blond hair had only just silvered over the last year or two.

Talking on the phone with a country club pal, Jonathan Stevens's voice boomed like no one else was in the room. "You've been running around on that old speedster too long. You really should consider my offer. I'll make you a good deal."

"Why do we need a new boat?" Casey asked his mom, poking through the box for his favorite ornament. It was a monkey playing a drum, and he'd picked it out for himself at Hallmark when he was four. "And why isn't Dad at the office?"

His mother, dressed in black jeggings and a stylish snowflake sweater, sorted through the box of mixed-up ornaments. "Heather needs to take better care when disassembling the tree," she muttered, smoothing her pixie cut around her ears. "She broke some ornaments last year." Then she smiled at Casey. "Your dad took today off to spend with you."

Casey's stomach dropped, and he glanced toward the clock. He had just enough time to help his mom decorate the tree, swing by Ham & Goody's for the sandwich and cookies he remembered Joel had once liked, and then get to Vreeland's in time for lunch. Assuming Joel ate lunch at noon like a normal person, and assuming Joel actually deigned to eat lunch with him. But he hadn't said *not* to come. And he'd seemed pretty into the kiss while it was going on, so Casey had reason to hope.

His entire body buzzed with excitement, like someone had caffeinated his blood, electrified his skin, and jazzed up his bones. There was no way he was going to cancel on seeing Joel at lunch today to awkwardly hang out with his dad and listen to him pontificate about the petroleum business. Casey chewed on his lower lip.

"What's wrong?" his mother asked.

"I have other plans."

"What sort of plans?" She blinked at him, her blue eyes glinting. "You know how much your father and I have been looking forward to your visit."

"I do, but…"

She lifted her pale brows. "But?"

"I'm meeting Joel. For lunch."

"Joel?"

"Yeah. Joel Vreeland."

Her voice tightened. "I know which Joel, honey. I'm just surprised. I thought you understood it was a good thing you'd let that friendship go by the wayside." She glanced toward his father, who was still pacing by the windows, nodding along to whatever Hank was saying. "Joel isn't ever going to be at your level."

Casey shook his head, refusing to engage in this line of conversation. He'd gone down that path with them before in high school, and he didn't see their opinion changing. But he was an adult now. It wasn't up to them. "I saw him at Vreeland's last night when I bought the tree and—"

"You went to Vreeland's? I sent you to Costco." She turned her gaze suspiciously toward the tree like she now suspected it of being infested with bugs.

"Does it matter? You said it was beautiful when I brought it in last night."

"It is," she agreed reluctantly. "I just thought… Never mind." Her shoulders sank. "I see. You went to Vreeland's where you saw Joel. You're still rebounding from Theo, so of course that old crush has risen to the surface. The holidays can make us nostalgic like that."

Ann had said to avoid arguments he couldn't win. She said he needed to learn to state his plans as a *fait accompli* and his parents would have to learn to deal with them—and him—accordingly.

"We're meeting for lunch," he said firmly. "So I won't be able to hang out with Dad today. Sorry."

His mom darted a glance toward his father to make sure he was still distracted before reaching out and taking his hand. "Joel's straight, Casey. Remember? I hate to see you hurt yourself this way."

Casey kept his face smooth, but it was harder than it used to be when he'd lived with his parents and *everything* rode on making them think he agreed with them.

"We were friends, Mom. And I wouldn't mind being friends again." He wasn't about to betray Joel's confidence by telling his mother the truth about Joel's sexuality. "I'm lonely in New York. It's a big city, full of strangers with lives that don't include me. I miss knowing people the way I did here."

It was true enough. He hadn't made the friends he'd anticipated when he'd gone away to college. He didn't know if it was his Southern accent, or his *nouveau riche* background, or his country-come-to-town awe of the city, but somehow he just never fit in.

Before he'd left Knoxville for NYU, he'd imagined four years of intellectual discussions, drunken parties, a dedicated friend group, and everything the Internet and TV had promised him about college. Instead, it'd been a lot of studying and casual acquaintances and being alone, aside from his doomed relationship with Theo. And meaningless sex via horrible hookup apps. Joel was right. What had the world come to?

He didn't necessarily regret any of his own experiences, but he was glad Joel had missed out on that rite of passage. Joel deserved better. He deserved to be loved by any man who touched him. Casey wanted to show him that truth.

"Well, you'll have to tell him," his mother whispered, shooting a meaningful look at his father. "I'm not going to be the one to say he took a day off for nothing."

Casey barely restrained his eye roll and marveled that he really must have lost control of his expressions by living alone. "I'm fine with that."

"Are you?" She raised a brow.

He raised one of his in return. "He can be pissed if he wants, but he didn't ask me if I was available to spend the day with him. That's his problem, not mine."

"What's this?" his father said, slipping his cell phone into his pocket, the conversation with his friend ended. He walked toward them, away from the windows. "Did you say I should have asked if you were available?"

"Did you sell your boat to Hank?" Casey's mom asked, moving aside the ornament boxes and reaching out to take his father's hands, squeezing them and giving him a bright, conciliatory smile.

"Hank said he'd think about it." He narrowed his brown eyes on Casey again and tilted his head. "I took today off to spend with you. Did I just hear you imply that you aren't available?"

Sweat broke out on Casey's forehead, but he held his tone steady. "Sorry, Dad. I have plans. Maybe you can still go into the office to get some work done and we can spend the day together tomorrow."

"I have appointments all day tomorrow. I had Natalie clear the schedule today."

"It's a misunderstanding, that's all." He returned to hanging the ornaments on the tree, his fingers shaking. He hated that his dad still evoked this reaction in him. "We'll see plenty of each other. I'll be here until the day after New Year's."

His father grumbled slightly but already had his phone out, placing a call. "Natalie, I'll be in today after all. Can you pull the files on the Branson deal for me? I want to double-check those numbers against last quarter's." He walked away still talking with his assistant. Casey took a slow breath and let it out even slower.

"That was lucky," Mom said softly. "He took that really well."

Casey shrugged. "He'd rather be at work anyway. We both know that."

She sat on the sofa, dangling an ornament from one finger, as she tsked at him. "I can't believe you'd say that. You're his pride and joy."

"He loves me, Mom, but that doesn't mean he likes me. I don't think he's ever really liked me."

"What nonsense! Of course he likes you and always has. He's your father."

Casey didn't argue any more, but he didn't agree either. He remembered far too well how frustrated his father used to get with him, how the time he'd spent with Casey always felt like it was more out of obligation than any shared interests or enthusiasms.

But Casey couldn't blame him entirely. He'd been a boring child and was an even more boring adult. At least as far as his father was concerned. He had no interest in social climbing, golf, or oil. Even less interest in his father's ideas for Casey's future.

He didn't want to work in a corporation. His dream, uncovered after months of talking to Ann about what he *didn't* want to do with his life, was to work in branding and marketing. He wanted to contribute to the growth of underdeveloped areas and help bring the shops and stores in a town or small city back to life. He loved working on marketing plans, and he enjoyed the idea of being part of a bigger social movement of shared vision for a community.

But it wasn't like Casey was going to confess his genuine interests or plans for post-graduation with his father anyway. The few times he'd made the mistake of thinking his father truly wanted to know his thoughts on anything, it hadn't gone well for him. It had always devolved into Casey being told he was wrong—back-to-front, top-to-tail wrong. And sometimes when he was younger…

He chose another ornament. The past was in the past and there was no sense dredging it up. His mother was right—he'd been lucky his father hadn't thrown a fit about Casey messing up his day. Maybe his father was mellowing with age. Unlikely but possible, he supposed. Or maybe he'd decided that temper tantrums, even in the privacy of one's own home, weren't classy.

Casey snorted. If only.

Shoving such mopey thoughts aside, Casey focused on decorating the tree. After all, it was the only thing standing between him and leaving to meet Joel for lunch. With a smile, he dangled his favorite monkey ornament, discovered beneath a trove of glittering balls. "Aha! Mr. Drummer Monkey. My favorite."

"He has such a sour face," his mother said archly, standing to hang a shimmery, gold ball on a mid-level limb.

"Nah. Mr. Drummer Monkey's adorable."

"I was talking about Joel."

Casey frowned and took his time choosing the perfect spot for his ornament. "I like his face," he said steadily. Ann's voice in his head told him to calmly stand his ground and protect his interests. "It's not like anyone else's face, and I like it."

"To each his own, they always say." She took up another ornament and frowned at a rip in the skirt of an ancient doll figurine ornament she'd brought to the marriage with her. It'd been a favorite from her own childhood. "I'll have to ask Heather to repair this when she arrives this afternoon to make dinner."

"About dinner," Casey said casually, "I might not be here for that either."

"But why?"

"I might have a date."

She blinked at him and sighed, shaking her head. "Chasing after a straight man is only going to cause you pain."

"Mom, it's none of your business. I'll let you know in plenty of time for Heather to adjust her cooking plans," Casey said.

The next song his mother's Christmas playlist offered up turned out to be "Frosty the Snowman," and excitement at seeing Joel later stirred again in his blood.

Irritable, grumpy Joel could be a Mr. Frosty Pants indeed. He might have been cold last night, but his lips had been warm for Casey's kiss today.

Casey sang along as they trimmed the tree, a bubble of irrepressible joy in his chest. His mother didn't offer any more objections, and they finished decorating with plenty of time for Casey to head out to pick up lunch.

Chapter Ten

JOEL'S STOMACH WAS in knots, and he couldn't stop checking the time on his phone. Ten minutes until noon, and who knew when Casey might show up? What if he didn't? What if he did? But what if he *didn't*? Joel wanted lunchtime to be here already.

"Why do you keep smiling like that?" Angel asked with her nose wrinkled like she smelled something rotten. She stood behind the register wearing a black T-shirt and black overalls, with new Sharpie tattoos decorating her exposed arms.

"Like what?"

"Like *that*. It's creepy. Like you'll be glaring, all normal and stuff, and then all of a sudden, you'll just…smile." She shuddered. "Like you can't even help it, and you don't know why you're doing it. Are you possessed?"

"*No.*"

"You are. You've got the devil in you." She waggled her dark eyebrows. "Call the priest! We'll exorcise this freakish happiness right out of your body."

"I'm not *happy*."

Angel tilted her head and examined him. "No, you're not. Which is what makes that smile so creepy."

Joel snorted dismissively. "Get back to work."

He knew the smile she was talking about. Ever since he was a little kid, when he was nervous about something, he'd break into what his pop called a "simpering face," like a whipped dog. He hated it. He resented having a nervous, anxious tic of any sort.

But he wasn't exactly *scared* for Casey to show up. Eating lunch with his old friend didn't terrify him. It was more about what Casey might expect or want from him now that they'd kissed, and even more what Casey *wouldn't* want from him. He didn't want to deal with the horrible confirmation that, yeah, he really wasn't worth anyone's effort after all. Or face the possibility that the kiss this morning was a bizarre hallucination born out of lonely, desperate insanity.

Joel left Angel behind the register where she was using a tiny stamp she'd brought in to add green Christmas trees to her black-lacquered nails. He should reprimand her for messing around at work, but he couldn't bring himself to care. He pulled on his jean jacket and headed out to straighten the rows of trees in the lot again. It'd only been a few minutes, but it was possible one had gotten blown out of line by a freak gust of wind. It gave him something to do at least, and that calmed his mind.

He'd just gotten to the end of the first row of Scotch pines when he heard footsteps and then Casey's warm, tenor voice. "I brought your favorite Ham & Goody's sandwich plus lemon cookies for dessert."

Joel turned around to find Casey holding a big white bag in one hand, as well as a paper tray with a few sodas in the other.

Joel's weird smile leapt onto his face again, and he tried to play it off with a joke. "Well, how gallant. It's almost like you're courting me now." He wanted to swallow his own tongue as soon as the words were out. Sure, Becca had said the same thing, but that was different. That wasn't him being an ass.

Casey's smile grew serious and his gaze grabbed Joel's and wouldn't let go. "Would it be terrible if I was? I think you deserve a little courting."

Swallowing thickly, Joel muttered, "Better than a kiss-n-run, I guess."

"Definitely." Casey's eyes drifted down to Joel's mouth and back up again. His tone softened. "Do you still hate onions? Because I asked them to leave those off."

"Still gross."

Casey grinned. "Some things never change."

Joel let out a slow breath, taking in Casey's tall form and muscular shoulders. "And some things do." He grabbed the white bag from Casey and motioned for him to follow. Pine filled his nose, and needles crunched under their feet.

They headed around to the back of the store, where the noon sun shone on a patio area. It was set up with winter-worthy deck chairs and a table. Because there was a view of the back of the store from the interstate, Joel and Brandon had decorated the patio for Christmas, including a large tree strung with white lights and golden, plastic balls that glinted brightly.

By the chairs and table, there was a privacy screen that shielded the area from the passing cars and dulled the road noise. A window into the store allowed Joel to keep an eye on things when taking his smoke breaks out here—back when he used to smoke enough to require breaks for it, anyway—but the view inside was currently obscured by faux frost Angel had sprayed on.

It was the most private place he could think of to eat with Casey without actually abandoning the store to Angel for his lunch hour. After last night, he had a lot to make up to her, so he really needed to stick around until Brandon relieved him in the afternoon.

"This is nice," Casey said, looking around. "I remember your dad kept a swing set out here for the kids to play on while their parents looked around the store."

"Huge liability. When I got rid of it, I was able to get our insurance down by enough to make it worthwhile, but not by as much as you might think. There are always safety hazards in a home-and-garden store. Lawn mowers, weed whackers, pruning shears."

"Insecticide."

"Exactly." Joel motioned at the table and then sat down with his back to the privacy screen and within eyesight of the door. Angel might come out and ask him for help with loading up a tree. Things sometimes got hectic around noon with people making quick stops on their way home for lunch. He should have told Casey to come at one or even eleven.

His hands shook as he reached out to grab a soda from Casey and started unpacking the bag of food. The sandwiches were wrapped up neatly with their names on each, and the cookies were enough to share. "This really is my favorite."

"I remember."

Joel shook his head. "Why? Surely you have better things to keep in that head of yours."

"I remember everything about you." Casey blushed like he'd embarrassed himself.

Joel said nothing, unwrapping his sandwich and poking a straw through the soda lid. He remembered everything about Casey too. "Sprite?"

"7-Up."

"Eh, it'll do."

"So..." Casey said after they'd both taken a bite of their sandwiches and washed it down with soda. He cleared his throat. "How've you been?"

"Busy. You?"

"Finals were tough, but next semester will be a breeze. I stacked my schedule that way from the beginning so I could have a relaxing last semester before I'm cast out into the cruel world to look for a job."

"No advanced degree then?" Joel was surprised. He'd thought for sure Casey would go to law school, or get a master's degree, or something hoity-toity to make him an exciting asset at some multibillion-dollar firm.

"No. Not yet anyway. Maybe never."

"What does your dad think of that?"

"He doesn't know." Casey smile grew tighter. "I got accepted at the Wharton School for their MBA program, and Dad thinks I'm going to attend." He shrugged. "But I'm not."

"Why?"

"Because I hate the idea of it." Mustard slipped out from the sandwich and slid down some of his fingers as he took a big bite. Joel wanted to lick it off. The thought unnerved him, and he flushed hot, sweating despite the chilly weather.

Casey wiped the mustard from his hand with a napkin. "I'm trying to figure out what *I* want, you know? All my life, I've done what was expected of me and what my parents wanted me to do, but that has to stop. It's no way to go forward."

"You can't claim you've always done what was expected. Being gay, for example. Being out about it. That had to be at the very least unexpected and, knowing your folks, probably unwanted." Joel's lips twisted up, and he took a sip of his 7-Up before saying, "Low-class, even?"

Casey laughed bitterly. "Yeah, like I said this morning, it didn't go over too well. But when I brought Theo home and my father realized that being gay with the right partner can open up unexpected doors? Well…" He shrugged. "He's never going to jump up and down that I'm queer, but he's mostly over it. Or he was before Theo and I broke up. But that's my point." Casey leaned closer, his sincerity ringing Joel like a bell. "In the end, it doesn't matter what he thinks or if he's happy with me. *I* need to be happy with me."

Joel lifted a brow. "And you're not?"

"No. I'm not."

Joel frowned. How was that possible? Casey was handsome, smart, and a decent person. He'd had a boyfriend, and he'd slept with men— probably hot ones. He'd gotten into NYU on his own merit. He had money, lots of it. If Casey was lonely, so what? He could buy friends, couldn't he? What other ingredients were necessary in life to whip up a batch of happiness? And why didn't Casey have access to them?

"Are *you* happy?" Casey asked, studying him carefully.

Joel tried to think. Had he ever been happy? Earlier with Casey's mouth on his, that'd been happiness, hadn't it? Or had it been terror? Or horrible, desperate need?

So, no. Maybe he'd never been happy. He didn't think happiness was a state of mind he'd ever had a real chance to entertain. Not since his mom died anyway. "I get by," he said.

"Getting by isn't loving your life and what you do and who you're with."

"That kind of life's a fairy tale."

"No, it's not."

"What do you know about it?" Joel shot Casey a half-hearted glare. "Happiness is a myth people convince themselves to believe in just so they can cling to hope during the all-too-real grim days. Name one person on earth who's happy."

Casey considered, "RJ's happy. Mostly. He loves playing in bands and traveling the world. He's got a boyfriend right now, and he seems to like him. I'm not saying his life is perfect, but RJ's a happy guy, I think. I mean, I'd be willing to bet on it." He frowned. "Probably."

"Well, good on him."

"My therapist says—"

"You have a therapist?" Joel snorted. "You really have gone New York on me, man."

Casey shrugged off the slight. "Ann, my therapist, says I deserve to find out what really interests me. I've saved the extra money my parents have sent me over the last four years, and I've got a little bundle. I'm thinking of traveling when school's out. Trying to see if somewhere out in the world calls to me."

"What? Like that *Eat Pray Love* lady?" Joel said, sneering.

"Did you read that book? Because it was pretty good."

"Bullshit."

Casey grinned. "The point is, I need to find my mission in life. I know what I want to do for my career, but I need to find the right place to do it. I want to live somewhere I'm passionate about too."

Joel rolled his eyes. "Passion is pointless."

"Well, you seem to have taken that sentiment to heart in every possible way."

Joel blinked, dropped his sandwich to the wrapper. "Did you really just mock me for being a virgin?"

Casey's lips smirked slightly. "You dish it out all the time. Always have. Can't you take it?"

"You know I can. Bring it."

"Okay, I will."

Joel waited expectantly for Casey to say something more about his poor virginal state, but instead, Casey asked, "So, did you ever finish that book?"

"Which book?"

"You know, the one back in high school. About the vampires."

"Oh, yeah. Ages ago. And I've written a few more trashy horror novels since," Joel said, lifting his lips in a half smile.

"Really?"

"Lots of ghosts, zombies, and gore."

Casey's eyes lit up, and he grinned. "Have you published any of them?"

"Rejection slips line the walls of my bedroom."

"Don't give up!"

"I didn't. But I took matters into my own hands in the meantime. I self-pub under a pen name. Joel Grimsbane." He chuckled. "It brings in a little extra each month. Not a lot."

Not nearly enough to make even a dent in the bills.

Casey poked a piece of fallen lettuce into his mouth. "Are they good?"

"How the hell would I know? I wrote them."

"Did you like writing them?" Casey tilted his head, gazing at him intently. "Would you read them again?"

"I guess. Yeah. Sure."

"Then they must be good."

"Becca read a couple." Joel picked a stray leaf of spinach from his sandwich just to keep from looking at Casey.

"Did *she* like them?"

Joel remembered Becca calling him after midnight, crying and hyperventilating, begging him to come to her apartment and spend the night. "*Since it's your fault I'm too scared to fall asleep, you sick, awful fuck!*" "Yeah, she liked them."

"Well, I'm still a horror fan, thanks to you making me read Amityville back in the day. So I'm definitely looking them up. You're on Amazon?"

"Enough about me and the books," Joel said, shifting uncomfortably. "Let's talk about something else now."

"Like what?"

"You're the one who's soul-searching for the meaning of life. What are your career plans?"

Casey's eyes brightened as he waved a hand toward the interstate. "Ultimately, I want to be part of a revitalization effort, like they did here in Knoxville with the downtown area. The way they brought it back to life and made it better is a beautiful thing. In the short term, though, I want to focus on setting up my own branding and marketing business. I think that's where my talent is and where I can help immediately. Now I just have to figure out where I want to do that."

"They're still making progress downtown. Why can't it be here?"

"Knoxville is always going to be home, but I can't live here. My dad…" Casey shook his head. "Anything I achieved here would be tied into him somehow, whether it was because of his reputation or his connections. I want someplace to call my own."

"I see." Joel frowned. He hadn't ever thought Casey would come back to Knoxville for good after he left for school, but disappointment stung anyway. "I'm sure school takes up a lot of your time. And all those hours of therapy."

Casey rolled his eyes.

Joel pressed. "But what do you do for fun?"

"In New York or here?"

"Anywhere?"

"In the city, I like to people watch." Casey took a sip of his drink. "It probably sounds kind of creepy and strange, but I like to find a comfortable place and watch folks go by."

"Why?"

"It's relaxing and reassuring. Everyone's got lives to live, places to go, you know? It makes everything I do seem a lot less important in the scheme of things. Also, since I study marketing and branding, I like to make note of what's popular. What attracts people into a store or a restaurant? That sort of thing."

"What else?"

"I really like the new Netflix show *Harkening*. I, uh, sometimes chat on Internet fanboards about where the storylines are going." Casey fiddled with his straw. "That probably sounds kind of lame, doesn't it?"

"Yeah. It does."

Casey shoved Joel's shoulder.

Joel chuckled. "But I like to read the *Harkening* fanboards too. So, I'm not sure I've got room to judge." He took a bite of his sandwich.

"Look," Casey said brightly. "We still have so much in common. I love horror novels, and you like *Harkening*."

"Oh, yeah. We're just rolling in commonalities." Joel set aside his sandwich and took a bite of a lemon cookie. Saliva rushed into his mouth from the tang on his tongue.

Casey licked his lips, eyes on Joel's mouth, before taking a big bite of his sandwich and chewing for a long time before he pulled his gaze away from Joel.

"So, I guess it's a feast for a queer guy in the city, huh?" Joel asked, though he immediately wished he hadn't.

Casey shrugged as sadness swept over his face. "Yeah. I've had some experiences. And I'm not ashamed of them. Still, I don't think casual hookups are really for me, even though it's hard to walk away from it entirely. I like sex."

"Nothing wrong with liking to sleep with people," Joel murmured. "Lots of folks are into all kinds of things. Consensual sharing and poly and all that modern jazz." Or so he'd heard.

It always sounded awfully complicated to him. But then he hadn't even had his dick sucked because he was so picky about the mouth attached to the pleasure. He wanted to have *feelings* for the person at least, if not love them devotedly. That might be old-fashioned or limiting, but he didn't see what was wrong with it.

"Of course not, if that's how you're built. But in the last few years I've discovered that my body is capable of enjoying a lot of things that don't bring me lasting satisfaction. And I want to respect what makes me truly happy. I think that involves finding someone to share deeply with—to share *everything* with. The whole of me." He shivered like a cold wind had swept over him, but the direct winter sun on their shoulders was flat and plenty warm.

"So casual hookups were sort of like smoking," Joel offered, wanting to smooth away the worried vulnerability that had crept into Casey's eyes. "You tried it out, didn't love it, and moved on. Youthful experimentation."

"I guess, in a way. Yeah. It's a decent analogy. I admit 'moving on' hasn't been as easy as it was with cigarettes. I never loved smoking. I just loved smoking with *you*."

Joel's heart did a fluttery little dance. "I wish I could say the same. I've been planning to quit for years. There's always some new reason to buy one more pack."

"What's your reason for smoking today?" Casey asked.

Joel laughed. "You."

"The kiss was that bad?"

Joel's insides turned gooey and hot, and he turned his face away. His throat closed up, and his hands went clammy. "You know it wasn't."

"Excuse me? I didn't hear you." Casey leaned closer, cupping his hand around his ear. "What did you say?"

"I liked it, okay?" Hope and want tangled up together and snaked through his gut, scaring the shit out of him.

"I could do it again," Casey whispered. He touched Joel's chin lightly, rubbing against his unshaven morning stubble. "Let me do it again."

Joel quivered and loosed an embarrassing sound as Casey leaned in and kissed him tenderly. Casey's tongue teased his lips open, and the tang of mustard exploded in his mouth.

Casey glided a hand to the back of Joel's neck, holding him in place as he slipped his tongue between Joel's lips and stroked sweetly, making him shiver, touching places that Joel had no idea could feel so awake, enervated, and needful.

The sweep of the tip of Casey's tongue along the top of Joel's mouth felt almost *too* good, and he trembled. His nipples peaked, and blood rushed in his groin, making him hard. He whimpered and pulled back, out of the wet, tender bliss of Casey's kiss.

His cock thudded against the restriction of his jeans as he held Casey's strong biceps to keep him from leaning in for another. "Wait," he whispered. "I need…" He trailed off. He didn't know what he needed.

"A smoke?" Casey's wet mouth glistened as he smiled.

Joel snorted and lowered his eyes, trying to control his breathing. He wanted to tug Casey in closer and try that kiss again, but it was all so much. So overwhelming.

And why was Casey even here? Joel didn't *want* to feel these things. Not if Casey was just leaving again—if Joel was some sort of experiment like hookups and cigarettes.

Casey leaned back. "I'm moving too fast. You're freaking out."

"Yeah, I'm pretty, well… I'm shook."

Casey whispered, "I can see that."

"You're an asshole. Coming here and stirring this up in me."

"Maybe I am." Casey rubbed his hands soothingly up and down Joel's arms. Joel trembled as Casey whispered, "Let's go on a date. Dinner and a walk. Downtown. Tonight."

Joel's head spun wildly. "Tonight?"

"Yeah. I'll pick you up at your place. What time?"

"A date?" Joel couldn't wrap his mind around his life all of a sudden, and typically stubborn Casey didn't seem to be asking so much as expecting. Joel should say no just for form's sake. Just to prove he could.

But there was no way he'd ever do that. Not now. He wanted to find out about Casey's idea of a date more than he'd wanted anything in years.

"I'm going to romance you." Casey smiled, touching Joel's chin again. "I know they still have ice skating in Market Square for the holidays. Have you been?"

Joel squeezed his eyes closed, willing his mouth to say no, to tell Casey to fuck off with his romance and his amber eyes and his sweet smiles. Instead, he said, "Brandon takes over today around five, I need to go home and take care of a few things, but I can be ready by six-thirty."

"Perfect."

Joel groaned as Casey's lips found his again. How did he do that thing with his tongue? It made Joel shiver and lean in closer.

"Sorry to interrupt, but I need help with a tree."

Joel jerked away to see Angel standing by the door with one dark brow raised and a shit-eating grin on her face. With his mouth wet and his heart racing, he rose shakily from the table, only to realize that his cock was hard and pressing against the front of his jeans. He jerked his jean jacket closed and buttoned it up over the evidence of what Casey Stevens's mouth did to him.

"I've got work to do," he said huskily. "You should go."

Casey stood and started bagging the leftover food. Joel realized he hadn't eaten his entire sandwich or more than one of the cookies. He regretted that Casey was probably just going to throw it away. But if he stayed even a second longer on the patio, if he asked to keep the leftovers so that he could put them in the small fridge in the back office for later, he'd end up kissing Casey again.

And if he kissed Casey again?

Then he'd probably be the one to initiate it. And somehow that felt too real to him. It was easier when kisses were things that happened *to* him.

Angel really did need help with the customer. The tree was awkward to fit on the top rack of the Mazda Z the middle-aged customer was driving, and by the time Joel had worked it up and started strapping it down, Casey walked out of the store with a poinsettia plant and a big smile.

"I left money for it on the counter, and I put the leftovers in the fridge in the back office," he called as he opened the door to his SUV. "I'll see you at six-thirty."

Joel said nothing, returning to his work and trying to shove down the riot of emotions in his chest—explosions of anticipation and fear and anger and frustration and horniness. He couldn't even catch his breath from one before the next began.

"So that's what your creepy smiles were about," Angel said from the other side of the car where she stood uselessly, grinning widely. "He's hot, boss. Congratulations. It's about time you got laid. How long has it been? A year?"

"Shut up and help me strap down the tree." Joel glanced toward the customer who'd wandered off to look at wreaths. "Or see if you can sell him one of those."

"More than a year, then," Angel said knowingly. "I'd say it's shocking, but then again, who'd want to sleep with a Mr. Frosty Pants like you?"

Who indeed?

Joel worked to make sure the tree wouldn't slide off at any sudden stops or starts. Maybe Casey Stevens wanted to sleep with him, and maybe he didn't. But if he did, and if Joel said yes, would his heart survive? He had his doubts.

He hadn't done too well the first time Casey left him behind.

Chapter Eleven

"BRUNO, DOWN," JOEL said gently.

He shoved his cold hands into his jean jacket's pockets and watched his happy, welcoming dog try to wreck Casey's nice clean jeans. "At least his paws are good, even if his behavior's not. Wrinkles and dog hair aren't a big deal, but red clay mud doesn't come out."

They stood by the stairs leading up to the front of Joel's mobile home, lit only by the front door lights. Bruno wriggled wildly at seeing Casey again so soon on the equally exciting heels of Joel's arrival home from work.

"Back inside, buddy. I'll give you something special later," Joel promised when Bruno gave him sad eyes and trotted up the stairs. He followed him up and stuck his head in the door and saw him settle down in his bed near the entrance to the kitchen.

"If you need us to stick around here awhile for Bruno's sake, I wouldn't mind having a beer or something before we head out," Casey offered.

Joel stiffened at the idea of inviting Casey into his trailer. It was messy, and he didn't have any beer, and, okay, fine—he was embarrassed.

Casey lived in that glittering hulk across the lake and drove a freaking Lexus. The idea of inviting Casey into his two-bedroom, one-bath mobile home made Joel sweaty all over. And no matter what Casey wanted with him, or how he felt about him, or how many times he kissed him, there was no way he wouldn't judge the way Joel lived. He wouldn't be able to stop himself.

"Nah, he's fine. Let's go." Joel stalked away from the trailer, hands in his pockets.

"You didn't lock up."

"Nothing to steal, unless they want some beat-up blue jeans and a crockpot." Joel tweaked a smile, hoping to defuse the weirdness of his refusal to invite Casey inside. "I guess they could take my decade-old computer and Goodwill TV set. Why not? Have at it." He reached out to jerk open the passenger side door of Casey's Lexus. "Besides, I figure a thief will take one look at Bruno and—"

"Get cuddled and loved to death?"

Joel snorted. "Probably. That beast thinks he's a lap dog."

Casey smiled and rounded to the driver's side. Joel wiped his sweaty palms on his jeans and willed his fluttery gut to calm the hell down. He was just going on a date. That's all. People did it all the time. There was nothing to be all worked up about.

"Nice ride," he commented.

"Thanks. It was a gift from my folks. It's not very practical in New York City between paying for parking and navigating the streets, but my parents have never cared about practical."

"Just whether or not it's classy," Joel murmured.

Casey snorted again.

The drive to downtown Knoxville was quiet. Casey seemed a little tired and Joel didn't quite know what to say either. He hoped the evening didn't continue on this way because it was verging on awkward pretty quickly. At least Casey's SUV had those amazing seat warmers that heated his ass up so fast that, for a second, he feared he'd somehow pissed himself. That was something.

"I've never been inside a mobile home," Casey said finally.

"They're pretty much like they look in the movies. Nothing exciting."

"Are you embarrassed for me to come inside?"

Joel sighed. "What do you think, Prince Moneybags? Of course I am."

"We should address this. It's not healthy. Ann calls this sort of thing internalized self-loathing, and most of us have some, but I don't want you to have it about where you live."

"Oh, what should I have it about then?"

"I don't know. Smoking?"

"You want me to loathe myself for smoking?"

"No!" Casey blew out an exasperated breath. "I don't want you to loathe yourself for anything. But if you have to internalize some kind of self-hatred, then maybe hating yourself over smoking is better than hating yourself over where you live?"

"Tell your therapist—what's her name? Ann?—tell Ann to get a new job. And tell yourself to never, ever, *ever* consider psychology as a future 'passion career' because you're terrible at it."

"I'm just saying that I'd like to be invited into your home, Joel. That's all."

"Weird. It sounded like you were judging me for my smoking and suggesting I must hate myself for where I live, but if all you really meant is that you want to come hang with me for a while in Down-Class-Burbia, then I can issue you an engraved invitation tonight. Maybe you can attempt to impugn my honor while appropriating my poverty and indulging your classist savior fantasy."

Casey bugged his eyes out. "Wow, are you sure you didn't attend my liberal sociology course up at NYU? Because you'd fit right in."

Joel scrubbed a hand over his face. "I should have invited you in for a beer and to hang out with Bruno a little. Yeah, okay, fine, I'm embarrassed about living in a trailer. It's not that I'm *ashamed.* There's a difference. I did what I needed to do for my father, but I'm not exactly proud of my circumstances either."

"At least they're your circumstances, created by your own choices." Casey's hands tightened around the steering wheel. "My circumstances are handed to me, and I don't even know if I want them or not."

"I didn't choose my father's stroke."

"No, but you chose how to handle it, and I'm proud of you. I think you've done a good job. You've kept Vreeland's going, and you have a shelter that keeps you warm, a dog that loves you, and I'm guessing you've taken the best care of your dad that you could."

Joel narrowed his eyes. "This conversation sucks. It feels more like a therapy session than a date."

"What would you know about dates? Or therapy sessions? Have you ever been to one? And yeah, I know you went on a lot of make-believe dates in high school, but have you ever been on a real date?"

"I've seen them on TV, and they don't go like this," Joel said, rubbing his hands on his jeans again. "No one starts out talking about their hardest, deepest, darkest thoughts and fears. Not on the first date anyway. Maybe at the end of, like, the second or third date. Just before they kiss."

"I'm doing things all out of order, apparently. I already kissed you. Twice."

Joel flushed hot as the memory of both those kisses swept over him. In the span of less than twenty-four hours, he'd gone from never-been-kissed to having Casey Steven's tongue in his mouth two entirely different times, and now he was on a *date*. Life was weird. He didn't even know if he liked the way that it was weird, but he was on the ride for better or worse now.

Rather than park in the garage near Market Square, Casey used his father's pass to pull into the private underground lot reserved for bigwigs at the petroleum company that held the top five floors of one of the tallest office towers in downtown Knoxville.

When they exited the echoing, empty garage onto a side street that led to the main road through downtown, the happily named Gay Street—inspiration for teenage boys' homophobic queer jokes for over half a century—Casey's hand brushed the back of Joel's. For a shivery moment, he thought Casey was going to take hold of it. In public. Like a couple.

His mind galloped with the idea, and he wondered if it was even possible. Knoxville wasn't the worst place in the world to be gay, but he didn't exactly see men holding hands in the city either. Not even the men everyone knew were gay because of their flamboyant hips and flying, birdlike hand gestures. What would happen if he and Casey held hands? Would anyone care? Would someone say something?

The sidewalks were more crowded than he expected for a Tuesday, but when they crested the hill and got a glimpse of Gay Street proper, he understood why. It was the night of the annual Christmas parade, and folks lined up and down the sidewalk, cheering as pickup trucks full of grinning cheerleaders and slow-moving floats of waving Boy Scouts drifted past.

Christmas carols combined and clashed between floats and trucks, rattling down the street and echoing from the buildings in a clamor of bells and horns. Almost against his will, a festive feeling descended, quickening Joel's heart, and his lips lifted in a closed-mouthed smile.

"Oh, look, baby ballerinas," Casey whisper-shouted in his ear to be heard over the cheers and music.

A class of about six five-year-old girls and two boys marched—or rather pranced, skipped, jumped, rolled, danced, and sang—their way down the street. They wore red, green, and white leotards, tights, and sweaters, and all of the girls and one of the boys wore white, glittery tutus. Five adults trying to corral them and keep them on track surrounded them on all sides.

"Cute," Joel said, laughing at the boy without the tutu. The child had shoved his hand into his tights to scratch his privates without a care in the world.

Casey slung an arm over Joel's shoulder, and Joel stiffened, looking around to see who was watching. But no one seemed to care. Everyone was too busy enjoying the baby ballerinas and their wranglers' struggle to keep them moving forward to notice two guys touching.

"C'mon." Casey tugged him away, heading north toward Market Square. "I have reservations."

It was too loud to talk as they walked on the main road, but once they passed the four-story, light-bedecked Christmas tree at the entrance to Krutch Park—a small swath of nature through the center of town—the noise level dropped drastically. The trees had been liberally decorated with white twinkle lights and additional decorated Christmas trees lined the walk past the creek, which babbled cheerily from the shadows.

"Romantic," Joel said. They hadn't spoken much since the conversation in the car had gone too deep for comfort, but in the illuminated darkness, the awkward vibe had dissolved into a kind of fluttery coziness. Like maybe this was a thing that was really happening, something they both wanted. At that thought, Joel tamped back a strange urge to yelp and run.

"I told you I planned to romance you. I don't know why you're surprised. Haven't I always been honest with you?"

"Uh, no?"

"Withholding information isn't lying. You, however? You're quite the liar."

Joel couldn't reconcile the tender fondness in Casey's voice with the ugly accusation. He swallowed hard, throat clicking nervously, and then he gasped when Casey really did reach out to take hold of his hand.

They weren't alone on the path, but it wasn't crowded either. A small family of four approached, and none of them gave a second glance to where Casey and Joel's fingers twined together.

"You're not going to argue it?"

"Why should I?" Joel said huskily. "It's true. I lied about myself—to myself even—for years. I can't pretend I didn't."

"Why did you lie?" Casey asked, pulling on Joel's hand until they came to a stop, standing face-to-face beneath the glitter-light trees, with the creek babbling next to them. "RJ was out as gay. Becca was out as liking girls. What did you think was going to happen if you told us?"

Joel's throat went tight. "You're one to to talk."

"True. I already told you what I thought would happen, though. I thought I'd lose you. If you'd have come out, I wouldn't have been so afraid of that. I lost you anyway, sure, but—"

"There you go again. Ruining my first date ever with all this deep digging. You're supposed to tell me things that make me laugh so I'll toss my head back and chuckle like this." He threw his head back and faked a laugh.

Casey mimicked him, though his laugh sounded genuine.

Dropping the too-real conversation, they continued walking. Joel pointed out the newest sculptures along the walk, and Casey began chatting easily about art he'd seen when he was in New York. "The best show was this insane one by Paul McCarthy—"

"The Beatle?"

"No. That's McCartney, you heathen. And to think you were ever in a band!"

"I was teasing."

"Right." Casey squeezed his hand. "Anyway, it was a perverse exploration of the story of Snow White and Walt Disney. Grotesque in this dark way that I associate with some of my uncle's descriptions of cinematic art from the 1970s and the early 1990s."

"Which uncle?"

"Robert."

"Oh, 'the pervert.'"

"He's gay. Like us."

"I guess that was hard, huh?" Joel asked. Along with the opinion that Manor Crest and Belmont Hills boys shouldn't be friends, Casey's dad and Joel's pop had shared a penchant for casual homophobia. "When you came out? Remembering how your dad had called Robert a pervert for all those years?" The things Pop had said about Joel's mom's brother had certainly always stung.

"That's third date conversation," Casey said teasingly.

"Sorry. I've never been on a date before. I'm taking my cues from you."

Casey shook his head wonderingly. "That blows my mind. Why hasn't anyone ever asked you out?"

"Something about my sweet and tender demeanor scares guys away," Joel snarked. "Maybe they think I'm too angelic to fuck or something."

"Ha." Casey pulled them to a stop again. They'd almost made it to the exit of the park near Market Square, but he held Joel back, just out of the brighter light of the street lamps. He touched Joel's chin gently. "Some guys just don't get how sweet a grumpy asshole can be." He glanced up then, dropping his hand quickly. He nodded at an elderly man and woman who stepped onto the pathway.

Joel got a distinct anti-gay vibe from the looks sent their way, but the couple said nothing, continuing their romantic Christmas walk without the taint of completely ruining someone else's.

"So, this show I saw. It was just filthy," Casey went on as they crossed the street from Krutch Park and into Market Square.

He described the art show at the Armory on Park Avenue, getting more and more animated as he did. "There was a video art component to it, with films on a loop, showing the most disturbing things you've ever seen. Snow White having sex with all of the dwarves and smearing herself all over with chocolate syrup, wearing a diaper. And then in another room, there was a video of Snow White's prince *masturbating*, and I just…couldn't look away. It was depraved, but I sat on the bench across from that screen and watched him for as long as I could stand it. It was compelling and somehow more intimate than porn. Like exhibitionism without the exhibitionist actually being present. People came and went, but a few women stayed to watch it too."

"That sounds messed up."

"It was. I didn't know anyone in the city at the time, so I was by myself. It was an intense thing to see alone. I had no one to talk it over with." He smiled, his teeth shining in the low light from the streetlights along the square. "Thanks for letting me tell you about it now."

"No problem, man. Happy to listen." And maybe a little aroused by the depravity.

Joel let go of Casey's hand as they immersed themselves into the nighttime of Market Square. The revitalized downtown center was alive with Christmas shoppers and kids eager for their turn on the small outdoor skating rink set up every year just after Thanksgiving until the second week of January. Luckily, it was a cold December. Some years, when the temperatures were in the sixties or even the seventies, the ice had to be put down every hour, and even then it was often covered in an inch of water within minutes.

Tonight the weather was a sweet, chilly forty-two, and while it was far from cold enough for snow to stick, it wasn't so warm the ice rink was a puddle either. Casey stayed close by as they walked around the square slowly, taking in the scents of the restaurants and glancing in the decorated windows of the stores. Piped Christmas music from the speakers stacked around the rink bounced off the low buildings and sent "Jingle Bell Rock" ringing out all around the square.

"So, Tomato Head or Tupelo Honey?" Casey asked after they left the oldest store on the square: Earth to Old City. It'd been there since Joel was a little kid, and he remembered his mother taking him inside to smell the handmade soaps. He'd spent some time smelling them tonight, thinking of her, while Casey explored small tea sets, mumbling some-thing about still needing a Christmas gift for his aunt Courtney.

"Whichever," Joel said. "You choose."

"No, you decide. I wasn't sure which you'd like better, so I made reservations at both. And I'm not picky either way."

"Well…" Joel confronted the reality he'd somehow avoided thinking about while he'd gotten ready for their date and up until this exact moment. How was he going to pay for dinner? He didn't have the cash, and the idea of not paying his own way felt wrong. "I'm not that hungry. So you choose. I'll probably just have water."

Casey shook his head. "No, no. It's a date. I asked you out, and I'm going to pay."

"I said I wasn't hungry."

"You also said you went down on Ally Cartwell and that she was a real blonde."

"That was in high school. What does that have to do with dinner?"

"Eating."

"Oh, good lord. Fine. Whatever. I'll let you buy this time, but I get the next meal."

Casey's face broke open with his smile. "So we're doing this again?"

"How else are you going to unlock the date where you're allowed to ask me hard questions?" Joel rolled his eyes. "Haven't you watched any movies? Read any books?"

Casey jerked his head toward the corner of the square across from a gaudily decorated Urban Outfitters. "Tupelo Honey, then. They make a mean rosemary lemon drop. I used to steal sips of my mom's."

"Girly drinks? Really?"

"Don't be a sexist, Joel. You'll lose all the credits from your self-taught liberal sociology course and then what'll happen? Besides, I thought you'd come so far since you used to throw girls' reputations under the bus for your social gain back in high school."

"Fine. I'll have two rosemary lemon drops in penance. Okay by you?"

"If you get drunk, can I still kiss you?"

"I won't get drunk."

"Aw, so what does that mean?" Casey raised a coy brow. "I can't kiss you?"

"Don't act all desperate for my honey now. I like a man who plays hard to get."

Casey guffawed. "Right."

"Fine, jerk." Joel's pulse went wild. "You can kiss me."

Casey's eyes drifted down to Joel's mouth, and he licked his lips. "Later. When I can do it right."

Then he grabbed Joel's elbow and steered him toward the welcoming lights of Tupelo Honey.

JOEL DID GET drunk, and Casey loved drunk Joel so much he thought his heart was going to escape from his chest and go running screaming with joy down the middle of Gay Street. Why had they never experimented with alcohol when they were kids? How had he not known that Joel was adorable like this?

"Yeah, so I said to Angel—my employee—I said to her, that's—well, that's the thing, right? I said you have to be ready to willy, I mean, really..." Joel lifted up the second empty rosemary lemon drop glass and stared at it. "Whoa. Talking is hard. What did they put in this? Straight alcohol?"

Casey held back on ribbing Joel about his opinion on girly drinks now. "Dinner should be here soon, and that'll help sober you up."

"Good thing you're driving," Joel muttered.

They were settled in a small booth in the middle of the crowded restaurant. Jazz renditions of Christmas songs played discreetly, the brassy tone of saxophone and trumpets soaring overhead, backed by a cheery snare drum.

"This is a good one," Joel said, cocking his head. "My old man used to play this at Christmas back when my mom was alive." He hummed a few bars of "The Christmas Song." "Dexter Gordon Quartet. He'd twirl her around. Call her his doll. It's one of my few memories of her."

Casey said nothing. In high school, Joel had almost never talked about his mother and hardly ever with the soft smile he was wearing now. Joel closed his eyes, and the song slipped around them, muffled by the sounds of conversations.

"This is nice," Joel said, opening his eyes and smiling crookedly. Casey's heart skittered and leapt to see that smile again. "Even if I am drunk on girly drinks."

Casey reached out to take Joel's hand, but just then the waitress delivered their plates.

After she confirmed they were satisfied with everything and walked away, Joel leaned over the table and whispered, "This is the Smoky Mountain Pork Infused Roll?" His outraged words were delicious with drunken sibilance. "What kind of place asks this kind of money for what amounts to a barbecue sandwich?"

"But wait until you taste it. It'll be so good."

"Hmmph." Joel frowned but took hold of the sandwich, trying to capture the messy insides before they fell out on his plate, and took a bite. "Oh. Well. How about that," he said softly, closing his eyes and moaning the way he had when Casey had brought the sweet potato casserole over all those years ago.

Casey swallowed, blood rushing south and fattening his cock against the inside of his pant leg. "Yeah?"

"Oh, yeah," Joel whimpered, licking his lips as his eyelashes fluttered. "Good God."

Casey bit into his lower lip, eyes trained on Joel, dying for him to take another bite.

Joel did, and the symphony of his pleasure was just as good the second time.

"So how is everything?" the waitress asked, swinging by to top off their water and check in. Her black hair was piled on her head in a topknot, and her blue eyes sparkled cheerfully.

"Great," Casey answered, his voice breathy even to his own ears. He hoped she didn't look in his lap because the way the front of his pants were distorted by his hard-on wasn't entirely hidden by his napkin. "Perfect."

"You didn't taste yours," Joel pointed out after she walked away again.

Casey glanced down at his plate of fried green tomatoes and Atlantic salmon and couldn't remember why he'd even ordered it. He could easily feast off the sounds Joel made when eating and be completely satisfied. "Right. I'm sure it's great, though."

"Come here a lot then?"

"No, not since high school. This actually is my first time back in Knoxville since I left."

"Oh, yeah? Why's that?"

Casey shrugged. "Being around my parents confuses things for me. I think more clearly when I'm away from them. But New York is lonely, so when they asked me to come down for the holidays this year, I caved." He sighed. "I'm not comfortable though. Nothing feels right at their house. In some ways, I just want to get back to my apartment in New York, but that doesn't feel like home either."

Joel appeared to consider what Casey had said for a long time. "I get what you're saying. I like the property my place is on, but living in a trailer was never my dream." He shrugged, wiping his mouth with a napkin and then taking another bite. After he'd chewed and swallowed, he said, "It's better than an apartment, though. I have my own space. Bruno's got land to run on. No rules or regulations about what I can and can't do and, best of all, no upstairs neighbors." Joel smiled. "Becca wants to murder the people who live over her. She swears they have family bowling tournaments on their wooden floors."

"Does Becca still drum?"

"Sometimes. She plays with a butch dyke group now and again, the token femme, I guess." Joel's eyes softened, and he seemed to cast back to an earlier time. "Did you know my dad thought Becca was my girlfriend? That was one of the reasons he let us have the garage for the band. That and... Well, there were a few other reasons too."

"I thought it was because he was the only parent who wasn't actually home in the evenings since he had to work at Vreeland's until it closed most nights."

Joel smirked. "That helped too."

"Do you still play bass ever? You were good."

"I was okay," Joel agreed fondly. "But I didn't really love it. Sometimes I play around on electric guitar with Becca just for fun, but it's been months since I touched the thing. I sold my bass guitars. My writing takes up most of my free time, and I like it better in terms of a hobby that pays."

"Why's that?"

"I don't have to rely on anyone but myself. A band requires cooperation. I had no idea how good our little group had it—you know, how well we got along—until it was over and I started playing with some other local bands for fun. Talk about a nightmare. Infighting, jealousy, posturing. It was exhausting. I was happy to step away."

The rest of their meal went by easily enough, their conversation having turned to memories of old times. The "whatever happened to so-and-so?" topic took up the better part of an hour and by the time the waitress asked if they'd like dessert, Joel had entirely sobered up.

"I'm good," he said, shaking his head. "Really, you've spent enough."

Casey didn't give a rat's ass about the money, but he still wanted to go ice-skating, and he figured he'd save the fight for the entrance fee on that instead. "I think we're finished. I'll take the check when you're ready."

The waitress nodded, and Joel excused himself to the restroom. Casey fished out his wallet and paid the bill while he waited for Joel's return. The music had changed to a particularly well-done jazz rendition of "Have Yourself a Merry Little Christmas," and he wondered if it was the Dexter Gordon Quartet, too. He'd have to ask Joel.

He couldn't get over how easy the date felt—how right. When he'd been with Theo everything had seemed like work. Conversation never flowed. The jokes hadn't tripped off his tongue. He'd never been sure of what to say, or even who he truly was when he was with Theo. Hell, even the fucking had felt like work, what with Theo being a demanding bottom who always acted like Casey just wasn't trying hard enough.

But everything with Joel was easy. Even when he was being a grouch or acting like he didn't really want Casey around, it was easy. Casey knew what to say and how to say it. He knew who he was and who he wanted to be when he was with Joel. And he knew that deep down, underneath the sometimes-dismissive gruffness, Joel absolutely felt the same. He had to. There was no way it could be so easy for Casey and be hard for Joel.

Speaking of hard for Joel, he couldn't help but wonder if the kiss he'd been promised would lead to more. If it did, he'd take his time, make it good. It was an honor to think he might get to be the first person to ever be with Joel like that. Casey wanted to make it perfect for him. Special.

"Ready to go?" Joel asked, standing by the table with his hands shoved in his jacket pockets, the colored lights strewn around the ceiling reflecting on his face and his arrow-shaped mouth lifted up in a gentle smile.

"Yeah. Let's go." Casey rose and followed Joel through the crowd by the bar and out the front door to the cool night on Market Square to find more fat snowflakes falling all around.

Lo and behold, some of them were sticking.

Chapter Twelve

"I SAID I'D watch *you* skate." Joel frowned at the ice skates Casey thrust at him.

"And I ignored you."

"You do that a lot." The two of them sat on one of the benches around the rink.

"Only about things like this." He'd never ignore Joel when it came to something serious. But ice-skating? He knew Joel wanted to go, deep down inside.

"We should probably have a come to Jesus about consent at some point," Joel said, lifting a brow. "Especially if you're going to kiss me again later."

Casey grinned. "I promise to honor every single 'no' or 'stop' you utter in that context. Swear on my soul."

"You better," Joel grumbled, crossing his arms and looking away toward the popcorn machine by the food trucks.

"I swear."

Joel nodded and then moved back to the topic at hand. "These people are extortionists. Twenty bucks to rent the skates and three dollars for a bag of popcorn? Insane."

"Come on. Skate with me."

Joel snarled his lip. "I don't know how."

"Oh." Casey's tummy flipped over. Joel was always adorably irritable when he was insecure. "Well, it's… I'm not going to lie and say it's easy. But you can hold on to the side, and I'll stay with you. You can lean on me."

"That'll look gay."

"Shocking."

"Yeah, well, this is Knoxville, not New York. Believe me, it'll be plenty shocking."

"Look." Casey nodded at two young men wearing baseball caps and what appeared to be fraternity sweatshirts under their jackets. They skated near each other, clutching arms now and again to keep from going down. They laughed and tugged each other along. "If bro-dude frat boys can get past their internalized homophobia to have a little fun, so can we."

But Joel wasn't done resisting yet, apparently. "I'm not going to be shown up by little kids." He jerked his head toward a posse of children zooming around like they'd been born with skates for feet.

"Yes, you are. And it'll be okay. Just put the skates on. Take two turns around with me, and if you hate it, then we'll go."

Joel snorted, but bent down to kick off his shoes. He glanced around at the glowing lights and dangling gold stars in the trees around the square as he tied on the skates, muttering under his breath, "Fucking Christmas."

"You don't like Christmas?"

"I don't like how it's got me feeling all…" He made a face and motioned toward his chest.

"All what?"

"All hopeful. Like this means anything tonight. Like this isn't just some holiday hookup for you with a bonus trip down memory lane."

Casey crossed his arms over his chest. "Oh, for fuck's sake, don't do that."

"What?"

"I've taken you on a romantic walk, wined and dined you, and now I'm asking you to ice-skate with me under the stars. Don't ruin our romantic date by calling it a holiday hookup. I already told you that I'm not into hookups."

Joel grimaced. "I just hate that maybe I want more."

Casey knocked him with his shoulder. "Maybe I do too. And maybe this is another 'not appropriate for a first date conversation,' but I'll forgive you since hearing that you want more is music to my ears."

"You were always too easy to please," Joel muttered, finishing up his laces. He heaved himself to his feet, and Casey had to grab his arm to keep him from going down. It was going to be impossible keeping him on his feet on the actual ice if he couldn't stand on the mat-covered floor. "Let's go bust my ass, I guess."

Casey led him toward the ramp up to the rink, his heart thumping hard. Joel's bicep flexed under Casey's grip, and he remembered the tattoos he'd glimpsed. Later, he'd find a way to ask about them. Maybe he'd get to see them, even.

After he'd gotten that kiss Joel had promised.

HE'D BEEN RIGHT, of course, and Joel grumbled as his ass hit the ice before they'd even reached the wall for him to hold on. Kids skated past, but none of them did more than shout, "S'cuse me, mister!" as they swerved to miss hitting him.

"You okay?" Casey asked, looming over, an annoying smirk playing on his lips as he reached down to try to haul him up.

Joel's feet skidded and slipped, and he almost pulled Casey down on top of him. But somehow he gained his feet and the wall at the same time. He gripped it with both hands, wondering how he was going to ever get back off the ice because every time he shifted his feet, he nearly went down again.

Christmas music played over the speakers surrounding the rink, and children zoomed by, along with adults who clearly had experience with ice-skating.

"It's okay," Casey soothed. "I've got you." He held Joel's arm firmly and didn't seem to have any trouble keeping himself upright on the ice.

"You better," Joel said, panting with the effort to stay standing. "I'm going to blame you for every bruise on my butt, just so you know."

"Now you're just flirting." Casey laughed. "Are you trying to turn me on imagining your naked ass?"

Joel huffed, but his cheeks heated, and his cock pulsed with a rush of arousal. "Shut up."

"All right, just try to move one foot slowly in front of the other. You've got this."

Casey encouraged and tugged, held and supported, until Joel moved gradually along the wall with barely any help at all. He was still afraid to let go for more than it took for him to get past the opening in the wall where the ramp connected to the rink, but by the time he'd made it around three times without falling, he was pretty pleased with himself.

Casey skated slowly alongside him, speeding up sometimes to take a loop around the rink at a faster pace only to join him again. The moments when Casey left him felt deeply lonely, though Joel enjoyed the opportunity to watch Casey's body move and to admire the way he'd grown since they were last together. He wondered if he'd ever get over having to look up to meet Casey's eyes.

"So," Casey said, swinging back up to Joel's side with pink cheeks and shining eyes. "Tell me more about your books. Are you writing one right now?"

Joel shifted his feet forward on the ice and moved ahead, using his arm strength to get some momentum going without freeing himself completely from the wall. "Yeah, I'm working on one called *Zombie Dog*, but I feel like it's not really coming together. I can't put my finger on why. I think it's a character development problem."

"You can't figure out the zombie dog's motivations?" Casey chuckled, taking Joel's elbow and steadying him before letting go to skate a circle beside him.

"No, I've got the zombie dog nailed. He's a zombie. He wants to eat brains. I guess I can't figure out why, in one crucial scene, the main character doesn't call for help. It feels too easy to say that his cell phone is dead or missing..." Joel trailed off, frowning. "But if he calls for help, that ruins everything."

"Maybe the zombie dog ate the cell phone."

Joel laughed. "Mistook it for brains?"

"Maybe the dude—I'm assuming the main character is a guy?"

Joel nodded.

"Maybe the dude panics and chucks his phone at the dog, who snaps it up and swallows it whole." Casey opened his mouth wide, mimicking the dog catching and eating the phone.

Joel laughed. "Might work. Hell, I can try it. See if it feels right. Writing's all about it feeling right, you know?"

Casey shook his head. "I guess. I took a poetry class one semester and, well, nothing ever felt right about what I wrote. I was horrible at it."

"Says who?"

"Says me and the fact that I barely passed. I scraped by with a C because I had perfect attendance and this professor was a dick who made that a third of our grade. Thank God."

Joel snorted, pausing in his efforts on the far side of the rink near the shining holiday lights on the rooftop of Preservation Pub. "I can't really see you writing poetry."

"I know, right? Do you ever write poetry?"

"Hmm...horror poetry," Joel said, tasting the words. "No, but that could be fun. I doubt there's a living in it, though."

"Is that why you write your books? To make a living?"

"It supplements. I mean, I'm not killing it out in the book market, but it brings in the money that I actually live on. Between the mortgage on Vreeland's and what it takes to keep the store running, I don't take any salary from the business myself."

"It's amazing that you make enough from writing to support your needs."

Joel shrugged. He wasn't going to tell Casey that some weeks he was hungrier than he'd like to be. That he had to supplement Bruno's diet, and sometimes his own, with fish he caught from the lake. One day, things would turn around for him. He just didn't know when or how.

"How's your dad doing?" Casey asked.

Joel shook his head. "Not great. But that's life. At least I'm not living with him anymore. That's the only good thing about it."

"RJ said—" Casey broke off, his mouth clomping shut like he was holding back something he regretted bringing up.

"RJ said what?"

"It's not first-date conversation material."

Kids swept by them, laughter rising into the night. The stars above twinkled dimly behind clouds that swept over them in a fine haze. The Christmas music bopped around them, and the bright decorations of the square somehow created a sense of intimacy. Enough that Joel leaned closer and said, "Tell me anyway."

"He said your dad used to hit you."

"Yeah. He did." Joel's stomach went heavy, like he'd swallowed lead. The cold night air stung his eyes, and he blinked rapidly. "He suspected I was queer. When he'd had too much to drink, I guess he thought he could punch it out of me."

Casey's eyes darkened, and his cheeks got even more ruddy. "That asshole."

"Yeah, well." Joel huffed, trying to loosen the tightness in his throat. "That was my life. I never wanted you to know about it."

"Oh, man." Casey glanced around them, pain etched into his expression. That look, that pity and hurt, was exactly why Joel had kept the abuse to himself. Well, that and fear that stubborn Casey Stevens would try to do something about it, and while being beaten sucked, the alternative—being put into foster care—had scared him shitless. Casey put his arm around Joel, tugging him away from the wall. "Lean on me. Let's get a beer, huh? What do you say?"

Joel had already had more to drink than he normally had in a month, preferring to avoid the substance that had turned his father so mean, though there was no evidence it did the same to him. Still, he could have a soda while Casey had a beer. "Sure. But I pay." He didn't know how, but he would.

"Let me get it."

"No. I'm paying. It's final."

Casey lifted his hands in surrender, and then grabbed Joel tightly so he wouldn't fall on the slippery ice. "Okay, you win. Let's go."

Joel leaned against Casey as they worked their way back to the exit of the rink. His feet threatened to shoot out from under him the whole way, but Casey's solid presence reassured him. The familiar scent of Casey's skin and laundry detergent warmed him more than his jean jacket or the cheery lights and music.

Casey's strong arm around his middle woke a strange need in him, something he'd ignored for a long time: a need to be cared for, to be protected. It swelled in him, huge and uncomfortable, pressing at his skin and threatening to burst through in a sudden, inexplicable wail. He shivered hard, cold terror creeping into his gut.

He swallowed again, shoving down the lump in his throat, and stumbled off the ramp from the rink, desperate to get away from Casey's touch before he did something stupid like let himself need it or, worse, pretend he could get used to it. He hurried to a bench and sat quickly, hoping Casey would keep his distance until he could regain his equilibrium.

Casey didn't seem to notice Joel's reaction as he dropped down beside him and started to casually remove his skates. Joel flipped his collar up on his jean jacket to hide his face as he bent down to work at the laces that had somehow become knotted. He took slow breaths, annoyed to find his fingers shaking again.

"Hey, about your dad—"

"Not now," Joel said. "Drinks first."

Casey squeezed Joel's shoulder reassuringly and then went back to removing his own pair of skates.

It was a date and nothing more. If he got another kiss from Casey, that would be enough—more than he ever expected to get anyway. Anything else was as impossible as it had ever been. He knew that, and he didn't really need for it to be anything other than what it was. A holiday fling was plenty.

Maybe when all was said and done, if he didn't let himself hope with Casey, he'd finally be able to move on. Though, honestly, deep down, he didn't want to. In the most secret part of himself, he knew he'd given his heart to Casey forever ago, and he had no idea how he'd ever take it back.

Once again, being honest was something he didn't plan to be.

He'd let Casey have this fling and give himself the gift of having the man he'd never thought he'd be with. It'd be a Christmas present to himself. Surely he deserved that much.

Maybe they both did.

And then, when it was over and Casey had returned to New York, he'd go back to his regular life. It wouldn't be that hard. He'd have memories to savor at least. And this time, he wouldn't blame Casey when he left. This time, he'd let him go with grace.

The knot came undone, and he quickly unlaced his skates. Tugging them off his feet was harder than he anticipated.

In the end, Casey had to help pull them free, laughing as he wrestled with them. "Some things go on easier than they come off!"

"Like Band-Aids," Joel muttered.

And you.

Chapter Thirteen

PRESERVATION PUB OVERLOOKED Market Square and boasted Knoxville's only rooftop bar. Once upon a time, Joel had played a few shows with local bands in the downstairs pub, but he'd always preferred the open-air space above. The snow from earlier had turned into the occasional flurry, but there was almost no accumulation, so everyone was bundled up in their coats on the roof, enjoying their liquor and beer.

Serendipitously, there was an open table giving a great view of the square, and Joel steered Casey into it, taking hold of his elbow familiarly. The overhead twinkle lights strung between the buildings on either side lent a glow to Casey's skin and hair, making him even more handsome than usual.

As Joel settled in the seat across from him with his soda, he smiled gently, remembering yet again the night Casey kissed the Virgin Mary figurine. "Do you remember Mr. Maples? I ordered a set of Nativity Blow Molds like his to sell in the store."

"I saw." Casey's eyes shone as he sipped his pale ale. "Do you make out with the pretty Mary when everyone's gone home at night? Or is it handsome Joseph for you?"

Joel laughed, tilting his head back and letting the giddy anxiety he'd been holding back rush through his veins.

"Oh, so you do." Casey laughed too, leaning closer.

"No, I'm afraid you still have the sole honor of having kissed the Mother of God."

Casey took another drink of his beer, lips and eyes curved with his smile. "I was an idiot."

"You don't have to convince me."

"I pretended she was you."

Joel's heart clenched, and he took a swallow of cola to wash the feeling away, but it didn't come loose. "Yeah? Funny. I wished it was me."

Casey leaned in even closer, eyes drifting down to Joel's mouth, but then he glanced sideways at the dark figures drinking and talking at other tables. "I'll save it for later, but I'd kiss you now if I could. Right here."

"You *could*," Joel said, raising a challenging brow. "It might not be the smartest thing you've ever done, but we just established that you're an idiot."

Casey's eyes took on that stubborn expression Joel knew too well, and he leaned across the narrow table, tilting his head and pressing a kiss to Joel's mouth. It was fast, lips plush and soft, a barely sticky thing, but it was enough to make his point.

Joel's toes curled up in his boots, and his fingers tingled. It was impossible not to smile helplessly.

"There. But that's not the kiss you've promised me all night," Casey said, eyes glowing. "That was an extra. A bonus kiss."

"Sure. Bonus kiss. For leveling up."

"Yeah? What'd I level up to?"

"At this point in the game, you're now playing for me to invite you in tonight."

Casey's brows rose. "Oh, that's on the table?"

"Maybe. It depends on how you do the rest of the evening."

"This isn't a game," Casey murmured, tracing the frosted glass of his beer. "Not to me."

"That's good because it's not a game to me either."

A fling, sure, but not a game. The most deadly-serious fling Joel could imagine having. It was the culmination of his life's romantic dreams thus far and the probable end of them too.

Casey grinned and reached across the table to take Joel's hand in his own. Their fingers fit together easily, and Joel tried to remember the last time anyone had taken his hand quite like this. Becca sometimes held onto his arm while they were walking, but no one since his mother had sat with his hand in their own just to feel a connection. He shivered, but he wasn't cold. His insides burned with joy and ached with anticipated pain.

But first the pleasure, Joel. Don't get ahead of yourself.

"I know we left the topic behind on the ice, but the whole reason I wanted to get away from there was so we could talk more privately about what you said about your dad."

"Ah." Joel snarled his lips. "Do we have to?"

"No, but…" Casey squeezed his hand. "See, the thing is… My dad never punched me, but when I was a kid and I disappointed him, he could be cruel."

Joel frowned. "Yeah, he always said such dick things."

"That's not…" Casey glanced away, his chest rising with a deep breath. He smiled ruefully. "I don't like to talk about this. Or think about, if I can avoid it."

"What?" Joel gripped Casey's fingers tighter, a sharp twist arcing through his giddy anxiety. "What happened?"

"When I was a kid, I went to see *Tuck Everlasting* at the theater with some friends. When my dad picked me up, I was still crying. Spoiler alert: it has a sad ending." Casey tugged his hand free of their connection and drank more beer.

Joel's fingers felt cold, but he didn't move them, keeping his hand outstretched in case Casey wanted them back.

"When we got home, my dad got out his belt."

"No." Joel's gut tightened.

"He spanked me with it. And that day I learned that boys don't cry, especially not in public, and good boys don't embarrass their fathers ever."

"Casey…"

"Between that time and the last time he hit me when I was twelve, he taught me some other stuff, too. Men don't give their neighbors reason to gossip, men don't make scenes, and men don't suck dicks. Unless they're rich, connected, famous dicks, apparently. But that part didn't become clear to me until college and Theo."

"Fuck him." Joel was flooded with cold. That wasn't how it was supposed to be for Casey. His dad was a prissy little shit, but he'd never thought Casey's father hurt him. Now he wanted to find the man and punch him into the ground, punch him until he begged. Punch him and punch him. Never stop.

"Yeah. After I turned twelve he never belted me again. I'm not sure why. But even after he stopped, whenever he'd give me a look or talk to me in an angry voice, it was like I'd been hit with the belt all over again."

"Shit. I didn't know." Joel reached out his hand farther, wriggling his fingers, begging for Casey to take hold. He exhaled in relief when Casey did.

Casey squeezed his fingers gently, his eyes sad but firm. "I'm only telling you because you should know that I get it. I mean, it's different because I guess spanking, with a belt or hand, is more socially acceptable than a punch. But it affected me. I never trusted that I was safe until I was away from him in New York."

"But you're in his house right now." Joel would have to seriously hurt Jonathan Stevens if he ever laid a hand on Casey again. Ever. His whole body burned with rage at the thought.

"He won't touch me." Casey shook his head. "I'm big enough to fight back. I think that's why he stopped, honestly. And my therapist is helping me cope with the past and the way I react to him. I'm getting better at standing up for myself."

"I'm glad. That's…that's good." Joel pulled his hand free of Casey's and ran it through his hair. The intense, scary feeling that had consumed him on the ice swelled again. It had a different feel to it, though. Something ugly.

"So, I get it," Casey went on. "The things we did and said back then as kids—and maybe even now—are partly because of what we lived with and where we came from. *Who* we came from. All of that stuff matters more than we want to admit sometimes." Casey reached his hand across again, wordlessly asking for Joel's touch.

Joel swallowed and blinked hard to get rid of the stinging in his eyes. He took a deep breath and slipped his hand back into Casey's, wanting to comfort as much as he wanted to ground himself with Casey's touch. "I can't make peace with my pop. Since the stroke, he's worse than ever. If he was physically capable of it, he'd still beat me up."

"I'm sorry."

"I don't think I'll ever get my peace with him. At least you can hope for that still with your dad." Did Joel even want Casey to have that, though? He didn't know anymore.

"Maybe. He's not too impressed with my life choices right now, and I don't know if he ever will be." Casey's voice dropped lower, and his lips started to tremble. Joel's heart clenched as Casey's eyes took on a previously unseen vulnerability. "But if he doesn't want to accept me as I am, and for who I'm going to be, then I guess it's better than pretending to be someone I'm not for some version of love that isn't even real."

Joel's whole body sang with an urge to protect and hold Casey, to heal him from the past and support him in the future. He said, gruffly, "Love. Yeah. What's that like, I wonder?"

"To be loved?"

Joel shrugged, forcing his gaze to fall to the skaters on the ice below. "I don't think my father ever loved me. My mom, Charlie loved, but me? I don't know. I was an inconvenience at best."

"It was always tense at your place," Casey said gently, and now he sounded the way Joel felt. Like he wanted to bundle him up and never let the past touch him again. "At least whenever I was there and your dad was around, it seemed really tense."

"That's because my dad knew how I felt about you." Joel met Casey's gaze again, his nerves jangling. "He knew it was you more than anyone else."

"What do you mean?"

"I don't know. I haven't felt… I don't feel…" Joel shook his head, searching for the words. "Becca says I'm demisexual, whatever that means." He rolled his eyes.

Casey nodded, squeezing his hand again. "I know about that. It means you're only sexually attracted to people you know well or have developed strong feelings for."

"I guess. That's what Becca thinks. I just know that I don't walk around wanting to fuck people. The only person I've ever wanted was—" He cut off the words.

"Was me?"

"Yeah." Joel exhaled slowly, his heart racing. Why hadn't he had a beer too? It would take the edge off this confession and all this emotion at least. "Not that I can't ever want someone else, I guess. I always thought I would eventually. One day. I hoped I'd meet someone, you know." He shrugged, pulse pounding. "But it was always you. And my dad knew."

Insane that he was trying to get the topic back to his least favorite subject in the world—his dad—rather than have to continue admitting to Casey how important he was to him, how singular.

"Is that why you always wanted me gone by the time he came home?"

Joel smiled grimly. "And the others too. RJ doesn't read as gay, but he was loud about it sometimes, and, like I said, my dad thought Becca was my girlfriend. The last thing I wanted was for him to hear the way she talked about girls. You? You were my temptation to be avoided. But

I couldn't avoid you. You just kept coming around."

"You're not so hard underneath it all," Casey whispered. "You're really soft."

"Great." Joel pulled his hand away. "Open up a little and suddenly I'm a pansy."

"I didn't say that. I'm grateful you trust me enough to tell me things after everything."

Joel laughed, taking another drink of cola to steady himself, but the caffeine just made his heart race even more. "After what? You left and went on with your life like a normal person?" He shook his head. "I was wrong last night to say the things I did."

"You? Wrong?" Casey teased.

"Yeah. Enjoy this rare admission. I shouldn't have treated you like that. You took me by surprise and..." He wasn't going to admit how much seeing Casey again had scared him.

"I'm glad you gave me another chance this morning. Lunch today and this date tonight have been amazing."

"They have." Joel zipped up his jacket and shoved his hands into his pockets. Everything inside him wrestled with what he said next. "Let's go now. I'm curious how the rest of tonight is going to be." He steadied himself, gathered his courage, and whispered, "I want you to show me."

BRUNO WAS THRILLED to see them again, but Joel didn't give him time to pull Casey's attention away. He dragged Casey back toward his bedroom, heart thumping and cock ragingly hard, and shut the door in his dog's face. Then he locked it, more to keep himself from running out than to keep Bruno from finding a way in.

Joel leaned back against the wood panel, doorknob digging into his back, heart pounding so hard he felt dizzy, and found Casey staring down at his unmade bed. The blue comforter was tossed half-on and half-off, and the sheets were a wrinkled mess. At least he'd broken Bruno of sleeping on his bed when he was gone, so there was no dog hair to contend with.

"Sorry. I didn't expect company." He bustled over, his dick softening, to smooth the sheets and tug the comforter into place.

"Don't apologize," Casey said gently, grabbing hold of his hands. "And leave it. Why does it matter?"

"Yeah. Okay." Joel tugged his hands free to rub his sweaty palms against his jeans. He'd tossed his jacket over the back of the sofa when they came in, and now he didn't know where to start. Did he just take his clothes off? Or…what?

"Come here," Casey whispered, pulling him close, and Joel's knees went weak as Casey wrapped his arms around him. "Just let me hold you. We don't have to do anything."

"Oh, hell no," Joel murmured, pressing his face against Casey's soft shirt and breathing in his scent. "We're doing something."

"Okay. Well, you don't have to twist my arm. But let's just see what happens."

"Do you have a condom?" Joel murmured.

"We don't need a condom."

"Uh, yeah we do."

Casey chuckled gently. "Because we're not having sex like that. Not tonight."

"No?"

"No."

"But I—"

"Hey. Let me just hold you. Don't be in a hurry. We've got time."

Did they have time? And why didn't Casey want to do that kind of sex with him? Was there something he needed to know? It looked really straightforward in porn. But maybe he should ask Becca. She knew stuff no lesbian had a right to know about men's bodies, and he never understood where she got the information. Maybe from her gay hairdresser friends? He should probably have more gay friends too. That kind of advice would be invaluable right about now.

Casey squeezed him closer. "I didn't think I'd ever get to hold you like this. For me, this is enough for tonight."

Joel frowned, rubbing his cheek on Casey's shirt again and trying to piece through the shards of emotions piercing him. Joy and arousal, but also disappointment. If not now, then when? Casey said they had time, but what did that mean? He was leaving for New York again soon. This was a fling. Joel's one shot to lose his virginity with his first love, and he didn't want to waste it. But it's not like he could make Casey take him like that either.

Or make Casey accept *him* like that.

Funny, Joel had always assumed he'd be the one on the bottom, but maybe that's not how Casey liked things. Maybe he liked to be the one getting plowed. God, Joel had no idea how to do that without hurting him. Porn usually skipped from blowjobs to penetration, with maybe a little rimming for prep. That couldn't be enough, could it? And how would he know what Casey liked? Did he ask? Or was he supposed to just be able to tell?

"Shh, turn that brain off. I can feel you thinking too hard."

Joel leaned back enough to get a good look at Casey's face, the sweetness of his amber eyes, and his mouth, curving into a tender, delicious smile.

"I *want* to do that with you, though," Joel whispered. "Anal, I mean. If you want it too. And if you have a condom. I'd do it either way—top or bottom. Whatever you prefer."

Casey shook his head and leaned closer, breathing against Joel's lips. "Stop talking about fucking and just kiss me."

Joel lifted on his tiptoes, his heart racing, and he pressed his lips to Casey's. Time stopped. The room around them dissolved into a haze as they kissed and clutched, their bodies moving toward the bed until they were horizontal on it. Their hands roamed, and their hips hunched, and

Joel found himself hanging on the edge of orgasm far too soon.

"Wait," he groaned, ripping his mouth from Casey's and staring up into his hot eyes. "Just give me a second."

Casey nodded, nuzzling Joel's throat. The slick wetness of his mouth left a tingling trail as he kissed the exposed bits of Joel's skin, tugging down the neck of his shirt to get his lips on Joel's collarbones.

Joel gripped Casey's soft hair and luxuriated in the sensations, soft whimpers tearing from his throat, until he shoved Casey up and back, demanding, "Shirts off. I want to feel your skin."

Casey didn't hesitate, and several hurried seconds later Joel gripped Casey's biceps to tug him down on top. They moved chest-to-chest, stomach-to-stomach, mouths open as their tongues teased and twisted. Joel shuddered when Casey's tongue tickled behind his teeth, a sensation overly sweet, like biting into a sugar cube: delicious but too intense, addictive but nearly hurtful.

Casey's sparse tufts of chest hair scratched enjoyably against Joel's nipples, and he shoved his hands down the back of Casey's pants, greedy for more skin and eager to get his hands on the mounds of flesh he found there.

"Here." Casey lifted up, fumbling one-handed with the buttons on his jeans. "Let me get them off. You too. Let me see your body."

Joel didn't know a simple request like that could be so hot, but his balls drew up hard, and he had to throw his head back and *resist* for all he was worth to keep from coming. When he felt the hot length of Casey's dick resting on his stomach, he gasped and opened his eyes again, watching Casey worm his pants down past his knees, trying to kick them farther.

Joel rolled out from under him, working on his own button and zipper. "Hurry," he said, his hungry gaze raking over Casey's body, anxiously trying to get another look at his dick.

"Yeah. Let me see." Casey fell back on the bed, hands outstretched, reaching for Joel.

Joel shoved his jeans down, his heart in his throat, and he kicked them clear of the bed. His cock slapped against his stomach and then swung out from his body when he turned and crawled across his queen-sized bed to reach Casey.

"Cut," Casey whispered, gesturing to Joel's dick. "My favorite kind."

Joel collapsed against Casey's body. He didn't want to hear about other lovers or other bodies Casey had enjoyed, but he was glad Casey approved of his dick, since there wasn't much he could do about it either way.

"I'm cut too," Casey said, gesturing down to where his thick dick swelled out of a pile of dark golden pubes.

"Shit," Joel groaned, holding back another urge to come now. "It's perfect."

Casey kissed him again, taking hold of Joel's hand and guiding it to his cock. The velvet heft of it was new and completely familiar all at once. Joel clutched Casey close and moaned as Casey's wet mouth moved on his neck. He grasped Casey's cock in his hand, afraid to let go.

JOEL WAS EVERYTHING Casey knew he'd be in bed—hungrily passionate and tremblingly vulnerable. His responsive noises and writhing body drove Casey wild, and he didn't want it to ever stop.

But nothing prepared him for the rush of being in love with the man he held in his arms. Joel might have been the inexperienced one, but Casey was just as undone by the riot of emotions that detonated in his chest, ramping up until the intensity overcame him, and he pumped his come out all over Joel's panting, arching body.

Joel's eyes glowed in the crystalline moonlight shafting in from the sole window, and his fingers shook as he ran them through the mess Casey had left on both of their chests and stomachs. "Holy shit," he whispered. "That was—you just—" He didn't seem to know what else to say. He brought his dripping fingers up to gaze at them. His chest was flushed, and his cock was still hard as his hips circled restlessly while he wonderingly pondered the mess on his fingers.

"Taste it," Casey whispered. "See what you think."

Joel's eyes flashed wide, and he swallowed hard before slipping one sticky finger between his swollen, red lips. Beard burn was blooming along his chin and jaw, and despite having not come yet himself—shockingly—he looked a debauched wreck.

It was beautiful.

Casey stared up at him, watching his every reaction: the flicker of doubt in his eyes just before tasting Casey's jizz, the stronger surprise at the flavor, and then dazed arousal after he shoved all three fingers in and sucked at them greedily.

"Christ, Joel," Casey muttered. "You're amazing."

He pulled Joel down to take another kiss and gloried in the flavor of himself in Joel's mouth. Gripping Joel's dick in his hand, he jerked him relentlessly as they made out, loving the soft curses, eager moans, and whimpers Joel released as he grew closer to his orgasm.

The heat of their bodies had warmed the room. Casey greedily took in Joel's dilated eyes, flushed face and chest, and the desperate twist of his hips as he worked himself higher and higher.

"Fuck," Joel whispered, eyes rolling up. "It's too much. I want to, but I'm too keyed up. I don't think—"

"Shh," Casey whispered in his ear. "Relax. Just kiss me. Let me do this for you."

Joel gripped Casey's hand with his own, guiding him to a different rhythm, and kissed him again. The pace of Joel's breathing changed, his kiss losing any attempt at technique, and then, just before he arched, Joel released Casey's hand and twined his fingers into Casey's hair, holding him fast so that he came crying out his pleasure into Casey's open mouth.

Trembling from exertion and shockingly renewed arousal, Casey held Joel tight and rutted against his hard hips and taut stomach. The come he'd already left there smoothed the way, and soon he gripped Joel, kissing his neck and shoulder while he shot another load out on their heaving bellies.

"Whoa." Joel clutched Casey tightly to him. "That was—whoa."

"Yeah," Casey agreed, and he buried his face in Joel's sweat-damp hair, breathing in the scent of him as tears sprang to his eyes. His throat was tight, and his body thrummed again with unstinted need for more of Joel.

"You okay?" Casey finally murmured when he could count on not breaking into overwrought sobs.

"Yeah. You?" Joel asked, insecurity tainting his tone.

"Great. Amazing." He nuzzled Joel's neck and ear. "I want to make you come again."

Joel huffed a laugh and motioned at his streaked, flushed body and his already hard cock. "Be my guest. I'll just be right here trying to figure out how to get my brains back. I shot them everywhere."

Casey flipped Joel over, and then slid down Joel's body, kissing his nipples and his sternum, making his way south. "And I'll just be down here showing you how it feels to have them sucked out this time."

"Oh, fuck," Joel breathed, his eyes wide and his legs trembling against the mattress. "Yeah. Show me all of that."

Casey's heart broke open with joy when he placed Joel's salty, come-slick cock on his tongue and tasted the combination of their pleasure.

The two of them together. The way it should have always been.

Chapter Fourteen

"I NEED A cigarette."

"I thought you were trying to give up smoking," Casey murmured, his sweaty skin still plastered to Joel's.

The idea of not having Casey's body against his was reason enough for him to laugh and agree. "Yeah. I am. If you want, I'll start now."

Easy enough to promise when he only had one cigarette left anyway and he should save it for the morning.

"I'd like that." Casey kissed his head. "I'd like that a lot."

Joel kissed Casey's shoulder and didn't remind him that he wouldn't be here long enough to like anything, really. For now, he'd let them both pretend that anything Joel did in the future was Casey's business and that his opinion on it mattered. Basking in the afterglow of his first orgasms with someone he loved, there was nothing he wanted to pretend more.

He heard snuffling at the door and laughed. "Bruno's worried. He's wondering what you're doing to me in here."

"He must think I've killed you after all that noise you made."

Joel huffed. "You weren't exactly quiet either."

"True. Did you know that when you come, your eyes scrunch up and you—"

Joel flicked Casey's arm teasingly. "Are you seriously mooning over my orgasm face?"

"I'd moon over your farts. Don't you know that already?"

"Let's not test that theory," he muttered, letting Casey gather him up close again. He'd never been held in bed before, and it was…weird, but nice. Cozy, a little overly hot, but sweet. He thought he liked it, and he wished he could have the opportunity to get used to it.

"I love the way you smell," Casey muttered, rubbing his nose in Joel's hair. "I love the way you taste. I love everything about—"

"Shh." Joel cut him off. "Just hold me. Don't talk anymore. Let's sleep now."

His heart thundered as he considered the declaration he knew he'd forestalled. It was too much, too raw. If Casey said those words, then there was no way Joel wouldn't hope. And if he hoped, it was going to hurt like hell when Casey left.

When this Christmas miracle was over and he went back to his regular, dreary, everyday life, he'd have a few good memories at least. That was more than he'd had before.

Even if it meant he was still, and might always be, alone.

PALE EARLY MORNING light streamed in through the open blinds of the mobile home's windows. Casey remained as still as he possibly could, his heart in his throat. Joel slept on his side next to him with his mouth open and drool slipping down onto his pillow. His dark beard was growing in, and his tattoos, clearly visible now in the pearly dawn, stood out against his pale skin. Casey had memorized every one.

Joel was beautiful. And Casey had made love to him. God, how amazing was that? He'd made love to *Joel Vreeland!* And it had been beyond his wildest dreams, better than any sex he'd ever had. And all they'd done was kiss and rut, grope and touch, and, there at the end, he'd watched Joel's face avidly as he'd sucked him off. That'd been *everything.* Absolutely everything.

The texts he'd quickly exchanged with his mother in the parking garage downtown—when he'd let her know he wouldn't be home all night—hadn't been fun, though. She'd even tried to call, but he'd declined to answer and switched his phone off. Why she thought it was her business who he spent the night with, he didn't know. He was a grown man, and he'd stay with anyone he wanted, and he'd love the man his heart chose. She'd have to suck it up.

"Mmfm," Joel mumbled, rolling over to his back and flopping his arm over his eyes to block out the rising sun.

Casey shifted, moving so he could more easily see Joel's face. His stomach fluttered, and joy pulsed inside him like a living thing.

Joel stiffened and his arm slowly lifted away, revealing his dark eyes staring wildly up at Casey. "Oh shit," he whispered.

Casey frowned.

"It really happened. I mean, you're here. Holy crap."

Casey didn't know if the nervous laughter pressing against his chest was safe to release or if he should actually be worried. He tilted his head, considering Joel's sleep-lined, wide-eyed morning look. Swallowing, he settled for saying, "You're cute in the mornings."

Joel sat up, reached to the nightstand, and clutched his nearly empty pack of cigarettes, tugging out the last one with shaking fingers. Casey's heart clenched, and he wanted to reach out and soothe him, but when he tried, Joel held up his hand to ward him off.

Watching as Joel grabbed a cheap, pink plastic lighter from the nightstand and lit up, Casey tried to radiate calm steadiness to combat Joel's likely oncoming crabby freak-out. He'd seen this before when they were teenagers and the band had been written up in a local paper as promising and up-and-coming. Joel had lost his crap and nearly quit—some sort of self-sabotaging panic overwhelming his common sense until RJ and Becca had talked him down.

Joel let out a slow breath. The tobacco smoke swirled around them both, making Casey cough softly. He resolved to say nothing about Joel's post-sex promise to quit. That would just piss him off now.

Joel's eyes narrowed. "You're still here."

"You invited me to stay," Casey reminded him. He shivered slightly. The room was chilly, having cooled down overnight after all the heat they'd generated together.

Bruno whimpered at the bedroom door, and Joel scratched at his dark eyebrow with his thumb, the cigarette burning perilously close to his unkempt, shaggy hair.

"Fuck," he whispered, tossing aside the bed sheets and rising. The pale morning light highlighted his light skin and the dark thatch around the soft cock between his hairy thighs. He grabbed his underwear from the floor and pulled them on, sucking another drag from his cigarette before jerking open the door.

"C'mon, buddy," he said roughly to Bruno, who bounced excitedly around Joel's feet. "Let's go outside."

Casey climbed out of bed, but he didn't dress entirely. If he did, then Joel would no doubt kick him out before they could even talk things through. With butterflies whirling in his gut, he carefully pulled on his boxer briefs and his shirt from the night before but left his pants pooled on the beige carpet. A train went by on the tracks near the trailer, and it shook slightly with the thunderous sound.

Exiting Joel's bedroom, Casey got a better look around than he had the night before. The mobile home wasn't particularly neat, but Joel had never kept his bedroom in Belmont Hills really clean either. In the kitchen, there were dishes in the sink with the remnants of some tomato-based meal on them. In the living room, there was a pile of folded clothes on the sofa next to a basket of what might have been clean clothes or possibly dirty.

Bruno's dog bed sat in the hallway midway between the kitchen and the living room doors. There were drifts of dog hair around it and scattered down the hall. Joel must have left the door open, because a burst of cold air rushed through the trailer, knocking out any semblance of warmth.

Casey saw there was a closed door that led to what must be a second bedroom, though he didn't know if it had a bed in it. The bathroom was on the right, and he ducked in to relieve his bladder so it wouldn't distract him while he tried to talk Joel down from whatever ledge he'd climbed up on.

After washing his hands, he walked to the open door of the mobile home and stepped out onto the small porch. Joel was off by the bushes, pissing into them, cigarette in his mouth, while Bruno tromped through the woods at the back of the property.

Smoke curled around Joel's head, and his naked shoulders shuddered in the cold air. Fog lifted from the lake and drifted low over the property, obscuring the edge of the water.

Joel turned around, spotted Casey, and narrowed his eyes as he took a final drag from his cigarette before stubbing it out on the closest tree. Tossing the extinguished stub into the woods, Joel stomped toward Casey with tight lines drawing down his mouth.

Where was the surprisingly sweet man Casey had made love to last night? In there somewhere, he had no doubt. He was just scared, that was all, and Casey resolved not to let Joel run him off before he reached him again.

"Pretty classy, right? Pissing in the bushes and littering?" Joel snapped.

"You wake up really grouchy. Did you know?" He aimed for merry and light. "Angel's onto something with her nickname for you. You're definitely a Mr. Frosty Pants."

Joel glared at him and shivered, wrapping his arms around his chest. His black-lettered tattoos stood out against his white skin, and the dark hairs of his forearms shifted in the light breeze. He kept his expression hard, the crookedness of his nose and mouth highlighted by the twist of his lips.

"Speak soon. Stay lucky," Casey said softly, inclining his head toward Joel's bicep where the swirling words were inked into Joel's skin alongside shading dots to make the statement pop. "What's that about?"

Joel arched a brow at him but stayed silent.

"What? Is that not morning-after conversation? I get to make you come, but I don't get to know about your tats?"

"I might be grouchy—*frosty* even—but you're annoying in the mornings, and that's worse."

Casey took a slow breath, determined not to be baited. Joel was just freaking out because he'd lost his virginity, and some guys had a hard time dealing with the vulnerability inherent in that. In his head, Ann reminded him to be gentle.

"I still respect you this morning, if that's what you're worried about," Casey said lightly, half-teasing in hopes of breaking through Joel's brittle defense.

"Respect?" Joel snorted. "Great. Whatever."

Bruno crashed through the woods, rushing toward Joel with a dirty tennis ball in his mouth. He dropped it at Joel's feet, wagging his hind end in excitement until Joel threw it for him.

"It's a lyric from a song I like," Joel said after he'd thrown the ball a few times. He touched the tattoo Casey had indicated. "Most of them are a reference to one Gaslight Anthem song or another."

"You still like them, huh? I do too. I saw them live a few years ago." Goosebumps rose all over as Casey shivered in the morning air.

One thing New York had taught him to appreciate were mild, Southern, so-called winters. He'd never step outside in NYC mid-December in just his underwear even if he wouldn't be arrested for it. Still, the air was bracing, and the excitement of being with Joel—even as irritable as he was—rattled him even more. He shook lightly all over.

"Yeah?" Joel raised his brow again, less hostile than before. "I saw them in Nashville. Becca took me for my birthday a few years ago."

"The lead singer is shorter than I expected. I don't know why, but he sounds so much taller."

"Yep. He's shorter than me even." Joel nodded and rubbed his arms, biceps and pecs bunching and releasing beneath his palms. "I'm cold.

Let's head inside."

Casey followed him, but it wasn't much warmer in the trailer since they'd left the door open. The cool air had funneled through and wiped out the tender warmth the small space heaters had created overnight.

Joel left Bruno outside and headed into the kitchen area. "I don't have much. I can make coffee, but unless you want some leftover chili for breakfast, you're out of luck."

"I'm fine. I'll grab something on the way home, but what about you?" Casey asked. "Don't you need to eat something before work?"

"I keep some beef jerky in the glove compartment of the Chevy. It'll hold me until lunch."

"Beef jerky?" Casey wanted to take Joel to breakfast, to woo him further with eggs, bacon, and pancakes covered in syrup. But there was a stiffness to Joel's back again, and Casey knew if he asked, he'd be shot down. And somehow he also knew that Joel would be insulted. "I'm a big fan of jalapeño-spiced beef jerky, myself," he added to offset the idea there might be any judgment in his words.

Joel didn't say anything, setting about brewing coffee with what looked like off-brand pre-ground beans from one of the local discount stores. Casey sat at the small wooden table he remembered from Joel's old house, though it was missing two of the chairs now. He supposed it would have been hard to fit them all into the cramped space allotted for eating.

Joel opened the fridge and stared into it, brows drawn low. Then he finally brought out a half-pat of butter before turning to a cabinet and tossing a packet of instant oatmeal on the counter. "There's some oatmeal. Just one packet. You can have it."

"No, I'm fine. Really. Don't worry about feeding me."

Joel leaned against the counter and dragged his hand through his hair. "Wish I hadn't smoked that last cigarette already."

"You don't have another pack in the truck or something? I'll go get it for you if you want."

"No, I don't keep extra packs. I only buy one every two weeks. That gives me one or two cigarettes a day. Yesterday I went over my limit." Joel glared at him. "Like I said, I'm trying to quit."

"If you really wanted to quit, then you wouldn't buy any packs at all." So much for not mentioning quitting again.

Joel snarled up his lip, but his eyes twinkled with a hint of amusement. Casey's shoulders relaxed to see the break in the near-constant hostility he'd exhibited since waking up. "Fine. I won't buy another pack."

"Really?"

"Maybe."

Casey grinned. "I always associated the smell of Winstons with you. There was a girl in my Strategic Planning class who smoked Winstons, and I used to purposely sit next to her and pretend she was you."

"Wow," Joel whispered, blinking slowly at him. "That's kind of creepy, man."

Casey shrugged, and Joel turned to pour the coffee into mugs he grabbed out of the cabinets. "It was a harmless fantasy. Didn't hurt anyone."

Ignoring that, Joel passed Casey a mug with a reindeer on the side of it. "It's not the best, but it has caffeine in it." He kept the mug with Frosty the Snowman on it for himself.

How apropos.

The coffee was hot, and that was the best thing Casey could say about it. Joel sat across from him at the small table and they sipped their steaming cups in silence for a long time. It was starting to get really uncomfortable when Joel cleared his throat and caught Casey's eye.

"Human piss keeps skunks away," Joel admitted quietly. "Bruno got sprayed a couple of times last year, and the vet told me if I piss along the property line, the skunks will keep off my land."

"I see. Next time I'm here, I'll avoid the bathroom and piss outside instead. Help out."

Joel's lips curved into the first genuine smile of the morning. He shook his head, saying nothing, but the contentment of that sweet flash of teeth filled Casey with more warmth than the coffee.

"So you think you'll be back, huh?" Joel said quietly after a while.

"If you want me to come back." Casey regretted the words as soon as he said them, fear gripping him that maybe Joel would take that out and forbid him to return.

"Last night was…" Joel cleared his throat. "I could do that again. In fact, if you're up for it, I'd like to do it again tonight." He smiled bashfully, leaving Casey's heart a mess of adoration. "Only if you want."

Casey nearly told him that he was ridiculous, that he'd wanted this forever, and he wasn't going to walk away now. But he managed to rein himself in and simply said, "Tonight works for me."

"Good." Joel wiped a hand over his face, his shoulders dropping in relief. Had he really thought Casey wasn't going to want to see him again? And again? And again forever? Did he not get what was happening here?

Probably not, knowing Joel. And if Casey told him, he'd just freak out. Now that he was being nice, Casey wasn't going to push it. There would be time for declarations and intentions later.

"You don't have a Christmas tree." Casey nodded toward the square, sparse living room. He sipped the coffee again, reminded of his Grandpa Stevens's thermos of cold coffee he always kept in his car. It'd tasted like this, watered down and cheap. "Isn't that like the shoemaker's children not having any shoes?"

"While Brandon, my assistant manager, was out of town I was too busy to bother. I got my outdoor stuff up in November but didn't manage to decorate inside." Joel shrugged. "It's not a big deal. There's no one here but me and Bruno."

"Do you have decorations?"

"Yeah. I kept my dad's old box of stuff from when I was a kid." Joel's dark lashes fell against his cheek, and Casey wanted to kiss his pale eyelids.

"Then let's put one up together."

"Why would you want to do that?"

"Because everyone needs a tree at Christmas."

"Jews don't. Muslims don't. Hindus don't."

"Asshole."

Joel grinned behind his mug but finally shrugged and grew serious again. "Don't feel obligated just because we…"

"Listen, I didn't kiss and run, and I don't fuck and run either."

"We didn't fuck."

"We had sex. Penetration isn't a requirement." Casey reached out across the table, palm up, and when Joel let his fingers rest in his hand, he couldn't resist asking, "So, how does it feel? You're not a virgin anymore."

Joel's cheeks grew red. "I already told you I liked what we did and want to do it again. What else do you want me to say?"

"I guess I just want you to say you're happy and you don't regret it." Casey could only credit Ann's coaching with his inability to stop being completely honest with Joel.

But he had to credit Joel too.

Because knowing him the way he did, and had, for so very long, deep down he knew Joel wasn't going to actually kick him to the curb. That's partly why Casey had to run all the way to New York, wasn't it? Because despite all of Joel's crankiness and words to the contrary, he never actually pushed Casey away in any meaningful way, and Casey couldn't stop going back for more.

As a teenager, Casey had thought it was just loneliness, but now he knew the real reason why: Joel was as in love with him as he'd been in love with Joel.

Probably.

God, he hoped.

"I told you already," Joel huffed. "You're the only one I ever wanted.

I still want you. Of course I don't regret it."

"But are you happy?"

"No, there you're barking up the wrong tree. I don't really do happy." Joel tugged back his hand to shove away from the table. "Sorry to kick you out, but I need to shower and go. My pop'll be waiting for his Egg McMuffin, and I was late with it yesterday. Plus Angel is shit at opening the store. I should get there pretty early on to make sure she hasn't screwed anything up."

Casey stood.

"But I'm not running either," Joel said with shaky vulnerability. "Okay? Do you get that?"

"I think so."

He headed back toward the bedroom and Casey followed him. As Joel gathered his clothes for the day, he said, "I'd let you shower first, but I really have to get on the move."

"I'll wait until I'm at home."

Joel lifted his brows skeptically. "You smell like cigarettes and come. What will your parents say?"

"My dad will be at work, and my mom will be..." He frowned. He didn't really know his mother's schedule anymore. She might be home, but she might be at tennis with her country club friends. Or at yoga. Or lifting weights. "It's fine. Get ready. I'll go ahead and get dressed."

Joel didn't argue more, and while he showered, Casey put on his clothes from the night before and turned on his phone. A barrage of texts from his mother came through. He gritted his teeth and didn't read them. He opened a very old thread with RJ instead and typed with this thumbs.

I'm in love. I can't tell Joel yet, so I'm telling you. Also, he's the most gorgeous man I've ever seen in my life. Especially naked. I'm in heaven.

RJ's reply came just as Joel turned off the water and Casey heard the shower curtain jerk back.

Well, hot damn. Def don't tell Joel about the love thing yet. He'll take off running for the hills. But I'm happy for you, man. You both deserve this.

Another text from his mother popped up on his screen, and he couldn't help but see the opening lines of it:

If you're not home by the time I'm back from tennis, I'll send the police out looking for you. And I won't hesitate to send them to Vreeland's to bother Joel if that's what it takes to get a response from you.

"Who are you texting with?" Joel asked, rubbing a towel over his wet hair. He was fully dressed now and smelled like drugstore shampoo, all fake fruit and yummy. Casey remembered being a child and standing in the shampoo aisle, carefully taking whiffs of each of the bottles, until his mother dragged him away.

"You smell good." He ignored the question.

"Garnier Fructis," Joel said with a teasing lilt to his voice. The shower seemed to have freshened his mood too. "I had a coupon."

Casey stepped closer, arms out to pull Joel close, but he found himself trying to embrace empty air.

"Sorry, you stink." Laughter underscored Joel's words. "Like I said, cigarettes and come."

Casey rolled his eyes, but he followed Joel out of the room and back toward the living room. Bruno climbed through the dog door, his paws messy and a half-chewed tennis ball in his mouth.

Joel turned to Casey, a flash of vulnerability surfacing in his dark eyes. "Brandon's got the store from noon on. I could see you again tonight."

"I'll bring dinner. You bring a tree."

Joel's mouth twitched like he wanted to dispute it. "Like I said, all I've got is leftover chili and more of this crap coffee. So I guess you *should* bring something for you to eat, if you don't want to starve."

"And like *I* said, I'll bring the food and you bring the tree. We'll call it even."

"Not sure how that works out, but I'm not in a place to argue about it with you." Joel grabbed his jacket from where he'd tossed it over the back of the sofa when they came in the night before.

Casey took his coat from the same sofa, and he and Bruno followed Joel outside. After Bruno did his business one last time, Joel shut him back into the trailer and started away toward his truck.

"Hold up." Casey jogged after him. "Don't I even get a goodbye kiss?"

"Goodbyes suck. Let's just skip that part."

"A see-you-later kiss, then."

Joel's crooked smile broke across his face. "You're demanding as hell."

"Or maybe kissing you makes me happy."

"Maybe so. But you won't be happy for long," Joel said.

"Meaning?"

"You're going to have to explain to your parents why you spent the night with me."

Casey's stomach soured, but he lifted his chin. "It's not their business what I do with you."

"They won't see it that way."

"Kiss me."

Joel rolled his eyes. But when Casey wrapped his arms around Joel and lifted his chin up, he saw the anxiety written on Joel's face.

"Don't worry about my parents," Casey whispered as he bent his head to take the kiss. "I don't anymore."

Joel whimpered softly, relaxing against Casey's body and clinging to his coat lapels. His soft lips opened, and Casey slipped his tongue inside, gently probing and tasting, teasing Joel sweetly.

Joel trembled as his hips jerked forward, pushing his hard cock against Casey's thigh. Casey smiled into the kiss, happiness bubbling up in him and arousal thickening his own dick in response.

"Gotta go," Joel said roughly, pulling away and turning his back on Casey. He climbed into his truck without another word.

Casey jammed his hands into his coat pockets and smiled after the

Chevy dreamily as Joel pulled out from his hint of gravel drive onto the dew-damp street.

"See you later," he whispered, solid determination filling him.

He'd tasted heaven, and he wasn't going to let it get away. No matter how skittish Joel could be. And no matter what it cost him with his folks. Joel would have to get used to being loved, and Casey's parents would have to get used to Joel.

Speaking of his folks, Joel was right about one thing. It was time to face the music.

Chapter Fifteen

"HEY, POP," JOEL said, rattling the McDonald's bag as he strolled into his father's room. "I brought your favorite."

"Where the hell were you yesterday?"

Pop sat in a chair by the window, gazing down at the cars whizzing by on the road below. The bald spot on the back of his head reflected the florescent lights of his room, and the gray fringe near his ears was mussed, like no one had come in to deal with him yet this morning.

"I was late. Sorry. Shit happens."

"Lack of discipline happened," Pop shot back, turning to glare at him with hard, blue eyes. "That's what you really mean, son. Isn't it?"

One of the things Joel had alway hated about his pop was the way he tried to get him to agree with his bullshit. It was one thing to have to listen to it, to endure it without reply, but it was another to be verbally prompted to agree with whatever nonsense his father was spouting on any given day.

"The line was short this morning," he said, ignoring the accusation entirely. "Hopefully the McMuffin is fresh." Joel pressed the bag into his father's hand before grabbing the comb from the nightstand by the bed. His pop sat stiffly, not opening the bag as Joel tamed the tufts of hair above his father's ears.

"If you're not going to come, you should call me. At least let me know that I'll have to eat the slop they serve here for breakfast."

"I left the bag on the bed."

"It was ice cold by the time I got back from physical therapy." His father somehow made his words sound like whips, shredding and violent, though he simply stated a fact.

"Did you get Katie to warm it up for you?"

"If you weren't a failure as a son, I wouldn't need to bother the nurses with crap like warming up my Egg McMuffin."

How had he fallen for it again? He always did. He couldn't just keep his mouth shut long enough to avoid the bait his father set. He walked into the trap of an argument every single time. Maybe he really did lack discipline since he told himself constantly not to engage, to keep his thoughts to himself, and to let his father say whatever it was he wanted to say without dignifying it with a response.

"I'm sorry, Pop," he said quietly, smoothing the last of his dad's messy hair down with his fingers. "I'll do better."

"Your mother wouldn't have left me hungry," his father snarled. "She'd have made sure I had plenty of food to eat. She'd bring full breakfasts, not this Egg McMuffin crap."

"You like Egg McMuffins. That's all you've ever asked me to bring."

Stop, Joel. Leave. Go on to work. Let him stew in it.

"Because I know you're so worthless you'd never bring anything else. It's the best I can hope for."

Joel put his father's comb back where he got it, keeping his voice calm. "Do you need something to drink? I'll get some water."

Rattling the bag, his father pulled out his breakfast and unwrapped it with gnarled fingers. "Get a Sprite."

Joel didn't really want to spend a dollar-fifty on a soda at the overpriced vending machine at the end of the hall, but he wasn't going to let his father get under his skin any more than he already had. He could already feel him wearing away at the magic Casey had left behind on him, or in him, like some kind of fizzy blessing on his nerves and skin.

When he passed the Sprite into his father's shaking hand, his eyes fell on the photo of his mother on the wall. Her dark hair and wide smile that crinkled up the corner of his eyes reminded him somehow of

Casey, and he wondered if his father had been as starstruck by her.

"When you met Mom," he started slowly, because his mother could be a volatile subject for his father, "was it love at first sight, or did it take time?"

His father chewed his breakfast, a frown creasing his forehead. "She was beautiful."

"Yeah."

"I knew I wanted her to be my wife the first time I held her in my arms. I met her at a wedding. We danced."

Joel let out a slow breath, softening his boundaries and allowing a tentative hope to blossom in his heart that he could have this conversation with his father without coming to regret it. "I figured it was like that. Did she feel the same way?"

"She did. Her father was another matter." He grimaced. "And her asshole queer brother. Both of them were like you—worthless nancies."

And there it was. Another hope dashed before it could come to full bloom. "Ah."

"Why? Did you finally meet a skirt that turned your head?" He narrowed his eyes speculatively at Joel. "Or... Shit, son. Better not tell me it's a faggot that's caught your eye. I'm not too sick and old to beat the snot out of you."

Joel let out his breath as slowly as possible, his heart twisting up hard even though he'd known what to expect from his father all along. He just wished he'd stop hoping for any evidence of a softening, a glimpse of unconditional love.

"No. I was just curious about you and Mom. You don't talk about her much. Not like that."

"You don't deserve to know about her. If it wasn't for you, she'd still be here."

"I wasn't even *there* that day." Joel swallowed hard, shocked the words had burst out of him before he could rein them in.

"If not for you, she would've been with me at the store, working alongside me. After you came, she stayed home. Never should have let her have you. I was weak when it came to her. And look how it ended up? Her dead. You a fucking faggot. You're my biggest regret. Wish you'd never lived to take a breath."

"You don't mean that. The stroke—"

"The stroke? Shit. I just don't bother hiding it anymore. Stopped feeling guilty about the truth. That's all the stroke did."

A nurse's shoes squeaked, and Joel's neck heated up as he glanced over and saw Katie standing in the doorway. Her wide eyes let on that she'd obviously overheard more than either of them were comfortable with.

"I'll come back later," she mouthed at him.

He nodded and turned back to his pop who was devouring his Egg McMuffin like it was the most delicious food he'd ever tasted, just like he did every morning. Part of Joel wanted to know why he came here every day, why he bothered at all, if that was truly how his father felt about him.

But a bigger part knew his mother wouldn't want Pop to suffer. She'd loved him. Hadn't she? He had to admit he barely remembered life before her death. How did he know what she would want? His father's version of her wasn't reliable.

Regardless, Joel was all the family Pop had, and if the doctors were right, it wouldn't be too many years before he joined Jennifer on the other side. Especially at the rate his father's heart disease was progressing. He'd feel too guilty if he stopped coming, even though he knew intellectually that his father didn't deserve the visits.

"Well, I need to get to the store, Pop. Make sure that Angel's handled everything this morning."

Eyes sparkling with naughtiness, his father looked up and asked, "That little slut putting out for you?"

Joel cleared his throat. "Angel's only nineteen, and she's an employee…"

His father's dark eyebrow popped up as he sneered. "And if I needed proof you were a pansy, that'd be it. If you weren't, you wouldn't let anything stop you from getting some of her pie."

"I need to go. I'll come by tomorrow. Do you want something besides an Egg McMuffin? I could swing by Perkins for an omelet or—"

"Just bring the McMuffin. I don't expect anything else."

Joel sighed and left without a goodbye. As he climbed into his car, his hands shook and his gut churned with the sick feeling being around his father always left in him. His phone buzzed in his pocket.

Just seeing Casey's name pop up on the screen made his throat convulse, and his eyes fill with tears. He was an idiot to dream that he could rely on the sweet feeling Casey had left him with, but, God, he wanted to. So much. It'd evaporated in the poison of his father's presence, but he wanted to find Casey and rub against him until he had it back.

Mom's got plans for me today. But I'll be at your place by 6. That good for you?

Joel thumbed in a positive response and wiped at his eyes. Ridiculous. He was overtired and overwrought after having Casey in his bed all night. He needed to get it together. Everything would be fine.

Or at least everything would simply *be*. He'd deal with whatever descriptor came afterward when it happened. For now, he was going to enjoy this Christmas gift of Casey's attention. As much as he could.

His phone pinged again. *Can't stop thinking about you.*

Casey's text summoned a frisson of that morning's magic again, and Joel's heart hesitantly rose in his chest. He typed in his response:

Ditto.

He knew it wasn't enough, but he also knew Casey didn't expect him to suddenly start spouting off about his feelings. Strong as they may be. Wrong as they had always seemed.

Right as they felt now.

"THE POINT IS, you have to stop embarrassing yourself by chasing after something you can't ever have." Casey's mother continued her lecture as they pulled into the parking lot of the newly built Astor Country Club and Golf Course.

The older country clubs were definitely considered higher class, and Casey knew that his father had long salivated to belong to one or both, but when his boss threw his weight, reputation, and money behind the construction of Astor, he'd shifted allegiances quickly enough.

Casey was tempted to tell his mother that she didn't know what she was talking about. He'd already had Joel last night, and he was going to have him for the rest of his life if he had anything to say about it. But Joel wasn't out to anyone yet, and it wasn't his place to share that news.

Still, sweetly simmering memories of the night before aside, he wasn't ready for the inevitable freak-out his social-climbing parents would bring when faced with a reality where Joel Vreeland was their son's boyfriend. He'd save that for another, less precious day.

"I'll take your words into consideration." Casey offered up the bland response Ann had coached him on before leaving New York.

Astor Country Club was decked from foundation to roof in glistening silver and gold decorations. The glare was nearly blinding in the late-morning sun, and Casey bit back a comment about his father's likely opinion of the garish holiday display. Money lived at Astor, so Jonathan Stevens probably gritted his teeth and bore the lack of classy simplicity.

"Good morning, Mrs. Stevens, may I take your coat?" The young, auburn-haired employee's nametag declared her to be Annika.

His mother gave Annika a gracious smile as she peeled off her Christian Dior fox fur coat—a gift from his father for her birthday—and handed it over.

"There's a Winter Wonderland luncheon in the Spring Room, ma'am," Annika went on. "Or are you here for the Santa Bowl benefitting the food pantry? It's in the bowling alley in the basement, obviously."

"Thank you, Annika, but I know where we're going. Come along, Casey." His mother's white-blond hair shimmered with some sort of glittery product beneath the incandescent lights of the grand entry. The broad walls and cupola above were painted in creamy, calming colors that soothed Casey's eye after the gaudy outdoor decorations.

The indoor decorations were sparse and tasteful, mostly greenery with red, silver, and gold bows, but there was a decorated tree in each room Casey peeked in as his mother led him down a quiet hallway toward the back of the building. He wondered if the trees came from Vreeland's, and the thought alone brought a smile to his lips again.

He followed his mother down a flight of stairs and smelled the greasy burgers of the golf pro shop's café before he reached the bottom.

"Isn't it early for burgers?" he asked.

She rolled her eyes and patted her short, pixie-cut hair. "Don't be silly. It's nearly lunchtime. Besides, they'll have other things besides burgers on offer."

It belatedly occurred to Casey that he probably should have wondered prior to this point why his mother wanted him to come with her to the country club, but he hadn't been able to break out of his dreamy, Joel-infused thoughts to consider it. Not until they were already in the highly masculine pro-shop café and the reason for her insistence became immediately and all-too clear.

"Casey, I want you to meet Walker Ronson," his mother said, pushing him forward to grip the hand of a handsome young man wearing expensive golfing clothes and shadowed by a middle-aged caddy. "He's Danny Ronson's son," she added pointedly. "You remember Danny, don't you, honey?"

"Ah, I see." His stomach tightened. "Of course I do." Danny Ronson, the CEO of the petroleum company where his father worked, and the man with whom his father was always trying to get in good.

Walker, blond and tall with teeth so perfect and white they had to be veneers, smiled warmly at him. "It's nice to meet you, Casey. I've heard so much about you from your parents over the last few years."

"We go to the Ronsons' house once a month for a dinner party." His mother smiled with all her teeth. "And Walker is always there now that he's joined on at the company."

"Oh, that's…nice." Casey really didn't know what else to say. His mother nudged him, and he smiled a little more widely, but he didn't have anything to talk to Walker Ronson about. His stomach tightened. He wished like hell he was back in Joel's mobile home, curled around his body under his sleep-warmed covers.

"So, how's NYU treating you?" Walker asked after dismissing his caddy and motioning toward an empty table close to the bar.

"Great."

Was he supposed to follow Walker? He glanced toward his mother, who made a shooing motion with her hand and winked at him. Then she turned on her heel and headed over to the bar. Grabbing a stool, she ordered a mimosa and an egg scramble.

Turning back, he found Walker holding out a chair for him. He searched his mind for any advice from his inner Ann about how to handle this situation, but she was strangely quiet. Casey accepted the seat with a low thanks and then took a menu from the server.

"I always enjoy their eggs Benedict," Walker offered. "I hope you don't mind that I chose the pro shop café instead of the upstairs luncheon room. Upstairs is the land of women and grannies. I prefer a man's world. Especially when I'm meeting with another man."

Casey cleared his throat. He was thrown. Walker talked as though Casey had agreed to be here with him. Was this a job interview or a date? Casey wasn't sure what to make of the situation until Walker spoke again. Thankfully, it was about Casey's post-college plans.

"Your dad tells us that you're graduating soon and headed to Wharton for your master's. That's impressive. You'll have plenty of companies begging for your application, no doubt, but hopefully you'll consider us first? After all, your father's been talking you up for years now. I know you'd hate to let him down."

Casey wanted to ask if that was how Walker had chosen to work with his father? Had he felt obligated because of his father's position? No doubt the opening salary for the son of the CEO wasn't bad, either. "I haven't quite decided how I want to move forward, actually. What made sense a year ago doesn't seem as important to me now."

"The fickleness of youth," Walker said with a grin, as though he was that much older than Casey.

"Yes, well. Recently, I've been thinking about focusing my marketing and branding skills on smaller businesses. Marketing mom-and-pop stores, along with artists and creative types. I'd like to make a difference in what succeeds in an individual town's landscape. That sort of thing."

"Oh?" Walker leaned forward, his eyes taking on an interested gleam. "Tell me more about that. I admit I enjoy the way Knoxville has seen a rebirth of late, and I agree that much of it is due to the ingenuity and creativity of our local small-business owners."

The rest of lunch passed almost painlessly. Walker Ronson wasn't an asshole. In fact, he was easy to talk to and knew a lot about marketing, given that he was the marketing and branding director at his father's company. When the time came to shake Walker's hand and offer thanks for lunch, it was easy to say, "I hope to see you again sometime. Maybe before I leave town."

"Yes, of course. Me too, Casey."

It was also easy to ignore the way Walker's hand lingered a bit too long in Casey's own because obviously Walker was straight. He'd flirted with one of the waitresses after all.

But that misunderstanding was put to rest when he climbed into the passenger seat of his mother's Mercedes. She laughed happily before declaring, "Well, that was an absolute success. Your father will be so pleased."

"Does Walker have that much power at the company?"

She shook her head, laughing still, her eyes sparkling. "Oh, honey.

You are so silly sometimes. Don't you see? Your father's been wanting to set you up with Walker since the week after Theo left."

Casey's stomach dropped. "Set me up? With Walker?"

His mother went on like she didn't hear him. "But I told him the time wasn't right. I admit I hoped Theo might return. But after our conversations since you arrived home and the way that you've been catting around after that Vreeland boy, it's clear to me now. You're ready to move on."

"He's gay?"

"Walker's bisexual, dear, with a preference for men. At least, that's what his mother told me." Her voice caught fire with enthusiasm. "You have a real chance with him. I could tell he found you attractive. And why wouldn't he? You're handsome, sweet, and smart. I love you, so why wouldn't he?"

"Mom, do you know what you've done?"

"Yes! I set you up with a handsome, wealthy, intelligent man. You can thank me later. And was Walker in on it? Absolutely. He was skeptical at first, but when he saw us walking up, I could tell by the look on his face." She nodded firmly. "He's interested after all."

Casey leaned back against the headrest as they whipped past leafless trees and evergreens along the Astor Country Club driveway. He kept his mouth shut, waiting for the right words to pop into his mind. Something less angry than the "mind your own fucking business" that filled it now. He pulled out his phone to text Ann. Maybe she would have time for a phone session later today before he had to leave for Joel's.

"So? Aren't you going to say anything about Walker?" His mother glanced at him out of the corner of her eye before they pulled onto the road that would take them home. "Casey?"

"I have dinner plans tonight. With Joel." He crossed his arms over his chest. "So I won't be around. Tell Heather I'm sorry to miss her delicious cooking two nights in a row, but it can't be helped. I might stay the night with him again. In fact, I probably will."

"But, Casey…"

"I'm a grown man, Mom. I can handle my own love life, all right? Stay out of it."

He closed his eyes and took slow breaths, willing his heart rate to slow down. A flash of Joel's crooked grin filled his mind, and he sighed softly. It was going to be okay. He would hold Joel again tonight, and no matter what nonsense his parents got up to trying to set him up with the boss's son, it wouldn't change a thing. He knew what he wanted. He just had to be patient and steady to get it.

"Fine. Be that way. We're just trying to help you. If you want to spend your break here flirting with someone you'll never have and who doesn't deserve you anyway, be my guest. But, young man, you *will* be at our Christmas party tomorrow night. Do you understand me? No excuses."

Casey kept his eyes closed and his mouth shut. He'd go to the party. Sure, why not? Maybe he'd ask Joel to come as his date. Get it all out in the open. And what better place than at a party where his parents wouldn't have the nerve to show their true feelings? They wouldn't want to make a scene in front of their friends.

"Did you hear me?"

"Yes, Mom. I'll be at the party. I promise."

Chapter Sixteen

A S IT TURNED out, Angel had done a wonderful job with the store. She was dressed in the holiday spirit in felt light-up reindeer antlers and dancing elf earrings. Otherwise, she'd maintained her head-to-toe black, but her lipstick was bright red, and she smiled at Joel when he came in like she was truly happy to see him.

"Guess what?" she squealed, racing around the sales counter to grab his arm.

"What?"

"My stepbrother came in last night to help out."

"Oh? Hope you're paying him out of your own pocket, because I don't have room on the payroll."

"He worked for free," she said gleefully. "Have you seen him?"

"No."

She waggled her eyebrows. "He's gay."

"Great."

"And cute."

"Uh-huh."

"And I think you'd like him."

"Why would you think that?"

"Because everyone says he's dreamy." She rolled her eyes.

Joel pulled free of her grip. "And I'm not interested."

She cocked her head knowingly. "Life's always feast-or-famine, isn't it? And you could be in a feast period, my friend. Enjoy it. Live a little."

"What are you talking about?"

She motioned at the beard burn on his chin, and he touched it gently. It stung. "That dude from yesterday and now, potentially, my stepbrother."

"I think you're getting ahead of yourself, Angel." For so many reasons.

"Hmmph. I just know Ashton was disappointed you weren't here to meet him. Listen, I know this sounds weird coming from me, but you have to understand. My stepbrother is *smoking hot*. Like whoa. A lot hotter than that guy you were macking on at lunch yesterday."

"I'm not sure what to make of that given the last guy *you* went out with. You thought he was smoking hot too." He made a face at her, ignoring the slight on Casey's looks. Angel's last boyfriend had been a string bean who'd always looked as though he hadn't showered in a month. And smelled like it too.

"I'm gonna let that go and just say this: my stepbrother is extra as all hell. Black stubble and green eyes. Prettier than me by far. Much prettier than any guy should ever be." She made a sour face, obviously irritated by that. "Disney pretty."

Several cars pulled into the parking area, and Joel raised his brow at Angel to let her know the conversation was over. He didn't care how handsome her stepbrother might be, or how extra. He didn't plan to entertain the idea of any other man until Casey had broken his heart again. And not for a good long time after that, either. He wasn't a fool.

He and Angel went their separate ways to help a solid stream of customers looking for trees, wreaths, and various outdoor holiday décor. The day passed steadily, but throughout Joel's stomach fluttered and flipped. He almost forgot to eat lunch, but when Angel took her break, he went out to his Chevy and grabbed a couple of sticks of beef jerky. They went down quickly enough, though he barely tasted them.

He couldn't stop himself from daydreaming when not actively helping a customer. In the few lulls, he wandered off to the back shelves, pretending to check the stock. Instead, he'd just stare off into space and remember the way Casey had held him tightly in bed, or the shine of holiday lights on his face as they'd walked in Krutch Park, or the passionate, blissed-out expression on Casey's face as he'd sucked Joel to orgasm.

God, that had been…something. Equal parts amazing and embarrassing and heartbreaking.

He didn't know why the memory made his throat ache and his chest hurt. He wanted so much for their night together to feel like something he could expect to have again and again, but he knew better than that. So, what was the point of being sad about it?

Knoxville wasn't where Casey Stevens belonged. He'd go back to New York City, graduate, and have more options than Joel could ever dream of. Joel wouldn't be allowed to go along on that ride even if he wanted to. He had Vreeland's to take care of and his father. He had Bruno and his grandma's land. He had a realistic grasp on what his future held, and this Christmastime with Casey was a beautiful blip.

Like the montage in a movie just before the lovers go their separate ways for good. Because life wasn't a fairy tale and some movies didn't lie.

He turned his back on the shelves of rosebush fertilizer, each can a silent witness to his musings, as his phone buzzed. Heart in his throat, he grabbed it from his pocket, sighing when it flashed with Becca's name instead of Casey's.

Becca's text was unambiguous: *Call me, asshole. We have things to discuss. Like immediately.*

He informed Angel that he'd be at the patio table out back if she needed him and then put the call through. He was curious how Becca'd found out about Casey staying the night with him already, because clearly she had if she was texting him at this time of day and with that tone.

"What the hell, Joely? I had to find out that you probably lost it last night to our very own Casey Stevens through a text message from RJ?" she said in lieu of a greeting. "What kind of friend are you?"

He took a seat at the patio table with his back to the door. Cars zoomed by on the interstate, obscured by the screen, and he stared at its blankness, trying to wrap his mind around the fact that Casey had apparently told RJ about what they'd done. "A freaked-out one."

"Well, that's no excu—" She gasped. "Oh no. Are you okay? Wasn't he gentle? Did he hurt you? I will bust his head if he hurt you."

Joel chuckled, his neck growing hot. "He was gentle."

"Did you like it? I hate anal. It's the worst."

Joel scrubbed his face. "Jesus, I don't even know where to start with unpacking that. Like, I just… Never mind."

"Start with whether or not you liked it." Becca sounded breathless but also worried. Her concern warmed him. Which was good since it was only in the upper thirties and a lot colder than it'd been the day before.

"I did like it," he confided. "But we didn't do *that*. By the way, when and, more importantly, how did *you* do anal, oh sweet lezzie o' mine?"

"Strap-ons, Joel. Please watch more porn. Jesus." She sighed, and he could just imagine that curtain of black hair flipping over her shoulder. "Okay, so you didn't get your ass cherry popped. Fair enough. Shows he really cares."

"Does it?" Joel blinked rapidly. "I mean, he cares. I know he cares." But Casey had told RJ about what they'd done apparently, and that made him nervous. Just because it'd been sacred to Joel didn't mean it had to be sacred to Casey too, did it?

"He loooooooves you."

"Shut up. Don't make a joke of this." Flurries started to drift down, and Joel stood up, pacing beside the windscreen, his heart racing like the cars on the other side of it.

"I'm not." Becca sounded contrite and still worried.

Joel tugged his jean jacket tighter, flipping up his collar to shield his face from the cool wind. "Let's back up. You said RJ told you? Why did he know?" He groaned. "I mean, obviously Casey told him, but why?"

"Duh. Because Casey's head over heels in love with you, idiot. And he's afraid he'll scare you off if he tells you. So he told RJ instead. And RJ told me."

"Why?"

"Because he thought *you'd* already told me, and he wanted to gloat over a stupid bet we made years ago about the two of you."

"A bet?"

"It was dumb. I didn't even think about it later. RJ forgets nothing. Unless he's high. And he wasn't high that day. Or this morning. Anyway, Casey loooooves you."

"No."

"Yes. RJ implied that Casey literally said he was in love with you." She laughed.

Joel groaned. "Casey doesn't...that's too..." He couldn't complete the sentence—*any* sentence—because his heart was beating so hard that it was going to flop out onto the concrete table like a landed fish.

Becca crooned soothingly. "Now, Joely, I can hear that you're on the verge of losing your sweet crap. Don't ruin this for yourself."

"He doesn't love me."

"Don't make me come over there and slap you until you cry."

"This is just a short-term thing," he whispered, closing his eyes and trying to get some of the prior night's magic back. It kept slipping away from him. "He's going back to New York."

"Sure. But what about when he graduates?"

"He'll either travel or go to graduate school. He has no intention of returning to Knoxville. He told me yesterday."

"Right, and what's wrong with that?"

"Nothing." Joel stared down at his dirty boots. His place was here. Casey Stevens was always meant for so much more. "But he should move on with his life. I don't have a place in his world. I don't *want* a place in it."

"What world?"

"You know what world, Becca!"

"Wow. You're totally going to ruin this." He could hear her pacing in her clompy high-heeled boots across what sounded like a wood floor. That meant she was at her girlfriend Andie's downtown loft apartment. "Don't you dare ruin this, Joel. This thing with you and Casey? It's meant to be. It's always been meant to be. Destiny. Fate. Whatever you want to call it. It's beautiful."

"Look, my life isn't a rom-com, okay? He's in town for the holidays. We're going to have a fling. Enjoy each other for what it's worth and then move on."

"First, that's literally the setup for half a dozen rom-coms, dude." He could picture her pointing her finger at him. "And second, he said that? This is just a fling?"

Joel groaned. "Please don't mess this up for me by sticking your nose in it. Just let me have this, okay? My way."

"Your way?" She fairly bleated with incredulity. "Only if your way means you'll tell him you love him too, and—"

"And what? Ask him to go steady?" He snorted. "Ask him to come back to Knoxville for me? Give up his dreams? Get a grip. We're grown men. Stay out of it."

"Mmm, maybe." Becca's uncertainty slipped through the connection. "But RJ says Casey's floating on cloud nine."

"So was I until this phone call." That wasn't true, but honesty wasn't his policy, especially when he was annoyed like this. His father had shot him down from the cloud earlier in the day, and despite his dreamy memories of the night before, he'd never quite floated back up.

"Always so stubborn."

"Not half as stubborn as Casey."

"And that, my friend, is the only thing that's going to save you." She sighed. Moments passed, and Joel listened to Becca breathe. "I should have hung up dramatically just then, but I blew it by staying on the line too long."

Joel laughed. "You're ridiculous."

"And so are you. I hope you won't ruin your whole life because you're embarrassed to be poor."

Joel scoffed. "I'm not poor. I'm a business owner, for fuck's sake. I'm solidly lower-lower-lower middle class."

"Hanging on by your fingernails." Becca groaned. He could hear her pacing again. "He could help you. His family—"

"Stop. No. There's no way in hell I'd take money from Jonathan Asshole Stevens. Besides, his folks have always hated me, so there's no way they'd offer."

Joel heard Andie's brassy voice call out to Becca that it was time for them to leave if they were going to make the movie. "Got the day off?"

"Andie's taking me to see some art flick she says I'll love."

"You'll hate it."

"Probably." She whispered, "I'd be out of this relationship in a heartbeat if I didn't want to ruin her holidays."

"So you've said."

She clucked her tongue at him. "If I had something like you have with Casey, I'd never let it go."

"Better go racing after Andie, then. We're a holiday fling, too."

"Wow. That's sad, babe. And utter bullshit." Becca growled when Andie yelled again. "Shit. Bye, Joely. I love you." She hung up, and Joel walked to the other side of the privacy screen to watch the cars zoom by.

He wished he saw a future where he and Casey could be together. But all he could imagine was Casey kissing him goodbye sweetly and his own heart breaking as he watched Casey walk away.

That's what always happened. People died, or they left. The story of Joel Vreeland's life.

Chapter Seventeen

"HO, HO, HO! Merry Christmas!" Casey stepped into Joel's place with a giant, green, nylon shopping bag tossed over one shoulder. He'd put on a red button-up shirt his mother had gotten him the prior year and which he'd never worn. He figured he looked enough like Santa to make a joke of it.

Feet bare, Joel wore a white V-neck T-shirt and a pair of black jeans, and he had a few scratches on his face and neck that hadn't been there when Casey had left that morning.

Casey dropped the food to the floor, and Bruno scampered to investigate the bag. "What happened?" he asked, gently thumbing the scratch on Joel's cheek. "How'd you get hurt?"

"It's fine. I survived Thunder Trees." Joel reached up to pull Casey's thumb away. But, to Casey's thrilled joy, he didn't let go of his hand, twining their fingers together instead.

"Explain."

"Two trees enter. One man leaves."

Casey shook his head. "I still don't get it."

Joel laughed. "It's dumb. I was distracted at work and tripped over a tree. It fell on me and brought another down with it. It's just a scrape. I'm fine."

"Did you put hydrogen peroxide or alcohol on it?"

"Yes, Mom."

Casey leaned forward and gently kissed the mark. "That should make it better."

Joel swallowed hard, and he darted his gaze away. "It did. Thanks." He bent to pick up the grocery bag. "Let's put this in the kitchen before Bruno decides to move from snuffling to chowing down."

Casey saw the new Christmas tree in the corner of the living room, already decorated with colored lights. His heart rose giddily. The spangles of color reflected in the mirror over the entry and on every shiny surface around. Next to the tree sat a box marked *ORNAMENTS* and some new boxes of bulbs that Casey recognized as being from Vreeland's Christmas stock.

"I put the lights on earlier," Joel said over his shoulder. "It's the least fun part, and it got my mind off... Well, I had some time to kill."

"It's great. I love colored lights." In that moment, he decided he'd only use colored lights on his own tree from then on.

As Joel unpacked the groceries on the kitchen counter, his eyes grew wider and wider.

"It's not a big deal," Casey hurried to explain. "Chips and salsa for a snack. And popcorn, of course, for stringing on the tree if we want. Or we can just eat it. But then I saw those doughnuts, and I figured if I was going to stay the night again—which you pretty much said I was?"

Joel nodded.

"Well, then I thought I might as well get breakfast. So... eggs, sausage, doughnuts, and some cereal, in case you thought the doughnuts were too sweet. I grabbed another box of oatmeal since I knew you were out. Got the same kind. And then I couldn't resist the Oreos since I know how much you loved them when we were kids." He pulled out the rest of the food as Joel watched. "For tonight, I thought I'd pan fry some steaks and roast the veggies. The cake is for dessert, and the beer and wine are for whenever."

"You must have spent a fortune."

Casey's gut twisted. He'd spent barely anything in his estimation, especially after acclimating to New York prices. How little must Joel be living on these days?

"Let me pay you for the oatmeal and half of everything else," Joel said, wiping a hand over his upper lip nervously.

"What'd I say? You bring the tree and I bring the food, and we'd be even. You've got the tree?"

Joel nodded. "The one that cut me."

"Well, then we're good. And we'll show that bitch of a tree. We'll dress her right up in ornaments and bulbs, and she'll never know what hit her."

Joel smirked. "I love yo—that." His dark eyes flicked up to Casey's face and then down again. "I love that idea."

"Right. I love *that* too," Casey said, but he jerked his chin toward Joel, hoping he'd accept the semi-declaration without a fuss.

Joel seemed eager enough to let his momentary slip of tongue fade away, so he started putting the groceries away. "This is too much, but I'll take it. It's Christmas, and you're a pretty cute Santa. I guess I'll pay you with sex later."

Casey laughed. "Only if you don't really mean it as a payment."

Joel grinned wickedly. It made Casey's blood race. "Oh, you know I'd do it for free."

"Just checking. I don't want you to feel obligated. That's not what this is about."

"I'm an asshole, remember? I wouldn't have sex with you for groceries. I'd sooner catch my dinner in the lake. As I have before, and I will again."

Casey frowned. The idea of Joel having to eat what he caught from the lake was awful.

Joel showed him around the kitchen. "The pans are there, the seasoning there, and potholders here. Let's get a couple of beers open." He grabbed the opener from a drawer. "*Yee-Haw*, dude? That brand's too rich for my blood." But Joel drank it, moaning sweetly when he took a big sip.

Casey's heart flipped over, and he quickly tasted his own beer to cover it up.

At the kitchen table, they worked together to prep the veggies for roasting. Bruno was busy being adorable at their feet, casting his wide eyes up at them hopefully.

After Joel got up to grab a second beer, he sat across from Casey, studied him for a long moment, and then asked, "Why'd you tell RJ about us?"

"What?" Casey's stomach caught. Joel didn't sound angry exactly, but he did sound wary.

"He told Becca. She called me because I hadn't told her myself. That's the chain of events, in case you were wondering."

"Oh." Casey's cheeks went hot, and if his ears could catch on fire, they'd be flaming.

"What did you say to him anyway?"

"Becca didn't know?"

"She did, but… Yeah, she did." Joel's pale cheeks pinked up, and he took a long swig from his beer. "I guess I don't mind. You didn't say anything bad."

"I thought… I mean, I thought he was trustworthy."

"He probably is. Usually Becca's like a steel trap. RJ tells her whatever, and it stays between them with no escape. But this time, since the gossip included me, and she considers me 'hers,' she let me know." He shifted awkwardly, like he wasn't telling the entire truth, but Casey didn't know why. "She's protective of me. Like a big sister who's magically the same age or whatever." He looked embarrassed to have a friend who cared about him.

"I'm sorry if I violated your trust by telling him what I did. For what it's worth, I didn't out you. He'd already figured out that you were gay a long time ago."

"I know. It's fine."

"I was excited when I left this morning. I thought I'd burst if I didn't tell someone how I was feeling."

Joel's sweet mouth crooked up. "I guess that's a compliment."

"It's more than a compliment, it's—" Casey took a deep breath. "My feelings for you are—"

"Not now. None of that." Joel's eyes twinkled as he sat back in his chair, pointing at Casey with his beer. "Make my dinner, slave."

Casey let all talk of feelings drop. Joel was still too skittish to go there. "Oh, you do role-play? Jumping right from virgin to advanced sexual kink. I'm impressed."

Joel snarled adorably. "You should be."

Casey laughed, grabbing the salt and pepper from the spices Joel had pulled down. He spiced the veggies and popped them into the warm oven before grabbing the package of steaks from the fridge.

After spicing the meat, he melted butter in the pan until it was sizzling. Then he placed the steaks side by side, filling Joel's entire cook pan with all four slices of meat.

Joel watched with a craving in his eyes that Casey wasn't entirely sure was lust so much as actual physical hunger. The idea of Joel not having enough money for food made him ache. Couldn't he take a salary from Vreeland's? Could the store really not afford it? Casey knew better than to ask that now, though. Not if he actually wanted to get laid tonight. That conversation would just lead to a fight.

But seriously, Joel's stupid pride!

Casey wondered what it was about the emotion that got under men's skin. His father was driven by pride, and so was Joel's dad. He'd be lying if he didn't indulge in excesses of it himself. Exploring his pride, and the way it limited him, was something he was doing with Ann to a degree—plus figuring out how to be a person to be proud of, and how to stop conflating his father's pride in him—or lack thereof—with his pride in himself.

"A penny for your thoughts."

"Ah, you wouldn't want them," Casey said, smiling. "They're totally fifth- or sixth-date material."

Joel rolled his eyes but didn't insist.

Dinner went quickly, with Joel stuffing himself on the steak and veggies. Bruno got some meat too, but the third steak went into the fridge as leftovers, and Casey could see that Joel was already eagerly looking forward to eating it tomorrow.

With both their bellies full, they turned to trimming the tree. Joel popped a copy of *National Lampoon's Christmas Vacation* in his old DVD player, and both of them were laughing before the opening scenes had even played out. As they watched, popcorn was popped and strung together with needles and thread. Four sore, bloody thumbs later, they strung the popcorn garland around the upper boughs and branches, leaving the lower ones free of temptation for Bruno.

"I should have brought Christmas cookies instead of Oreos," Casey lamented as they cracked open the boxes of ornaments. "Why didn't I think of that?"

On the small screen, Chevy Chase and his family continued to mess up Christmas for everyone, but Casey was having the most perfect Christmas experience of his life in Joel's cozy trailer. Aside from the lack of cookies.

"I have some frozen cookie dough," Joel offered. "I bought it from Brandon's son for his school's band fundraiser today. Expensive as hell, but I couldn't tell him no. Not as his dad's boss."

"Get them out!" Casey hung up a bright orange ball with the words "Tennessee Volunteers" scrolled in white. It was from the box of older ornaments from Joel's pop's house. "Make some!"

Once the scent of baking cookies filled the air, they finished up the tree and eventually collapsed on the sofa with a plate of delicious chocolate chip cookies and grins of satisfaction.

"It looks great." Casey put his arm around Joel's shoulder, dragging him in close before grabbing another cookie from the plate. "Beautiful."

"It's festive," Joel agreed. "I wonder what happened to the star, though." He frowned up at the bare top branch. "I thought I packed it with all the rest."

Casey shrugged. "It still looks good."

The Griswolds finished up their Christmas adventure, and the screen went blank. Joel aimed the remote and turned it off. "And that's all I've got for entertainment. My streaming services are all turned off for now." He scooted away from Casey and grabbed his phone from the coffee table. "I have Internet still and a free Pandora subscription. If you don't mind ads?"

"I don't mind them."

"Christmas music or…?"

"Let's keep with the theme for the evening."

Joel got up and turned on a small Bluetooth speaker placed on a shelf of books by the only overstuffed chair in the room. Casey made a mental note to look for any Joel Grimsbane titles there the next time he was alone in the room.

"Pandora is always a mixed bag. No promises."

The first song began with the clomping of reindeer hooves and a big band swinging beat. A 1950s-sounding woman's voice broke into the familiar words of "Sleigh Ride."

Joel laughed, his head falling back. "Christ, it's merry as shit up in here."

Casey stood and gripped Joel's hand. "Dance with me."

Joel shook his head, but he didn't pull away. "I can only do the swaying thing. Nothing fancy."

"So? It's a fun song. Let's dance."

Joel's elbows were a health hazard, and their ridiculous dance moves drove Bruno out of the room and out his dog door. The next song was Perry Como's "Silver Bells," and they kept on with their awkward movements, laughing and bumping into each other in the close quarters.

"You're lame," Joel muttered, sweaty and apparently finished. He collapsed on the sofa with another beer in one hand and a cookie in the other.

"You loved it."

Joel shrugged, filling his mouth with cookie so he wouldn't have to answer. Casey dropped down beside him and grabbed his own beer from the side table. It was lucky they hadn't tipped it over with the "dancing."

"I looked up your books this afternoon."

Joel swallowed his chocolatey mouthful. "Yeah?"

"I bought one, even. The werewolf one? But I admit I didn't have time to read any of it yet. My Kindle was charged and ready to go, but I had to listen to another lecture from my mother instead."

Joel's mouth quirked. "About what?"

"About... You know what? Never mind."

Joel shook his head, pointing at Casey with his beer again. "You brought it up. Tell me."

Casey sighed, kicked his feet up onto the coffee table, and leaned his head back on the sofa. "She tried to set me up with the son of my father's boss. I wasn't interested, and she's not impressed with what she sees as the reason why."

"Me?"

Casey shook his head, staring up at the smooth, white ceiling. "She doesn't know about us. But she does think I'm chasing after you fruitlessly. She thinks I'm making a fool of myself."

"Funny. Today must be a day for setups." Joel snorted. "My employee, Angel, is trying to fix me up with her stepbrother."

"Oh." Casey didn't like the way his stomach curled up at that.

"I'm not interested," Joel said, nudging Casey with his elbow. "I've already got my holiday fling sorted."

"I told you, let's not call it a fling."

"It's definitely not a hookup," Joel said primly, which made Casey want to laugh through his own jealousy.

"No. It's not."

"Let's not call it anything." Joel's voice took on a vulnerable quality that made Casey's insides quiver and his cock get hard. "Not yet."

"Okay," Casey agreed, but he really wanted to argue. He wanted to pin Joel down and make him say words about their feelings and their potential future. Because, if he could have this, maybe everything else in his life was negotiable. If he could have Joel, the rest of his so-called "life plans" could go suck a dick.

Speaking of…

"Hey," Casey whispered. "Want to fool around on the sofa? Or should we head back to your room?"

Joel set his beer aside. Casey followed suit, ready to stand and let Joel lead him back to his dark room again.

"Here's good," Joel muttered, leaning over to take hold of Casey's chin before kissing him hard.

Casey moaned, surprised at Joel's aggression, and even more so when Joel climbed onto his lap, grinding his jean-clad ass down against Casey's trapped, hard dick.

"Fuck, you're so hot," Joel whispered, rubbing his stubble against Casey's cheeks, shivering at the combined scratch of their evening stubble.

A warm, slow-jazz version of "Have Yourself a Merry Little Christmas" slipped around them, and Casey groaned as Joel's kiss slowed to match the vibe of the song.

"Get it out," Joel whispered wetly in his ear. "I want to see it."

Casey fumbled with his pants, trying to get them open with Joel still half on his lap and distracting him by sucking on his earlobe as he made impatient little noises.

Finally, Casey's pants were down around his hips and his dick was free. Joel whistled low and quiet. "It's so nice," he murmured, running the tip of his finger up the shaft and circling under the helmet. "Can I hold it again?"

Casey nodded, moving his hand aside to allow Joel to take control. Joel sat back, ass on Casey's knees, gazing solemnly down at it. Casey's heart pounded, and his cock thudded, growing harder and harder in

Joel's hand. He could feel his pulse rising, and he squirmed, trying to get Joel to stroke or do something. Anything but just hold him like his cock was delicate.

"I want to suck it." Joel's voice was gravelly. The lights from the Christmas tree sparkling in his dark hair.

Casey's cock ached already, hard and needy in Joel's hand, but those words robbed him of breath.

Joel's dark eyes met his, dark pools of defenselessness and lust. He shifted off Casey's lap to stretch out on the sofa, sprawled on his stomach, his hand never leaving Casey's cock. He gazed at him worshipfully. "Please? I want to try."

Casey nodded dumbly, slipping his fingers into Joel's hair before guiding him slowly to his cock. Joel's breath against the head was almost too much. Casey squirmed, and his hips bucked up, bumping his cock against Joel's lower lip.

"Sorry," he whispered. "Take your time. It's okay. You're just so sexy, Joel. Fuck."

Joel took a slow, deep breath. He swallowed hard, and then opened.

Casey's toes curled up as Joel's hot, wet mouth surrounded his leaking cockhead. He groaned softly, biting his lower lip and trying to hold perfectly still when all he wanted was to get further into Joel, to fuck into his throat.

Joel took him in. Saliva slipped out of his mouth and down Casey's length, wetting Joel's fist where he gripped Casey at the root.

"Yeah, that's…" Casey threw his head back but kept his eyes slitted on Joel, watching him work to take more of him in, to go deeper.

Joel gagged and pulled off, his eyes watering and his cheeks flushing.

"Don't worry," Casey whispered, twining his fingers in Joel's hair a little tighter. "It's perfect."

He wasn't lying. Despite the occasional scrape of teeth and the lack of expertise, Casey had never felt anything as perfect as his cock in Joel's mouth.

Blinking away tears from the gagging, Joel bent back to work. He licked Casey's slit. Casey's legs shook, and he begged Joel to suck him again. Casey glimpsed Joel's self-satisfied smirk before he complied.

It was too good, too much. Casey's pulse roared, his cock stiffened even harder, and he felt the rush of orgasm barreling his way. Joel's tongue and soft inner cheeks were a gorgeous torment, and he wasn't going to last much longer.

"That's it. I'm close," he warned. "Oh, fuck. Now. It's...now."

He let go of Joel's hair, freeing him to pull off, and yet Joel only took him in deeper, choking gently, his dark eyes glowing with feeling. When the first spurt landed on Joel's tongue, he cried out in surprise, backing off Casey's cock in shock.

Casey held Joel's wide gaze as orgasm grabbed him. He convulsed in pleasure, pumping jizz into Joel's open mouth, spilling it down his chin, and shooting a thick stream of it all over his face.

"Holy shit," Joel sputtered, his dark eyes pools of wild lust. He scooped come from his cheek and forehead and shoved it into his mouth. "You taste so...fuck."

He knew what Joel meant. When Joel had come in his mouth the night before, it'd been perfect: sweet and dirty, filthy and pure, all at the same time.

Their taste was everything. *They* were everything.

On Joel's sofa, beside the colored lights of his starless Christmas tree, Casey had never been happier.

JUST LIKE THE night before, Casey's come tasted kinda gross but also so fucking good. It was a paradox Joel couldn't quite understand. He scooped another finger-full from his chin and pushed it in his mouth, his cock ragingly hard in his jeans and his eyes rolling back in his head. He moaned gently.

Casey's mouth was on his again before his brain un-frazzled, and he let himself be tugged up again as they mauled each other while trying to get their clothes off. Finally, naked and hard as a rock, he rutted up against Casey's stomach and pubes, hungry for his own orgasm.

"Fuck, Joel, you're hot as hell, babe," Casey muttered, dropping down on top of him as they stretched out on the sofa.

Joel gripped Casey's butt, reveling in the fleshy mound of it as they kissed and licked and bit. He moaned as Casey sucked a kiss into his neck hard enough to leave a mark later. Squeezing his eyes closed, he breathed in the scent of Casey's skin and licked the sweat on Casey's shoulders.

"You're perfect," Casey grunted in his ear. "Squirmy and hot. So fucking eager... Jesus, Joel, you're just—"

"Shut up. Suck my dick."

Casey laughed, kissing Joel's breath away, and he moved slowly down, pressing wet, shivery kisses along Joel's chest and neck and teasing his nipples, which made Joel bark with laughter until he pushed Casey's head down closer to where he wanted it.

Casey resisted, slowing down, licking along Joel's dark treasure trail and kissing the soft part of his belly before sliding his hands beneath Joel's knees, shoving them back and smiling filthily.

"I bet I know something you'll like," Casey whispered. "Close your eyes."

Joel stared at him, heart pounding, cock thudding, and pre-come pooling on his stomach. Nervous saliva filled his mouth, but he swallowed it down, closing his eyes on Casey's shining face and the glittering tree beside them. In the darkness behind his lids, he could see his pulse beat in colors firing rhythmically in the darkness.

"Shh, just relax," Casey murmured, his breath caressing the inside of Joel's thighs.

Joel knew what was coming. He'd seen porn. And yet when he felt the heat of Casey's breath against his butt cheeks, he squirmed and covered his face with his hands.

"Oh, fuck, Casey," he whispered. "You can't. That's…oh, Jesus."

Casey murmured reassurances and then licked a slick, hot stripe from one butt cheek to the other. Joel groaned as Casey spread him wide. "Look. You're perfect here too."

Joel felt tears push up behind his lids, and he pressed his hands even tighter over his face. His heart beat hard in his throat. A cry of fear and desire, of need and old hurt he couldn't even understand, began to slip from his mouth in a slow keening.

Casey's tongue was gentle on his asshole, and Joel quivered all over as Casey kissed him there again and again, with too-good teases that surpassed the ticklish bliss Casey's tongue had demonstrated on the roof of Joel's mouth. Joel spread his legs slightly, inviting Casey deeper, squirming and tensing, his hips moving in a seeking rhythm he couldn't stop. The sensation bore into him, body and soul, tearing open something inside that left him begging and shameless even as he broke. Tears of pleasure and fear slipped out and tracked down his cheeks.

Casey didn't stop, though he hummed soothing sounds that trembled inside Joel through the sweet instrument of his questing tongue. Joel's cock convulsed, spilling pre-come, and he circled his hips in a vain attempt to find a less overwhelming position.

"It's too—oh fuck!" He whimpered, lifting his hips greedily as Casey swathed his hole with broad sweeps and then went back to painting delicate designs over his spasming anus.

Clenching one fist in Casey's hair to keep him in place and holding his other hand fast over his own sweaty, tear-wet face, Joel let go of the last of his pride. Shaking harder than he could ever remember, Casey's tongue on his asshole became the center of his world. He whispered desperately, "Need to come. Please, help me come."

Casey took Joel's cock and stroked it feverishly as he shoved his tongue deep into Joel's ass.

"Oh, fuck!" Joel cried, his body clenching all over. He roared with pleasure. Come spewed from his cock and spattered his chest and stomach. He whimpered and moaned, his heart thundering as Casey milked every spasm out of him before bending low to lick and kiss his hole gently again.

"Stop," he choked out, tugging on Casey's hair. "Too much now. Stop."

Casey climbed up his body and peeled Joel's fingers away from where he still hid his face. "Oh, Joel," he murmured, his eyes soft with adoration that Joel couldn't pretend he didn't see. "Oh, baby."

Casey kissed him, and Joel cried quietly as Casey gently caressed his mouth with his tongue and lips. His heart broke open, a shattering that splintered through him. Shards of hope and fear pierced him and made him cry harder.

Casey was there, holding him, whispering in his ear. "Are you okay? What can I do?"

Joel clung to him, words gone, unable to translate his vulnerability into vowels and consonants. "Hold me tighter," he finally got out.

Casey did just that, squeezing him tight enough that they both fit side by side on Joel's couch. Staring at the Christmas tree, watching the lights sparkle in the dark room, he leaked tears as the moon ripened in the sky out the window. Slowly, he came back to himself.

Casey's lips pressed gentle, undemanding kisses against his shoulders, holding Joel tight in uncompromising arms. The sound of Bruno coming back in through the dog door broke the spell, and Joel sat up, his limbs still trembling, to grab his shirt from the floor. He wiped away the mess of come drying against his skin.

"Hey," Casey said from behind him. His voice was so gentle that Joel felt it like a caress down his back. "You all right?"

"I'm fine," Joel snapped. Shame gurgled in the pit of his stomach, and he stood without looking at Casey. God, he'd cried like a little kid. "I'm going to wash off."

Bruno came around the corner warily, and he eyed them like they'd been doing something he didn't approve of. Casey huffed a laugh. "Your dog thinks I was murdering you."

"Yeah. Maybe you were."

Casey rose from the sofa. "Joel, wait. Let's talk."

"I just want to shower off." Joel walked briskly, naked and exposed, toward the bathroom. "Just give me a minute."

He heard the impatient, worried sound Casey made, but thankfully stubborn Casey Stevens didn't make an appearance, and Joel locked the bathroom door behind him before sitting down on the toilet and covering his face.

"What the fuck?" he whispered. He scrubbed his still-damp cheeks with his fingers and reached to start the water. As steam filled the small room, he stared down at his bare feet outlined against the linoleum floor.

What had Casey Stevens done to him? Fucking asshole. He'd ruined him. That's what he'd done. He'd irrevocably and completely ruined him.

Now what was he supposed to do? How was Joel ever going to let this be over now? He'd have to cut out his own heart to make it out of this "holiday fling" alive. How could he have been so stupid?

He wished he had his phone to call Becca. She'd talk him down from this ledge. Probably. Or she might push him off it, actually, knowing her.

"Joel?" Casey's voice came from outside the door. "I'm not trying to invade your space. But I've really gotta piss."

"Um, right." Joel wiped at his face again and rose to put his hand on the door. He caught a glimpse of his red, tear-stained face in the not-yet-fogged mirror and pulled his hand off the knob. "Skunks, man. Piss outside."

"Oh. Right. You okay in there?"

"Just washing off."

"All right. I'll just…piss outside."

Joel glared at himself in the mirror and whispered, "Get it together, asshole. You're fucking this up." The worry and insecurity in Casey's voice twisted those painful shards that had pierced him so thoroughly.

He stepped under the water stream, washed the come away, closed his eyes, and tried to wash his panic away too. Yet it clung to him, and he grabbed some soap, trying desperately to scrub it off.

Chapter Eighteen

AFTER CASEY DRESSED and pissed on the bushes along the property line, he headed back into Joel's trailer. Hanging his coat up on the rack, he wondered if he was going to be donning it again soon—if maybe Joel was about to kick him out.

He'd had sex with a lot of guys over the last few years but none of them affected him the way Joel did. And none of them had broken down while being rimmed. Casey was at a loss about what to say or do, but he wasn't going to leave unless Joel actually told him to go.

When he resumed his place on the sofa, Bruno padded over to him with wide, worried eyes. Casey ran his hand soothingly over the dog's head and back, whispering, "It's okay, buddy. Our pal Joel gets scared sometimes, and when he's scared he gets prickly."

"Sorry." Joel's voice came from behind him. Casey looked over his shoulder to find Joel standing there in just a pair of fresh jeans. His dark, wet hair reflected the colored lights of the tree like hidden flames, and his pale torso glowed, dark hair swirling down the center of his chest and the hickey Casey had given him glaring red on the curve of his neck and shoulder. "Got a little freaked about losing my frosty pants there for a minute."

"Hey," Casey said, standing up, relief pounding in him at Joel's small joke. "I'm sorry, I shouldn't have—"

"Yeah, you should have. I wanted you to. It was great." Joel swallowed hard, but his lips wobbled again, and he rubbed a hand over his face. "I'm just… It's been… I've never…"

Casey abandoned Bruno to go around the couch and tug Joel into his arms. "You've been lonely."

Joel nodded.

"Really, deeply lonely," Casey added.

"My mom," Joel started and then stopped.

Casey hugged him tighter and cupped the back of his head.

Joel cleared his throat and began again. "My mom was the last person to hold me or love me. No one's wanted to make me feel good. Ever. And…" His voice broke. "I like it. But it's… a lot."

"It's scary."

Joel nodded again, like he didn't want to admit the word out loud. Casey guided him back to the couch, where Bruno jumped up beside them both, pressing his worried face against Joel's exposed chest and peering up at him.

Joel snorted a laugh. "It's okay, Bruno. He didn't hurt me."

Casey could have sworn Joel's tone somehow implied an unspoken "yet." Joel's muscles moved like coiled ropes under his skin, the shadows compelling. Casey wanted to trace them with his fingers.

"Can I give you a massage?" Casey asked when Bruno finally conceded that Joel was all right and moved to lay on the floor at his feet. "Feeling good doesn't just have to be about sex."

"But I like sex," Joel said, his crooked lips tweaking up. "At least, I like it so far. With you."

Casey grinned, the heaviness that had pressed on his heart since Joel had bolted for the shower lifting. "You do?"

"Yeah. Rimming is better than it looks in porn, and that's saying something. Because it looks pretty great in porn."

Casey laughed outright and hooked his arm around Joel's shoulders to drag him in close again. "Oh yeah? What else looks good in porn?"

"Fucking. Especially getting fucked."

"Yeah? You like the idea of a guy fucking your ass?"

"Don't you?"

Casey shrugged. "Sometimes. I like to be the one doing the fucking usually."

Joel's throat clicked. "Did you bring condoms?"

Casey shook his head. "We're not doing that yet. We've got plenty of time. We don't need to rush into it." Especially not after Joel's emotional reaction to rimming. Casey wasn't ready to push limits when Joel was still so fragile. "Fucking isn't second-date material," he joked, though he'd fucked plenty of guys he'd never even gone on a first date with. But Joel didn't need to know that.

Joel scoffed. "We don't have a lot of time, Casey. You're going back to New York after Christmas. Which, for the record, is the day after tomorrow, and, if I like getting fucked, I'd like to do it more than once." He was wide-eyed and earnest, his expression of resigned determination burrowing into Casey's flesh.

"I'm staying through New Year's Day," Casey murmured, his brain circling around the words Joel had spit out so sincerely. "But, are you saying... Do you want it to be over when I go back to New York? It doesn't have to be."

Joel shook his head. "Just stop." He cleared his throat. "It doesn't matter what I want, Casey, because we've got no future. So, let's just have this time and be happy we got it." He rubbed his face. "Fuck, I need a cigarette."

"You know, when we were kids, you used to boss me around and most of the time I took what you said as the God's honest truth."

"Ha. Could have fooled me. You did whatever you wanted when it came to me."

"If that was true, I'd have kissed you back then and made love to you a million times in the years since."

Joel closed his eyes.

"But I'm telling you right now, this doesn't have to be over when I go back to school. Maybe that sounds safer to you. Something with a beginning and an end that you can see from the start. But that's not what either one of us really wants."

"You think you know what I want?" Joel gritted out.

"I know that you trust me more than you trust anyone else in the world."

"Oh yeah? What makes you think that?"

"Because you let me lick your ass, man." Casey grinned. "And you haven't kicked me out yet. And you're sitting here looking at me like you hope like hell that what I'm saying is true."

"So what?" Joel ran a hand into his hair. "It doesn't make it true."

"What's your big fear? That we make a go of this and...what? What's so scary about the idea of us carrying on when I go back to school?"

"We can't work out. What you want, who you are? It's not what my life is going to be."

"Who am I, Joel? If you know the answer to that, tell me now. Because I'm just figuring that out for myself. I started seeing a therapist to get to the heart of what I wanted and who I am, but I haven't felt more me in my entire life than I have when I'm holding you, making you feel good, letting you be you too. Fuck, why would I want to let that go? Why do you?"

Joel vibrated beside him on the sofa, arms around his knees and his eyes focused on the top of the starless Christmas tree. "You'll leave me. In the end, you'll leave me."

"I won't."

"You don't know that."

"And you don't know that I will."

Joel shuddered. "What's your future going to be? You already said you don't want to live in Knoxville because of your dad. You want a fresh start. Well, guess what? I don't get a fresh start. I've got Vreeland's, and I've got my pop to take care of."

"Those plans are negotiable. I'm not committed to any of them. I just want something for myself, to know who I am and what I want.

And now I know. I want you. I want this." He touched Joel's bare shoulder, but Joel shrugged him off.

"Where will you live? In your parents' house across the lake while I'm here? How will you feel introducing me to your friends or their friends? I'm not like your family."

"Where I want to live isn't really second- or third-date conversation material," he tried to joke.

"You think you want to live with me?" Joel gestured at his living room. "Look around, Casey. Do you really think this is what I want for you?"

"There's nothing wrong with this place."

"For me, maybe. But for you? No. Don't you get it?" Joel's voice pitched up desperately. "You're Casey Stevens, son of Jonathan Stevens, vice president of one of biggest petroleum corporations in the country. You're going to *NYU*, man! You can't just…" He waved his hand. "You can't."

"None of that matters to me."

Joel sputtered. "It matters to *me*. You think I'm going to let you throw away your degree and move into a trailer with me?"

"Throw away my degree?" Casey snorted. "I can work on branding and marketing in Knoxville."

But Joel was caught up in his rant. "What kind of love is that? Letting you give up so much potential to be with me? Who would I be if that's the kind of love I gave you?"

Casey's heart flipped in a scary roll that took his breath away. When he caught it again, he asked slowly, "Now you're ready to talk about love?"

Joel threw his hands in the air and turned away. "Forget it."

"You love me?"

"What do you think? I've loved you since we were kids." Joel glared at him over his shoulder. "Sometimes I really think you're an idiot, you know that?"

"You say I'm Casey Stevens, right? Do you think that means any-thing important to anyone who isn't you? Don't you get it? I've been living in New York City, and no one gives a shit about who I am, Joel. I come home, and I'm here just a few days with you, and I feel…alive. For the first time in forever. For the first time in my entire life, it's awesome to be Casey Stevens. Because of *you*. Not NYU or my apartment in the city. It's because Joel Vreeland loves me." He touched Joel's chin, lifting it to stare into his eyes. "You love me."

"Don't use it like a weapon."

"I'm not."

"The hell you're not. You've got me quaking here, man."

Casey took Joel's hand and pressed it against his chest so he could feel his pounding heart. "And you've got me terrified that you're going to throw this away—throw us away—because you hate my parents' money, or you're ashamed that you don't have as much."

Joel didn't pull his hand away. "Get serious. If you really moved in here with me, can you imagine your parents coming to visit you here?"

"No. And that's fine with me." Casey shrugged, releasing Joel's hand. "But if you don't want me to live here, I wouldn't have to. I could get an apartment. Until you were ready for us to be something more, and we could figure out what we want our living arrangements to be then."

"Fuck you," Joel whispered. "You're—" He scrubbed at his face. "You're here stirring up all kinds of shit in me, and I can't hold still for it. I feel like I'm going to explode."

"I feel the same way. Right now, the idea of going back to New York seems like hell. I want to stay here with you and be with you all the time. I'm in love with you. And, like you said, I have been forever."

Bruno sighed heavily at their feet, and Joel used his bare foot to scratch along the dog's side until Bruno rolled over onto his back, begging Joel to rub his belly.

Casey reached out and rubbed Joel's back. "Can I give you that massage?"

Joel was silent a long time, but he finally replied, the fight gone out of him. "Only if you're planning to seduce me again."

"I promise."

"And I promise not to cry this time." Joel's chest flushed. "Sorry about that."

Casey scooted closer, pressing his lips to Joel's shoulder and then whispering in his ear, "Cry if you need to, baby. I don't mind. I love you just the way you are."

THE NEXT MORNING, the sun rose before Casey was ready to relinquish his hold on Joel for the day, but there was nothing to be done about it. Joel had an Egg McMuffin to deliver to his father and a store to open, so Casey crawled out of bed with him and ate a quiet breakfast of dough-nuts, eggs, and coffee. He was grateful when Joel let him share the shower.

They didn't mess around, though. Both of them cleaned as best they could in the tight space with all the elbows, knees, and asses in the way. Joel laughed when Casey accidentally clipped his jaw while washing his hair, and he swatted Casey's ass on his way out of the shower to grab a towel from the rack.

"When I graduate, this could be every morning," Casey said, rinsing the shampoo from his hair, thrilling inside that he would smell like Joel's Garnier Fructis all day.

"Dreamer," Joel said, studying his own face in the mirror and grab-bing a razor. Despite the mild whisker burn that decorated his chin and upper lip, Casey noted that he was efficient in his strokes. Soon the dark stubble that had left nice scratches all over Casey's neck and chin was scraped away.

"One of us has to be." Casey turned off the water, grabbing the second towel Joel must have put out for him.

"I dream plenty, thank you. Who's the writer here? That's like dreaming while you're awake."

"Horror writer. Your dreams are dark and grim. I'm here to lighten them up."

Joel snorted and rinsed off his razor before splashing at his face. "Will I see you again tonight?"

Casey grimaced, rubbing the towel over his dick and balls and then sliding it down to get his feet. "You could. If you're willing to take a risk."

"I already told you I want to get fucked. Buy some condoms. Make it happen."

Casey swallowed hard, eyeing Joel's apple ass on top of his taut, firm legs. He licked his lips as he took in the various tattoos he'd finally had a chance to eyeball up close. Each of them held a lyric, just like Joel had said, and Casey was going to Google the songs from the ones he didn't recognize.

"Not that kind of risk," Casey said, coming up behind Joel to press kisses along his shoulders. He'd noticed the night before how Joel melted when he did that, and he wanted him soft as putty now in hopes he might actually say yes.

"I don't know how much more risk I can take," Joel said, his dark eyes in the mirror sparking anxiously. "I'm already putting my heart out there, and it's gonna get squashed, so what more can you ask of me?"

"Come to my parents' house tonight. They're having a Christmas Eve party for their friends, and I want you there with me. As my date. As the man I love. I want to ring in Christmas with you."

Joel tensed in Casey's arms. "What? Are you insane? Hell no. Not a chance."

Casey nuzzled Joel's neck.

"If you think that's going to convince me, you're wrong." Joel pushed away from the sink and, evading Casey's wandering hands, headed back into the bedroom.

Casey pulled Joel's brush through his hair and grabbed the new toothbrush he'd picked up with the groceries, concentrating on designing a new argument while brushing his teeth. By the time he finished and went to pull on his own clothes from the night before, Joel was already dressed and stuffing his pockets with a key ring and his wallet.

"Yeah?" Joel asked, like he was ready for whatever Casey was going to say.

"If you don't come, then I guess I can't see you tonight. What's your schedule tomorrow?"

Joel frowned. "Can't you come over after?"

"I've spent the last two nights here. I want to stay again, obviously," he said conciliatorily when he noticed Joel's shoulders inching up. "There's nothing I want more. But Aunt Courtney's arriving this afternoon for the party, and my parents will give me a hard time if I try to bail on seeing her." Casey's heart leapt wildly, and he didn't know what possessed him to say it, but the words were out of his mouth before he could reconsider. "We have two guest rooms. Come to the party. Spend the night in my bed. Then you can have Christmas breakfast with my family in the morning. It's worth the pain of dealing with my folks."

"Even if I wanted to do that, which I don't, I've got Bruno. I can't leave him for the night."

"You could feed him before you come. Plus, he has the dog door."

Joel shook his head. "You're barking up the wrongest tree that ever grew." He turned to face Casey and smiled, his eyes crinkling at the corner, "But you're cute to think I'd ever consider it." He pressed a kiss to Casey's mouth. Then, like he almost couldn't believe he was allowed, he did it again.

"Joel," Casey started, but Joel pressed his fingers to Casey's lips and shook his head.

"Let's not fight. I've got to go. Let yourself out whenever you're ready. We'll talk later."

"If you change your mind, it's casual dress. You don't have to wear anything fancy. And I'd be proud to introduce you as my boyfriend."

"Would you?" Joel asked. "I wonder."

"Handsome, smart, funny, and in love with me? What more could I ask for?"

"Oh, I can think of a few things," Joel said bitterly. He grabbed his coat from the rack, pressed another kiss to Casey's mouth, patted Bruno's head, and was outside before Casey could plan a new assault on his commitment not to come to the party.

"Text me," he called out the open door.

Casey lingered with Bruno as long as he could, not eager to return home and face his mother, or possibly his father. At least Aunt Courtney would be there soon to pull some focus.

Besides, they always had to play happy family when there were witnesses around.

Chapter Nineteen

"HEY, POP." JOEL stepped into his father's room at the nursing home with some measure of trepidation. He'd been walking a razor's edge of insane joy and utter terror all morning, and he knew there was no one better suited to tip him over to the terror side than his father.

"About time," his father barked, frowning. Christmas carols played from the small speaker Joel had set up for him to use with an old iPod he'd scored for more than half off at McKay's. "What's wrong with your face?"

Joel touched his sore chin. He hoped whisker burn healed quickly. That was another thing porn didn't get even close to the reality of: the pleasure-pain of prolonged kissing with a stubble-faced man.

"Get in a fight?"

"With a tree, yeah." Joel moved his finger to the scrape on his cheek from the tree and shrugged. "Some branches got me good."

His father narrowed his eyes, but he said nothing.

"Brought your Egg McMuffin." Joel held out the bag.

"There's something wrong with you today," his father said after he'd chewed and swallowed his first bite. "You look..." He leered. "You got laid?"

Joel swallowed and shook his head. He wasn't going to let his pop taint what he'd done with Casey. Not now. Not ever.

"Finally found a pussy willing to spread its lips for you?"

Joel wrinkled his nose. "Pop, could you be more crude?"

"Faggot," his father hissed.

"And I'm out." Joel backed toward the door, waving goodbye.

There was a time he'd have stayed to try to calm his father, but he'd learned over the years that the best course of action was retreat when his dad started up with the name-calling.

"Pussy!" his father yelled after him as he turned and made his way into the hallway.

He grimaced as he ran into Katie as she approached his pop's door with a tiny plastic cup of meds. "Bad day," he said to her, shuddering as his father screamed more obscenities from his bed.

"Aren't they all with him?" Katie asked gently, putting her hand on his arm. "You do more than you should for him. More than he deserves." Her eyes went wide, and she flushed bright red. "I'm sorry. I shouldn't have said that. It was out of line."

Joel huffed as Pop's endless curses still rained against his back. "It's true."

He walked stiffly out to his truck and sat with the heater blasting, staring up at the nursing home building, thoughts roaring through his head like a storm.

"IT SOUNDS LIKE things are progressing quite fast," Ann said, though her calm voice resonated with her usual lack of judgment on Casey's choices. "You sound confident and, dare I say it, happy?"

Casey lolled on the soft guest bed he'd claimed as his space when he'd first arrived home. The windows beside the bed looked out on the lake and, if he squinted against the morning sun on the water, he could see Joel's mobile home on the other side.

"I know it seems fast, but I've known him forever. I've loved him since the beginning."

"I didn't say your feelings were fast, Casey. Just the progress of the relationship. You're talking about returning to Knoxville now, something you were adamantly against before, and you're discussing living with him in his home." Ann hesitated. "I'm not against it, mind you. It's simply, quite objectively, fast."

Casey laughed. "It is, I guess. But I don't want to be away from him. And Knoxville is where he needs to be. He has his family's store and his father to take care of."

"And who knows what the future might bring…"

"Exactly. We're young, and his father isn't well. I don't have my heart set on anywhere else. You know that. Well, now it's set on Joel."

"I've never heard so much excitement in your voice. I'm happy for you, Casey. Though I do urge you to take things as they come. Don't push for too much, too fast. Like you said, you're both young. There's time to breathe in this relationship."

"It just feels like we've already wasted so much time."

"You haven't. You've found each other sooner than most. You've got your whole lives ahead of you."

Casey smiled and rolled onto his back, gazing up at the smooth, white ceiling and the decorative crown molding all around the edges of it. "Thank you. I know you thought coming here was a bad idea. If I hadn't manned up and gone to see Joel, it probably would have been. But I'd never have found the nerve to do it without our work together. So, thank you."

"Of course. And I'm not too proud to admit when I was wrong. Going home to Knoxville and facing your feelings for Joel has been a long time coming. I'm proud of you."

"Thanks, Ann. I guess our hour's mostly up."

"I'll charge my phone rates to your bill. And, genuinely, I'm thrilled for you. I hope your happiness only grows. See you in a few weeks when you're back in New York and I've returned from my vacation."

Casey placed his phone on the nightstand and grabbed his laptop. Opening it up, he fiddled some more with the marketing plan he was putting together for Joel's books. He'd read a few chapters of the werewolf book when he got home, and it'd been so much better than the cover art and blurb had led him to believe. So, he'd taken it upon himself to mock up something sexier and gripping. Something he'd one-click if it ever popped up in his Amazon search.

When he'd made something he was proud of and was convinced Joel would like too, he moved on to researching a little about the horror-book market. Everything he found for indie authors stressed what he already knew: social media and getting the word out about the book was key.

And those were two things he knew Joel wasn't doing.

He did a fast Google and Facebook search for Joel Grimsbane and found almost nothing. Just the original sales site links, a couple of enthusiastic but low-quality reviews, and some pirated copies.

It didn't take long after that to make a list of things Joel could do to improve his books' visibility. A Facebook page for Joel Grimsbane first and foremost, and then a website, and a list of horror review sites and contacts to send review copies off to. This was easy stuff. Casey could do it all in his sleep.

He sat back and considered his next semester's course load and smiled. He'd be able to do almost all of the marketing for Joel, if his crabby lover (*lover!*) was willing and didn't put up a fuss. Not just for his books, but for Vreeland's too. Casey double-checked that there was nothing online for the home and garden store, not even a website, and shook his head when he was proven right.

After cleaning up his list into bulleted to-do items with deadlines for execution, he decided to take a little rest. So he closed his eyes, letting sleep steal him away into Joel's arms again. He woke not too long later to the sound of his aunt's squeals and his mother's laughter drifting up the stairs.

Yawning, he stretched and rose, checking his hair and face in the mirror over the dresser. He hadn't shaved yet, and his chin was still scrubbed pink from Joel's stubble the night before. He grinned and flattened the places where his hair stood up before heading down for hugs and the obligatory exclamations about his height.

"Here he is," his mother said, with a hint of disapproval sneaking into her tone. "Casey, honey, look who's here."

Aunt Courtney squealed again and met him halfway down the stairs, pulling him into her arms and hugging his middle for all she was worth. Twelve years younger than Casey's mom, she was smaller than Casey by half a foot, with strawberry-blond hair and hazel eyes. But dang if she wasn't strong!

Casey grunted as the breath crushed out of him. "Hey, Aunt Courtney," he gasped when she released him enough to breathe.

"You got too tall," she scolded, slapping at his shoulder and going up on her tiptoes to kiss his cheek.

"Sorry. I tried to stop growing back when I was ten, like you asked, but no luck."

Courtney giggled and slipped her arm through his, letting him guide her back to the first floor and his mother's tense smile. "Your mom was telling me on the way from the airport that she has to meet with one of her charity clubs this afternoon, but she's volunteered to let you entertain me."

"Perfect. What do you want to do?"

"Go shoe shopping. I brought a red dress for tonight, but I don't have any heels that are right for it."

"I thought it was casual," Casey said, turning to his mother.

"Of course it's casual, but that doesn't mean we shouldn't look our best," his mother said, sending him a gleaming smile. "Take her to Off Broadway shoes. They have some decent brands at good prices. If she can't find anything there, take her to the mall." She leaned forward and whispered, although it was still loud enough for Courtney to hear. "If the pair she wants seems above her budget, just use your credit card. I'll pay you back."

"But first, let me unpack my bags and freshen up," Courtney said with a big smile. "Which room should I take?"

"All of the rooms upstairs are available, except for the one Casey chose. If you don't see his stuff all over the place, feel free to claim it as yours." His mother squeezed her sister's arm and kissed her cheek. "I'm so glad you're here. I've missed you. There's nothing like family at the holidays."

Once Courtney disappeared upstairs and Casey had delivered her bags to the room she chose, his mother cornered him in the kitchen where he was dreaming of Joel and waiting for his aunt to be ready for shoe shopping.

"What is going on with you and Joel Vreeland?" his mother asked, crossing her arms over his bosom. "I'm tired of making excuses to your father about where you are every night."

"It's only been two nights, and why haven't you just told him I've been staying at Joel's?"

"Why would I do that? It would upset him. He's never liked that boy."

"Because he thought my crush on him meant I was gay, which I am, and we all know it now, so what's the problem?"

"Joel Vreeland's not a good connection for you. Unlike Walker Ronson, who could take you far in life. Even if you're not attracted to him—though how could you not be?—you should at least strive to be his friend. He's the kind of man that will elevate you to the next echelon socially. If things really are over with Theo, then we should set our sights on something almost as good."

"Deanna, for heaven's sake, are you trying to force that boy to marry up?" Courtney's laughing voice echoed around the kitchen, and when Casey turned around, she met his gaze with an eye roll. "He's not even out of college. Give him a chance to live a little."

"I would, honey. But he's trying to kindle something that isn't ever going to catch fire."

"Mom, Joel is—"

"Joel Vreeland?" Courtney's strawberry-blond brows arched up. "That sour-faced little boy who used to live behind you at the old house?"

"He's still cranky," Casey conceded. "But he's grown up as much as I have. I wouldn't call him little. And we've rekindled our friendship recently. For some reason, that bothers Mom."

"Uh-huh," Courtney said, glancing down at Casey's chin. She shot him a knowing look and then turned to her sister. "Okay, don't you need to get going?"

His mother cursed lightly when she glanced toward the clock on the microwave. "I'll be back in plenty of time for the party. Don't you two be late! Do you hear me? Jonathan will do his thunder god impression if Casey isn't ready when the Ronsons get here."

"Mmm-hmm," Courtney said, tossing her hair and smiling sweetly. "Have a good time, Dee. Love you."

As soon as the door out to the garage shut on his mother's back, Courtney grabbed Casey's hand. "Oh, wow. So, she hasn't figured out that you're totally hooking up with that crabby kid?"

"He's twenty-two, like me."

Her eyes glowed. "Did he grow up hot?"

"Aunt Courtney," Casey scolded. "What are you getting at exactly?"

"Why are you being coy? I'm not stupid like my sister. You've spent the last two nights there. You're not a child anymore. These haven't been slumber parties. Your old friend Joel is queer as a two-dollar bill, and you're tapping that." She frowned. "Do the kids still say 'tapping that'? Or do they say 'getting it'? What do you say these days?"

Casey ignored her question. "I'm in love with him." His heart giddy-upped in his chest, and a smile broke over his face. He knew he probably looked as silly as he felt, but love was an undeniable emotion.

"Ah! Well, Deanna will have to put her romantic machinations aside, won't she?"

"How bad is it?"

"The Ronson heir is going to be here tonight. Apparently, you made a good impression on him when you last saw him." She waggled her brows. "You've grown up to be a real man-killer."

"Aunt Courtney... Stop." Casey sighed.

"Why don't you just tell your mother what's really happening with you and this boy?"

"Because he's not out. I shouldn't have even told you."

"You didn't. I guessed."

"But I think he'd come out if he was sure of us, or more sure of us. I'm trying to convince him that I'm serious and that this isn't some kind of holiday fling. I invited him to the party tonight, as my date. As my boyfriend."

She gasped. "Oh, my. I mean, yes, you should let your folks know you're involved before they dig themselves deeper into this Ronson setup, but springing it on them at their Christmas party? With their friends and co-workers, and their boss and his son? Couldn't you have just told them this morning? The drama that's going to bring!"

"Don't worry, he turned me down. Said there was no way in hell he was going to come to a party where everyone would look down their noses at him."

"Smart kid."

"He runs his own store. He's not a child. And I'm not either."

"No, no, of course not. I'm just... I remember when you were born, and, to me, you'll always be that baby. But you're right. You're a grown-up now, and you know what you want and who you love. I'm here for you. If things go pear-shaped tonight, or, well, ever? Your Aunt Courtney has your back."

His heart swelled with love for her. "Let's get those shoes."

"HEY BOSS," ANGEL sang, following Joel as he entered the store. "I cleaned the drawings off the Blow Mold Nativity scene, like you asked."

"Good." He headed toward the back, hoping she'd already started a pot of coffee because he was feeling bleary-eyed and shaky. Maybe it wasn't good for the system to get so much touch all at once, especially after years without it.

"You have a visitor," Angel said, still following him through the rows of merchandise.

His heart leapt. Casey? Had he been unable to stay away?

"My stepbrother."

"What?"

"Ashton."

Joel frowned, his lip coming up in a sneer. But just then he rounded the corner and clapped eyes on the most insanely good-looking man he'd ever seen outside of his television screen. The guy picked up a container of rosebush fertilizer and cocked his head, reading the directions on the back carefully.

"Do the right thing here," Angel whispered.

"What the fuck does that mean?"

Just then Ashton turned around. Joel didn't see any resemblance to Angel, but then he wouldn't since he was a stepbrother and not related by blood.

"Hi, I'm Ashton," the faultless face said from a pair of lush lips surrounded by perfectly sculpted stubble. "Angel said you might be able to help me out."

Joel patted his hair, hoping he didn't look as discombobulated as he felt in the face of gorgeous bright eyes of some indiscernible color between green and gray. "Uh, hi. I'm Joel. Yeah, so how can I help you?"

Angel giggled behind him, but she scampered off when he pointed toward the register and the customers that had lined up there with purchases in arms.

"I know this sounds insane, since I literally just met you and all," Ashton said, blinking long lashes that couldn't possibly be real, "but I have a problem." He laughed nervously. "I have to go to this family Christmas party tonight, and I'm in desperate need of a date. That would be you. Hopefully."

"Me?" Joel grimaced.

"Yes, you." He smiled even brighter. "Angel said you were gay and liberal-minded. Hopefully she's right."

"Angel said… *Angel* said…" Joel sucked on his teeth and turned to glare toward his employee as she rang up five poinsettias for a small, brunette woman with two strangely well-behaved children.

Now that Angel knew he was gay, he should have known better than to think she'd keep it a secret. Now it would get out. News of his homosexuality would spread like wildfire in a town the size of Knoxville. Soon all of his customers would be eyeing him strangely—if they even still came in to make their purchases once they knew. They'd all speculate about what he did with other men. He closed his eyes and waited for the panic to hit.

Instead, a wave of relief seized him, and he felt like his knees might go out.

Fine. They'd all know. It'd be done and over with. He'd be honest about himself for the first time in his life. He'd be a big giant queer and own it. He would *not*, however, wear eyeliner, like he was pretty sure Ashton was wearing.

And was that lip gloss? Christ. Angel was right when she'd called this guy extra.

Ashton chewed on his shiny, plump lower lip. "God, this was already awkward, but now it's downright humiliating. You're not gonna hit me, are you?"

"Look, I'm…flattered?" Joel cleared his throat and tried again. "Yeah, I'm flattered that you'd ask me as a date to a party—can't say I really get why, or why you'd even need to ask someone like me when you look like that, but anyway. It doesn't matter. I'm not—"

"Has Angel set me up with some kind of humiliating prank?" Ashton's eyebrow went up.

"No, I don't think so." Joel rubbed a hand over his upper lip. "I'm just not available. I've got a—" He swallowed. "I'm involv—" What was he to Casey? Had they declared a relationship yet? He chewed on his lip and laughed under his breath. "Christ, I'm in love with a guy. All right?"

"Oh, is that all?"

"And we're monogamous." He hoped.

Ashton's eyes twinkled as he shrugged. "I understand, and I guess it didn't hurt to try. Angel did seem overly optimistic about my chances with you." Ashton laughed. "Oh well, there's always Grindr. There's more than one way to lure in a man to solve my problem."

Grindr? For a date to a family Christmas party? That seemed chancey. And why did a guy as handsome as Ashton need Grindr or help getting a date anyway? He supposed he'd never know. "Couldn't you go alone?"

"My grandma is a total homophobe. This is going to be my last Hudson family party ever because I'm coming out to them all tonight. I'm going for massive emotional explosions. I need someone to go with me who'd be willing to put on a good show. If you know what I mean?"

"And Angel thought *I* was that guy?"

"She said you have enough grit to survive the family meltdown when I show up with a man on my arm."

Maybe Angel was setting *him* up for the prank, not Ashton. "Yeah, well, sorry. I hope you find someone."

"Me too. I want to see my Grandma's head spin around as Bible verses spew out of her mouth."

Joel coughed. "You and Angel have a lot in common. Sure you're stepsiblings?"

"Absolutely sure. But she and I get along great."

"I see why."

Ashton smiled prettily. "Well, thanks for even entertaining the idea. You don't have any queer friends that might be up for scandalizing old ladies on short notice?"

"Sorry. I'm not much for friends."

Ashton laughed like Joel was joking. "If you fall out of love or find it's not all it's cracked up to be, give me a call." Ashton pushed a card into Joel's hand. "I'm always up for a quick pull and suck. Or more. I'm easy like that."

Then the most handsome man Joel had ever seen in his life swept by him like some kind of six-foot-tall Christmas fairy from a story. Joel shook his head, returned to his quest to find coffee, and considered Ashton's proposition.

He wasn't the least bit tempted. If he was going to cause drama at any Christmas party tonight, it was going to be at Casey's folks' party.

And he'd need a decent tie and shoes.

Jesus, he was insane for even considering it. Wasn't he?

He wondered if he still had shoe polish in one of the unpacked boxes from the old house. It'd be in the one marked for the contents of his father's closet. There'd be ties in there too. Decent-looking ones, and he had a clean, white button-up and a navy sports jacket he kept ironed in the closet in case he needed to attend a funeral.

Would Casey's mother's head spin when he showed up? And what, if not Bible verses, might spill from her mouth? How did a meltdown look on Casey's class-obsessed father?

Maybe it was time to find out.

Chapter Twenty

SNEAKING INTO THE kitchen and away from his parents' newly arrived party guests, Casey checked his phone again. He hadn't heard back from Joel since their last text exchange around five-thirty, and he worried that in Casey's absence Joel might be getting cold feet about their relationship—or whatever they had now. It made him twitchy.

His father had hired a trio of classical guitarists from the university's music program to play from the broad upstairs balcony over the living room. The upbeat, plucky carols, no doubt chosen by his mother for the evening, pattered over the guests, smoothing over the clinking glasses and bursts of laughter like a waterfall of Christmas joy.

Normally Casey would have enjoyed the infectious spirit of the party, but his phone remained stubbornly still. He read over their text exchanges from the day, trying to see if he'd inadvertently said something to piss Joel off.

Around noon, after watching Courtney try on fifty-nine thousand pairs of shoes, he'd texted Joel with: *I already miss you.*

You'll be okay. You're a big boy.

He'd manfully restrained himself from making a joke about how Joel was gonna feel just how big he really was before too long if he kept begging to get fucked. Instead he'd said: *I'm out with Aunt Courtney. She thinks we're a couple.*

Cool.

Really? You're okay with that?

Sure. Then there'd been a pause and the clarifying question: *I mean, if we're a couple?*

Casey's heart still flipped over remembering the way his fingers had trembled with excitement as he'd tried to reply quickly. Autocorrect was his enemy, though, and he'd sent: *Yes, we're a coupe.*

Then: *Coupe.*

Then: *COUPE.*

Then: *COUPLE. Damn it, autocorrect.*

Joel had sent a crying-laughing emoji and asked: *Spend a lot of time texting about four-door coupes, do you?*

Screw you, Casey replied, but included a winking emoji to make sure Joel knew he was teasing. *Autocorrect is demented.*

I know. One time I accidentally texted Angel that we needed to restock deck cleaner, and autocorrect changed it to dick cleaner. I'm lucky she didn't charge me with sexual harassment.

He'd replied with his own crying-laughing emoji, and they'd gone radio silent for nearly two hours after that. Casey had felt like he was walking on air the rest of his shopping trip with Courtney, even letting her talk him into buying a new "ugly" Christmas sweater for him to wear to the party. His dad would hate it, which gave him a twist of satisfaction.

They'd texted lightly off and on for the rest of the day. Then, around five-thirty Joel had texted asking, *When does your folks' party start? Sure you can't come over after?*

7:30. Sure you can't come to it? I'd be so proud to introduce you as my boyfriend.

Joel hadn't replied after that. Had Casey messed up by pushing the issue of the party? Or was it the word "boyfriend" that had sent Joel running? Or was he just really busy selling Christmas trees to people who'd waited until the very last minute to decorate for the holidays?

Casey typed in a message and hesitated only a moment before sending it.

I still miss you.

He rounded the corner back to the living room and stepped right into Walker Ronson. Their collision sloshed Walker's wine and narrowly missed staining their clothing.

"Oh, man. I'm sorry," Casey said, gripping Walker by the elbow to steady him. "I didn't see you."

"Well, I was hiding in a corner, trying to avoid talking to people, so I can't blame you for that."

"Oh yeah?" The confident young man he'd met at the club for breakfast the other morning didn't seem like the type to hide from a party. But what did he know? "Not a fan of crowds or just allergic to meaningless chatter?"

"I'm avoiding my father," he said, chuckling into his glass. "We don't agree on many things, but politics we disagree on most of all. He started praising our current president to Nancy Kilmer-Jones from accounting, and I had to make an exit from the room before I said something we'd both regret." He gave Casey a long once-over. "Nice sweater."

Casey glanced down at his newly purchased joke that was only truly meaningful to one other person in the world and smiled. His sweater was blue and white, with a buff, sculpted snowman on the front and the words I'M WITH FROSTY in gold holiday lettering across the chest. It was ridiculously perfect, if a little warm, and he felt closer to Joel just wearing it.

He should have taken a picture of himself in it and texted that to Joel. It would have said more than his last text message. He met Walker's eyes and realized he'd never responded to the compliment on his sweater. "Thanks. You look nice too."

Walker smiled warmly, his eyes taking on a gleam Casey recognized from many hookups past. "So, is there a private place you and I could go to talk?"

"No," Casey said, smiling with as much friendliness as he could muster while shooting down his father's boss's son. "Afraid not. We'll have to just brave the crowd."

Walker laughed. "C'mon, Casey. I'm attracted to you, sure, but I'm not talking about anything like that. Let's just head out to the deck for some fresh air and to escape this endless round of 'God Rest Ye Merry Gentlemen'. I don't think these guitarists know when to quit."

On the back porch, Casey gazed out across the lake to the Christmas lights lining the edge of the rectangle that was Joel's trailer. The interior lights were out, and he squinted, trying to see through the darkness, looking for Joel's Chevy. He leaned against the porch railing as the cold night wind off the water raked through his hair and stung his eyes.

Walker leaned against railing beside him, his wine glass still grasped loosely in his fingers. He took a sip and murmured, "Nice. Your parents should buy that property across the way, though. Control the view."

Casey pressed his lips together. Circumstances having led to Joel being their backdoor neighbor once again seemed like fate. Separated by a lake instead of a fence this time. He hoped that wasn't symbolic. And even if it was? He'd deal with it. After all, he could swim.

"I know earlier I said I was avoiding my father," Walker murmured, his voice pitched in a decidedly seductive tone that made the hair on Casey's neck stand up. "Which is true in a way, but I was also looking for you."

"Why's that?"

"I enjoyed our breakfast the other morning, and when your mother let me know that you needed a date for the night, I was happy to fill the spot. But you don't seem to be in on the fact that I'm your date, so I'm wondering what's going on."

Casey sighed. "Walker, you're right. I need to clear something up. There's been a mis—"

"Casey!" Aunt Courtney's head thrust through the door from the house, her eyes wide. "You need to come inside. Now."

Casey's heart jolted at the wild seriousness in his aunt's eyes. "What's going on?" She didn't wait to tell him, leaving the door open behind her.

"Excuse me. Sorry," he said to Walker, pushing through into the house. He heard raised voices coming from the entryway as soon as he crossed the threshold. The words were indistinct, muffled by the ongoing chatter and still-playing guitar trio, who were, yes, still doing rounds of "God Rest Ye Merry Gentlemen."

Casey pushed through the guests, following Courtney's strawberry-blond head weaving through the crowd. Walker Ronson was at his heels, and as he drew closer to the front entrance, his heart started to race.

"I was invited. By your son." Joel's dark eyes burned in his pale face. His hair was carefully combed and held back with some sort of product. His crooked mouth was set in a frown, and he clutched a bottle of wine. The one Casey had bought for him.

"Courtney's trying to find Casey now," his father said uncomfortably, glaring around the room and not inviting Joel in. Finally, his gaze landed on Casey. "Son, your friend is here."

"Why didn't you tell us you invited him, honey?" his mother asked. It sounded like she was trying to be lighthearted, but her voice was tense around the edges in a way that caught the attention of the other guests around them.

Casey slid in beside his mother, feeling flushed and breathless. Irritated and excited all at once. "Joel. You came."

"And I shouldn't have, according to your old man."

"Young man, that's not what I said. I simply didn't realize an invitation had been issued. That's all. Casey should have told us. Your mother asked for RSVPs, son."

"So did the guy who ran the inn where Mary and Joseph dropped by," Joel said tightly. "He was big into RSVPs apparently."

"Come in, Joel," Casey's mother said brightly, glancing at the guests who were going quiet to listen in all around them. "Don't be silly, Jonathan. RSVPs aren't that important in this day and age. We have plenty of food and drink. I'm sure Casey knew that, and of course you're welcome here." She took the bottle of wine from Joel and said overly sweetly, "Oh, this is lovely. Thank you for bringing it. I'll just go put it with the rest to be served out tonight."

Joel stepped over the threshold slowly, as though it might be a test and a steel trap might snap around him at any second.

Casey's father clapped Joel on the shoulder and shook his hand, but somehow it came across as a warning more than a welcome. Casey glared at his dad, but Jonathan Stevens had already turned his attention to another guest, and he moved across the room with single-minded focus.

The rest of the guests went back to their regularly scheduled conversations, and Courtney engaged Walker Ronson, taking him by the elbow and moving him away from Casey and Joel.

"Hey," Casey said softly in the dubious privacy of his parents' suddenly empty entryway. He wrapped an arm around Joel's shoulder and pulled him into an awkward hug. Joel was stiff in his arms and pushed his hands firmly against Casey's chest, keeping them about half a foot apart.

"Hey." Joel moved out of Casey's grasp. "You should have seen their faces when they opened the door and saw me instead of one of their hoity-toity rich pals."

"You look amazing."

Joel glanced down at his black jeans and tugged the cuffs of his pressed shirt from beneath the sleeves of his sports jacket. He adjusted his silk, paisley-patterned tie.

Casey kept his arm around Joel's shoulders and steered him away from the main rooms and toward the side stairs that led up to the bedrooms. He wanted to get Joel alone, kiss him, and check him over for damage before sharing him with anyone else.

"Oh, so *he* gets to go upstairs. I see how it is now," Walker said from where he leaned in the doorway to the dining room. He'd apparently gotten away from Courtney, and he smirked at them, his wine refilled and his eyes amused. He stepped forward with his hand out to Joel. "Walker Ronson, and it looks like you're stealing my date."

"Joel Vreeland." Joel's eyes narrowed as he shook Walker's hand. "And are you sure he's you're your date? I thought he was mine."

"Just a misunderstanding," Casey said, smiling at Walker. "I'm really sorry. My mom wasn't aware that I already had a date for the night."

"It's a shame. For me, of course. A stroke of luck for you," Walker said to Joel with a smirk.

"I'm the lucky one," Casey said, putting his hand on Joel's lower back. He was relieved when Joel didn't move away from it but instead scooted closer to Casey's side.

"I'll manage." Walker winked, lifting his glass their way. "Guess I'll get back to working the room. Nice to meet you, Joel."

Casey sighed in relief as Walker headed back into the living area to join the people mingling there. He herded Joel up the stairs to the guest room serving as his room and shut the door behind them. "Oh God, I'm so glad you're here." He pulled Joel close, burying his face in Joel's hair. "You smell so good."

Joel chuckled in his arms. "You smell pretty okay too."

"Why did you come?"

"I don't know. I wasn't going to, but then Angel's insanely hot stepbrother asked me to go a party with him, and all I could think was that if I was going to any party, it was going to be this one, with you."

"Her stepbrother is insanely hot?" A curl of jealousy started in his gut.

"Smoking. Like 'holy crap, how are you not a movie star?' kind of hot." Joel pulled back, gazed at Casey's sweater for a minute, and then broke into a sly grin. "You're with me, huh?"

The jealousy died, and Casey puffed out his chest. "I am. And I'm proud of it."

"Are you ready to face the music?" Joel said, nodding toward the door.

"First I want to show you something. I was going to save it as a surprise for later, but now's a good time. And I can keep you to myself for a few minutes longer."

Joel followed him across the room toward the laptop resting on the desk by the window that looked out on the lake. He got Joel seated in the chair and leaned over his shoulder as he woke the computer and clicked his way to what he wanted to show him first.

"What do you think?" Casey asked. Anxiety balled up in his chest next to excitement and hope. He felt like he had as a kid in Joel's garage, watching Joel play and hoping he'd get to stay.

"You made this? A new cover for my book?" Joel leaned a little closer to the screen. "It's so...professional."

"I took some digital arts classes in college and, obviously, my focus is on marketing and branding. I loved what I read of your book, but—don't take this the wrong way—I only bought it because you wrote it. The current cover doesn't do a great job representing what's inside. This one is so much tighter and thrilling than what you currently have. I thought, maybe, if you were willing, you'd let me redesign all your covers for you. Make them more exciting, memorable, and marketable."

Joel stared at the screen in silence for a long moment, and Casey had a horrifying feeling that maybe he'd overstepped. But then Joel sighed. "I don't know what to say. I made the other cover myself with my limited skills, and I know it sucks. But I can't afford to pay you what this kind of work is worth, no matter how much I love it."

Casey's heart rose. This objection he could handle. "You'd be helping me actually, if you'd let me do this—and more—for you. I have a pretty easy course load next semester, but one of my classes requires that I implement a branding and marketing effort and track the results. I was thinking of offering free help to one of the many small-time actors in New York, maybe help them get a better Facebook presence, a cool website, and a tighter resume, but that didn't really correlate to what I want to do after I graduate. But this—you, the books, and Vreeland's—does. And you'd be able to report back to me about any change in profits and income stream for real, dynamic data to track my results."

"So, you're saying you want to make new covers for me for free?"

"That and more. I'd do covers, set up a website, get you going on Facebook—"

"I hate social media."

"A lot of creative types do, but you can't opt out of it if you want to succeed. It's okay if you don't want to do it yourself. I could run it for you at first."

"I don't know."

"Look." Casey stood at Joel's side and clicked around the Internet, showing Joel the websites and Facebook pages of indie horror authors he'd found who seemed to be pulling in a strong income, given that they'd given up their day jobs in order to write. "All of these folks have healthy social media accounts and online presence. They solicit reviews from sites and promote those reviews. They have a Twitter."

"Hell no."

"Look, just give me a chance. You'd be helping me more than you know. And I could do the same thing for Vreeland's. I haven't mocked anything up, but with some work on ads and online presence, I think we could get the store's profitability up in six months' time, easily."

Joel laughed. "Says the college boy who's never done any of this in the real world for a day in his life."

"Tell me what you have to lose," Casey said, turning to Joel seriously.

Joel took control of the laptop then and clicked back to the new cover Casey had made for his werewolf book. He stared at it for a few moments. "Okay. Let's start with books. If I see an increase in profit there after a month or so, I'll give you leave on Vreeland's too."

Casey grinned. "You like this cover, don't you?"

"It's like you read my mind. It's what I saw in my head when I wrote the book. It's perfect."

Casey puffed up. "I'm going to do a great job for you. I believe in your books, Joel. And I believe in Vreeland's. Thank you for trusting me to help you."

"I thought I was helping you." Joel raised a brow.

"You are. I've been dreading trying to find some narcissistic actor to try to spiff up. This is so much more my speed. This is the kind of thing I want to *do*."

"Yeah," Joel agreed. "I remember when you had that sketchbook full of doodles. Half of them were re-imagined ads for local businesses. You always loved thinking about this sort of thing."

"And I love doing it."

Joel swallowed hard. "I feel like I should offer you something, though. Like a piece of any increase of profit. Twenty-five percent."

"I don't need money, Joel."

"I don't want to feel like a charity case."

"You're not, you're doing me a—"

"I know." Joel cut him off and leaned against him. "Thank you."

Casey put his arm around Joel. "I'm ready to go downstairs now if you are. I want to show you off."

Joel glanced around the room like he might jump out one of the windows to escape going back downstairs, but then put his shoulders back. "I'm ready."

"Can I say you're my boyfriend?"

"Probably safer than calling me the love of your life and personal sex god."

Casey grabbed Joel close against him. "You are, you know."

"Your personal sex god? Of course. I'm pretty good for being so recently a virgin," Joel said, smirking. "Just wait until I have a few years of experience under my belt."

"The love of my life."

"You can't just say things like that."

"Why?"

"Because you can't mean them."

"But I do. I mean everything I say to you."

A knock came at the door then, and Casey pulled away reluctantly. He wanted to tip Joel's head back and kiss him until Joel *felt* how much he meant his words, but instead he crossed the room and yanked the door open to see who'd disturbed them.

"Mom. Hey."

"Your father would like you and your guest to come downstairs," she said tightly. She didn't smile, and her eyes bore into him with the "you're in trouble, young man" look he remembered from childhood.

"Why?"

"It isn't seemly to have you and your…friend…alone upstairs when everyone knows you're gay, dear. You wouldn't want people to gossip about Joel, would you? Don't put him in an awkward position like that."

"Like what?" Joel asked, coming to stand just behind Casey.

"People will make assumptions. They already are. There's talk downstairs that you're Casey's date, and I know you don't want that getting around." She smiled again, all faux brightness and even more faux concern.

"Why wouldn't I?" Joel asked.

His mother tilted her head. "Because you aren't gay, honey." Then, more slowly, like Joel was stupid, "People will think you're gay."

"I am gay," Joel said, lifting his chin. "And I *am* Casey's date. We're together. And I do want people to know that."

"I see." She blinked hard and fast for a moment and then spun on her heel. "Regardless, your father wants you downstairs. Now."

"You didn't tell her?" Joel whispered as he followed Casey from the room.

"It wasn't my news to share. Besides, it's not her business anyway. Or it wasn't until you were ready for it to be."

Downstairs, many of the party guests bordered on intoxicated, and the trio of classical guitarists up on the living room balcony had moved on to playing "Santa Claus is Coming to Town."

Casey grinned at Joel and whispered, "Here we go. Are you ready?"

"I guess I better be," Joel said, smiling strangely as Tawnie Dobbins, the company's CFO, approached with her hand outstretched and obviously looking for an introduction. "Hi, I'm Joel Vreeland." And then, before Casey could say a word, he added, "Casey's boyfriend."

Joy was a brilliant emotion, bright and almost blinding. Casey put his arm around Joel to steady himself as he almost burst with it.

JOEL SAT IN a ridiculously comfortable chair in the corner of Casey's parents' living room, sipping an amazing glass of wine and eating from a small plate of cheese Casey had brought to him. To his right was Walker Ronson, chatting endlessly to another young man about golf and the price of cable television ad spots in the age of streaming media. It wasn't boring so much as soothing, a running pitter-patter of pleasant noise that lacked any sharp edges or wicked points.

Unlike some of the other conversations he'd overheard that night. Especially with Casey's mother.

"*Joel is Casey's special friend,*" he'd heard Mrs. Stevens whispering pointedly to one of her friends. "*A real step down from Theo, I know, but we assume he's a rebound relationship.*"

Her friend had looked Joel up and down and murmured, "*Lord knows we've all had one of those.*"

He'd almost said, "*I can hear you, you realize,*" but he didn't want to upset Casey, and what had he expected? A "welcome to the family" hug? Of course not. The shock and outrage had been half of why he'd come. Though the idea of it had been a lot more fun that the reality. It turned out that maybe he really did want to be loved and accepted by the people close to Casey. Who'd have thunk it?

How annoying.

He sipped the wine again and thought back to the moment he'd seen the cover Casey had mocked up for his werewolf book. He still worried about not paying Casey for the work, but he couldn't afford it, and something had ignited in him when he saw that cover. It'd been so perfect for the story—so professional and real. For the first time since he'd hit publish on his first book, he truly felt like an author and not just an imposter pretending to be a writer.

How was it possible that Casey could come back into his life and turn it around after just a few days? But he had, and every moment things kept getting better. It was more than Joel ever thought he'd have and more than he deserved. It was worth putting up with all the catty comments from Casey's mother and more.

As his eyes swept over the room again, looking for Casey, he caught the eye of Casey's aunt instead. He'd always liked Courtney when he was younger. She'd been nice to him back then. He straightened up and smiled as she headed in his direction. He hoped she'd be nice to him now.

"You've got our little Casey swoony as a lovesick schoolboy," Courtney said, dropping into the chair next to him, a pink, foamy cocktail in hand. Her red dress poofed around her thighs, and she smoothed it down as she grinned at him from between glossy, ruby lips. "Are you equally smitten?"

"He's cool. I like him," Joel said, shrugging. "I could do worse."

Courtney laughed, tossing her head back as she did. "So it's love then."

Joel smiled into his wine. It'd been the weirdest few days of his life. He didn't know what to say. "A Christmas miracle is more like it."

And just like a Christmas miracle, unlikely to outlive the holidays. But it was nice to believe. To let them both believe for a little while. And, maybe if they were lucky…

Not that Joel had ever been lucky a day in his life.

Sitting close to the gas fireplace and thinking of the chances that he'd be fortunate enough to make this work with Casey, sweat slipped down the side of his face.

"So, you run your old man's store now?" Courtney asked.

"I do."

"It's probably a good investement, too," Courtney said. "In Atlanta, some of the older mom-and-pop stores are really making a comeback. My friend Mark's parents just sold their home-and-garden place to a young hipster couple hoping to keep it going. They've retired on the profit they made."

"Oh yeah?" Joel tilted his head, an inkling of an idea scratching at his mind. "How long had they been in business?"

"It's warm in here," Courtney said, fanning herself with one hand as she took another sip of her drink. "Do you want to step outside for some fresh air, and we can keep talking?"

"Sure." He looked around for Casey but didn't see him. "He said he was going to the bathroom. But that was a while ago."

"He probably got waylaid by a mouthy guest on his way back. He'll find you. Don't worry." Courtney led the way toward the French doors that opened to the back porch. The reflection in the windows along the back of the house showed the party was winding down, as guests had dropped off through the night.

"Oh, let me grab my coat," Courtney said as she pulled open the door. "I'll meet you out there."

Joel stepped onto the porch and took a slow, deep breath. The night air cleaved through the stuffy heat of his lungs, and he sighed, wishing desperately for a cigarette.

"He lives in a trailer, Casey. A filthy, rundown trailer."

"It's not filthy, Dad. For God's sake, you don't even know him."

Joel's heart stopped. Casey and Mr. Stevens's voices rose from the patio beneath the porch.

"You think I don't know this boy? I *was* this boy. Or could have been." Mr. Stevens's voice shook with anger. "Do you have any idea how hard I worked to climb up out of the poverty I was born into? And now you're asking me to just watch you turn around and climb into bed with it? No. Absolutely not."

"Joel isn't—"

"It doesn't matter what you think he is or isn't. What matters is I hold the purse strings to your future. Your tuition? Your apartment? Wharton? All of that is up to me. My money. My way."

"Joel isn't up for negotiation," Casey said sharply. "I love him."

"Then un-love him. Because this isn't happening, Casey. We've worked too hard to get where we are as a family for me to watch you get involved with someone who doesn't have any kind of future in this world. Take my word for it: he'll be on dope before the end of the year, if he isn't already. Like my brother Donny. Like my cousin Jon in Pikeville. People like that are all the same."

"People like *what*?"

"People like Joel Vreeland."

"What the actual hell, Dad? Joel isn't on heroin, and he's not like Donny or Jon at all. Why are you being such an asshole? It's Christmas. Can't you just love me for who I am and rejoice in what makes me happy? For once?"

"Why *him*? What was wrong with Theo? You should have chased after that boy and begged him to stay with you. He cared about you! And now you'll never do better than him. Walker Ronson isn't even close to his league. But no. Instead of doing the smart thing, you let Theo go, so you can rub willies with riffraff."

Casey's voice rattled with rage. "Joel is a business owner and an author. He's smart and funny, and I've loved him for as long as I can remember."

"So long as you're with him, you won't have my support, financial or otherwise. I scrambled my way up, and I won't have you grabbing my ankles to pull me back down. Even having him here tonight was an embarrassment. After we told everyone about Theo last year? How do we explain this step down for you? It's humiliating."

"Dad, you need to think very carefully about what you're saying."

"No, you need to think. That therapist we pay for? Done. That school? Finished. Degree or no degree."

"You're not serious."

"I'm serious as a heart attack. If you're with Joel Vreeland, or someone like him, I won't provide you with a single dime. Not now. Not ever."

The light footsteps behind him drew Joel to attention. Courtney's arm slipped around his waist.

"Come on," she whispered. "Neither one of them would want you to hear this."

"Too late."

"Joel," she said softly when he tugged free of her and went back into the house.

The steam on the windows and laughter bouncing off the walls along with the ceaseless guitar carols smothered him. He pushed through the room, bumping into people, searching for the place Casey's mother had taken his coat. Finally finding a pile of them on a counter in a small room off the kitchen, he grabbed his and checked the pockets for his keys. Then he was out the front door with the frigid air slapping his face. The Chevy's seat was cold on his ass, but the steering wheel took him where he needed to go.

The credit card he'd used too much lately was put to good use again. At the gas station he filled his tank before ducking inside for some cigarettes and other essentials for the upcoming night and morning.

His newly lit cigarette tasted like misery as he pulled the heat into his lungs and exhaled it out the open window while he drove aimlessly down dark country roads with Jonathan Stevens's threats rattling around between his ears.

He needed to go somewhere safe. Somewhere he knew he was cared for. He barked out a laugh. That sure as hell wasn't with his own family. Hearing Casey's dad's threats reminded him of his own father's abuse, and, fuck, he wasn't going to take it anymore. He'd put up with that kind of thing for way too long. He was a grown man and he was done with begging to be loved. He'd never try to convince his father—any father—to love him again. And speaking of love, he needed to forget about loving Casey Stevens. It'd been stupid to think he could have him for even a little while. He pressed on the gas, the night speeding away behind him. He'd always known forever was off the table.

Chapter Twenty-One

C ASEY GROANED IN frustration as he pulled into the Vreeland's parking lot and was forced to admit Joel's Chevy wasn't there either. He'd already been to the trailer, and he had no idea where else to look.

He checked his phone again, but there were no missed calls and no new texts from Joel. He scrolled through the fifteen texts he'd sent in the last hour and a half, all some rendition of the same thing: *Joel, I'm so sorry you overheard any of that. Let's talk.*

There were some that were more pleading, some that went on about his father being an asshole, and some that were just: *Are you okay? Please call me.* But Joel hadn't responded, and Casey completely understood why.

What would he have done back when he was with Theo if he'd ever overheard Theo's parents saying things like that about him? He'd have been out of there faster than a New York minute. Just imagining it made his stomach curdle with humiliation. He couldn't blame Joel for doing the same.

He parked in the Vreeland's lot to brainstorm. What should he do? Where would Joel go? He pulled out his phone again and texted RJ.

Hey, man. What's Becca's number?

He left it at that and got out of his car to pace the length of the Christmas tree lot while he waited. The scent of the trees filled his nose, and the cold air made his eyes burn, but it was only two trips down and back before his phone buzzed with RJ's response.

He gave the number first and then said, *Hope things are going well for you and Joel. Will be in NYC in March with Pearl Necklace if you want to hang.*

He didn't bother replying right away, clicking the number RJ had sent and going straight to a voice call. He hoped Joel was with Becca or, if not, that she might have some idea of where he might be. She was obviously his closest friend and Casey's only shot.

"This must be Casey," Becca said in lieu of a normal greeting. "RJ texted to ask if it was okay to give you my number," she explained when he confirmed his identity. "But, sweet cheeks, you just missed him if it's Joel you're looking for."

"Crap." He climbed back into his SUV, turning on the heat to warm his cold fingers and nose. He'd left in such a hurry he hadn't bothered looking for his coat or gloves. "How was he? Is he okay?"

"Believe it or not, Joel's not so fragile that your daddy's assholery is gonna break him completely. But I'm glad you're looking for him all the same. I wasn't sure about you."

"Do you know where he was going?"

"Why? What do you plan to say or do to make up for what he heard?"

"He heard my father making my life all about him. That's all he heard. I don't know what Joel needs, but I'll say anything, do anything, so long as we're okay."

"Wow. Is it his cranky-ass attitude you love best or his weird, crook-ed smile?"

"All of it."

"Aw, such a sweetheart, aren't you?" Becca laughed.

"Has he gone back home or...?"

"Home. He's not actually avoiding you so much as doing that thing he does. You remember that thing he does, don't you?"

"The big shove?"

"The big shove," she agreed. A woman's voice sounded in the background, and Becca sighed. "Coming, dear." Sarcasm rolled through her tone. "Gotta go. I'm being summoned."

"Thanks, Becca. I'll head over to Joel's now."

"Listen, if it's not going to work out because of the things your dad said, just be honest with yourself and with him now. Don't drag it out, okay? Make it quick and complete. He'll live. And you'll live too. But if you're going to do this thing? Do it all the way. Because he deserves someone who'll go all in for him. Who'll give up everything and everyone to be with him. He's that good of a guy. Understand?"

"I do."

"God, Andie, I'm saying bye now. Chill. Bye, Casey. Let's talk again sometime when life isn't a drama-rama, and we both don't have places to go."

On the drive back to Joel's, Casey took his time, lining up his words carefully, trying to guess what Joel would do or say when he got there.

Stepping up to the front porch of the trailer, Casey heard the Gaslight Anthem's signature grunge guitar and Brian Fallon's gravelly-voiced lead vocals vibrating against the door. The lyrics to "Get Hurt," a song represented on Joel's forearm with an upside-down red heart like the album cover, came through loud and clear. Casey rested his forehead on the door for a second, listening and wondering what Joel was doing, thinking, *feeling* in there.

Finally, he raised his hand to knock, but before he could, the door jerked open and Joel stood there with his eyes narrowed, dark hair hanging in his face, and a cigarette between his lips. "Hey," he said, sucking deeply and exhaling a stream of smoke up between them.

"Can I come in?"

Joel stepped back and motioned for Casey to enter. Bruno greeted Casey with his usual enthusiasm, but Joel just turned and walked into the kitchen, where he'd apparently baked more chocolate chip cookies from his frozen stash. Casey followed and sat at the table, where there was a pack of cigarettes, a tube of lube, and a box of condoms.

He swallowed hard. "I see you've been shopping."

The music pounded around them, coming from the speakers in the living room.

"I didn't know if you'd come tonight," Joel said, raising a brow challengingly and taking a drag on his cigarette. "But I figured if you did, no matter how things go from here, we'd want these."

Casey's heart pounded as he stood, took a step closer to Joel, and stole the mostly-smoked cigarette from his mouth. He felt the damp paper against his own lips and shivered. Taking a drag, he then put it out in the sink and tossed the stub into the trash.

"I thought you were going to quit."

"I was. But..." Joel shrugged, eyes narrow and hard, his lips wet from his nervous tongue. "I broke down and bought a pack after I left your parents' house. I figured if you didn't come by tonight, I'd at least have the satisfaction of a smoke."

"I called Becca. She told me you'd been at her place."

Joel's mouth tightened. "She's my person when shit goes bad. That's all."

"And has shit gone bad?"

"What the fuck do you think, Casey? Your father said he was cutting you off if you stay involved with me and—"

"It's not his business. He doesn't have to know."

"You want me to be a secret?"

"No. It's just... No. I don't want that at all. What I want is for us to agree to see what happens. My dad said some things. So what? They're things he probably doesn't mean. I know him. He'll have regrets later."

"Believe me. I know all about dads who say and do things they regret later, or at least pretend to regret, but what if he does mean it? What then?"

Casey swallowed hard. He'd done well at NYU. But if his father wasn't going to pay for his final semester, then he'd just have to find another way to complete his education.

"It doesn't matter," Casey said quietly, trying to calm Joel down again. "I'll get a job. I'll go to school here in Knoxville. Or I won't graduate at all. That's fine too."

"Are you insane? That's not *fine*. You're too good for that, Casey. You need a degree."

"Why? All I really want is to get involved with people's businesses, with a community, and contribute to good people's growth and prosperity. Hell, if I could help you with your books and turn Vreeland's into a successful store, that'd be satisfying enough to me. If I could help you make the store part of the fabric of Knoxville—"

"It already *is* part of the fabric of Knoxville."

"I know, but there are ways to capitalize on that and—"

"And I haven't done a good job with it," Joel agreed, his fingers trembling as he raked his hand into his dark hair, messing it up even more. "I'm not a great manager or marketer, I know. I'd rather be home, working on books. Which I'm also no good at marketing."

"I've already said I'd help with that."

"But you have so many more opportunities ahead of you. You can't leave school to try to shore up my failing life."

"Your life isn't a failure. It's just that it's too hard to do this all alone." Casey stepped closer. "You don't have to be alone, Joel. I could be there with you, for you. We could work together."

"From what your asshole dad was saying, it sounds like the least of it is your schooling. You'd be giving up *them*, as well. The family. *Your* family."

"And that's on him." Casey's stomach rolled at the thought of not seeing his parents anymore, of not being part of their life, of losing his connection to them. He was an only child. They were all he knew.

He wished he could call Ann and get her advice on how to move forward with all of this, how to talk to his father. But if his dad wasn't paying for her services anymore, then he didn't want to rack up additional expenses. Of course, he'd owe her at least a call or email in explanation of what was going on and to cancel their future appointments.

"You don't mean that. You'll regret it, and then you'll hate me. Right now, living here seems exciting and fun. A place with just the two of us, where we can be alone. A love nest, or whatever the fuck. But that's not reality. I'm broke, Casey. I can't support myself, much less you. I catch fish out of the fucking lake to supplement my meals, and sometimes I go hungry. I don't want that for you. I never want to see you eating ramen for a week because that's all we can afford. It's not what I want for you. Ever. Don't you see? If you're not going to be reasonable for yourself, then I'll be reasonable for you."

"What are you saying?"

"I'm saying that we can have tonight. But tomorrow you'll go home to daddy and tell him you're accepting his deal. I'll be out of your life, but you'll at least *have* a life—the life you were always supposed to live. Without me in it."

"So you think I'm going to…what?" He tapped the box of condoms. "Fuck you and then just leave?"

"It'll be a nice memory for us both."

"A nice memory?" Casey shook his head. "For one thing, no. For another thing, you've never even been fucked before. It might not be a 'nice memory' at all. You might hate it. Some guys do."

"I won't hate it."

"This is so not the point! But how the fuck would you know?"

"Because it's all I've ever wanted. To be with you. Like that. And if I get that? Tonight? Then it's a gift. A Christmas miracle. And that's more than I ever thought I'd have. Don't ruin this by making it more than it needs to be. Don't ruin your life or your relationship with your parents—"

"What relationship with my parents?"

Joel threw his hands in the air. "The one where they don't hate and hurt you every damn day."

"Like your dad does to you?"

Joel shrugged. "He can't put his hands on me anymore at least. But he still manages to get in some abuse. His mouth is good for that."

"You don't have to take that."

"I know. Believe me, I get it." Joel shivered.

"My parents think they can tell me what to do and who to be. That's not the life I deserve either, is it? Don't I deserve a life I choose? One of my own design and making?"

"You're special. You could have the entire world if you want it."

"You say that because you love me. I know because I feel the same way about you, and I want you to have the whole world too."

"The difference is, you *can* have it!"

"There is no difference at all because I don't want it if you're not with me."

Joel scratched at his eyebrow with his thumb, obviously searching for something else to say to convince Casey that they couldn't work.

But Casey wasn't going to hear it. Maybe he was naïve, and maybe he was spoiled, but he didn't really believe he'd be cut off, and even if he was…so what? They'd find a way to survive. He believed in the two of them. They were magic together.

"Can we stop fighting now?" Joel asked sullenly. He flicked the condom box with his finger. "Will you please just fuck me?"

Casey rubbed a hand over his face, calming himself. "I won't 'just fuck you,' but I'll make love with you, if that's what you really want right now."

"That's what I want."

"You're sure?"

"I'm fucking sure, Casey." Joel snatched up the cigarettes, but Casey pried them out of his hand and tossed them onto the table. Instead, he grabbed the condoms and the lube. "Let's go then."

JOEL KICKED THE door closed behind them, his body trembling as he clenched fistfuls of Casey's sweater and tugged him into another heated kiss. Casey tossed the box of condoms and lube onto the bed, but Joel kept his eyes on Casey's, diving deep into his dark, dilated pupils. Casey's hot breath puffed against his mouth, and they kissed again. They shucked their clothes quickly, stopping only to click on the space heaters against the chill of the room.

Bruno whined outside the door, but Joel ignored it, shaking all over as Casey gripped his biceps and took another brutal kiss. Their cocks pressed against each other, hard and leaking slippery pre-come that streaked over his stomach. When Casey pressed him down onto the bed, Joel closed his eyes, moaning at the friction of their body hair over skin and the delicious slide of their bodies as they moved together, cock-to-cock, gripping and kissing and biting as they grunted and moaned.

Casey's hand slipped down between Joel's legs, bypassing his cock and taint to rub against his asshole. Joel clutched him closer, wrapping his arms around Casey's neck, kissing him hard as he spread his legs wider, giving more access. Casey's fingers were dry and his nails blunt on Joel's tender anus, and Joel shivered as Casey stroked him there over and over until his asshole quivered and his cock flexed, pushing out a bead of pre-come.

Joel's eyes rolled up as Casey sat back, shoved his legs up, and lowered his mouth to kiss Joel's ball sac and the sticky head of his cock where it pulsed against his belly. Then he slipped down to lick and kiss the exquisitely enervated ring of his ass.

Joel groaned, his body shaking as he held his knees back and let Casey lick him there. He squirmed when Casey pushed his tongue inside, the sensation so good and so intense, tingling and too much all at once. He shoved one knuckle in his mouth, trying to hold back his shout as Casey worked his tongue deeper and then drew out to lick the trembling edges of his asshole.

Tears pricked his eyes again, and he couldn't hold in a small sob when Casey gently, sweetly kissed his inner thighs and whispered, "I love you, Joel. Let me show you how much."

Joel's thighs shook, and his toes curled when Casey pressed a spit-slick finger inside, awkward and perfect at once, and hooked up to rub against his prostate. "Oh, fuck," he whimpered. "That's…" How did it feel so good and so different when it was someone else's finger probing inside? His own never quite got the right angle, and Casey knew exactly what he was doing.

Joel's knees quivered, and his hips jerked up, his cock spilling more pre-come onto his dark treasure trail as Casey kissed his taint and balls. Joel's cock was harder than it'd ever been, an aching, needy thing that left his head swimming in lust.

Casey drew his fingers back and reached for the lube and condoms. He broke open the tube while Joel watched through wet, slit eyes. Casey slicked two fingers, then a third, and kissed Joel's knee as he leaned in close and pressed inside up to the first knuckle. Joel gasped as his ass tightened in resistance.

"Shh," Casey soothed, taking hold of Joel's cock finally and stroking it gently. His own cock pressed hard and hot against his firm stomach, and Joel watched as Casey rolled his hips to get some friction on it. "Just relax. I'm going to make this good for you."

Joel nodded and closed his eyes again. His body shook enough that he worried Casey would stop, but he didn't. He pressed firmly, and soon he had two fingers inside, rubbing against Joel's prostate, making him gasp and cry out, roll his hips, and release small wads of pre-come— enough that it slipped down the side of his stomach, a slick track of his need.

"Have you done this to yourself?" Casey whispered.

Joel nodded.

"Used toys?"

Joel shook his head. He'd always meant to get a dildo, but money was tight, and the good ones were ridiculously expensive. He'd made do with his fingers, and he'd worked up to four inside himself before. Though that had hurt.

"I'm going to open you up wide for me," Casey said, his voice gruff. He massaged Joel's leg with his free hand. He pushed the third finger in, and Joel hissed low and hard, the sting harsh enough to make him go tense. "Breathe for me. That's it."

Joel grunted, reaching down between his thighs to feel where Casey's fingers went into him. He held onto Casey's wrist, keeping him steady, and when he could breathe without tension, he let go. He writhed on Casey's fingers as he started to move them inside, hitting his prostate, massaging him open, pressing against his inner walls and stretching his anus as he finger-fucked him confidently.

"That's it," Casey whispered. "Fuck, I'm going to come just watching you like this."

Joel forced his eyes open, gazing up at Casey, who stared at him with a flushed, wild-eyed expression and a wet, open mouth. His cock responded to that beautiful sight, and his balls drew up tight. Casey pushed forward on his knees, shoving his fingers deeper, and took Joel's mouth with a hungry kiss.

Joel squirmed on his fingers as their tongues slid together, and the overwhelming sensations from his mouth and full ass left him undone, lost on emotion and pleasure-pain until Casey withdrew his fingers and sat back on his heels, staring down at him needily.

"Ready?" Casey asked, reaching for the box of condoms.

Joel nodded, his heart thudding in his throat, his legs shaking worse than they had when they'd first started. He watched as Casey rolled the condom onto his red, thick cockhead, and then slicked it with liberal amounts of lube.

"This might hurt, but just breathe and it'll get better," Casey murmured, lining his cock up between Joel's ass cheeks and pressing the head against Joel's slick, tingling hole.

Joel nodded, words so far beyond him now that he didn't bother to try. Casey's gaze captured his own. He held it as long as he could, until the intensity of penetration took his breath away, and his eyes rolled back, his breath escaping him in a cry of pain and pleasure, a shocked gasp that pierced the bubble around them.

"Fuck!" Joel shouted, his body quaking, his asshole spasming hard around the intrusion.

Casey gripped Joel's thighs and shoved his legs up higher. He backed out a little, and when Joel had caught his breath, he pushed back in. Slower, harder, and thick as fuck, until Joel was thoroughly taken over, penetrated deeply, the root of Casey's cock all the way inside and his pubic hair pressed flush against Joel's ass.

"You feel so good," Casey moaned, dropping carefully onto Joel, keeping his legs spread wide by hooking them under the knees with his elbows. "So hot inside. So tight."

Joel felt hot tears leak from his eyes, but he couldn't be ashamed of them, not when he was convulsing with pleasure and need. His asshole gripped and released Casey's cock in a rhythm he couldn't control, and his hips jerked in small circles, wanting more and less at once—wanting everything, wanting to come and scream and get fucked like an animal. Wanting Casey to make love to him. Slowly. Quickly. Whatever it took.

"Just move."

Casey laughed against his mouth, kissing his joy into Joel, and he swallowed it down as they finally moved together. Casey was gentle, and Joel was grateful because when he moved, everything got good and scary all at once, the pleasure so intense and the stretch so big that he couldn't do anything but hold on and feel.

He buried his face in Casey's neck, breathing in his sweet scent, crying out against his skin and taking Casey's thrusts hungrily while tears spilled out of him uncontrollably. Tears of joy, tears of need, and tears he didn't understand the source of.

"Love you," Casey murmured, taking his time, moving his hips at a strong, steady pace and making Joel feel like he was going to break open under his patience and affection. He released Joel's legs and wrapped his arms around Joel's body. Joel's aching cock rubbed between Casey's stomach and his own, a hot, sweat-slick tunnel that left him on the verge of coming, but not close enough.

Casey kissed his shoulders and neck, murmuring love constantly, and Joel wrapped his legs around Casey's waist, holding him inside, making his thrusts shorter, sharper, and tighter. His asshole burned and spasmed, his body opening more with each plunge of Casey's thick cock, which jammed against his prostate with nearly every thrust.

He felt like his was going to break apart, his emotions and body joined together in an ecstatic understanding of sex and love and fucking, of need and want and pleasure. Of being loved, and of feeling that love in his body, in his soul, and giving himself entirely in return. Trusting that he wouldn't be hurt. Not right now, and not with this.

Joel reached between their bodies, taking hold of his cock, and he jerked himself as Casey moved inside him. They kissed again, and Joel's blood pulsed in his veins wildly as he rushed up into orgasm, gripped by it hard and suddenly.

Agony-pleasure roared through him, and he cried out, gripping Casey close with his free arm and squeezing him into his body with his legs. His asshole gripped painfully as he came, and came again, the fat wads of come splattering hot heat between them.

Casey shook in his arms and then whimpered before he convulsed, shouting and moaning with pleasure. As Joel rode out the remnants of his own shaking orgasm, he felt Casey's cock expand in his ass and the pulse of his dick as he came too. Veins stuck out on Casey's flexed neck as he was wracked with pleasure. He collapsed on top of Joel, quivering in his arms, sweaty and gasping, for several long, unreal, beautiful minutes.

"I love you," Joel whispered when his voice worked again.

"I love you, too," Casey answered, his smile evident in his tone, even though his face was pressed to the pillow beside Joel's head.

The disengagement of Casey's body from Joel's was weird, and when he had pulled free, Joel wanted him back in. But Casey was softening, and the condom needed to be disposed of, so Joel lay back and played with the come that was drying on his chest and stomach while Casey took care of the necessities. His asshole felt tender and stretched, and he clenched it gently, as he brought the come up to his nipples, outlining them with the slippery remainder of his climax.

Casey's eyebrows went up, and a smile lifted his lips. "You're so hot," he whispered, dropping back onto the bed and scooping more of Joel's come up, helping to smear it on his nipples.

Joel said nothing, only arched his back when Casey bent to suck and nibble his way from pec to pec, and then down to lick clean the come from his ticklish tummy. He spread his thighs as Casey went lower still, taking Joel's limp cock into his mouth and sucking it gently. It wasn't long before he was hard again and Casey had two fingers inside, making him crazy, making him beg for it.

Then Casey was making love to him again, until Joel didn't know where his body ended and Casey's began.

Chapter Twenty-Two

WITH JOEL QUIVERING in his arms and the most sweetly vulnerable expression on his crookedly handsome face, Casey was consumed with gratitude. He'd never thought he could ever be this lucky—to have someone trust him so much. To have *Joel* trust him so much—with everything: his virginity, his heart, their lives. Though he still needed to convince him on that last front.

"You okay?" Casey asked, nuzzling Joel's sweaty hair.

They'd fucked again, and Joel had reacted almost the same way as the first time: hungrily, passionately, and with tears. He hoped Joel wouldn't get weird about that like he had the first time he'd cried. It was intense sharing intimacy with someone you loved, and if Casey were a different person, he'd probably cry too. He was honored to be the one who got to see Joel undone like that.

"Yeah, I'm fine," Joel said, his voice ragged out and gentle with exhaustion.

"Everything feel okay?"

"I said I'm fine." He sounded too tired to be as snappish as he obviously wanted to be.

Casey snuggled in closer. "What did you think?"

"I was too busy feeling and then coming my brains out to think." Joel yawned and twisted in Casey's arms to face him. He kissed Casey's chin and then shrugged. "I could do it again. I mean, if you're up for it already."

Casey snorted. "You're tired."

"That's okay. You could do all the work. I'd just lay here and let you make me feel good."

Casey's heart clenched, and he whispered in Joel's ear, "I love making you feel good."

Joel shuddered and closed his eyes, rolling into Casey and pressing his face against Casey's shoulder. He didn't say anything, but he let Casey continue to hold him, so Casey took that as a good sign.

"It felt good to me too," Casey said. "Being inside you. It was amazing."

"I have all kinds of questions for you I shouldn't ask," Joel murmured against his skin. "Like who touched you first? Who got to be your first kiss? Who had the honor of teaching you to fuck like that?"

"No one that mattered. You're the first person I've ever been with that I've loved, so… In a way, maybe I was a virgin too."

Joel leaned away enough so that Casey could see him roll his eyes. "Was it that Theo guy?"

"No. Let's not talk about it right now."

Joel nodded and went back to pressing his face against Casey's skin, rubbing his stubble against his shoulder like a cat.

"It should have been you, anyway," Casey said. "No one else matters because it should have been you."

"I'm glad it wasn't. You're thick as fuck, and if you'd tried that on me without knowing what you were doing, I'd probably never let a dick near my ass again."

Casey laughed. "But since I did know what I was doing?"

"Like I said, I'm ready for round three when you are."

"And like I said, you're tired."

"And like I said, you can do the work."

"And like I said…" Casey couldn't remember what he'd said. "My dick's tired."

Joel laughed and rolled up to a sitting position. "I have to piss."

Casey felt cold in the damp, sweaty places where their skin had pressed together. "Don't go outside. It's too cold."

Joel dragged himself free of the tangled blankets and shuffled toward the door. "I'll be back. Don't worry."

The sound of Bruno heaving himself out of his dog bed reached him along with Joel's gentle tones as he spoke quietly to him, and then the splash of Joel's piss in the toilet. Casey rolled onto his back, his skin and bones alive with joy, and tried to wait patiently. As the sound of Joel washing his hands drifted into the room, Casey's cock thickened, and he touched it with the palm of his hand, stroking it lightly.

When Joel returned, careful to shut the door on Bruno again, he paused in the doorway, watching Casey stroke himself. He whispered, "I'm going to be honest right now, and that's not something I always do easily or well."

"Okay." Casey's heart clenched, but his cock stayed firm.

"I'm scared to let you fuck me with that thing again, but, also, if you don't I'll be pretty pissed off too."

"Come here," Casey whispered. "Ride me this time."

Joel swallowed hard and approached with wide eyes and his mouth slack. He watched as Casey rolled another condom on and applied the lube, and then he crawled up Casey's body, thighs shaking, and let Casey guide him onto his cock.

He threw his head back as the tightness of his anus gave way to the determination of Casey's thrust up, and he rested his hands in the middle of Casey's chest as he slid down, slow and hot, until his asshole had taken every inch of Casey one more time.

"Fuck," he moaned again, just like the first time.

Casey rubbed Joel's thighs and took hold of his burgeoning cock, stroking him to full hardness. Joel tipped his chin forward and gazed down at Casey with his dark-brown eyes, and then he moved, lifting and falling slowly until he finally dropped down to clench Casey's biceps and started riding him hard.

Casey gritted his teeth and let Joel take him deep again and again, harder and harder until he groaned and came again. Joel moaned, collapsing on Casey's chest and sliding off his spent cock. Joel hadn't come again, but when Casey made a move to jerk him off, he batted his hand away. "You're right," he whispered. "I'm too tired."

After disposing of the third condom, Casey curled up behind Joel, making him the little spoon. "Well?" he asked again. "You still okay?"

"I'm great." He reached behind to take Casey's jaw in his palm. "Don't worry so much. I liked it."

"If you ever want to try it the other way, I'm willing to do that," Casey said.

Joel shrugged. "Maybe. I like it this way."

"Me too." Being the guy who got to see Joel Vreeland fall apart on his cock? Yeah, he liked that plenty.

"Tomorrow is Christmas," Casey murmured.

"Yeah." Joel shifted in Casey's arms, questions in his eyes.

"There's supposed to be a Christmas morning breakfast with Aunt Courtney. Then we were supposed to open presents, and, after that, Mom was going to start on thawing out the Christmas dinner Heather prepared last week."

Joel's eyes held his, but he said nothing.

"I guess they'll do all that without me."

"You can go home, Casey. You don't owe me more than tonight."

"I don't think I'm welcome there, and even if I was..." He trailed off, not sure if Joel wanted to hear what he had to say about it.

"It's your family. Of course you're welcome there."

"But I don't want to be." Especially if Joel wasn't welcome, if he couldn't bring Joel with him and have everyone be happy about it. "I can't go there like nothing happened."

"It's late," Joel finally said, his voice gravelly with exhaustion. "Why not wait to see what the morning brings?"

Sleep hovered around him, and Casey knew they should talk more, nail something down, either about their relationship or about Casey's parents, but he also knew it wasn't going to happen tonight. He pulled Joel close, let his eyes slide shut, and when he woke to a clear, bright Christmas morning, he was beyond grateful to find Joel still in his arms.

"MERRY CHRISTMAS," CASEY said, kissing Joel's cheek. His hair was wet from the shower, and he smelled fresh as he gathered Joel in a hug from behind.

"I'm trying to cook here," Joel muttered, but he tilted his head to the side so that Casey could kiss the crook of his neck.

When Casey released him, Joel quickly flipped the strips of bacon he was frying in a too-small frying pan. He'd bought the bacon at the gas station on his credit card when he'd picked up the condoms and cigarettes, to go along with the carton of eggs Casey had purchased before. He smiled as Casey greeted Bruno and plopped down at the small kitchen table with the half-eaten box of doughnuts he'd brought yesterday.

Glancing over his shoulder, Joel's heart raced. Casey looked delicious in his boxers and nothing else. There was even a red mark on Casey's shoulder that Joel had put there himself, and there was a strange puff of pride inside whenever he looked at it.

Joel had put on his jeans and T-shirt after showering while Casey slept in. He felt stronger somehow in his clothes while Casey lounged in his underwear. He raised his brow pointedly as Casey took a doughnut out of the box and chomped a giant bite from it. Powdered sugar floated around his mouth, coating his beautiful lips.

"What? Doughnuts are totally a healthy breakfast," Casey said with a smile.

Joel went back to frying up more strips of bacon and ignoring Bruno's drops of drool as they landed on his bare feet. The mobile home was toasty warm, which was good, since the weather had dropped well below freezing overnight.

"So, what are you going to do?" Joel asked. "Are you going to call them?"

"I'll call them," Casey said, but the joviality was stripped from his voice, and his shoulders sagged a little. "I guess I'd better do it now."

Joel's breath came in a little faster. "What are you going to tell them?"

"You'll see."

As Joel plated the eggs and bacon, Casey found his phone and frowned at the touchscreen. "There sure are plenty of texts from Mom and Aunt Courtney."

Joel didn't know if he was supposed to ask what they said or not, so he didn't.

"Okay. Here goes," Casey murmured, placing the call. "Hey, Mom. I'm okay. I'm with Joel."

He almost wished he could hear Mrs. Stevens's side of the conversation, but most of him knew that would be a terrible idea. He couldn't quite let go of the things he'd heard Jonathan Stevens say the night before, so he didn't need to add to them. He shook some pepper over the eggs on both plates and then carried them to the table.

"I understand that," Casey said archly. "Dad says a lot of things he doesn't mean when he's upset, but I think he meant a lot of what he said too." He paused while his mother spoke. "I don't think so, Mom. I don't want to be there today. I'm sorry, but no."

Joel put the plate in front of Casey and took a seat across from him. Part of him wanted to tell Casey to forget everything, to go home. But part of him wanted to keep Casey close, to have this holiday together and seize everything he could for a few more days. Maybe then he'd have the strength to send Casey back home to his parents, who would surely accept his apology and pay for his return to NYU.

What was a fling with a guy from the wrong side of the lake in the scheme of life? They'd forgive Casey for that, wouldn't they? And he'd have a beautiful memory of the time he and Casey had had together. His stomach knotted up, and he could barely swallow the bite of bacon he'd taken.

"That's just it, Mom. This isn't about you and what you want. It's not about what Dad wants either. This is my life. And after a long time of trying to do things the way dad wants me to do them and not being happy? I'm done. I'll do the rest of my life my way."

Casey pushed his uneaten plate of food back and stood, pacing by the table. Joel couldn't eat either. He wished Casey hadn't taken his new package of cigarettes and hidden them at some point, because he sure could use one right now.

"Crying won't change this, Mom. If you're upset, I'm not the one to talk to. Talk to Dad. So long as the man I love isn't welcome in your house, then I don't consider myself welcome either."

Joel shook his head, wanting to stop Casey from making these declarations, but it was done, and he couldn't shove the words back into Casey's mouth now.

"Find a way to enjoy your day," Casey said more gently. "Hang out with Aunt Courtney. Have a merry Christmas. It's going to be okay, Mom." He rubbed his face and shook his head. "I don't know what to say about the presents. I guess if Dad's not going to continue to pay for my school or my apartment, then he probably won't want me to have whatever's under the tree either." He laughed bitterly. "No, I'm not being a brat, Mom. I'm being myself. It's a new thing, and I know you'll probably find it surprising, but I'm done minimizing who I am to make things easier. And I won't minimize who I love. Ever."

Joel pushed the eggs around with his fork. They looked rubbery already. It was a shame to waste good food since he so rarely had the money for things like eggs and bacon, but he couldn't possibly chew it up now. Not with the tension rolling off Casey like steam from a train. He scraped most of it off for Bruno who ate it with delight.

"Fine. Tell Aunt Courtney I'm sorry. And I'll stop over tomorrow to get my things and then, sometime before I'm supposed to drive back to New York, we can schedule a time to talk as a family about whether or not that's even going to happen now."

His lower lip trembled a little at whatever his mother had to say. "I know, Mom. I love you too. And it really will be okay. One way or another. I promise."

Then he disconnected the phone and wiped a hand over his face again. The light that'd been in his eyes when they woke had died.

"So?"

"I'm spending Christmas with you. Hope that's okay."

Joel cleared his throat, trying to come up with the right response.

"Please tell me you aren't thinking I should apologize to them, throw you under the bus, and grovel at their feet," Casey said, frowning into his coffee cup before grabbing another doughnut and ignoring the now-cold bacon and eggs completely.

"Aren't you thinking that?"

"No. Not even a little." He glanced up at Joel sharply. "I'm thinking that we'll have a great Christmas here. You, me, and Bruno."

"I'm not seeing the problem with that." Joel smiled, though his stomach still hadn't loosened up. He wished he could tell Casey's father where he could go stick his bullshit.

Bruno pranced by Casey, hoping for his uneaten food. But Casey stared off into space, his expression falling through several phases of emotion, starting with optimism and ending with a gloomy despair that Joel knew all too well.

"I have a little money put aside," Casey said. "I was saving it for travel after I graduate, like we talked about before, but I can use it to pay for tuition at UT and keep us in groceries for a little while. It won't last long, though. So, I'll need a job. At least my car is paid for and in my name."

Joel picked up a strip of cold bacon from Casey's plate and chewed it slowly. He didn't have an answer to the money problem, no way to soothe Casey or bring him down for a gentle landing. If he chose this path, he'd land hard, and that was all there was to it.

"You should go home," he finally murmured as the silence stretched on. "You've got too much to lose. I'm not worth it."

"Fuck that." Casey sat up straighter. "Other people do this all the time. Their parents kick them out or give up on them, and they make it work. They get jobs and figure their shit out. I'll do the same."

"Casey…"

"Joel. Stop. I'm not going to break things off with you just because my parents told me to, okay? That's not happening."

"Stubborn."

"So what? I'm right. They're wrong."

"They're the ones with the purse strings. I don't want this for you."

"You said that yesterday. Let's not have the same fight." Casey's lips quirked. "Unless you want it to end the same way?"

"With your dick up my ass?"

Casey smiled, his eyes dilating slightly and darting down to Joel's mouth.

"You don't seem that upset," Joel commented. He kept waiting for Casey to lose his shit and start bawling and sobbing. But he didn't seem likely to break even a little bit. Was this the stubborn surety that had let Casey go to New York and not contact Joel for nearly four years?

"I'm upset." Casey's brows creased. "I'm hurt, but I'm not *surprised.* Dad did basically the same thing when I came out to him. Said he wasn't going to pay for NYU, said he'd cut me off." Casey rolled his eyes. "He said all kinds of things he didn't mean. At least, he didn't mean them for more than a few days. But it still sucked flying off to start school without knowing if he was really going to jerk my funding or turn his back on me. Mom told me not to worry back then, and she was right. He came around."

"What if he doesn't come around this time?"

Casey's eyes tightened at the edges. "I almost don't want him to. I'd almost like to see what it would be like if he didn't. I believe in us, Joel. And I believe in myself." He lifted his chin. "I have what amounts to a degree from NYU in marketing and branding. I have talent, and I'm *good* at what I want to do. Once I finish up at UT, I could get some references from my professors, both in New York and here, and I could start hunting for starter positions." He shrugged. "Sure, it'd be easier to achieve my dream with my dad's help and support. I'd be able to start my own firm if I wanted to, focus on the mom-and-pop stores, local products, and artists. But I never wanted my own firm to begin with, and he was never going to support me in that anyway. He wanted me to go to Wharton. He wanted me to come aboard at his company. So what if we've sped up the inevitable? It's better than living under his thumb and giving up what's most important to me to satisfy his idea of who I am. Who he wants me to be." He thrust up his chin again. "Let him see how strong we can be together."

Joel wished he believed the way Casey did. He'd do anything for an ounce of Casey's certainty. But when he looked into a future where Casey moved in with him and gave up his family, their money, and his degree, all Joel could see was struggle and poverty—and the fire of conviction going out in Casey's eyes.

"My father doesn't get it, and everything he said to me last night only made me more sure," Casey went on. "Every objection he raised? Just made me more certain that I could never live in the future he envisions for me. Never, ever."

"I get that, but you don't have to decide now."

"I've already decided. Or don't you want me here with you? You get a choice too, Joel. If you don't want me, you should say so now." Hurt tinged his voice.

"I don't have to decide now either," Joel said quickly. "Let's not fight on Christmas. Let's just enjoy the day the best we can and see what the future brings."

It wasn't his usual way to brush reality under the rug, but he was willing to do it now. If Casey wasn't eager to go home, then Joel was going to milk this time together while he could. But he wasn't ready for the man he loved to throw over his entire life to live in poverty, running on caffeine and dreams, either.

As Joel stood to put his somehow-empty dish in the sink, a new thought crossed his mind. Maybe Casey wouldn't go running to his parents, but Joel could. Not today, necessarily, but if things didn't right themselves soon... It wasn't like Joel had nothing to say to Jonathan Stevens.

"I've got to get to the nursing home." Joel swallowed hard. "I'd ask you to come, because I'm not ashamed of you or what we're doing." He dumped his coffee down the drain. "But if you think last night was a shit show? Bringing you into my dad's nursing home room on Christmas Day would probably result in him stroking out." He shrugged, turning toward Casey and catching his sad eyes. "So, unless you want a death on your conscience today..."

"That's all right. I get it." Casey smiled. "I have things I can do here. If I can borrow your laptop, that is."

"Sure. It's not nice like yours, but..."

Casey stood up and gathered Joel close. Joel buried his nose in Casey's neck and took long, deep breaths. He pushed Casey back and murmured, "I won't be long."

"Take your time. I'll clean up the kitchen. Can I feed Bruno the leftovers?"

"The eggs, yeah. But keep the rest of the bacon. We'll want that later." Joel moved away to grab his coat, thinking about the day ahead and their lack of any ingredients for a suitable Christmas dinner. He flipped the collar up as he tugged it on, nerves about his visit to his father clawing at his gut.

"You're hot when you do that," Casey said, raising a brow and stepping closer. He licked his lips, and his wet mouth glistened in the morning light through the mobile home's kitchen windows. He mimicked flipping up a collar and grinned. "Mysterious and sexy."

"I try," Joel snarked.

"When you get back, I'm going to show you how hot you are. For hours."

"Don't have to twist my arm," he whispered, grabbing for his keys as Casey drew closer again, tempting with his warm body and acres of exposed skin. Joel took a deep breath. "Later, do you want me to try? You know, the other way? Where I do it to you?"

"If you want to, sure."

Joel frowned, his stomach balling up. He didn't know why he didn't want to do it to Casey, but he just didn't. He shrugged. "Okay, if you want me to, I will."

Casey rolled his eyes. "I already told you. I like to be on top, so if you don't want to switch, we don't have to."

Relief punched through him, and he took Casey's chin in his fingers before going up on his toes and kissing him hard. Casey moved in closer, pressing his tongue into Joel's mouth and slipping his hand down toward Joel's crotch.

"I have to go," Joel muttered as his dick fattened up fast and traitorously in his pants. "I'll see you later."

Casey released him with so much reluctance that Joel nearly gave in and dropped to his knees to suck him off. But he stopped by the Christmas tree and pulled out one of only a few gifts he'd tucked underneath it the prior afternoon.

It may not have been time for Casey to move on from his family, but, like he'd realized the night before after leaving Casey's folks' house, it was past time he made a clean break from his own. His stomach churned, and he wanted to turn back to Casey and tell him what he was about to do, let Casey take him in his arms and hold him until Joel stopped stupidly shaking.

But no. It was his dad, and he could do this. Casey would be waiting when he got back.

Chapter Twenty-Three

"HEY, POP." JOEL entered his father's room without an Egg McMuffin as usual. Even the local McDonald's franchise allowed its employees the day off. He held out the present he had for his father instead. "Merry Christmas."

Charlie, as Joel had decided to think of him from now on, glared at him from the bed. "I hoped you wouldn't bother showing your face today after the crap you've pulled this week." He didn't reach out for the present, content to glare and sneer.

"Funny, I almost didn't come." Joel put the gift on his father's nightstand and shoved his hands in his pockets. He didn't bother pointing out that Charlie had been the real monster this week, abusive and humiliating. He just said, "Go ahead and open it."

Slowly, Charlie reached for the present like it might bite him. "What's in it?"

"The last thing you're getting from me," Joel said easily, like it didn't pull hard at his insides to speak the words he should have said when he turned eighteen. "So, I hope you enjoy it."

"What's that supposed to mean?" Charlie's fingers stilled in the ripping of the wrapping paper, his weak eyes narrowing into another glare.

"It means I've already let you have too much."

Charlie stared at him like he didn't understand before turning his attention back to the gift. He opened it and pulled out a framed photo. It was a picture of the outside of Vreeland's Home and Garden, done up for the holidays and dated on the bottom as the year before Joel's mother had passed away.

"I found it in some boxes when I was looking for the tree ornaments. I thought you might want it."

His father sneered. "Why would I want a crummy picture of a place that stole the best years of my life?"

Joel felt the wound open, but he thought of Casey's stubbornness, closed his eyes, and stitched it back up with his own determination and will.

When he looked at Charlie again, he said calmly, "It's a thank you, in a way. Vreeland's is the best thing you ever did for me. It may not be my dream career, but it's going to be my way to my dream."

He'd realized the night before during his brief discussion with Courtney that he didn't have to stay at Vreeland's forever. He could sell the place to someone who could love it and use the proceeds, slim as they might be, to start on the log cabin or, hell, to live on while he wrote more books.

He didn't *have* to remain at Vreeland's unless he wanted to. And right now, he did want to. But the job had an escape hatch. One that he could use when or if the time came. That realization had opened the world up for him, relieving the trapped sensation he'd been stuck in for so long.

"Your dream? More faggy talk already?" Charlie tossed the photo onto the bed. It nearly slid off to the floor, but he made no move to catch it. Joel didn't either.

Joel walked around the room, going to every photo of his mother and taking a snap with his phone.

"What are you doing?" his father asked stiffly.

He didn't bother giving him an answer. Talking never did any good with Charlie, and it wasn't going to do any good now. Besides, this wasn't a threat or a negotiation. He'd made up his mind, and there was no discussion, pleasant or abusive, that was going to talk him out of it.

Maybe he understood where Casey was coming from with his father more than he wanted to admit.

"Goodbye, Pop," Joel said gently, calling him by that name one last time. He came to stand near him, but out of cuffing range. "I won't be back again. You'll need to eat the breakfast food they serve you from now on."

"What?" Charlie's face reddened incredulously. "You're going to leave me here alone? To rot?"

"You're not alone, and you won't rot. You've got the nurses, and they'll take care of you."

He took a step back, his heart twisting in his chest and adrenaline screaming through him. Was he really doing this? Did he dare? Was he allowed? Would he be able to stick to it later without drowning in guilt?

"Just because you're my father doesn't mean I have to take your abuse. I watched someone I care about stand up for himself and for me today in a way I never expected. It's about time I do the same." He lifted his chin. "I'm gay."

Charlie stared at him, mouth open, his face growing purple.

"And I'm sorry you never loved me, because I couldn't help but love you." Joel's lips twisted and his throat clogged. "But I'm done now. No more. I'm gay, and I'm in love, and I'm not going to be your whipping boy or let you tear me down. I'm through with you. The nurses have my number, and they'll call me if I'm truly needed."

Joel turned away, but he paused in the doorway. "Goodbye. I hope you find a way to not die a miserable fuck."

He didn't look back.

CASEY CLOSED JOEL'S laptop on the notes he'd made for a social media strategy for the Joel Grimsbane pen name. After petting Bruno for a bit and thinking, he found some blank paper in a kitchen drawer and started mocking up branding for Vreeland's Home and Garden and jotting down ideas for drawing in a younger crowd.

Things like: fresh coffee to sip as customers strolled the store and checked out the outdoor plants, a sandwich chalkboard at the front entrance with a daily quirky quote and drawing (that Angel girl could be in charge of that), and monthly "medicine in your garden" meetings for instruction on the uses of herbs and other plants. He knew there had to be plenty of people in Knoxville who could speak on that subject. Local Osteopaths or chiropractors or herbalists or something.

He also made notes about seeking out locally made garden ornaments to feature during a "local craftsman day" where the artist could come in and show off their work. It could be a real draw to have some bearded hipster redneck carving their wooden garden sculptures with a chainsaw in the Vreeland parking lot where everyone could see.

And there was more.

Casey was bursting with ideas for how to get Vreeland's on the Knoxville millennial hipsters' map. He was certain he could turn the store around in less than six months.

Bruno, who was stretched out at Casey's feet, looked up at him and sighed.

Casey stroked his silky ears. "We're going to do this, Bruno. No matter what my folks say or do, or what Joel thinks now, we can make this work. His books, the store, our relationship. All of it. Don't you agree with me?"

Bruno stared soulfully at him, sighed again, and dropped his head down, closing his eyes.

Casey hoped that was a yes. He kept swinging between ecstasy and terror, and optimism and despair. He couldn't let Joel see anything but his hope, though, or he'd use it to try send Casey home. And he wasn't going home. Not yet. Not when he truly felt alive for the first time and knew Joel loved him.

He stood and stretched. Bruno opened one eye and looked up at him, then closed it again. Casey meandered over to the tree, checking out the ornaments again, remembering them from Joel's old house in Belmont Hills.

Glancing under the tree, Casey found two small packages wrapped up with his name on them. And another package for Bruno. He wondered when Joel had had time to do that.

Casey had picked up something for Joel when he was out with Courtney the day before. God, had it only been twenty-four hours ago that he was joyfully telling his aunt all about Joel while watching her try on more shoes than he could count?

Shit. His gift for Joel was in a bag in his bedroom at home. Casey had thought he'd have plenty of time to wrap it and bring it to Joel in the afternoon on Christmas Day.

Sucking his teeth, he paced around the living room before grabbing his phone. There was a text message from RJ including a photo of him relaxing in a hotel bed with a tall, skinny, shirtless guy who must be Pan Soldier.

Wishing you a Merry Christmas, dude. Give Joel my love. Hoping for the best for you both in the new year.

Casey sent back a smiley emoji and an all-caps MERRY CHRISTMAS and then fielded his next new text, which was oddly from Theo. It was simply a Christmas tree emoji and the words, "Merry Christmas." Casey replied the same way he had to RJ, sans the all-caps, and quickly moved on.

Pulling up his last text stream with Aunt Courtney, he scanned everything she'd sent the night before, all outraged for him and worried. He'd messaged her in the morning to let her know he was all right, but now he needed a favor. He thumbed in his request and hit send.

After her response came through, he grabbed his jacket and headed out. It smelled like snow was coming, and he took a deep breath of the ozone scent before ducking into his SUV and turning the heater on full blast.

At the local Starbucks, one of the few places open on Christmas Day, he dropped into his seat with a maple pecan latte in the signature red cup and waited, checking out the weary-looking travelers who shared the space and were apparently on their way to grandma's house for Christmas dinner. But it wasn't long before Courtney breezed in wearing a red coat, carrying his laptop case and the shopping bag from his bedroom.

"Hey," she said after she kissed his cheek. "I've got about ten minutes. I told your mother I was taking a post-Christmas breakfast drive to Starbucks."

Casey's gut churned. "I'm sorry I missed breakfast."

She sighed. "Me too. But I get it." She gave his hand a squeeze. "Anyway, your mom was distracted enough trying to figure out how to defrost Christmas dinner not to question me. She's talking irrationally about halving the defrosted servings since you won't be there and crying into her many mimosas. Oh, Casey. Your mother is so upset with you."

"Just with me?"

"And your father. Let's put it this way: there's enough upset to go around. No one's spared. Not even me, since I knew about Joel before she did."

Casey kept his mouth shut, mainly because so many thoughts tumbled through his head at once that he didn't know where to start. Old childhood hurts shoved up next to the most recent ones, and he sat there with them, solid balls of pain in his belly.

"It was a good idea to stay away, though," she said soothingly. "It'll give all of you time to cool off."

"Even though I've ruined Christmas?"

"You didn't ruin Christmas." She snorted. "Your father did that."

"I won't argue there," he muttered.

"Although you didn't have to spring Joel on them the way you did. It wasn't fair to Joel, and it wasn't fair to them."

Casey sighed. He'd already figured that much out for himself. He'd thought the surprise of it would force them to treat Joel nicely. In a way it had, but he hadn't counted on his father getting him alone and Joel overhearing it all. He'd also thought it would give them the opportunity to see how good he and Joel were together—how Joel could fit in if they just gave him a chance. But they hadn't given him a chance, had they?

"So, what are you going to do now?" Courtney asked.

"Spend Christmas with Joel. He was going to be alone for it, so now he has me." His heart fluttered, and he smiled a little.

"I'm glad you're happy with him. He's a sweetheart. I talked with him just a little last night and even I could see how desperately he adores you. Stand your ground and keep your man." She glanced at her phone. "Time to place my order here and head back. Before I go, I want you to know your mother loves you and so does your father. They're trying to wrap their minds around your defiance, as they see it, but I have faith they'll get it together. They're not actually bad people, Casey."

He knew that was true, but it didn't take away the sting from the night before.

She waited in line for her drink and swung back around to kiss his cheek one more time before leaving. Her whispered parting rang in his ears, cliché though it was, even as she and her red coat disappeared out the door, "In the end, love is all that matters."

Chapter Twenty-Four

C ASEY PACED THE trailer from living room to Joel's bedroom again and again, with Bruno watching him patiently from his dog bed. It was almost two o'clock now, and Joel still wasn't home from visiting his father, nor was he answering his texts. Had something happened with his dad? Had his car broken down or worse? What if he was getting cold feet again and was avoiding Casey?

He'd headed out earlier to one of the few places open on Christmas to grab a takeout dinner for them both. Shoney's wasn't high class at all, and that was part of the reason he'd chosen it. Cheap, greasy comfort food—turkey, gravy, green beans, and pecan and pumpkin pie—seemed like the right way to show Joel he was ready and willing to take his lifestyle down a notch. Besides, it'd smelled amazing when he'd grabbed the takeout bag from the girl working the register.

Now when he opened the Styrofoam containers to check on the cold food, he grimaced to see the congealed grease collecting at the edges of everything. Zapping it in the microwave would undo the damage, most likely, but he couldn't do that until Joel got back, and just where was he anyway? Casey was hungry and worried, and ready to get back to the feeling of being wrapped up in each other again. Surely Joel was too?

He checked the time again.

What if there was an accident? He looked out the kitchen window to see that it is starting to snow. Folks were so bad at driving, even in just flurries, in Tennessee; what if Joel had gotten caught in some sort of Christmas traffic-related, snow-panic accident? He texted Joel again.

I'm worried. Where are you?

He stared at the phone, willing the three little dots to appear that indicated Joel was replying. Nothing. He groaned and shoved the phone in his pocket, and then put the Styrofoam containers of food back in the fridge, resuming his pacing of the hallway.

Suddenly Bruno hauled himself up, an excited wriggle in his hindquarters, as he jolted out the dog door. Casey followed, his heart in his throat, and a sweaty excitement grabbing him hard.

Joel squatted in the flurrying snow patting Bruno and passing him a new red Kong chew toy. He rose up to his feet and gave a strange smile to Casey, a kind of simpering grin that made Casey's insides flip over.

"Sorry I'm late," Joel said, approaching slowly like Casey might pounce. "I should have texted. I didn't mean to make you worry. I just needed to clear my head, so I drove around for a while and then stopped by the pet store. There's one still open on Chapman Highway."

"That's a long way from here."

"Yeah." Joel swallowed and met Casey's eyes sadly. "Sorry."

"C'mere?" Casey opened his arms, and Joel nearly dove into them. Casey held him close, smelling his hair and kissing his ear. "I love you."

"I know."

"Do you?"

Joel nodded and clung even tighter. Casey tried to infuse him with his devotion, to fill whatever holes his father had left in him with his own affection.

"I got dinner for us. Shoney's."

Joel huffed a wet laugh, and when he pulled out of Casey's embrace he quickly wiped his cheeks with the back of his hands. "Oh goodie. My favorite."

"Super classy," Casey said with a wink, letting Joel's emotion slide by without making a big deal of it. It wasn't the time. He needed to help Joel feel safe before he probed whatever raw wound had been opened.

"The pinnacle of class," Joel agreed, shoving his hands into his jean jacket.

They followed Bruno back into the trailer and past where he collapsed on his dog bed with his new toy.

After dishing out the food and microwaving it warm again, they settled down at the little table for their Christmas meal. "To Christmas," Casey said, lifting his beer for a toast.

Joel clinked and then dug in. Based on the little sounds he made, it wasn't too bad in his opinion. Casey tried a bite of the turkey and gravy first. It wasn't bad.

"How did it go with your pop?" Casey asked once they'd both eaten enough to offset the pangs of hunger.

"It could have gone worse. In fact, I'm surprised it didn't. I think I shocked him."

"In what way?"

"I told him I'm gay and in love. And I told him I wouldn't be coming to see him anymore."

"Joel…" That was a huge decision, and Casey didn't know what to say.

"I know you probably think I'm a dick to ever walk away from my pop, but…" Joel held up his phone. It showed twenty missed calls, all from his father. His voice was raw, almost broken as he whispered, "My voice mail is full of his ranting." When he opened up his texts, he passed the phone to Casey so that he could read them.

The invectives and insults were so abusive they made Casey nauseous. He handed the phone back to Joel and whispered, "I'm so sorry."

"It's not like this is new. And it's definitely not your fault." Joel rubbed at his eyes and sighed heavily. "I just wanted you to see what it is that I'm leaving behind." He chewed on his bottom lip and looked away, like he was ashamed to meet Casey's eyes even as he went on to say, "I'm not a cruel person, and it's not like I don't care about him. But I won't take this kind of treatment anymore. From anyone. Not from him, and not from…" Joel trailed off. "I won't."

"I'm glad," Casey said, reaching out to take Joel's hand and squeezing, relieved when Joel met his eyes again. "I mean, I'm not glad that he's the kind of man who treats you this way, but I don't want you to take it anymore either."

"You don't think I'm a terrible son?"

"No." Casey stroked Joel's hand with his thumb. "You deserve to be treated with kindness, Joel. Only ever kindness. And love. Because I love you, Joel."

Joel ducked his head like he was trying to believe Casey's words.

"I know it was hard," Casey said. "I know you didn't do this lightly. You never do anything lightly."

"Yeah." Joel tugged his hand free and pushed his food around on his plate. "I hope I did the right thing."

"You're a good man. If this feels right, then it is." They ate in silence for a few minutes, the weight of Joel's day coming down on them.

"It was easier than I think it should have been, actually," Joel confessed. "Especially for doing it on Christmas. But being with you the last few days, thinking about the future—with or without you in it—I realized that I can't keep subjecting myself to his abuse. When I'm with you, when you talk to me like I'm…" His mouth twisted up, and he looked away.

"I know."

Joel searched Casey's eyes again, and his shoulders relaxed. "You really get it? I don't need to say it?"

"No, baby. I understand."

They were silent again then, the only sound Bruno chewing on his toy and the hiss of snowflakes hitting the windows and roof. A train went by, rattling the trailer and waking them from their pondering. They returned to eating, though the meal had become cold again.

Finally, Casey asked, "What will you do if the nursing home calls you in to come see him?"

"It depends on what they need. I still have his Power of Attorney, so if it's a health issue, I can handle that over the phone if necessary. If they really need me to come in, then I'll deal with that when it happens. Right now, I'm just looking forward to not hearing his abuse every day." He tilted his head. "How about now? Do I sound like an asshole now?"

Casey scoffed. "No. I'm proud of you for standing up for yourself."

Joel's smile wavered.

"It's okay if you cry or get upset."

"I know. But I don't want to. Not right now." Joel leaned forward and licked his lips. "I want to be here with you. That's all. Let's just be here together. No outside world at all. Just us."

Bruno made a disgusting sound with his toy, and they both laughed. "Just us and a big old dog," Joel said. "C'mon, Bruno. Outside." Casey watched as Joel lured Bruno into going out into the pale afternoon light by filling his new Kong toy with peanut butter and then tossing it into the yard. Bruno bounded out amongst the descending snow, eager to claim his treat.

"Will he be too cold?" Casey asked, shivering as the cold air carved into the heat of the trailer.

"He's got the dog door. Besides he likes to romp around out there in this kind of weather. He'll be fine." Joel shut the door on his dog tossing the Kong toy up and catching it again.

Casey drew Joel into his arms, pushing his hands under his shirt to stroke down his smooth skin. He gripped his narrow hips and kissed him. They made out for a while against the front door and then slowly moved together toward the sofa in the living room, leaving a trail of clothes behind.

Once they were naked, they collapsed on the couch together. Joel straddled Casey's lap, groaning as he took both of their erections in his callused hand and jerked them together. Casey added his hand to tighten the tunnel their cocks moved through, and watched avidly as Joel's head tipped back, his eyes squeezed shut, and he came with a sharp cry, spurting come across Casey's stomach and chest. It wasn't long before

Casey broke open too, grunting in pleasure as his white jizz joined Joel's on his skin.

"Let me," Joel whispered, getting on his knees between Casey's feet and bending down to lick it up. He grimaced a few times, and when he finished, he wiped at his lips. "Mine doesn't taste as good as yours."

"Cigarettes," Casey said breathlessly. "But it's okay. I like that it's yours."

Joel frowned a moment, but then crawled up to straddle him again, collapsing against Casey's body, and nuzzling his neck and hair. "All the more reason to quit."

"I don't mind. Really. But you should quit for your health. That's what's important."

"I want to make it good for you," Joel whispered.

Casey wrapped his arms around Joel's torso, holding him tight. "Baby, you *are* good for me. I promise."

"I like that." Joel shuddered against him, as if the words cost him.

"What?"

"You calling me baby."

"I like it too." He paused and kissed Joel's neck before whispering, "Baby."

Joel dug in deeper, holding Casey tighter with both his arms and his thighs, like he was desperate and skin-hungry, and Casey wanted nothing more than to indulge him.

Eventually, they broke apart and decided to use Casey's streaming login ID to watch the *Harkening* Christmas special on Casey's laptop. Bruno came back inside still carrying his slobbery toy. They heated up the takeout again and curled together on the sofa with more greasy food, more cookies, and Bruno dozing at their feet. They laughed and groaned at the storyline of the show, agreeing that it was schmaltzy as hell, but somehow they both loved it anyway.

As the afternoon waned and darkness crept in, Casey cued up the live action version of *How the Grinch Stole Christmas*. They sprawled and laughed, holding each other close. The lights on the tree and the yellow glow outside from the rising moon lent a softness to the room that seeped into Casey, leaving him so warm and comfortable—so happy—that he never wanted the night to end. So long as he stayed right here, he wouldn't have to face his parents or negotiate a future. They could be content.

When Joel got up to grab a couple of beers, he stopped in his tracks, his gaze glued to something outside the living room window. "Holy shit."

Casey tensed, leaping up, Bruno immediately on guard too. God, was it Casey's parents? He wasn't ready for this confrontation. Couldn't he and Joel just have their Christmas in peace? "What?" He joined Joel at the window and gasped out loud. "Whoa."

The snow that had been flurries earlier was sticking, lining tree limbs in white and covering the grass.

"No way," Joel said. "A white Christmas? In Tennessee? This is crazy."

"It's a sign." Casey grinned, his heart full.

"A sign that climate change is real? Yeah."

Casey rolled his eyes, and they laughed as Bruno shot out of the dog door again and bounced around, leaping to catch snowflakes in his giant maw. They put on their coats and shoes and joined him, making snow angels by the colorful lights strung along the trailer.

When they were soaked, with fat snowflakes caught in their hair, they hurried back inside, leaving Bruno to run around as much as he liked. Shivering, they stripped to their boxers and hung their wet clothes in the bathroom. Casey was relieved they'd left the space heaters on high so the trailer was warm and toasty.

Joel let out a long breath. He reached out for Casey as though seeking comfort. He pressed his whole body against Casey, tucking his head beneath Casey's chin and holding on tight.

Skin against skin aside from their boxers, Casey wrapped him up in his arms and rubbed his cheek across the top of Joel's head. He wanted to kiss him again but wasn't sure if that's what Joel was going for or not.

"C'mon," Joel said, breaking away and pulling Casey toward the living room. "We almost forgot presents. I've got something for you. Something special."

Casey sat on the sofa and gestured toward the box he'd put under the tree earlier when Joel was away. "I have something for you too."

Joel distributed the gifts—two for Casey and one for Joel. Casey immediately wished he'd spent more on Joel. At the time, he hadn't wanted to go overboard or make Joel feel stingy, so he'd just bought the one thing. But now he wished he had more.

"Go first," Casey said. "I got it for you yesterday. I hope you like it."

Joel opened the gift and grinned, holding up the gold glitter-dusted tin star. "It's perfect. Thanks."

"Do you really like it? No pressure."

Joel stood up and placed it on top of the tree, going up on his tiptoes to do it. "It looks great. Perfect, like I said. Thank you."

Casey let out a breath of relief. It could have been worse. Joel seemed to genuinely like the star. He stood beside the tree and admired it for a minute before clapping his hands together and sitting by Casey again. Casey loved the way the Christmas lights played on Joel's pale skin.

"Okay, your turn. Open the big one first."

Casey worked open the tape and shoved back the paper to reveal a miniature Blow Mold Nativity set, about one-fourth the size of the one in Mr. Maples's yard or Joel's store. "Is this...?"

"So you can kiss Mary every year." Joel laughed.

Casey grinned. "I'd rather kiss you every year."

Joel shrugged. "I'd be okay with that."

Casey's heart somersaulted. "Do you mean it?"

"Yeah."

"I was an idiot to kiss Mary instead of you."

"Yeah, well, we were both idiots back then. I'd say I was worse with all the bullshit stories about making out with girls and trying to keep you at arm's length."

"I get it. You were scared. It was for your safety."

"It was." Joel shrugged, his shoulders rising and falling. "Anyway, I grabbed that from the stock at the store. I thought it'd make you laugh, and it's small enough to fit in your place in New York. Or wherever you end up."

Casey looked around the living room. "It'd look pretty good in that corner."

"Yeah, like I said." Joel scratched at his eyebrow with his thumb, but he spoke clearly despite his shaking voice. "Wherever you end up."

Casey smiled. "Thank you."

Joel tapped the smaller package. "And now that one."

Casey opened the gift and stared down at a black jewelry box. "It's... Is it?"

"Just open it."

Casey pried it open and found inside a wide silver ring with a J imprinted within a circle on the middle. "What's this?"

"My mom's ring," Joel said, a tense smile on his lips. "Her dad gave it to her. It was his ring originally. His name was James, and hers was Jennifer. I'm Joel, obviously, so she put it aside for me when I was just a little kid. She rarely wore it because it was so big, but there are a few shots of her with it on her thumb when I was a baby and she was still carrying some weight from the pregnancy."

"I can't take this."

"Well, I'm not asking you to keep it forever, unless it works out that way. I'm giving it to you like a promise ring. So, when you go back to New York to graduate—because you will—you can look at the ring and know I'm right here waiting. That I belong with you. Okay?" Joel's cheeks flushed. "Or is that too big of a thing?"

"No. I love it." Casey never knew happiness could hurt so much, but damn if his heart wasn't being carved out by sheer joy. He took the ring out of the box and slid it onto the ring finger of his left hand. It fit perfectly, which seemed to be an omen.

A good one. A freaking *amazing* one.

Casey flexed his hand in the light from the Christmas tree, studying the swoop of the J and the way the silver shone against his skin. "Thank you."

"It's okay?"

"It's perfect. Whenever I look at my hand, I'll think of you."

Joel took hold of his fingers, stroking his thumb over the ring. "J for Joel's. I'm staking my claim. For as long as you want me. If you decide to move on, you can just return the ring. I'll live." He didn't sound like he'd live at all, though, with his voice vibrating so hard.

Casey laughed. "Dude, I just tried to move in with you. I don't think you need to worry about me giving the ring back."

"Good."

"When did you change your mind? About us? About continuing on even if I go back to New York for school?"

Joel flushed. "I don't know. Somewhere between overhearing your dad's bullshit last night and walking away from my dad's crap today, I realized that it's too late. I've already gone all in with you. Fighting it just seems stupid now. And having your dick in my ass might have persuaded me, too." Joel flushed. "I don't know how I'm going to do without it, so…"

"Baby, you'll never have to do without that. Never," Casey said, tugging Joel closer. "Not so long as I'm around."

"I…fuck, Casey, but I really want you around."

Casey ran his hand down Joel's chest, the metal of his new ring reflecting the Christmas tree's lights across Joel's pale skin. "Tell me how much."

"So much. I…" Joel's voice broke, but he went on. "I need you."

Casey growled and jerked Joel into his arms. "Fuck, yes. I need you too. Let me show you."

"Yes."

"Let's go to bed."

JOEL'S COCK BEAT with his pulse, thudding on his quivering stomach as he tried to hold back the tears of pleasure that slipped out of his eyes. He wondered why he kept crying every time they did anything anally.

Rimming and being fucked broke him down in a way he could barely take but then craved again as soon as it was finished. It was embarrassing, but Casey's gentle words and tender kisses made him feel okay about it, like maybe Casey took his emotional reaction as a compliment.

Casey thrust his cock in hard again, and Joel arched up, his legs shaking on Casey's shoulders and his cock spurting pre-come onto his treasure trail, leaving a slick spot that his cockhead rubbed in with each involuntary hump of his hips.

"You're beautiful," Casey whispered, holding Joel's wrists down against the mattress as he screwed him.

"You're in so deep."

"I'm in all the way." He flexed so his balls slapped against Joel's ass for emphasis. "You've got all of me. Do you feel me?"

"Fuck yes." How was he supposed to feel anything else? With each drag out and hard thrust back in, Joel's nipples pebbled and chills broke over his body. His eyes leaked more, and he moaned. Pleasure ricocheted through him, tightening his skin and making him shake like he was going to burst free from himself or maybe die if the goodness didn't stop. But also like he'd tumble into an endless well of frustration and disappointment if it did.

"That's good. Open up. Yeah. Like that." Casey fucked into him harder, making his body jolt on the mattress and his cock bounce against his stomach.

"Oh God," Joel moaned, tossing his head and clenching his hands in fists. His hole clenched and released around Casey's dick, an uncontrollable rhythmic spasm that felt so good. He writhed, trying to hold back, to hold on, but orgasm was tightening in him, aching in his balls. He gasped, "Close. I'm close."

Casey jerked his cock free of Joel's ass, sweaty and panting, his gaze never leaving Joel's face. Scrunching his eyes closed, Joel wailed, a shock of emptiness and loss rocking through him, and Casey squeezed his wrists hard against the mattress, before hushing his cry with a kiss. Then he pushed back in, slow, slow, slow, and Joel quivered under him, impatient and a little scared.

Releasing one arm, Casey took Joel's cock in hand as they moved together, gazing down into his eyes. Shifting his legs to Casey's hips, he dug in his heels, trying to get Casey in deeper and deeper.

"Fuck me," he whimpered. "Hard."

Casey did as Joel asked.

As the pummeling thrusts came, he couldn't hold Casey's gaze anymore. Laid bare and seen, loved and touched, taken and given to without reserve, Joel reached up for Casey, dragging him down for a kiss. He dissolved into the pounding bliss, the rhythm that gripped him and took him over inside and out. Thundering pulse, aching cock, and his hole gripping and releasing needily as Casey's cock slammed in and out. Casey's grunts grew louder and louder, the sound of their sex an echoing slap and moan around the room, and the bed shook hard.

Joel clawed at Casey's shoulders, trying to grab hold and make it last, but the pleasure built and grew, his cock dragging between his stomach and Casey's in a sweaty, hot press of friction. "Please," he said, holding on. "More."

Casey gripped his shoulders harder and shoved into him with a force that rolled Joel's eyes up into his head. His balls drew up tight, and his legs clenched around Casey's pumping waist. He reached down to take hold of his cock and stroke it, but he barely touched it before his pleasure exploded over him, in him, and out of him. He spasmed as he came, and a rough, haggard cry launched from his throat.

Casey shouted too, his cock swelling in Joel's ass, and Joel felt the pumping of Casey filling the condom. He dragged Casey down for a kiss, moaning into his mouth and whimpering in exhausted, but somehow unsatisfied, need. Would he ever get enough? Now that he'd had Casey, had this love, he didn't want to let it go. *Ever* let it go.

He held Casey inside as long as he could, and after Casey pulled out to dispose of the condom, Joel reached for him until Casey collapsed on top of him, sweaty and still huffing with exertion.

"You okay?" Casey whispered, touching where the tears still leaked from his eyes.

"I don't know why it happens."

Casey kissed his nose and mouth and then each eyelid. "Ann says crying just means you're feeling something big. So long as it's a good something, I don't think we should worry about it."

"It's good." Joel's throat ached, and he squeezed Casey in closer. "Everything about this is good."

Casey kissed him gently. "Let's get some rest. I'm going to want to do that again later."

"Yeah. Me too," Joel admitted. He breathed in Casey's scent and snuggled in close.

"Now do you see why people are so into it?"

"Only with you," Joel murmured, closing his eyes as his body slowed its shaking and finally relaxed so he could sleep. "I still only want to do it with you."

"Me too." Casey kissed his hair before tenderly kissing the ring Joel had given him. "Me too, baby."

Chapter Twenty-Five

T HE NEXT MORNING, they rose to a winter wonderland by Tennessee standards. A foot and a half of snow covered the lawn and piled on tree branches sturdy enough to hold the weight. Bruno was delighted by it and dashed in and out of the dog door, tracking wet, muddy footprints all over the kitchen floor and hallway. Joel sighed and stared at them, thinking about how now he'd have to mop.

"He's crazy about the snow," Casey said, coming in from having gone out to piss on the bushes.

Joel wasn't sure how much skunks really got out and about in the snow, but he didn't bother telling Casey to urinate inside. He'd rather piss outside every day of the year than deal with Bruno covered in skunk stench ever again.

"What are your plans today?" Casey asked, rosy cheeked from the cold as he kicked off his boots and hung up his jacket.

"Gotta run to Vreeland's for a few hours. We're open at ten. We won't have too many customers, but we'll have some. And my assistant manager Brandon and I need to make sure Angel re-priced all the Christmas stuff for the sale and discuss what we're going to stock for spring."

"Ah." Casey shifted uncomfortably.

"You going to hang out here or…?"

"I've agreed to see my parents this afternoon. My dad had to go into the office this morning."

"His office downtown?"

"Yeah. I'm going to head over to the house early to pack up a few more things I left there. Talk to my mom. Feel her out about what to expect from my dad. And before that I'll work some more on the book-marketing stuff. Speaking of, I need to get your approval on it so I can move forward, and get your password so I can upload the new covers and update your seller account. And I need to start a Facebook page, a Twitter account, an Instagram account, and—"

Joel shuddered. "Start whatever you want, but I'm not keeping up with it."

"I'll do it. Like I said, this is perfect for my project. I've even started a few spreadsheets for keeping track of any changes in sales." Casey cocked his head. "Though some of the marketing has to be about the actual writer. People want to know things about you, Joel."

"Start with the general marketing, and if that goes well, I'll consider doing more, okay?"

Casey smiled, breaking out his laptop and pulling a sheaf of papers from his bags. "These are my plans. The main things I need your approval on are the covers, the branding designs, and the changes I've made to the blurbs. Getting those changed out, if you approve them, will take most of the morning."

Joel looked through everything and was vaguely surprised that he didn't hate any of it. He shouldn't have been, though. Casey's work in his sketchbooks of yore had always been impressive and well-considered. There was nothing he could really balk at, so he gave Casey a shaky smile and a mostly enthusiastic thumbs-up.

"Go for it." He stood up, kissed Casey's cheek, and grabbed his coat. "I'm going to be late if I don't go. I have a few errands I need to run first."

Casey grinned up at him. "By the time you get home, I'll have this all changed out." Then his expression went a bit queasier. "And I'll know what my folks have to say about everything. I'll have a better idea of what the future holds."

Joel touched Casey's cheek, feeling the line between smooth skin and stubble with this thumb. "If it turns out they are stubborn assholes, you can stay here until we get things figured out. Maybe not technically move in, but I'm not going to leave you high and dry."

"Thank you."

"But it won't come to that," Joel murmured.

Casey shook his head. "No. I don't think it will. Dad said a lot of things he'll come to regret, if he doesn't already. I don't think he'll really disown me."

Joel nodded, lingering to feel the drag of stubble over his thumb for a few moments more before kissing Casey's mouth. He broke away, groaning when Bruno darted back through the dog door bringing more snow with him.

"I'll get it," Casey said, indicating the footprints. "You go on to work."

Joel nodded and left, his heart tripping and a new plan for his morning formulating in his head. He texted Brandon when he got to his truck, and once he was sure the store was taken care of, he headed off in the opposite direction instead. Just because he wasn't going to have to field an uncomfortable meeting with his own father for the first morning in way too many years, didn't mean he couldn't choose to have an uncomfortable meeting with *someone else's* father.

What would a morning be without one?

DOWNTOWN KNOXVILLE GLISTENED with frost as Joel gazed out from the wide windows of Jonathan Stevens's sixteenth-story office. A tall, pretty woman named Aditi with dark brown skin and lush, wavy hair had led him here and asked him to wait while she located Mr. Stevens.

He could see the Sunsphere, the distinctive Knoxville iconic building, from where he stood—round and shining with morning light on its reflective gold glass. Looking down at his work boots, he knew he didn't belong here. This was the land of suits and skirts, polished shoes, and ties. It wasn't the place for callused, dirty hands and frayed blue jeans.

Still, he had to try. For Casey. And for himself.

He wasn't devoid of pride, after all. He still had some left in there somewhere. And he'd show Jonathan Stevens what it meant to have a working man's pride, what someone like him was willing to give up for the happiness of the man he loved.

"Joel." Jonathan Stevens's voice held all the disapproval that a father could muster for a friend deemed a bad influence on a beloved son.

"Mr. Stevens." Joel turned around to put out his hand. "Good morning."

Jonathan tilted his head and considered Joel a moment but took his hand after only the briefest hesitation. His handshake was firm, and Joel tried to balance his end of it.

Releasing Joel's hand and moving behind his desk, Jonathan asked bluntly, "Why are you here?"

His throat went dry, but he stood his ground. "I wanted to talk to you about Casey."

"Unless you're here to tell me that you see the sense in ending things with him, then I don't think we have much to say, and you can see yourself out."

Joel sat down in the chair opposite Jonathan's desk. "That's just it. I think we do agree on some important things. Like that Casey won't be happy with me. Not in the long run, anyway."

He hoped deep down that wasn't true. There was no way he could deny to himself what he'd seen the night before in Casey's eyes: the love, the devotion. Nor could he deny his own returning feelings for Casey, or his new, optimistic hope that Casey was right, and they could, in the end, be happy together forever. But for Casey's sake, he could fake this certainty in Casey's eventual loss of interest to convince Jonathan Stevens not to cut him off.

Jonathan stared at him, disbelieving. "So, you're here to…what? Ask for some money to bug off and break his heart? Because if that's the case, name your price. Six hundred? A thousand? Five thousand? If it's reasonable, we have a deal."

Joel stared at the man behind the desk—his well-ordered in-and-out boxes, his tidy hair and slick suit. What sort of monster was under all that co-opted "class" that he'd think Joel could be bought? "No, I don't want any money from you."

"What then?"

Joel lifted his chin. "Just give him time to realize it on his own. How long will it be before he gets the picture? A month? At most a year, right? Casey's not an idiot. He'll see how little we have in common, and when things have cooled off between us—" Jonathan visibly winced, and Joel resisted the urge to smirk. He continued, "He'll go on to find a wealthy, handsome man like Walker Ronson to be with." Saying the words hurt, but hearing them stated aloud, he was even more certain they weren't true. Casey *loved* him. He loved him wholeheartedly, and Walker Ronson and men like him couldn't compete with what they shared.

"You don't really believe that, do you?" Jonathan asked, snorting incredulously. He rolled his eyes, and his blond brows lowered darkly. "Have you met my son? He's stubborn and has his heart set on you."

"If that's the case, then what do you hope to accomplish by cutting him off? You're just going to make him dig his heels in even more. You should have heard him this morning. He's determined to go out and get a job, use his savings to pay for tuition at UT, and move into my trailer with me!" Joel leaned forward, speaking slowly. "Don't you see? You're pushing him away, and if you'll just let this happen, it will end on its own."

Joel willed Jonathan to believe that his and Casey's romance would end in a natural death. On paper, the outcome made sense because love didn't fix everything and it didn't make them a good fit. No matter what his heart said, no matter how much they loved each other, arguably they *shouldn't* work. Never mind that they did work, and they *would* work if Joel had his way. It was still worth a try to convince Jonathan that he and Casey wouldn't make it if it meant Casey could graduate from NYU.

"I told your father back in the day. I warned him that the two of you were drawn to each other like magnets. I should have moved us out of that neighborhood before Casey set his stubborn sights on you."

Joel kept quiet.

"You're an idiot, but it's also clear that I'm an idiot as well." Jonathan leaned forward and steepled his fingers together. "So, what are you proposing? I give my blessing and leave it to you? So you can, what? Sabotage this relationship in some way?"

"It won't need to go as far as sabotage. It will naturally self-destruct," he lied. It seemed absurd that he'd believed these words himself just a day ago. But now he felt certain that no matter how hard he was trying to sell this to Jonathan, both of them probably saw the truth: he and Casey were too far in, and always had been, for their love to die.

Jonathan laughed and shook his head. "Ah. Well, I'd call that short-sighted on your part. Do you really lack so much confidence in my son's affections?"

Joel frowned. It almost sounded like Jonathan wanted Joel to fight for Casey. Like he wanted Joel to believe he *could* have Casey forever. Why?

"Mr. Stevens, please. Allow Casey to return to NYU to finish his degree."

Jonathan raised a brow. "He's supposed to start at Wharton in the fall, but he's told me he plans to stay here. With you."

"I know. I understand why you want him to go to Wharton. Trust me, I'll be in his rearview before it's time for him to start there." The lie felt so obvious. Jonathan had to see through it.

Joel already had a plan for the Wharton contingency: he'd sell Vreeland's and follow Casey to Pennsylvania if he decided to follow his parents' wishes and attend. Hell, Joel would follow Casey to the ends of the earth if he had to. But he couldn't afford to pay his last semester at NYU; only Jonathan could do that.

Jonathan shook his head in obvious disbelief, his tongue clucking in his closed mouth, and Joel wondered if he'd failed in his mission. "Who made you feel so worthless? Your father?" He sighed. "I can believe it. He was always a bastard."

Look who's talking. Joel stayed silent.

Jonathan stood and turned to look out the window behind his desk. His powerful shoulders stretched out his suit jacket. "Well, whatever the case. Deanna isn't happy. With me, I mean. She wants her boy home for the holidays. She wants him home whenever and however he'll agree to come. Even if that means bringing you along with him. Say I do this. I just let you be together." He kept his voice calm. "What guarantee do I have that you'll cut him loose?"

"I won't cut him loose. He'll walk away. It's just a matter of time."

"For some reason, I don't think that's a bet I'm willing to make. But I'll tell you what," he said, turning back around. "I'll add something to this to sweeten the pot. I'll pay you ten thousand dollars if you break it off with him by New Year's Eve."

Joel shook his head, sickness rising within.

"Eleven thousand. Twelve thousand."

"No." Joel's stomach churned. He wanted to punch the man for thinking Joel would turn his back on Casey for cash. "All I'm asking of you is that you have faith."

"In what, exactly?"

"In my ability to fuck things up."

Jonathan shook his head. "Let me tell you a story about Casey."

Joel swallowed and kept his mouth shut.

"When he was a kid, he was stubborn as hell. He'd throw tantrums on his mother and me when he didn't get his way. So, I did what my father did when I was a kid. Took a belt to him. Tried to force him to conform to what I wanted."

Joel clenched his fists. He couldn't believe Jonathan talked about that so casually. God, he really wanted to punch the smug bastard.

"It didn't work. All it did is make him quiet. Now he doesn't talk to me. Now he keeps his opinions and his life to himself. Now he goes behind my back and falls in love with the likes of you."

"You knew he cared about me."

Jonathan smiled bitterly. "I had eyes. And a parent knows their child, even when they don't know them at all."

Joel frowned but didn't push it with questions.

"When he was twelve, I put the belt away, and I never used it again. Do you know why?"

"No."

"Because I realized that every time I used the belt, I lost. It just drove Casey farther from me and from what I wanted for him." His shoulders slumped, and he turned back to the window. "The threats I made the other night are just another belt. I know that. I felt it when I was saying the words. I love my son. I truly do. But some part of me won't easily accept that I can't force him to be the man I want him to be."

Joel stared at the back of Jonathan's blond head. It wasn't an apology, and it wasn't a promise, but it was close enough, maybe. Bittersweet pain washed over him. He'd never see his own father in a moment of self-reflection like this one. The closest he'd ever get would be the dark ruminations of regret when his father wished him never born. Casey's father was an asshole, but he didn't seem to be an irredeemable one. Not yet anyway.

"So, Joel," Jonathan said, turning back around, the backlighting from the window hiding the exact expression on his face. "You can have your way. We'll let this thing go on naturally. I don't think I have any choice in the matter really, between my son and my wife. But I want you to make a bet with me."

He frowned, rising from his seat to meet Jonathan's gaze better.

"What's that?"

"If you're still around by next Christmas, you'll come to me and apologize for having so little faith in him."

Joel's throat tightened, confusion churning in his chest. "And if I'm right? If he does leave?" *Shh*, he soothed himself internally, *Casey loves you.*

"Then I'll send a note with my condolences and a very nice Christmas bonus."

Joel shook his head. "No money."

Jonathan shrugged. "We'll see." He put out his hand. "Do we have an agreement?"

Joel studied his face, seeing the tired lines around his eyes and mouth and the resignation in his expression. "Yes. It's a deal."

They shook on it.

As Joel left the office, he wondered how it was that he'd come to bet against Casey, and that Jonathan, who made no bones about his disapproval, had come to bet on their relationship actually succeeding.

His heart quivered with hope and desperate love. He'd never wanted to lose a bet so much.

"CASEY?" DEANNA ASKED through the closed bedroom door. "Can we talk?"

He'd arrived earlier than his father's expected return from work for the express purpose of feeling out his mother. Now that she was here, though, returned from taking Courtney to the airport, he wasn't sure he was ready to talk with her.

Casey took a slow, deep breath and remembered what Ann had said about standing his ground. He opened the door and gestured for her to come in. She wore a pair of soft jeans and a flowing, crushed-velvet shirt with long, bell-shaped sleeves. Her hair wasn't styled with product, and she looked as tired as Casey felt, but not nearly as wild.

Deanna sighed, smoothing down her hair as she sat gingerly on the side of the guest room bed. He continued to sort and pack up what he'd brought. He bit the side of his cheek rather than ask what he should do about all the stuff in his apartment in New York if they weren't paying for it anymore. He guessed he could ask his landlord to deal with it, but that would be pricey and… Well, he just didn't know what was going to happen now.

"Joel isn't my first choice for you," his mother said softly, her eyes filling with tears. "But I don't agree with what your father said the other night either. I don't think cutting you off and kicking you out of our lives is the right way to handle this."

"Me either," Casey agreed, stopping what he was doing to turn the desk chair around and have a seat, willing to listen.

"Courtney is furious with him."

"I'm not too happy with him either."

"And I imagine Joel must feel…" She shook her head. "I'm sorry for how he must have taken all of this."

"Dad made him feel like the scum of the earth, like he wasn't worthy of sharing the ground we walk on. And frankly, you weren't much better. Couldn't you have been a little more welcoming? A little more understanding?"

His mother's shoulders drew up tight. "What about *you*? You couldn't have, oh, I don't know, been honest with me? Letting me believe you were just friends with him when all along—"

"Not all along. This is brand new. We were just friends back in high school, and I hadn't talked to him for years until I came home on this trip."

"Regardless, you didn't even tell me what was happening. Instead you just let me find out there with everyone watching when he showed up on our doorstep."

Casey sighed. "That's a valid point. But if it had been Theo, you wouldn't have minded."

"No. I wouldn't have," she agreed, her eyes cast down again. "But Theo was different. He was—"

"Wealthy. High class. What else was he?"

"Charming."

"And not the man I love," Casey said firmly.

"Yes. That seems to be true." She sighed and shook her head distantly. "Courtney says I've become a snob."

Casey laughed outright. "You think?"

"When I married your father, I was a nothing, you know. A little nobody from nowhere. Uneducated and working at the grocery store in Friendsville. He was out there for a business meeting, working some petroleum accounts, and he stopped in to buy some apple juice for his drive home. That's when he saw me. He said he knew the moment we locked eyes that I was the one for him."

Casey had heard this story before, but he let her tell it again.

"It took me a few months to believe that a man like him, a man with a good job and a big future, was interested in a poor, ignorant girl like me. And then, when I finally started to believe it, I let myself fall for him too." She shrugged. "I felt so bad about myself back then, like I'd never be as good as these women he kept introducing me to, the wives of his business associates. But it wasn't long before I found out where he came from, the poverty and the despair he'd been raised in too. And that's when I understood he felt exactly the same way I did." She smiled sadly. "We've spent years trying to stop feeling like imposters, to prove to ourselves and everyone around us that we belong here."

"Mom…" Casey sighed. "Joel's just the same as you once were. A normal guy trying to make his life. He's not trying to ruin our family."

"I know," she said carefully before taking a deep breath and blowing it out. "That's what I'm trying to tell you. I realize that, and while I can't pretend to understand what you see in him, I'm still sorry for my part in all of this mess."

Casey wished that was enough, but it probably wouldn't be. Not for a long time. But it was a start, and that was more than he could say for what Joel had with *his* father, which was nothing but endings.

She smiled sadly. "So, you really do care about him?"

"I love him. And he loves me."

"Love?" She tilted her head. "It's so fast. Just a few days."

"You just said dad knew the moment you met."

"Yes, but… Well, yes." She reached out to take Casey's hand and touched the ring. She looked up at Casey with questions in her eyes.

"I've known Joel for years, really. We know everything important about each other. And I've always loved him."

She nodded. "I suppose that's true."

He pulled his hand away and smiled down at the ring on his finger. She stared at it, too, but said nothing more.

"So, what happens now?" Casey asked when the silence grew too long. The worry that had gnawed at him despite the joy of new love took another bite into his gut.

"Your father isn't going to cut you off. That's absurd." She rolled her eyes. "I'll make sure of that. Don't worry. Everything is going to be okay."

"Deanna!" His father's voice echoed up the stairs, and they caught each other's eyes. "Deanna! Casey! Time to talk!"

Tension filled the space between them. "It'll be okay," Casey said, wondering why he was the one saying it and not her.

She took hold of his arm, her nails digging in hard.

They left the room together, and Casey wondered if he would ever have a sense of easiness with his family again. Surely once he proved to his parents that Joel was good enough, smart enough, and wonderful enough to be part of their family, things would go back to normal. Or maybe even better than they'd been before. Maybe they'd find a way to really love each other, for their true selves.

He ran his shaking hands through his hair and descended the stairs beside his mother, praying he wasn't wrong.

Chapter Twenty-Six

JOEL PULLED HIS Chevy into the driveway well after dark, but there were lights on in the trailer, and he could see Casey's shadow in the kitchen window moving around, probably making some kind of dinner.

It was a new experience to come home to someone. He sat in his car, looking at the half-melted snow and the shadow moving inside, trying to decide if he liked it or if he loved it. His heart fluttered, and he couldn't stop his grin.

"Hey honey, I'm home," he said sardonically as he pulled off his coat and hung it up, patting an almost demure Bruno on the head. He was much calmer having had Casey with him already and not having spent the whole day alone.

"Hey there." Casey came around the corner in fresh jeans and a *Harkening* T-shirt he'd clearly picked up that day from his parents' place. "I'm making burgers and veggies. Hope you saved room."

Joel had texted Casey from the Starbucks on his way home asking if he wanted anything, but Casey had said no. Joel had picked up a box of decent instant coffee for the next morning and some iced snowmen cookies for dessert, it was still Christmas after all, and a splurge to fight his nicotine craving seemed fair. But he hadn't eaten them yet.

"I'm plenty hungry." He grinned, taking a kiss from Casey, his heart warm and his blood pumping happily. "This is good. Coming home to you. I could get used to it."

Casey's smile softened, and he nuzzled Joel's hair briefly before turning back to the kitchen. "Don't want to burn the meat."

Joel followed him in and sat at the table. Bruno begged at Casey's feet while he pan-fried burgers.

"I made an extra one to cut up for Bruno's bowl," Casey said, looking down at Bruno fondly. "He'll like that."

"Keep that up, and he'll like you better than me before long."

Casey took the burgers off the heat, pulling buns out of a package and roasted potatoes from the oven, and plating them all. He cleared his throat anxiously. "Yeah, well, it looks like he won't have time to get used to me before I have to go."

Joel went cold as a wave of disappointment crashed down. This was what he'd wanted, wasn't it? It was why he'd gone to Casey's dad today. So why was he regretting that now?

"They forgave you?" What a weird way to put it, like being with Joel was something that required absolution, but they both knew it was true.

"I don't know about that. But they're letting me return to NYU to graduate and keep my apartment for the next semester. They're also not going to fight me on whether or not I go to Wharton this fall. They say that's up to me. So long as I understand that Christmas a year from now they expect me to be self-sufficient if I'm not going to follow their wishes." Casey sat the plates on the table and took a seat.

Joel swallowed, staring down at the burger and potatoes on his plate. "Do 'their wishes' include breaking up with me?"

"No. Just school."

"Ah. So, you have half a year to get on your feet if you don't go?"

"Exactly. But I already know what I want to do and with your help—between the books and Vreeland's—I'll have some success under my belt to help draw in new clients." He smiled broadly, putting a potato piece into his mouth. "I'm going to open my own local marketing firm. Hipster-sized at first: just me, myself, and I. But who knows what might happen? That'll allow me to do what I love most: work with mom-and-pop stores and participate in the growth of the community. It'll be perfect."

"And your dad was on board with that?"

"In a way." Casey shrugged, getting up to grab two beers from the fridge. He popped the lids and handed one to Joel. "He even suggested I talk to Walker Ronson about my plans since we hit it off as friends."

"I bet he did."

Casey's eyes grew tender and reassuring as he took his seat again. "I think he really understands that I'm not interested in anyone but you, Joel. He gets it now. And even if he didn't, I'm absolutely not interested in Walker. Period."

Joel darted his gaze away, staring at the snow melting on the floor from his boots. Heat rose through him, embarrassment at having revealed his jealousy and insecurity. He took a pull from his beer bottle. "What makes you think your dad gets it?"

Casey smirked. "Because I made a massive scene today, said everything I've needed to say for a long time, and I made sure he heard me. Loud and clear. He knows now that I love you and that you're not going anywhere." His chest puffed up. "I gave *him* the ultimatum this time: It's me *and* Joel, or it's not me at all. Mom was basically calling you her second son by the time the conversation was over in hopes of pleasing me." Casey sounded a little power-drunk.

Joel chewed on his bottom lip, watching Casey dig into the burger hungrily. He thought of his own father and how he'd never come away from any of their conversations feeling powerful. Not even their last one. "Wow. I, uh, guess you're a pretty persuasive person. Speaking from experience and all."

"I suggested we all needed some space still, and Mom wasn't wild about that, but she conceded to it." Casey gestured at Joel's plate. "Eat up."

Joel took a bite of the burger. It was so good he closed his eyes. When he opened them, Casey was smiling at him.

"Then, after all the yelling and crying was over, we exchanged gifts and had a small family Christmas. I told them goodbye and that I'd call them when I got back to my apartment in New York. Between now and when I leave on January first, I want all my time to be devoted to you."

Joel's heart kicked, and he swallowed another swig of beer. "I want to spend that time with you too, but I have to work."

"I know, and because of you, I have work to do as well. Today I got a lot accomplished before I headed over to my folks' place." He fed a potato piece to Bruno, who sat at his feet drooling. "Operation New-Covers-and-Blurbs is complete. I believe that alone will make a difference in your sales, but now we have to increase visibility on your back catalog. Tomorrow I'm going to start soliciting various book review sites. Then it's time to work on Joel Grimsbane's social media presence."

Joel crinkled his nose.

"Don't worry, I'll keep that simple for you. But you can see I have a ton to do. I won't be bored while you're at Vreeland's."

"Twenty-five percent of any increase in profit seems like too little to pay you for all that you're doing." He ate more of the burger, hoping to cover up how much he wanted Casey's dream to come true. After all, it was what he'd bet against with Jonathan Stevens, and, boy, did he want to lose.

"I've told you before, it's for my semester project. And I want to do it. I'm *excited* to do it. In some ways, I'll get more out of it than you do. I promise."

"You always were kind of a nerd about this stuff."

"And you believed you weren't worthy of people helping you, of being loved even, but you're wrong." Casey's brows lowered, and he spoke seriously, like he wanted his words to penetrate to Joel's core.

Joel's palms grew sweaty. He didn't know what to say, so he kept quiet, drinking more beer and popping a potato wedge into his mouth.

"My dad told me you came by his office," Casey said seriously. He scrubbed a hand through his hair and then pushed his plate back, apparently done. "He told me you don't have any faith in us lasting and that I've put in all my chips on the table for someone who didn't have what it takes to pony up with their own. Those were his exact words."

Joel's mouth went dry, anger shooting through him along with a hot, messy sense of humiliation. He shoved his own plate away. He should have known Jonathan Stevens wouldn't keep their conversation a secret. He just hadn't realized exactly the way Jonathan would try to use it against him. "I gave you my mom's ring," Joel pointed out. "I promised to be here whenever you come back. I'm committed."

"But you don't think I'm going to stick around." Casey's eyes flashed hurt. "Dad said you were adamant that he should let me graduate from NYU, and not cut me off financially, because 'this will die a natural death.'"

"I..." Joel didn't have any defense for himself. It was true. He'd said those things, but no part of him believed them. "I did say that, but Casey—"

"And you know what's hilarious? He was offended on my behalf." Casey snorted, shaking his head. "He was more offended than I was, to be honest."

Joel scrunched down in his seat.

"Do you know why I'm not offended?" Casey asked, sliding down to kneel on the floor by Joel's feet. Bruno scooted away to make room for him there. Casey tilted Joel's chin up, forcing him to meet his eyes. "Because, unlike my dad, I know you, and I realize your fear has nothing to do with me or how you feel about me. It's all about that self-loathing we talked about."

Joel whispered, "The one you said should be focused on my smoking?"

"That was dumb of me and I apologize."

"You've been in therapy too long, man." Joel shook his chin free of Casey's grasp. He wanted out of this conversation now before Casey said something that made him split wide open, that broke him down, the way rimming or fucking broke him down. "I was lying to your dad. I do believe in us, Casey. I just wanted him to send you to New York for your last semester. That's all. I'm a liar, Casey. I tell lies when I think it can help."

"Maybe. And maybe you're lying to me right now. I don't really care either way, Joel."

"You don't?"

"No. The only way I can change your belief about us is to prove it to you."

Joel croaked, "How will you do that?"

"By not leaving you." Casey's eyes bored into him.

"You have to graduate. I want you to."

Casey smiled. "I mean by not leaving you emotionally. Yeah, I have to go back to NYU for a few months, but I'll fly down to visit some weekends and during Spring Break. You can always come up to see me, too." He touched Joel's lower lip with the pad of his thumb. "And I'll text and FaceTime every day. I'll fly you up for my graduation, and you'll see my apartment before I give it up. I'll show you the city."

"You always make me want to believe in your dreams, Casey."

"You make me believe in yours, too. You dream in books and writing and in fantasies about the log house you're going to build here on your land. You're not alone in your dreams, Joel. You're a living, breathing, striving human being, and I believe in you. I believe in us."

"I believe you. I do. But—"

"But nothing. It's been four years we've been apart, and nothing about how I feel about you has changed for me. I don't see why it ever would."

"It's early days," Joel muttered. "Give it a minute."

"I'm planning to give it multiple decades, actually."

Joel scoffed, but tears pricked his eyes. Christ, he'd never been such a crybaby as he'd been this week. "I guess I'll let you prove it to me, then."

"I will." He kissed Joel's chin and then sat back on his heels. "By the way, I hear you and my dad made a bet."

Joel rolled his eyes.

"I'm making a bet, too. I bet we'll be together next Christmas, and the one after that, and the one after that, and for dozens of Christmases to come. And, if I'm right, then for every Christmas we're still together, you have to kneel in front of me and say aloud that you're sorry you doubted me. You'll have to say that you know I'll love you until I die."

Joel snorted. "That's absurd. I never doubted you. Not really."

"And then you'll have to give me a blow job."

"Right after I say those things?"

"Yes."

"Oh." Joel shivered, his cock taking interest.

"You like that?"

Joel grumbled, "Maybe."

"I thought you would." Casey stood up and put out his hand. "In the meantime, I'd like to seal this bet. Shake on it."

Joel reluctantly took Casey's hand and shook.

"And now I want to make love to you."

Joel rolled his eyes. Who even said "make love to you" anymore? Casey Stevens, that was who. And it made Joel's insides quiver.

"I need to shower first."

"Go ahead then." Casey started back toward Joel's room, calling over his shoulder, "I'll be waiting because I'm not going anywhere."

"I'm not either," Joel said. "And I believe you."

He'd never believed anyone more.

Chapter Twenty-Seven

MARKET SQUARE WAS full of people, lots of them happy and many of them drunk. Joel stood next to Casey with his hands stuffed into his pockets, his eyes directed up to the big, round ball of light dangling from a crane above the small stage at one end of the square. The snow had melted for the most part days before, but there were still some clumps of it here and there. Combined with the pile from the ice rink, there was plenty of "snow" for some teens to make snowballs to threaten each other with.

Pop music played over speakers spaced around the square, and a countdown clock was displayed on a big screen behind the MC from a local radio station, who periodically interrupted the revelry to announce the time left until midnight.

It was a festive atmosphere, and Joel felt loose and merry himself, having allowed Casey to buy him a few rosemary lemon drops at Tupelo Honey. But beneath it all, he felt a little sad too.

Casey was leaving the next day. And while Joel absolutely believed in the promises Casey had made to him and he felt secure in his place in Casey's life, the reality was that only time would tell.

"There you are!" Becca cried, popping up beside him with a happy cry. She wore purple eye makeup that perfectly matched her lipstick and the scarf around her neck. Her red wool coat covered her legs, but she wore stompy, high-heeled boots that made her almost as tall as Joel for once.

He hugged her, and Casey came in for a hug too.

"Long time, no see. I missed you, Bec. Wow, you look gorgeous," Casey said, grinning. "Where's your girlfriend?"

"We didn't make it to the New Year." Becca popped one of her brows. "But that's okay. Guess who did make it?"

"Who?"

She pulled out her phone and pushed a few buttons. Leaning over her shoulder, with Casey leaning over his, they spotted RJ's face, nostrils first, on the screen. He appeared to be in a hotel room. It was loud and crowded in Market Square to do a group FaceTime, but Joel's heart warmed up at the sight of his old friend, a sense of familiarity washing over him.

Greetings were exchanged, and Joel listened while Becca, RJ, and Casey chatted. He threw in his own comments now and again, but, for the most part, he just enjoyed being part of something bigger than himself for a few minutes. The sensation of belonging was unfamiliar and something he didn't want to let himself take for granted.

RJ was apparently somewhere in Germany playing for a group called Pearl Necklace, and it was basically morning there. He'd been up all night partying after their New Year's Eve gig, and he looked haggard but happy. Casey and Becca shouted questions to him over the noise of the crowd, but sometimes the reception froze and they missed what he had to say in reply.

Joel put his arm around Casey and leaned in, taking a deep breath of his scent in the warmth emanating from the skin above his soft, plaid scarf.

"So, I'm thinking this time next year, I'll be ready for a break," RJ said, glancing over his shoulder as the hotel room door opened and a skinny, long-haired dude walked in wearing nothing but a towel. RJ gave him an up-nod before turning back to the screen. "What do you say? December of next year, if we're all in Knoxville, we can get together and play a few gigs. Get the band back together."

Joel snorted. "I sold my bass. I have a few guitars, though."

"You can play rhythm, then."

"What about Casey?" Becca asked.

"It's the triangle for him," RJ said, laughing.

"Nah, I'll make sure there's an audience for the shows," Casey said. "Marketing is my specialty."

Joel shrugged. "I could be in practice by then, probably."

The conversation grew impossible to follow in all the hubbub, and Joel closed his eyes, feeling the jostle of the crowd around them. He held tight to Casey, enjoying the vibration of his laughter against his own body. He wondered what his pop was doing. Was Charlie asleep or was he struggling to stay awake to watch the *Rockin' New Year's Eve* on TV like he had when Joel was a kid?

Joel let himself drift back into his memory, touching a few old ones, including the one of his dad dancing his mom around in the kitchen. It ached like pushing on a bruise, but he took a deep breath, opened his eyes, and let Charlie and the past wash away with the murmur and rumble of the crowd.

"One minute to midnight, y'all!" the MC called out, his deep voice amplified over the crowd. "Bring on the new year!'

They disconnected with RJ and crowded together. Casey and Joel with Becca next to them and all their eyes affixed to the glowing ball as it jiggled and started its slow descent.

"I can't believe I'm here with you," Casey said in his ear, his hot breath tingling, making Joel shiver. "This is going to be our year, baby. The best one ever. I promise."

Joel shuddered. Promises like that were foolish, but he had one of his own to make too. "I promise that I'll be here waiting for you, even if it isn't."

Casey took off his glove, the silver ring on his finger glinting in the holiday lights. He gripped Joel's chin as the crowd started shouting the final countdown. Joel didn't look at the ball any longer, content to stare into the lights reflected in Casey's eyes. He put his arms around Casey's neck, and as the cries of "Happy New Year!" filled the air, he surged up to meet Casey's kiss.

Whoops and hollers rose around him. Becca's screams of delight were close by and piercing, and yet he let the kiss go on. The joy of a new beginning rattled through him, and he gripped Casey's lapels, dragging him down for a deeper kiss. Who gave a damn if people were watching? Let them all see.

When the strains of "Auld Lang Syne" gave way to "Rocky Top," he broke loose and grinned at Casey, who stared back down at him with a face full of joy.

Tomorrow might not be a great day. Saying goodbye to Casey before he flew back to New York City was going to be tough. And trusting that Casey's interest in him would last once he was alone again would be even harder, but he had faith. He believed in Casey. In *them*.

Right now, Joel had the boy of his dreams in his arms, his best friend shouting with joy beside him, and a whole new year coming his way.

Right now, life was good.

Epilogue

Christmas Eve, one year later

C ASEY WRAPPED A few more presents, pushing them under the Christmas tree, admiring the way the colored lights sparkled on the shiny paper he'd picked up at Costco while buying ingredients for pumpkin pie.

He glanced at the time on his phone, wondering if maybe he should have ignored Joel and gone with him to the graveyard anyway. There were things that a man shouldn't do alone and maybe putting an Egg McMuffin on his father's grave was one of them. It was so hard to tell sometimes where the line was between what Joel wanted because he didn't believe he was worthy and what Joel wanted because, well, he truly wanted it.

Casey wrapped another gift, hoping he'd made the right choice.

Bruno drowsed next to him, watching him through bleary, gold eyes. He huffed a sigh whenever Casey rolled out the paper, obviously wishing Casey would hurry up and be done with whatever this nonsense was because he was tired and wanted to sleep.

"Don't worry, Bruno. This is the last one."

The door opened with a creak, and Bruno hefted up to go greet Joel. Casey stayed where he was and waited. Christmas music played on the new Bluetooth stereo he'd purchased for Joel's birthday. He gazed around the living room of the trailer, taking in all the changes since the prior year.

There was a desk now, holding a laptop with multiple tabs open to the social media accounts Casey ran for Joel Grimsbane and Vreeland's Home and Garden. He'd updated them earlier and was pleased with the continued participation for both accounts, but especially by the readers of Joel Grimbsbane, who often left long, excited comments about the books, all of which he read aloud to Joel in the evening. Those never failed to get Joel at the actual computer, typing up a stunned reply for himself.

"Hey," Joel said, stepping into the room. He'd removed his coat and shoes, standing there in just his jeans and T-shirt, muscles showing and tattoos on display.

"Hey." Casey rose to plant a kiss on his mouth. "How did it go?"

"It was okay. Wish I still smoked. A cigarette would have taken the edge off. But I don't, so..." Joel sank down on the new sofa he'd purchased with six months of increased royalties. He hadn't smoked in over six months, either, which did Casey's heart good, but even he missed the scent of cigarette smoke sometimes. Joel didn't smile, but he relaxed, reaching out for Casey. "I said my goodbyes. My relationship with my dad will never be what I wanted or needed. That's the hard part. But that was true whether he was alive or dead."

"But while he was alive, there was still hope."

Joel shook his head. "No. And that's why I had to walk away in the end. There was never any hope." He tugged Casey down to the couch beside him, and Casey was grateful that Joel huddled against him, seeking the reassurance and affection he needed. The old Joel—the one Angel had called Mr. Frosty Pants—would never have done such a thing.

Casey kissed the top of Joel's head while Joel played with the silver ring Casey always wore on his finger.

"My folks will be expecting us around five for the Christmas party," Casey reminded him.

"My second Stevens family Christmas party," Joel said softly. "I'd say I was looking forward to it, but that'd be a lie."

"Walker will be there. He likes you."

"He doesn't suck."

"And you and my mom get along great these days."

"Yeah, but at some point between tonight and tomorrow at Christmas dinner I'll have to apologize to your dad for underestimating you." Joel squirmed a little. "Even though that was a lie, too."

"True. And then later you owe me an apology for ever doubting me at all."

Joel went still. "On my knees."

"Yeah."

"And then a blow job."

"Hell, yeah."

Joel laughed. "Good thing I've gotten better at those."

"You're the best I've ever had. Always have been. Always will be."

Joel snorted softly, obviously doubting it, but he didn't argue. "I'm tired. It was cold out there. Will you hold me for awhile?"

Casey tugged Joel down until they were lying on the sofa together, staring at the tree. Satisfied, Bruno flopped down on top of the wrapping paper still spread out for the last gift and started to snore.

"I love you," Joel whispered.

"I love you too."

Joel rolled on top of him, nuzzling his neck. "Show me."

"You want me to fuck you?"

"Yes."

Casey grinned. "All right. Where?"

"Here. On the sofa." Joel's lower lip tucked into his mouth and he looked almost bashful. "By the way, I have a gift for you. Something just for us."

"What's that?"

"I got a physical for that insurance I purchased recently—the insurance for the store."

"Right, I remember."

"My lab results were good."

Casey nodded.

"And you got a physical before you left NYU. There's no reason to think any of those results would have changed."

Casey's eyes lit on fire, understanding dawning. "That was months ago, but no. I've only been with you since last year."

"And I've only been with you ever."

"I know."

Joel swallowed hard. "We don't need condoms, do we?"

"No. We haven't ever needed them, really. I just wanted you to feel safe."

"I feel safe with you, Casey." Joel's lips trembled slightly as he whispered, "I believe in you. In us. Forever."

Casey's stomach somersaulted. "What convinced you for sure?"

"I don't know. All of it. You keeping your promises when you were at NYU. Then moving in here instead of going to Wharton. Making my dreams come true by marketing my books. Turning Vreeland's around. Helping me save enough to start building the log cabin—"

"We'll be in it by next Christmas."

"Telling me you love me. Showing me."

"Fucking you."

"Yes."

Casey nuzzled Joel's neck. "Baby, I love you so much."

"I know you do. And I believe it," Joel whispered, sitting up to straddle Casey's hips. "I shouldn't have ever doubted you."

"You had a lot of good reasons to doubt me. Like almost four years of reasons."

"Well, don't remind me of them!" Joel exclaimed, laughing. He leaned down and kissed Casey, rough and playful, demanding and still hiccupping with joy. "Fuck me instead. Just fill me up. Make me come my brains out."

"Such a dirty mouth you have," Casey muttered. "But don't worry.

I'll fuck you until you're screaming and shooting all over me."

Bruno huffed like he could understand what they were saying, got up, and stalked into the kitchen to collapse on his bed there.

"Bruno doesn't appreciate your dirty talk," Casey said. "He's appalled."

"Let him be appalled. Just get your dick up my ass."

"You're always such a sweet talker, baby." He ground his hips up, pushing his erection into Joel's jeans-clad buttocks. "You don't know what you do to me."

Ten minutes later, Joel shook and sobbed as Casey licked his hole. He'd never stopped dissolving into tears when he was rimmed, and Casey liked having the power to strip Joel down to raw emotion. He loved that he was the only one who ever had.

Entering him bare was bliss. His entire body sang with the joy of being united with Joel, skin to skin, and nothing between them. The heat and lust escalated with each thrust. Flipping so that he was on top again, Joel rode Casey hard, the colored lights of the Christmas tree glinting on his sweaty, pale skin and in his dark hair. He was healthier than when Casey had found him again a year before—stronger and meatier, with a little bit of jiggle to the flesh over his strong stomach speaking to the increase in fortune and good meals. It was beautiful to see.

Casey squeezed Joel's hips and held him down hard, shoving up at the same time until he was deep in Joel's hot, squirming body. He slid his hand up Joel's stomach and chest, over the dark hair, and tugged him down by the back of the neck for a kiss.

Joel whimpered at the change of angle and stiffened against him, hot come shooting over Casey's stomach as his hole squeezed Casey's dick so tightly that he gasped into Joel's mouth. He convulsed beneath Joel and came hard too, his come spurting into Joel's body and his cries of pleasure echoing around the living room.

Panting in the aftermath, come slick between them and the scent of sex rising, Casey held Joel close. The golden tin star he'd bought as a gift the year before shone on top of the tree, and he gazed up at it, sated and happy, stroking Joel's hair and shivering in the aftermath of shared joy.

Christmas Day

AFTER THE TRADITIONAL Stevens Christmas breakfast, Joel cornered Jonathan Stevens on the back porch of the Stevens's carefully decorated house across the lake. "I owe you an apology," he said, stuffing his hands into his jean jacket pocket and straightening his shoulders.

"Do you?" Jonathan said, turning to him with a gleam in his eye. He wore a Bloody Mary-softened smile and a thick coat against the cold. He nursed a third one. "I was rather thinking I owed you the same thing."

"Last year, I promised that I'd be out of your life by today. That didn't happen." *Thank God.*

"I knew it wouldn't then," Jonathan said. "If anything was going to make my son determined to be with you, it was your lack of certainty in him. But he's devoted to you. He's like me in too many ways, I suppose. He saw what he needed in you, and he wasn't going to let you go." He nodded toward the windows of the house. Joel saw Casey, Courtney, and Deanna laughing in the kitchen as they decorated Christmas cookies together. "That's how it was with Deanna."

"I'm sorry that I…" Joel trailed off. He wasn't sure what he should apologize for anymore. "I guess I'm not sorry that I was wrong." He also wasn't sorry that he'd been less than honest entirely with Jonathan to make sure Casey got to finish at NYU.

"I'm not either. I am, however, sorry for what I said last year. The way I behaved. I'm sure I have a lot to still make up to you both, but it looks like I'll have a lot of years ahead to do that."

"If Casey has his way."

"And if you let him."

Joel smiled and nodded. "I plan to."

"Come on," Jonathan said, motioning with his nearly empty Bloody Mary glass. "Let's go inside. They'll want help eating the cookies."

Taking one last look at his trailer across the lake and the unfinished first story of the log cabin that would be his and Casey's home soon enough, Joel followed Jonathan inside.

"WHERE ARE WE going?"

"You'll see."

Casey drove Joel through the old neighborhood, past the bus stop and toward Mr. Maples's yard where the Blow Mold Nativity scene stood. "Remember when we stole the baby Jesus?"

"What? Are you planning on doing it again?"

Casey stopped the car in front of the house and got out, his heart pounding.

Joel jumped out behind him. "Seriously?"

Casey shook his head and took hold of Joel's hand and dragged him toward the scene. As they reached Mary, Joseph, and the baby in the manger, he got down on one knee.

"Marry me."

"I... Well... Okay." Joel gazed around in confusion. "Why here? Why now?"

"I was already in love with you, but I knew it without a doubt that night we stole the baby Jesus and I kissed this Mary for 'practice,' wishing like hell I could kiss you instead."

Joel laughed. He squeezed Casey's hand. "I knew I was in love with you when I was jealous of your lips on that plastic glowing statue."

"I want to be with you forever."

"I know."

"So, say you'll marry me."

"I'll marry you." Joel grinned his crooked, happy smile, the one that made Casey's heart sing. Then he dropped to his knees as well. "Only if you agree to marry me too."

Casey laughed, gripping him by the lapels. There, in sight of Mary, Joseph, and the precious glowing baby Jesus, he kissed Joel silly, basking in their love and determined to hold onto it forever.

THE END

Letter from Leta

Dear Reader,

Thank you so much for reading *Mr Frosty Pants*! It was gratifying to write this holiday novel of childhood friends to lovers, and I hope you enjoy reading it as much as I loved crafting it.

Flip on through to get a gander at the first chapter of *Mr Naughty List*, the second book in this series, featuring a teacher who wants to be spanked by his hot former student.

Be sure to follow me on BookBub or Goodreads to be notified of new releases. And look for me on Facebook for snippets of the day-to-day writing life, or join my Facebook Group for announcements and special giveaways. To see some sources of my inspiration, you can follow my Pinterest boards or Instagram.

If you enjoyed the book, please take a moment to leave a review! Reviews not only help readers determine if a book is for them, but also help a book show up in site searches.

Also, for the audiobook connoisseurs out there, *Mr Frosty Pants* will be available in November 2019, narrated by the amazing John Solo. More and more of my books are now available for listening! I hope to eventually add my entire backlist to my audiobook roster over the next few years. Check for the books on Audible!

Thank you so much for being a reader!
Leta

MR. NAUGHTY LIST
by Leta Blake

A cute teacher gets a spanking this Christmas.
How hot can it get being on his former student's Naughty List?

Is Aaron allowed to want a hot holiday fling with his young former student? Even more forbidden, is he allowed to want this student to spank him?

It's another Christmas, and Aaron is still in the closet as a gay man and a natural submissive. With one youthful indiscretion blacking his ethics record, he can't afford to indulge his desires no matter how pent up and needy that leaves him.

Until his former student comes home for the holidays.

Dominant and charming, RJ knows what Aaron needs—intense, steamy encounters and a firm hand. As Christmas nears, RJ helps Aaron unlock his true self. But family and fallout await, and all good things must end.

Or can their hot holiday affair turn them into lasting lovers?

Mr. Naughty List is a steamy Christmas MM romance set in the *Mr. Christmas* series that began with *Mr. Frosty Pants*, but **can be read as a standalone**. Featuring light D/s, spanking, an older sub with a younger Dom, former student/teacher dynamics, and, of course, warm, sweet holiday feels complete with a strong happy ending.

Book 3 in the Mr. Christmas series

MR. JINGLE BELLS
by Leta Blake

Opposites attract as frosty business partners become fake boyfriends in this Christmas gay romance!

After an emergency forces Ashton Sellers from his apartment, all he wants for Christmas is new lipgloss, zero contact from his abusive family, and a place to stay for the holidays. Cue his business partner begrudgingly taking him in.

Walker's a fuddy-duddy with no sense of fun, but he does have a safe, warm home with four adorable dogs and delicious food on the table.

If it turns out Walker's also a secret softy with a tender side and a hot body beneath his endless parade of golf shirts? Great, good, cool. And if Walker wants Ashton to pretend to be his boyfriend for his sister's Christmas-themed wedding? Awesome, amazing.

Could Walker be the safe haven Ashton missed out on as a child? Could they be falling in love for real?

But when Ashton uncovers a painful mistake in Walker's past, it hits too close to home. As the jingle bells quiet and the snow settles, will Ashton be able to forgive Walker, or will their relationship be over before it ever truly begins?

Mr. Jingle Bells is a gay Christmas story by Leta Blake featuring forced proximity, opposites attract, fake dating, office romance, steamy scenes, and a taffy-sweet happy ending. It's set in the *Mr. Christmas* universe, which began with *Mr. Frosty Pants*, but **can be read as a standalone**.

Content warnings for childhood abuse, past addiction issues, PTSD episodes, and gambling.

Standalone novel featuring winter holidays

SMOKY MOUNTAIN DREAMS
by Leta Blake

Sometimes holding on means letting go.

After giving up on his career as a country singer in Nashville, Christopher Ryder is happy enough performing at the Smoky Mountain Dreams theme park in Tennessee. But while his beloved Gran loves him exactly the way he is, Christopher feels painfully invisible to everyone else. Even when he's center stage he aches for someone to see the real him.

Bisexual Jesse Birch is a single dad with no room in his life for dating. Raising two kids and fighting with family after a tragic accident took his children's mother, he doesn't want more than an occasional hookup. He sure as hell doesn't want to fall hard for his favorite local singer, but when Christopher walks into his jewelry studio, Jesse hears a new song in his heart.

Smoky Mountain Dreams is a heartfelt gay romance with a single dad, winter holiday highlights, found family, and steamy scenes to warm even the coldest heart!

Full-length novel featuring winter holiday scenes

TRAINING SEASON
by Leta Blake

Can a cowboy's firm hand help discipline this feisty figure skater—on and off the ice?

Matty Marcus fears he doesn't have what it takes to achieve his Olympic dream. His self-esteem is at an all-time low after figure skating coaches and skating judges have told him he's not skinny enough, good enough, or masculine enough to win.

Matty wishes he could afford the kind of coach he needs, a top-notch one who specializes in keeping their skaters focused. But those coaches are ridiculously expensive, and Matty is financially strapped.

Until a lucrative house-sitting gig brings him to rural Montana.

And to Rob.

No one has ever looked at Matty the way rural cowboy Rob Lovely looks at him. No one has ever touched him, loved him, and healed him from the inside out. No one has ever made him feel so valuable and adored. Worthy. Strong.

No one has ever taught Matty how to fly. Or how to lose.

Rob might be a cowboy and a single dad who knows nothing about figure skating, but after only a few months, he's trained a new kind of bravery into Matty's soul.

But to achieve his Olympic dream, Matty will have to face the ultimate test. Has he truly learned what it means to win—on and off the ice—during his training season?

Training Season is a MM romance with a feisty, flamboyant figure skater and an easy-going dominant cowboy, opposites attract, hurt-comfort, single dad, winter holiday highlights, love beyond reason, multiple steamy scenes, and a well-earned happy ending. *This book contains some BDSM elements.*

Standalone

ANY GIVEN LIFETIME

He'll love him in any lifetime.

Neil isn't a ghost, but he feels like one. Reincarnated with all his memories from his prior life, he spent twenty years trapped in a child's body, wanting nothing more than to grow up and reclaim the love of his life.

As an adult, Neil finds there's more than lost time separating them. Joshua has built a beautiful life since Neil's death, and how exactly is Neil supposed to introduce himself? As Joshua's long-dead lover in a new body? Heartbroken and hopeless, Neil takes refuge in his work, developing microscopic robots called nanites that can produce medical miracles.

When Joshua meets a young scientist working on a medical project, his soul senses something his rational mind can't believe. Has Neil truly come back to him after twenty years? And if the impossible is real, can they be together at long last?

Any Given Lifetime is a stand-alone, slow burn, second chance gay romance by Leta Blake featuring reincarnation and true love. This story includes some angst, some steam, an age gap, and, of course, a happy ending.

Gay Romance Newsletter

Leta's newsletter will keep you up to date on her latest releases and news from the world of M/M romance. Join the mailing list today.

Leta Blake on Patreon

Become part of Leta Blake's Patreon community in order to access exclusive content, deleted scenes, extras, bonus stories, rewards, prizes, interviews, and more.

www.patreon.com/letablake

Other Books by Leta Blake

Any Given Lifetime
The River Leith
Smoky Mountain Dreams
Angel Undone
The Difference Between
Omega Mine: Search for a Soulmate
Raise Up Heart
Heat for Sale
Bring on Forever

The Mr. Christmas Series
Mr. Frosty Pants
Mr. Naughty List
Mr. Jingle Bells

The Training Season Series
Training Season
Training Complex

Heat of Love Series
Slow Heat
Alpha Heat
Slow Birth
Bitter Heat

Stay Lucky Series
Stay Lucky
Stay Sexy

'90s Coming of Age Series
Pictures of You
You Are Not Me

Co-Authored with Indra Vaughn
Vespertine
Cowboy Seeks Husband

Co-Authored with Alice Griffiths
The Wake Up Married serial
Will & Patrick's Endless Honeymoon

Gay Fairy Tales
Co-Authored with Keira Andrews
Flight
Levity
Rise

Audiobooks
Leta Blake at Audible

Free Read
Stalking Dreams

Discover more about the author online
Leta Blake
letablake.com

About the Author

Author of the bestselling book Smoky Mountain Dreams and the fan favorite Training Season, Leta Blake's educational and professional background is in psychology and finance, respectively. However, her passion has always been for writing. She enjoys crafting romance stories and exploring the psyches of made up people. At home in the Southern U.S., Leta works hard at achieving balance between her day job, her writing, and her family.